Thomas E. Lightburn served twenty-two years in the medical branch of the Royal Navy, reaching the rank of Chief Petty Officer. He left the service in 1974 and obtained a Bachelors (Hons) degree at Liverpool University. After teaching for sixteen years, he volunteered for early retirement. He then began writing for *The Wirral Journal* and *The Sea Breezes*, a worldwide nautical magazine. He interviewed the late Ian Fraser, VC, ex-Lieutenant RN, and wrote an account of how he and his crew crippled the Japanese cruiser, *Takao*, in Singapore.

Thomas is a widower and lives locally pursuing his favourite hobbies of soccer, naval and military history, the theatre, art and travel.

Published work

**The Gates of Stonehouse**
*(Vanguard Press 2005)*
*978 184386 203*

**Uncommon Valour**
*(Vanguard Press 2006)*
*978 184386 301 4*

**The Shield and The Shark**
*(Vanguard Press 2006)*
*978 184386 350 2*

**The Dark Edge of The Sea**
*(Vanguard Press 2007)*
*978 184386 400 4*

**The Ship That Would Not Die**
*(Vanguard Press 2008)*

**The Summer of '39**
*(Vanguard Press 2009)*
*978 184386 561 2*

**A Noble Chance**
*(Vanguard Press 2010)*
*978 184386 647 3*

**Beyond the Call of Duty**
*(Vanguard Press 2011)*
*978 184386 714 2*

**The Russian Run**
*(Vanguard Press 2012)*
*978 184386 840 8*

**Deadly Inferno**
*(Vanguard Press 2013)*
*978 184386 736 4*

*To
Margaret
Best Wishes
[signature]*

# MISSION INTO DANGER

Thomas E. Lightburn

# MISSION INTO DANGER

Vanguard Press

VANGUARD PAPERBACK
© Copyright 2014

**Thomas E. Lightburn**

The right of Thomas E. Lightburn to be identified as author of this work has been asserted by him in accordance with the Copyright, Designs and Patents Act 1988.

**All Rights Reserved**

No reproduction, copy or transmission of this publication may be made without written permission.
No paragraph of this publication may be reproduced, copied or transmitted save with the written permission of the publisher, or in accordance with the provisions of the Copyright Act 1956 (as amended).

Any person who commits any unauthorised act in relation to this publication may be liable to criminal prosecution and civil claims for damages.

A CIP catalogue record for this title is available from the British Library.

ISBN 978 1 84386 994 8

*Vanguard Press is an imprint of*
*Pegasus Elliot MacKenzie Publishers Ltd.*
www.pegasuspublishers.com

**First Published in 2014**

**Vanguard Press**
**Sheraton House Castle Park**
**Cambridge England**

Printed & Bound in Great Britain

This book is dedicated to my mother, the late Cora Lightburn, whose kindness and love sustained me throughout my life.

# Acknowledgements

My grateful thanks to the staff of the library at the Liverpool Maritime Museum and also to the patient work by the staff at Imperial War Museum, London.

I am indebted to Captain Lars Juel Kjeldsen, who as Commanding Officer of the SS *Boudicca* kindly gave me the navigation details of a voyage to the Cape Verde Islands. I wish to thank John F. White for using information from his book, *U-Boat Tankers*, and Terence Robertson's excellent story of the exploits of Captain J. Walker is his stirring biography entitled *Walker, R. N.*

Last but not least, I am grateful to the criticism and suggestions by Doctor S. K. Muckherjee MBE, for correcting the medical details of the manuscript.

# PROLOGUE

Captain Robert Henry Stirling, Royal Navy, DSO and Bar, stood staring out of the porthole in his cabin. Outside was the cobbled-stoned quayside of Gladstone Dock, gleaming wet after a recent downpour of rain. The time was just after 1700, the date Monday 2 September 1941. From his jacket pocket he took out a packet of Players and lit one with a match. Breathing out a steady stream of smoke he turned around and sat down at his desk, cluttered with folders and papers. Except for the monotonous hum of the generators everything was quiet. Suddenly he felt nervous. In a few minutes he would go into the wardroom and meet the officers of his new command.

Stirling stood well over six feet with the broad shoulders of an athlete. He was forty-two with thick, dark wiry hair streaked with grey. His deep-set penetrating brown eyes, heavily wrinkled at each corner of his gaunt, weather-beaten features, gave evidence of hours exposed to the elements on a ship's open bridge.

HMS *Sandpiper* had recently undergone an extensive refit. The mottled red lead on her three-hundred-foot superstructure had been replaced with a dull grey and dark green camouflage together with her pennant number S21 painted boldly in black.

It was a far cry from 1917, when as a young sub lieutenant Stirling joined HMS *Sarpedon* based in Dover. It was onboard this ten-year-old destroyer that his great interest in anti-submarine warfare began. *Sarpedon*'s task was screening the Grand Fleet against U-boat attack. He couldn't understand why the destroyers simply waited for the enemy to be detected before attacking them. Why, he wondered, couldn't they leave the convoy and seek out the enemy before the U-boats managed to slip among the convoy and do their damage. He mentioned this to the First Lieutenant, a frosty, self-opinionated officer, who told him in no uncertain manner to leave the anti-submarine tactics to his betters. Stirling angered the Torpedo and Depth Charge officer by suggesting a more concentrated pattern of depth charges fired by *Sarpedon* and the other destroyers might prove more successful. Once again he was told to mind his own business. However, his comments must have reached the ears of the ship's captain, who was secretly impressed by Stirling's enthusiasm. Consequently, in 1920 Stirling was sent to HMS *Osprey,* the navy's anti-submarine base in Portland, for specialist training in amphibious warfare. With the outbreak of World War Two he would become dedicated to the destruction of Doenitz's U-boats, a task he tackled with unbounded relish.

Stirling turned around and with a weary sigh sat down at his desk. He stubbed his cigarette out in a heavy brass ashtray and stared longingly at the framed photograph of his wife Pamela, a petite, attractive woman with short dark hair and a radiant smile. Next to this was another photograph of a tall, slim, fresh-faced nineteen-year-old sub lieutenant in the Royal Navy.

'To think we've been married for over twenty years,' he muttered, smiling to himself. 'Such a lot has happened since we first met in Plymouth at that cocktail party in 1918 and married a year later.' Mark, their only child, was now eighteen and had volunteered for service in submarines. The irony of this was not lost on Stirling. Mark would soon be serving in the very types of warships he was determined to sink.

With a slight shrug of his shoulders he took a deep breath and lapsed deeper into thought. After the First World War had ended no one seemed to think conflict could happen again. In 1919, the three services were reduced due to a mixture of complacency and financial stringency. Nobody in the navy thought the U-boat menace would rear its ugly head once more. Kaiser's surface fleet lay at the bottom of Scapa Flow. Their U-boats had surrendered and had been scrapped. How wrong the government and admiralty had been. Now, here he was about to take command of one of the navy's newest warships, carrying forty depth charges, each containing 450 pounds of amatol, determined to sink as many U-boats as he could.

Stirling remembered sitting in the front room of his father's house in Mutley Plain, Plymouth, where he was born forty-two years ago. The date was Monday 20 September 1939. Robert had managed to get a weekend off duty. James Stirling was a retired naval captain, having commanded a destroyer flotilla in the First World War. Matilda, his wife, had died in an outbreak of influenza that had decimated Europe in 1920. Like his son, he was tall, dark-featured with intelligent brown eyes and thinning grey hair combed neatly across an almost bald head.

"Believe me, Robert, my boy," the captain had said warming a brandy glass in his hand before taking a sip, "Winston is right. The damn U-boats will be our greatest menace. It'll be up to you and your colleagues to deal with them once and for all."

Robert stubbed out his cigarette in an ashtray and sat back in his chair. His father's words, uttered a day after war broke out, were very true. The sinking of the passenger liner SS *Athenia* on the 3 September with the loss of 112 lives shocked the nation. Fifteen days later 500 men died when the aircraft carrier HMS *Courageous* was torpedoed and sunk. Over 800 men were lost when HMS *Royal Oak* was sent to the bottom of Scapa Flow. The sinking of several merchant ships had followed this. The time had come for Stirling to put into practice the tactics he had devised at *Osprey* to combat the U-Boat menace.

# CHAPTER ONE

The aromatic aroma of Old Holborn permeated the warm air of the room where Commander Robert Stirling was sat smoking a cigarette. He had managed a few days off from his duties as Planning Officer on Admiral Ramsay's Staff in Dover Castle. Because of the heavy bombing of Dover, Stirling and his wife, Pamela, had rented a two-storey, red-brick cottage in Emsworth, a picturesque village outside Portsmouth. They were sitting in the lounge feeling the warmth of the log fire crackling in the open grate. The time was just after three o'clock on Saturday 22 February 1941.

Built at the turn of the century, *Silveroaks* was comfortably furnished with a neatly trimmed thatched roof, and small, squat chimneys that would have done justice to the lid of a biscuit tin. The low-slung oak-beamed ceilings and open fire grates gave the rooms a feeling of close-knit warmth and cosiness. The upper floor contained two bedrooms and a bathroom tastefully decorated in pastel colours. The cottage was surrounded by a high evergreen hedge. The view from the deep bay window in the lounge showed a narrow gravelled pathway leading through a small, well kept garden and a wooden gate, painted bright yellow, that opened onto a leafy lane. A deep, solid looking washbasin and well scrubbed wooden draining board occupied the far end of the kitchen. From a long shelf above the sink hung several shiny brass pots, pans and bottles of various shapes and sizes. Although the black iron cooking stove gave the kitchen a distinctly Victorian appearance, a modern gas cooker and a large metal icebox lying close by offset this. The floor was tiled in black and white squares and a large pale green lampshade hung from the ceiling. Oak panelled cupboards with marble tops lined the base of one wall. A stout wooden door led onto a back garden that ordinarily grew a variety of flowers. With the help of Mark, when he was home from Dartmouth, they had uprooted the flowers and in response to the Government's cry to *Dig For Victory,* planted untidy lines of potatoes, carrots and cabbages. Close by was a small red-brick garage housing a brown box Ford.

With a sigh of frustration, Stirling angrily stubbed his cigarette out in a round silver ashtray and said, 'I can't take anymore of this Pam. Sitting behind that bloody desk is driving me crazy.'

'Now, darling,' Pamela replied cautiously while lowering her knitting onto her lap. 'From what you've told me your job helping to protect Dover and the Channel from submarine attack is very important.' She was a small, attractive woman whose clear complexion contrasted sharply with her husband's heavily lined dark features.

'Maybe so,' Stirling answered feeling the soft warmth from the log fire caressing his face. 'But all those fishing vessels, ferryboats and such, looked so vulnerable sailing out of the harbour towards Dunkirk. How I wished I'd been onboard one of those corvettes escorting them across the channel.'

'But Robert, dear,' said Pamela, her dark blue eyes wrinkling into an understanding smile. 'Remember, you were part of Admiral Ramsay's staff that organised the rescue of those 300,000 men from the beaches. So please try not to sound so discontented.'

With a slight conciliatory shake of his head, Stirling replied, 'At least last year our lads managed to bloody the Luftwaffe's nose. I hear they're calling it the Battle of Britain. But if Doenitz and his so-called Wolf Packs have their way, the battle has only just began. I warned them against this when I was commanding officer at the Anti-submarine School in *Osprey*.' With a despondent shrug of his shoulders, he added, 'I tried to tell them about my ideas to combat the U-boat attacks, but nobody appeared to be interested.'

Pamela reached across and gave Stirling's hand a comforting squeeze. 'Don't worry, darling,' she said encouragingly, 'even though you've had requests for a ship turned down, I'm sure you'll have one approved soon, just try and be patient.'

But Stirling's patience was running out. With pent-up feelings of frustration he had to sit in his office and read about other men, some junior to him, being promoted. The main reason, he told himself, was during the inter-war years the Admiralty mistakenly considered the menace from the U-boat was of lesser importance to the construction of warships. This led to the country being exposed to the growing might of the German Navy. This belief was strengthened when battle ships such as *Bismark* and *Tirpitz* were built, thus competing in firepower with HMS *Hood*, the pride of the Royal Navy. At times, his despair was so overwhelming he even considered retiring from the service, and might have done if Pamela hadn't convinced him otherwise.

'What would you do, darling,' she had said half mockingly, 'sell insurance? Your place is in the navy, doing what you do best.'

'If only they would let me,' he replied, a look of determination in his eyes, 'anyway darling,' he went on, 'as you know I have a two o'clock appointment in London next week with George Creasy. Maybe he can use his influence to help me get back to sea. I'll return to Dover directly afterwards. I only hope he remembers my ideas about tackling those damned U-boats.'

Captain George Elvey Creasy, Royal Navy, and Stirling were old friends having worked together at HMS *Osprey*. Creasy was now Director of Anti-Submarine Warfare and was well aware of how badly the Battle of the Atlantic was going. At a recent meeting he had attended along with Sir Dudley Pound, the First Lord, and Admiral Tovey, Winston Churchill had openly confessed that the war against the U-Boat must at all costs be won.

"Gentlemen," the prime minister had said in his usual stentorian manner. "The situation is grave. If it continues, food shortages and vital material will cease to arrive and the country could be brought to its knees. It is therefore imperative to use the best men to combat the U-Boat menace."

On Monday 1 March, Pamela drove Stirling to Portsmouth Harbour station. His thick naval overcoat worn over his uniform, offered scant protection from the bitterly cold wind blowing down the Solent.

'Now remember, dear,' Pamela said in a stern yet sympathetic voice, 'do try and be a little diplomatic. Remember you have upset too many admirals in the past with your aggressive attitude.'

'I'll do my best,' Stirling replied, a wry smile playing around his mouth as he climbed out of the car. 'Now off you go and drive carefully. I'll phone as soon as I can and send my love to Mark when you write to him.' After giving his wife a quick kiss on the lips, he grabbed his brown canvas holdall and gas mask and hurried away.

Pamela watched the very tall, slightly stooped figure of her husband walk up the steps leading into the station and return the salute of a petty officer standing next to the ticket collector. In her heart she knew more goodbyes would follow if he were sent back to sea. Once again she would sit in her chair listening to the latest news on the wireless. Once again, lying in bed at night, she would pray for his safety. It was an experience she and thousands of service wives never got used to. On her journey home the low-lying dark clouds and misty rain added to her sudden feeling of loneliness.

The time was 1300 as the train, bellowing steam, shunted to a halt at Waterloo Station. During the two-hour journey, Stirling gave a good-mannered nod to two elderly ladies in his compartment then concentrated on reading *The Times*. The headlines telling of the Royal Navy sinking eleven German ships during a raid on the Lofoten Islands off Norway not only filled him with pride, but also made him more anxious for a sea-going appointment. President Roosevelt had signed a Lend Lease agreement with Britain promising war material and fifty old, but much needed, destroyers to supplement the paucity of Royal Naval escort vessels. He smiled to himself wondering what Pamela would think when she read that the Minister of Labour, Ernest Bevin, had announced women of a certain age would be mobilised for factory work.

Stirling helped the two ladies out of the compartment then made his way through a concourse, crowded with servicemen and women. After a quick cup of tea at a kiosk, he left the station and took a taxi to the Admiralty Buildings situated in Whitehall. The drizzle had stopped but the sky remained dull and overcast. Evidence of *Operation Steinbock*, Hitler's code-name for the Blitz, was everywhere. Along the Strand several large buildings lay in smouldering ruins. Windows of stores and theatres were cross-crossed with tape protecting them from bomb blasts. In Trafalgar Square, Nelson, perched imperiously on his famous column, looked defiantly across the city. The surrounding buildings included the National Gallery, open only for afternoon musical recitals while its mass of valuable paintings were stored away in a secret locality in Wales.

The taxi driver turned left at Northumberland Avenue and drove down Whitehall.

'The Admiralty, you said, sir?' enquired the taxi driver stopping outside a large, imposing Victorian building on the right hand side of the wide road. 'No charge, sir,' he added, his heavily lined face wrinkling into a broad smile, 'me son's in your lot. Buggered if I knows where he is though. Good luck to you.'

Stirling thanked him and climbed out the taxi, and after showing his identity card to a sailor wearing white webbing and armed with a .303 rifle, he entered the building.

Captain Creasy's office was on the third floor overlooking Horse Guards Parade. A shiny wooden sign on the door painted in neat gold lettering stated Creasy's name and rank. Stirling knocked and went inside. A pretty dark-haired Third Officer Wren was sat at a desk typing. Close by was a closed door with a sign that read *"Director Anti-Submarine Warfare"*. She looked up as Stirling entered and stopped work.

'You must be Commander Stirling,' she said with a smile. 'Captain Creasy is expecting you.' She paused and pressed a button on a small machine and announced his presence.

'Thank you, Linda,' came a deep, but clear, voice. 'Please ask him to come straight in.'

Stirling gave the Wren officer a polite smile then opened the door and went inside. The office was quite spacious, heavy with the smell of tobacco smoke and tastefully furnished. The floor was covered with a dark blue carpet embellished with small gold anchors. From a high, stuccoed ceiling hung an imposing crystal chandelier. A wide bay window, criss-crossed with white tape occupied most of one wall. The oak panelled walls were lined with leather bound books and ornately framed photographs of warships past and present. A glass drinks cupboard rested in one corner next to a green metal filing cabinet. Close by was a comfortable looking brown leather Chesterfield and two matching armchairs. On the wall behind the captain's red leather desk were a black and white photograph of King George VI and Queen Elizabeth, and a large, coloured map of the world. Stirling noticed that numerous red pins dotted the central areas of the North Atlantic Ocean.

Sitting behind a desk was a fifty-five-year-old man whose once thick dark, receding hair was almost grey. The four gold rings on each sleeve of his immaculate uniform indicated his rank. From his breast pocket peaked a white handkerchief. Above this was a row of First World War medal ribbons. On his desk next to a small stack of folders was an open letter. Upon seeing Stirling he stood up revealing a burly six-foot frame.

'Do come in and sit down, Bob,' he said, 'how's Pamela and Mark?' As they shook hands Creasy's sharp brown eyes and pale craggy features wrinkled into a broad smile.

'They're fine, thank you George,' replied Stirling, sinking into an armchair. 'Mark graduates this year. He tells me he intends to join the navy.'

'Following in his father's footsteps, eh?' Creasy said smiling as he sat down. 'Good for him.'

The captain lent forward and opened a silver box and pushed it towards Stirling who took a cigarette. Creasy did the same and lighted both with a small, gold lighter.

'I have a very good idea why you asked to see me, Bob,' said Creasy, relaxing back and exhaling a long stream of smoke. 'A week ago I wrote to Sir Percy Noble. As you know he's the C in C Western Approaches in Liverpool. I told him experienced officers trained in anti-submarine warfare were in short supply and recommended you for a sea-going command.'

Creasy's words sent Stirling's pulse racing. This was the news he longed to hear.

Seeing the look of anticipation in Stirling's eyes, the captain quickly added, 'The admiral agreed with me and has given you the command of *Sandpiper*, a Black Swan Class sloop.'

Stirling gave a short gasp of excitement, clenching both fists as he did so. 'That's... that's wonderful news,' Stirling replied, his face breaking into a wide grin. 'I can't thank you enough, George.'

'You can thank me by putting those ideas we discussed at *Osprey* into practice and bagging those bloody U-boats that seem to be sinking our shipping almost at will. Those red markers you see behind me,' he added, 'show that between January and March this year 975,000 tons of shipping was sunk. Intelligence tell us the bastards have the audacity to call it, "The Happy Time". This cannot go on. Somehow, they have to be stopped,' he stressed emphatically, 'or God knows what will happen.'

'Where is *Sandpiper*, George?' Stirling asked, trying his best to sound calm.

'In Gladstone Dock, Liverpool, undergoing a refit,' Creasy replied taking a deep drag of his cigarette before stubbing it out in an ashtray. 'Her captain, Commander Fearnley, has left to take command of a destroyer. Therefore, you are to join her on 1 September. You will be senior officer in command of a flotilla of five sloops. At present *Redshank* and *Curlew* are on escort duty to Mumansk, *Petrel* and *Shearwater* are at Plymouth also on escort duty. In September they will form the 15th Escort Group under the overall control of Sir Percy Noble at Western Approach Headquarters in Derby House, Liverpool. Your main task will be to protect convoys as well as destroying the enemy. You'll receive all these details by special courier. Any questions?'

Stirling quickly brushed away a flurry of cigarette ash that had fallen down onto the front of his jacket, and sat back in his chair. A surge of excitement ran through him. At last he would be able to put into practice the ideas to combat the U-Boat menace.

'Sloops, sir?' Stirling said with a sly grin. 'I'm told they would roll on a bowling green and were only armed when the war broke out. Before that they were used for survey work.'

With a slight frown the captain sat forward and clasped his hands in front of him. 'You're quite right, Bob,' Creasy replied tersely. 'However, despite being somewhat uncomfortable for the crew, sloops are very seaworthy and are especially manoeuvrable. Their exceptional endurance is due to the economical use of oil. Therefore they can out do corvettes and destroyers making them ideal for long voyages and convoy duty.' Captain Creasy stood up and handed Stirling a large buff-coloured envelope. 'The details of your officers are in here. Except for your Number One, Lieutenant Commander Bill Manley, the rest are RNVR. Many of them have recently joined the ship but seem an efficient lot.'

'Isn't a two and half a bit senior to be a First Lieutenant?' Stirling asked with an inquisitive frown.

'Yes, it is,' answered Creasy, pursing his lips, 'Manley was in command of a minesweeper when it went aground off the coast of Dover. The reason for this was put down to a faulty steering mechanism. Unfortunately it was spotted by a Messerschmitt and attacked. Luckily nobody was hurt. Manley was exonerated by a court of enquiry, but it didn't bode well for his future promotion.'

Hmm... like myself, another misfit, Stirling thought. We'll probably get on quite well. With a warm smile Creasy proffered his hand and said, 'Good luck, Bob, give my love to Pamela and good hunting.'

# CHAPTER TWO

As soon as Stirling left the Admiralty Buildings he looked around and saw a telephone kiosk. After fumbling in his pocket he unhooked the receiver and inserted sixpence into the slot. Pamela answered and he immediately pressed button A and spoke. She received the news of Stirling's appointment with a mixture of stoicism and equanimity.

'I knew this would happen, dear,' she said quietly, 'and I realise how much you've yearned to go to sea again.'

During the next five months Stirling was kept busy ensuring the extensive minefields around Dover were kept intact thus denying passage to U-boats. Looking out from the heavily taped window of his office, Stirling witnessed the daily bombing of convoys as they passed through the English Channel. Stirling clenched his fists in frustration wishing he were onboard one of the convoy escorts sending up a punitive barrage against the enemy. A patchwork of grey explosions littered the dull sky as ship after ship passed through a deadly wall of spray. To this cacophony was added the constant bombing of Dover and the terrifying whine of the Stukas, looking like big black spiders descending on their prey. The only mental relief he had from this carnage was the comfort of Pamela's correspondence. In her latest letter he learned that Mark had now passed out from Dartmouth and was a Midshipman awaiting a sea posting.

At 0900 on Monday 1 September 1941, Stirling left Dover Castle. His gas mask and steel helmet were slung over his left shoulder and he carried a small brown leather briefcase containing details of his new command. The morning was bleak with low-lying, dark grey cumulonimbus clouds presaging rain. He was met at the castle gate by a driver and taken by tilly, (nickname for blue naval vans called utillicans used extensively by the navy) to the station and boarded a train for London.

Everywhere was crammed with service personnel including the First Class compartment occupied by Stirling. The atmosphere was smoky, warm and humid, causing the windows to cloud over with foggy condensation. As the train rumbled through the leafy Hampshire countryside, the ticket collectors had to fight their way through passageways blocked with kitbags and cases. Arriving at Victoria he took a taxi to Euston. Five hours later, following a tedious journey, he arrived at Lime Street Station. Making his way along a crowded platform he found the RTO (Railway Transport Office). Inside a thickset, red-faced petty officer sat behind a desk reading a copy of the *Liverpool Echo*. Next to him stood a tall, sallow faced able seaman with black smudges under his sleepy dark eyes, smoking a cigarette. Upon seeing Stirling, the PO quickly put down his paper and rose to his feet. The seaman hurriedly straightened his cap and palmed his cigarette.

'Welcome to Liverpool, ser,' said the PO in a broad, Scouse accent. 'I've been expecting you. There's a tilly outside to take you to Gladstone Dock. Able Seaman Jackson 'ere, is the driver.'

Jackson hastily stubbed out his cigarette and in a thick northern voice, said, 'This way, sir.'

A bitterly cold northerly wind invaded Stirling's face as he followed Jackson down the steps of the station. The bustle of the city, despite the regular air raids, mingled with the rumbling of trams and motorcars. Deposits of manure from dray horses pulling carts littered the wide road. The pavements gleamed with a slight drizzle descending from an overcast, grey sky.

Opposite the station was St George's Hall with its thick, Corinthian columns giving the imposing grey-stoned structure the appearance of a mini Acropolis. Two lions flanked the entrance to the cobbled courtyard and not far away stood a majestic equestrian statue of a Boer War cavalryman, sword raised in the air in defiance to the enemy. However, signs of recent bombing were everywhere.

'That building used to be Lewis's store,' remarked Jackson, pointing to a large, burnt out shell at the corner of Ranlagh Street. 'It were hit last week,' he added as they climbed into the tilly. 'Luckily only a few were killed.'

'The city's taken quite a pasting, hasn't it?' replied Stirling as he sat down next to Jackson.

'Yer right there, sir,' Jackson soberly replied as he started the tilly. 'You ought to see Lord Street and Church Street. The place has been razed to the ground, so it 'as. Nowt left but a mass of rubble and rows of ruined shops.'

Continuing through the city centre, Stirling looked up and saw the tall grey edifice of the Liver Building with its twin towers jutting into the dark, cloudy sky.

'People coming to the 'Pool thinks those birds you see perched on each of those towers are seagulls, sir,' Jackson remarked with an all-knowing air. 'In fact they're actually cormorants. They say the one at the front points seawards to welcome the ships, the other looks inland to warn the judies.'

'Do they indeed,' replied Stirling, giving a short laugh.

'Old Lord Haw Haw reckons if the Luftwaffe knocks 'em off their perch we'll lose the war.'

'Well,' mused Stirling, glancing furtively upwards, 'they're still there, thank goodness.'

They continued down Water Street, passing the ruins of bombed buildings stained black with smoke.

(Over 4,000 people were killed on Merseyside during the Blitz. This was second only to London where 30,000 lives were lost.)

'Do you know where Derby House is?' Stirling enquired, as they turned right into the Strand. This was a long stretch of cobbled road paralleling the many small roads leading onto the main dockland area.

'We've just passed it, sir,' replied Jackson. 'It's just off Water Street on your right. It's part of Exchange Building, you can't miss it.'

Across the murky waters of the Mersey, Stirling could see the cranes and docks of Cammel Lairds in Birkenhead. Then came a long line of houses dominated by the dome of Wallasey's Town Hall, stretching along the promenade to New Brighton.

'The Mersey seems especially busy today,' said Stirling, observing a convoy of several merchant ships, their bulkheads covered in rust and low in the water. With the help of a small fleet of tugs they were slowly making their way towards the various dock entrances.

'Aye, that's right, sir,' Jackson replied solemnly, 'but I wonder how many of the poor buggers have been lost wherever they've come from.'

The driver's poignant remark served to remind Stirling that from this great seaport sailed convoys across the turbulent Atlantic, the ice-bound Arctic and the Cape of Good Hope.

They continued along the Strand then turned down a wide road leading into Regent Road. The road was bustling with lorries, delivery vans and dray horses pulling wagons loaded with beer barrels. Women wearing woollen shawls bent against the cold wind and pushed prams while dragging the hands of small children. Elderly men in overcoats and flat caps stood on the corners of the road smoking and talking.

'The masts and yardarms of those merchant ships you can see over the wall on your left,' replied Jackson, 'are in Hornby and Alexandra Docks, packed like sardines ain't they, sir?'

'Indeed they are,' Stirling replied dryly, then added, 'how far to Gladstone Dock?'

'Right at the end, sir,' replied Jackson, glancing confidently at Stirling. 'We'll be at the main gate in a few seconds. The *Sandpiper* has had its re-fit and is alongside in number two Branch Dock.'

'How do you know all this?' Stirling asked, giving the driver a searching look.

'Because I'm usually one of the ship's quartermasters, sir,' Jackson replied with a short laugh. 'The tilly's on loan to us and I'm the only bugger on duty wot can drive.'

They arrived outside a set of tall, pointed iron gates guarded by two stout policemen and an armed soldier. Upon seeing Stirling's gold encrusted peak cap, the soldier snapped to attention, shouldered his rifle and performed a perfect parade ground butt salute.

Stirling returned the salute as one of the policemen opened the gate. The noise of activity could be heard as they drove into the dockyard. The place was teeming with industry. Burly stevedores staggered down gangways humping heavy sacks and wooden boxes. Riveters clattered and chattered their deafening noise along the hulls of the ship; welders' torches hissed defiantly sending up white sparks reminiscent of Roman candles; railway goods wagons creaked and shunted alongside merchant ships. To this cacophony was added the cranking sound of cranes unloading cargo from the many, rust-encrusted freighters.

The peppery smell of diesel oil, dust and dirt stung the back of Stirling's throat and made his eyes water. Nevertheless, he could see four destroyers moored alongside the quayside. From the upper deck of one of them, its superstructure splotched with red lead, came the intermittent, sharp shudder of a pneumatic drill, while on the quayside, coils of wire, rope and crates awaited strong hands to carry them onboard; it was as if everyone knew the war was going badly and were in a hurry to do something about it.

Stirling felt his pulse quicken as they arrived at the next dock basin.

'That's the *Sandpiper,* sir,' cried the driver, shooting Stirling an excited glance. 'Tied up aft of that minesweeper.'

Stirling immediately recognised *Sandpiper* from consulting *Jane's Fighting Ships* a few weeks previously. Launched in 1937 and built by William Denny in Dumbarton, he knew that her maximum speed, generated by steam engines on two shafts, was a little over eighteen knots. This was faster than a corvette and most destroyers. And with a bit of luck, thought Stirling, she might be able to catch one of Doentiz's latest U-boats in a surface engagement. *Sandpiper*'s complement of 125 men included himself and four other officers. The ship's pennant number, S21, painted black, was barely visible against her green and grey camouflage. As they drove along the quay he took in the ship's sharp bows, the small fo'c'sle and A and B turrets each with their single 4.7 inch gun barrels poking menacingly upwards into the grey sky. Directly behind was the bridge, open to the elements. For a fleeting moment Stirling could almost sense the deck swaying under his feet and feel the wind and rain whipping against his face.

Behind the bridge was the crow's nest perched midway up the mainmast like a huge bird sanctuary. Behind this he could see the twin set 20 mm Oerlikons. Then came the wide quarterdeck with its depth charge guardrails and white ensign fluttering lazily from the jackstay. To Stirling this was the most important part of the ship's armament. It was from here that he intended to attack the enemy with all the might he could muster.

# CHAPTER THREE

At the top of the wooden gangway stood a tall, athletic looking officer and a small, stout petty officer. Close by was the duty quartermaster, a stocky, three badge Able Seaman. Next to him was the QM's runner, a young, pale-faced junior seaman. All four were stood smartly to attention ready to welcome their new captain.

Stepping onto *Sandpiper*'s deck, Stirling saluted as the shrill sound of the bosun's pipe echoed around the ship. This was quickly followed by, 'Attention on the upper deck,' being announced over the tannoy.

'Welcome aboard, sir,' said the officer, saluting while staring at the tall, lean individual facing him. 'Lieutenant Commander Manley, First Lieutenant,' he added, the corners of his deep-set dark blue eyes wrinkling into a nervous smile. 'I received a telephone message from Derby House earlier today, sir. Sir Percy Noble would like to see you tomorrow at 0900. I've ordered a tilly to pick you up at 0830.'

William Manley stood six feet tall with a weather beaten complexion, a legacy of hours spent on the open bridge. Stirling guessed Manley's age to be in his late twenties, but the grey hair on his sideboards suggested he could be older. He knew Manley was married to Patricia and had a two-year-old son called Kevin, both of whom lived in Reddich, a small town outside Coventry. The straight, two-and-half gold rings on Manley's sleeves showed he was regular navy. 'Thank you, Number One,' Stirling flatly replied. 'That'll be fine,' he paused and gave the PO and the QM a cursory nod, then in a slightly impatient tone, went on, 'now let's get on, shall we?'

'Of course, this way, sir,' Manley said, indicating with his hand. 'Your trunk arrived yesterday, it's in your cabin.'

The 'Carry On' pipe echoed around as the two officers made their way towards the citadel. Manley unhooked the clips of a hatchway and they entered the ship's main passageway. In doing so they were met by the warm, aromatic smell of paint, diesel oil and mansion polish. From below, the dull throb of the generators penetrated the soles of their shoes. Stirling sniffed the air and felt relaxed, at last he was back in the navy he had missed so much.

The two officers climbed down a hatchway and walked a short way along a narrow, stuffy passageway. Several ratings, dressed in their number one uniforms, stood back allowing him to pass. The time was 1600.

'I take it the ship is ready for sea?' Stirling anxiously enquired as he followed Manley down a flight of metal stairs onto the wardroom flat. They were interrupted by the strident voice of the duty QM piping over the tannoy, 'Secure. Liberty men fall in on the quarterdeck.' This was followed by the clatter of footsteps along the passageway and the upper deck.

'We completed ammunitioning and fuelling yesterday,' Manley answered firmly. 'The Chief ERA and Chief Stoker have tested the engines and they report all is well.'

'Good,' Stirling replied as they arrived outside the cabin door marked "Commanding Officer". Opposite was another door with a sign, painted in small gold lettering that read, "Wardroom".

Manley opened the cabin door and pulled back a curtain, stepping back to allow Stirling to enter. In doing so he took off his cap to reveal a head of fair hair parted neatly on the left. Stirling turned to him and in a firm but understanding voice said, 'I just want you to know that I'm aware of that problem you had when your minesweeper went aground,' he paused, allowing his words to sink in, 'and it cuts no ice with me. Do your job well and maybe you'll get a command of your own. Is that clear?'

'Yes, sir,' Manley replied, somewhat taken aback by his new captain's forthright manner. But was quickly pacified by the mention of him obtaining a command, something he longed for.

'Right,' Stirling said breezily. 'Now that we understand each other, I'll meet the officers in the wardroom at dinner tonight.' The clock on the bulkhead close to his desk read 1615, then added dismissively, 'Thank you, Number One, please carry on.'

After the First Lieutenant left, Stirling took off his overcoat, gas mask and steel helmet and hung them up behind the door. He smiled, realising that the gleaming black oilskin hanging next to them would no doubt be put to good use.

Painted in a pale shade of green, the cabin was larger than he expected. A glance upwards showed two strips of encased neon in a deck head covered with wires and piping, providing clear, shadowless lighting. On the port side were two open scuttles. Together with small curtains dawn on either side they helped to ventilate the cabin that smelt strongly of mansion polish. Above a small drinks cupboard was a small shelf containing a few box folders and books. These were kept safely in place by a wooden crosspiece. A made-up bunk resting on a long oaken chest took up most of the starboard side. Attached to the bulkhead next to an overhead light were a telephone and a voice pipe. Next to this were an oaken wardrobe and small writing desk with and a shaded electric lamp. Lying close to a heavy-looking round brass ashtray was a small red button. For a fleeting second Stirling was tempted to press it, but thought better of it.

On the bulkhead behind the desk was a gilt-framed photograph of King George VI and Queen Elizabeth. Next to this was the ship's wooden crest showing two sandpipers facing each other. Underneath was the motto, *Endure and Ye Shall Find,* written in Latin. Close by was a large coloured map of the world. A collapsible wooden chair was folded neatly under the desk. This was in sharp contrast to a comfortable looking, well worn brown leather armchair nestling at the side of the desk. Beneath this was a glass cabinet containing sets of keys and a small cupboard. Stirling later discovered this contained a few bottles of whiskey, a legacy of his predecessor. An open door led into a toilet and bathroom, also decorated in green. Finally, his eyes fell on his black, metal chest lying in the middle of the deck and covered in highly polished brow linoleum. With a sigh, he unbuttoned his jacket, took out a key, unlocked the top and started to unpack.

Ten minutes later a knock came at the cabin door and a tall, rangy steward with a pasty complexion and a mop of wavy black hair came in. He wore a short white jacket with shiny brass buttons. In one hand he held a white mug.

'First Lieutenant thought you'd like a cuppa tea, sir,' he said in a thick Geordie accent, his dark brown eyes wrinkling into a welcoming grin. 'I hopes you take sugar. The last captain didn't take any.'

Stirling had just finished hanging his clothes in the wardroom. He turned around and gave the steward an appreciative smile and said, 'Well I do, thank you, and tell Number One that's just what I need,' he replied, accepting the mug and blowing over the top. 'And who are you?'

'Steward Potts, sir,' he answered, 'I'll, er... be looking after you, so to speak, sir. Just press that red button on the desk if you need anything.'

'Hmm, I wondered what that was for,' said Stirling taking a careful sip of tea. 'My compliments to the First Lieutenant and ask him to meet me outside the wardroom at nineteen hundred.'

'Yes, sir,' answered Potts, who, with a broad smile, added, 'and welcome onboard, sir,' then left.

Stirling sat down at his desk and opened the envelope given to him by Captain Creasy. By the time he had read its contents he had a good idea about the background of his officers.

At precisely 1900, Manley met Stirling and they entered the wardroom. Inside, five officers were standing around, shuffling nervously while talking and smoking. My goodness, thought Stirling, noticing their youthful appearance, maybe it's me getting old, but they look so young! He could tell by the anxious looks on their faces they were just as nervous as he was. After all they knew only too well that a new captain could make their lives either miserable or otherwise.

The wardroom, painted in pale cream was surprisingly large. In the centre the table, complete with a pristine white tablecloth, was laid for dinner. Behind the door, caps, canvas gas mask valise. Steel helmets and a few overcoats hung from hooks. Strips of neon provided clear, shadowless lighting and a dark blue carpet embossed with the ubiquitous small gold anchors covered the deck. Close by the door was a glass cabinet containing sets of keys. Two leather armchairs lay near a small table cluttered with magazines and newspapers. A long settee draped in multi-coloured chinz material stretched along the base of the port side. Above this were three closed scuttles.

At the far end, near the open door leading into the galley, stood the wardroom Petty Officer Harry, "Slinger" Wood. A small, dapper man with a milk-white complexion, beady brown eyes and well-groomed dark hair. He wore a pristine white jacket with shiny brass buttons and carried a small white cloth neatly folded over his left arm. Nearby was a wooden cupboard on which rested an assortment of alcoholic drinks.

After a quick glance to Manley, Stirling moved towards the first officer, a sturdily built man in his mid twenties, with light brown, wavy hair and intense dark blue eyes.

'Lieutenant Anderson, sir,' the officer said, as they shook hands. 'Gunnery Officer.'

'Pleased to meet you, Guns,' replied Stirling feeling Anderson's firm grip. 'You're married with a young boy. I believe he's just started school. How is he getting along?'

'Andrew's just turned seven and finds it all rather confusing,' replied Anderson, somewhat surprised at Stirling's concern for his son. 'Thank you for asking, sir.'

'Not at all,' Stirling answered with a smile. 'I remember my son, Mark's first day at school. It was all very nerve-wracking. How is your wife?'

'Janet's fine, sir,' said Anderson, 'a bit lonely like most service wives.'

Standing next to Anderson was a tall, athletically-built surgeon lieutenant. Stirling judged him to be in his mid twenties. His healthy-looking features complemented his thick, dark, brown hair, neatly parted on the left side.

'Doctor Coburn, I believe,' Stirling said accepting the doctor's hand. 'I see your parents are dead and you're single. Any matrimonial prospects in view?' Stirling added with a slight mischievous smile.

'Ahem…' coughed the doctor, nervously clearing his throat. 'I am sort of engaged to a Third Officer Wren, sir.' He was about to tell him that Fiona was stationed at the Admiralty, but thought better of it. They had met at a cocktail party in the Royal Naval

Hospital at Chatham four months ago. Her mother had died a few years ago and she lived with her father in Stansfield, where he was the local vicar. His strict religious regime imposed on her since childhood had made her determined to get away from home as soon as she could. The war had provided her with a perfect reason for doing so.

'It's not that I'm against religion,' he remembered her saying somewhat disdainfully, 'but a lifetime of prayers before every meal, regular bible readings and church three times on Sunday, especially during holidays, is enough to put anyone off.'

He guessed, correctly as it turned out, her age to be twenty-four. She was not pretty, but beautiful with strong porcelain features with high cheekbones. Her eyes under curved brows were a captivating deep violet, her nose slightly aquiline. When she smiled her wide sensuous lips parted to reveal a set of white even teeth. After a few hastily arranged dates they realised they were falling in love. Courtesy of the navy she was billeted in a small, ground floor flat on the Gloucester Road. It was here that they first made love on a warm July evening a few weeks before he joined *Sandpiper*.

'Ah,' Stirling replied, raising his eyebrows, 'a man paying his romantic cards close to his chest eh? And what made you join the navy?'

In a well-modulated northern accent Coburn replied, 'My late father was a naval surgeon in the last war, sir, and I thought it would be more interesting than being a GP treating coughs and colds.'

'I see,' Stirling replied with a smile. 'I only hope you're not kept too busy.'

So far Coburn hadn't experienced being under fire and often wondered how he would react when it came. He would find the answer to that out sooner than he expected.

Stirling glanced up at the circle of electric bulbs embedded in a wooden plate on the deck head directly above the table. 'I only hope you won't have to use those,' he remarked warily. 'As you know, the wardroom can be used as an emergency operating station if necessary.'

'Yes I do, sir,' Coburn replied soberly, 'and I entirely share your sentiments.'

The officer standing next to the doctor was a small but heavily built man with thick, wavy black hair and a heavily lined face that made him look older than his twenty-four years.

'And you are?' Stirling asked as he offered his hand.

'Sub Lieutenant Weir, sir.' His accent was straight from the Scottish Highlands and as they shook hands his dark blue eyes wrinkled into a grin, 'Engineer officer.'

'You're from Castletown, I believe?' Stirling said, 'and did your degree at Glasgow University. This is your first ship, is it not?'

'Right on all three accounts, sir,' Weir firmly replied, 'and my stokers will be ready to flash up for sea, whenever you're ready.'

'Glad to hear it,' Stirling replied. 'They may be needed sooner than you think,' he added, glancing warily at Manley.

A small officer with a pallid complexion and whose long dark hair badly needed cutting stood next to Weir. His deep-set dark eyes half hidden behind horn-rimmed glasses made him look distinctly professorial.

'Sub Lieutenant Hailey, I believe,' said Stirling shaking the officer's hand. 'My secretary and the ship's supply officer. I do believe you're a Cambridge graduate, am I right?'

'Yes, sir,' John Hailey answered, glancing nervously at the deck. 'I hold a masters degree in medieval history.'

'Indeed,' Stirling replied, suitably impressed. 'I expect we'll be seeing quite a lot of one another.'

'And you must be Lieutenant Peter Graves, my Navigating Officer,' Stirling said, turning to a tall, fair-haired officer with a pair of strikingly pale blue eyes and a clear-cut, handsome face.

'That's correct, sir,' replied the officer, nervously running his tongue along his lips.

'You were married eight months ago, I believe,' Stirling said, giving the officer an inquisitive smile. 'When was the last time you saw your wife?'

'A week ago, sir,' Graves answered, suddenly feeling self-conscious. 'Most of the officers and crew had ten days' leave while the ship was in dry dock.'

'And where's home?' asked Stirling.

'Bayswater, London, sir,' Graves answered dryly, avoiding Stirling's eyes.

'Everything all right?' asked Stirling, detecting a slight look of concern on Graves' face.

'Er... yes, sir,' Graves replied, trying his best to sound convincing. How on earth could he possibly explain to Stirling or, indeed, anyone that everything *wasn't* all right? How could he tell him that his marriage to Dorothy had never been consummated? They had been introduced a year ago in London at a cocktail party. At that time Weir was stationed in Chatham Barracks awaiting a posting. Dorothy had just turned twenty-one and stood five feet plus with short blonde hair that curled neatly around the nape of her neck. He vividly remembered how ravishing she looked wearing a glittering pearl chocker and a low-cut black dress that did little to disguise her full figure. As they spoke her soft dulcet voice and beguiling turquoise eyes captivated him. He knew instantly he would fall in love with her. However, her father, a retired gentleman farmer, didn't approve of him.

'You can't trust sailors, my dear,' he had once overheard him say to her. 'A girl in every port. You can hardly expect him to be faithful to you.' Not that Dorothy had shown any interest in the opposite sex. The men in Biggleswade, a small village outside Cambridge, reminded her of country yokels in a Victorian novel.

Since Dorothy's mother's death three years ago, her father had become completely dependent on her. Dorothy kept the cottage neat and tidy and did all the shopping and cooking. However, even though she loved her father, she had long felt enclosed and unfulfilled. Graves realised later she had used him to get away from her father's influence. During there brief courtship she had never allowed him to touch her intimately. 'No, Peter,' she would say when his hand strayed. 'Wait until we're married.' However, on their wedding night she told him she had her period and insisted on separate beds. Shortly after he was appointed to *Sandpiper* he was granted a week's leave while the ship was in dry dock. By this time they had moved into a small flat in Bayswater. While he was away she had become friendly with a pretty dark-haired girl named Janet who lived in the flat above and had, on a few occasions gone out with her. *"All very innocent and above board",* she had written. When he was granted a week's leave, Dorothy complained of constant "tummy pains" and a headache. He was so frustrated that he almost forced himself upon her. Instead, he had to show her how to masturbate him. Now he would be going to sea and God knows when he would see her again.

At that moment, 'Mail will close in ten minutes,' echoed over the tannoy. This reminded Graves that he hadn't had a letter from

Dorothy for well over a week. Too busy gallivanting around with Janet, no doubt, he added with a touch of jealousy.

The last officers were two young sub lieutenants. One was tall and awkward-looking, whose wavy ginger hair contrasted sharply with his pale blue eyes set in a dark, narrow, face whose cheeks were spotted with acne. The other officer was small of stature, heavily tanned with straight well-kept brown hair and dark brown eyes that looked decidedly nervous.

'Now don't tell me,' Stirling said, staring inquisitively at them while shaking their hands. 'I know you are both not married but which one of you is Oliver Amery?'

'I am, sir,' the smaller of the two replied, nervously licking his lips. 'Asdic and fo'c'sle officer, sir.' His voice sounded plummy, like a BBC announcer.

'I do believe your father, Sir Charles Amery, is an MP for Chiswick, isn't he?'

'Er... yes, sir,' muttered Amery, feeling his cheeks burn.

'And your mother, Lady Amery, is she well?'

'Yes, thank you, sir,' Amery answered, feeling as if he was back at school standing before his headmaster. 'She's at our family home in Richmond.'

'And have *you* any political ambitions?' Stirling asked, raising his eyebrows and smiling.

Taking a deep breath, Amery replied, 'None at all, sir.' Inwardly he was petrified in case he failed to live up to his father's expectations.

"Blessed if I know why you joined the navy, my boy," his father had said dismissively one day, reclining in his favourite Chesterfield armchair. In one hand he held a copy of the *Financial Times* while smoking an expensive cigar. "You've always had a weak disposition and I'm sure the rigors of sea life will prove too much for you. If that is so, I'll see if I can't get you a cushy shore job somewhere."

For the past six months Amery had served onboard *Sandpiper* and been exposed to rough seas and wet, uncomfortable living conditions. How often while on his knees being violently seasick in a toilet bowl, he had thought about taking up his father's offer. But he was determined to prove his father wrong about him being weak. Gradually, with the help of a few pills, he slowly became accustomed to the turbulent motion of the ship. His vomiting became less frequent and he began to enjoy his new life.

'Good man,' said Stirling, nodding his head in agreement. He paused, cleared his throat and as if he had been reading Amery's mind, went on, 'I want you to remember that small ships like *Sandpiper* are the backbone of the navy. If you're unhappy about anything, come and see me. Understand?'

'Yes, sir,' said Amery. Stirling's veiled reference to small ships, suggested he knew about his dilemma.

'And you must be Henry Harper-Smyth,' Stirling said, shifting his gaze to the taller officer suffering from acne.

'Yes, sir,' the officer answered. He spoke with a distinct, but quiet West Country burr. 'Deck and Depth Charge Officer, sir.'

'And a fellow West Countryman,' said Stirling. 'In case you haven't heard I'm a Plymouth man. You're from Penzance, I hear?' Stirling said, pursing his lips. 'I do believe they have damn fine sailing club there. Is that right?'

'Indeed they have, sir,' Harper-Smyth replied. 'And I was a member before the war.'

Stirling gave a slight cough, then in a stern voice said, 'Yours is the most important job onboard. If your team are not up to scratch it'll mean the difference between sinking the enemy and allowing him to escape. I'm sure you understand that?'

'Yes, do, sir,' replied Harper-Smyth. 'And I can assure you, sir, we'll be ready for them.'

'That's very reassuring,' Stirling answered dryly. 'I only hope you're right.'

The sly old devil, Harper-Smyth thought. He knows I was barred from the sailing club after crashing a yacht against the harbour jetty while celebrating my twentieth birthday.

'Now,' Stirling said, staring hopefully into his empty cup. 'Perhaps I could have another cup of coffee before I continue my talk. And do sit down.'

A few minutes later Petty Officer Wood appeared and handed Stirling a cup and saucer. Stirling took a good sip then placed the cup and saucer on a nearby table. He then took a deep breath and looked around staring at the faces of men he would soon recognise as well as his own.

'Now that we've met, gentlemen,' Stirling said, placing both hands in his jacket pockets allowing his thumbs to show, 'I have a few things to say before dinner. Firstly, for the time being, the Standing Orders of my predecessor will remain,' he paused, before continuing, his brow deeply furrowed and his gaze steady. 'With the help of everyone here my intention is to destroy as many U-boats as possible. In order to do this, every department will have to be doubly efficient and work to its full capacity. This can only be achieved by constant drilling night and day until I'm satisfied. I will not tolerate any form of slackness. However, I will encourage everyone to make decisions on the spot and learn by your mistakes. In a few weeks we will be joined by four other sloops and form the 15th Escort Group, based here in Liverpool.' He paused, looked around then said, 'Any questions?'

'May I ask when we're going to sea, sir?' Lieutenant Coburn asked, anxiously leaning forward in his chair.

'I'll be able to answer that after I meet Sir Percy Noble in the morning,' Stirling replied staring directly at Coburn.

'Any idea where we'll be going, sir?' Sub Lieutenant Weir asked, raising a hand.

'Your guess is as good as mine,' Stirling replied, 'but when the other ships arrive, I expect we'll have to do a work up. Now,' he went on, 'if there's no other questions, I suggest we have dinner.'

# CHAPTER FOUR

Derby House was situated just off Water Street not far from the iconic Liver Building. This was the headquarters of Combined Operations, responsible for control of the Western Approaches. Originally housed in Plymouth, the organisation was transferred to Liverpool in February 1941. This was because shipping travelling to Britain was vulnerable to U-boat attack and from the Luftwaffe stationed on the French coast. Shipping, therefore, had to be redirected around the northern tip of Ireland.

The Citadel or Fortress of Derby House with its seven-foot thick roof and three-foot thick walls was designed to be bomb proof. The 100 rooms covered an area of 50,000 square feet. The Germans had a good idea that such a place existed, but failed to find out exactly where it was – hence the devastation that had occurred around the area during the bombing.

The man responsible for this was Admiral Sir Percy Lockhart Harnam Noble, Royal Navy. He was a thickset man whose pleasant but firm disposition made him easy to work with. It was a trait his wife Celia admonished him about during his rare periods of leave at the family home in the Lake District.

'Nonsense my dear,' he invariably replied, kissing her softly on the cheek. Although born in India in 1880, his clear, well-modulated voice had a distinct Old Etonian tone. 'I find being pleasant to people brings out the best in them.'

The admiral's once thick dark hair was now greying at the temples. The pallid colour of his fleshy features was off set by a firm chin, an aquiline nose and thin lips, all of which gave his appearance one of solid determination. A thick gold ring below four thinner ones on each sleeve of his immaculately tailored uniform designated his rank. And on his breast pocket, standing out among the slightly faded row of First World War medals, were the scarlet and mauve colours of his CBE and KCB (Commander of the British Empire and Knight Commander of the Bath).

While awaiting the arrival of Stirling the admiral was sat behind his wide oak desk cluttered with official documents. In front of him lay a report marked TOP SECRET. After he had finished reading it, he looked up and with a worried sigh, slowly shook his head. He then sat back in his chair and allowed his keen, but tired grey eyes to take in the room in which he spent at least fifteen hours a day. Despite being enclosed well below the surface of the road he was always surprised at the clarity of the atmosphere provided by an efficient air conditioning unit. The floor was covered with the usual dark blue carpet embossed with small gold anchors. Coloured maps of every ocean and continent almost obliterated the walls painted a boring dull cream. What space remained was taken up with shelves containing box files and official books. A framed black and white photograph of King George VI and Queen Elizabeth hung on the wall behind the desk. In one corner close to an oak door rested a tall, green metal filing cabinet above which stood a white vase with a bunch of wilting daffodils. Next to this was an oak drinks cupboard with glass panels. In front of the desk rested two brown leather armchairs, a sofa and a shiny walnut table containing a small silver cigarette box, a matching lighter and heavy brass ashtray. The only item of sophisticated living was the small crystal chandelier that hung from a high, stuccoed white ceiling. The admiral smiled and realised that if everything was removed, the place would resemble a cell in Walton Prison.

At precisely 0850 the tilly stopped outside Derby House.

'I may be some time,' Stirling told the driver before sliding open the door and climbing out, 'but you'd better wait.'

Returning the salute of the armed Royal Marine he entered the building then walked along a narrow balcony. The atmosphere was warm, slightly claustrophobic and smelt strongly of tobacco smoke. On his left were doors marked "Telecommunications", "Decoding Room" and "Operations". Directly below the balcony was a very large area on the walls of which were chalked the names of ships in convoys in various areas of the Atlantic and North Sea. Nearby, officers of the Royal Navy, Army and RAF, equipped with headphones, waited to receive the latest convoy information. In the centre was a wide rectangular table with a map showing the numbers, names and deployment of the ships. Close by, Wrens and WAAFs, wearing service slacks, stood on moveable ladders near the walls making notations of convoy movements. This information, received via the Operations Room by the officers, was passed to the female personnel who, using long-handled markers, leaned across the table and removed small wooden models of ships that were reported sunk. Alternatively, they plotted the progress or otherwise of the convoys. Faced with the reality of lives being lost, the women tried not to think of the sorrow that awaited wives, parents and sweethearts. It was a feeling each one tried to hide, only to be spoken of in quiet moments of reflection.

A sharp, but clear female voice from the desk intercom announcing the arrival of Commander Stirling interrupted the admiral's reverie. The time on the clock above the door read 0900.

'Send him in, please, Joan,' replied the admiral, sitting back in his chair.

Stirling came in nervously holding his cap in his left hand; after all, it wasn't every day he was called before such a distinguished officer.

'Do come in,' said the admiral, raising himself up to his six feet plus height and offering his hand. 'Hang your coat and gas mask behind the door and take a seat. Coffee?' His manner, warm and courteous, immediately made Stirling feel relaxed.

'That's very kind of you, sir,' Stirling replied as they warmly shook hands. 'But no thank you.' He then hung up his gear and lowered himself into one of the armchairs.

'Then help yourself to a cigarette, I don't use them, for visitors only you understand,' the admiral said, indicating the silver box. 'It's Robert, isn't it, or should I call you Bob?'

'Bob will do fine, sir,' Stirling answered as he leaned forward, opened the box, took out a cigarette and lit it. Exhaling a steady stream of smoke he relaxed back in his chair. Anticipating the admiral's next question, he confidently added, 'And *Sandpiper* is fully stored and ready for sea, sir.'

'I'm very glad to hear it,' the admiral replied, smiling pleasantly as he sat down. 'And I expect you'll want to see how she handles and get to know the crew.'

'Indeed, sir,' said Stirling, flicking his ash into the ashtray.

'Then I suggest you sail the day after tomorrow at 0800,' the admiral replied, 'and I'll send for you when you return.'

'Convoy duty, sir?' Stirling enquired, raising eyebrows and smiling warily.

'Perhaps, my boy,' the admiral said, then forcibly tapping the report with his finger, went on, 'the blasted Hun is taking a terrible toll of our shipping. A convoy of forty ships left Halifax three weeks ago. By the time they arrived in Britain, eighteen were lost with several others severely damaged. Another one containing fifty-five merchantmen from Nova Scotia lost over half of its vessels,' the admiral stopped talking for a few seconds and furrowed his brow, 'that's over 90,000 tons in just over a month. Winston maintains the country needs 70,000 tins of food a month to survive, so you see, the situation if not checked, will soon become desperate.' He paused and raising his thick, greying eyebrows, sat forward and placed both hands on the table. 'Now,' he went on, taking a deep breath, 'when you were at *Osprey* you proposed a few rather unusual tactics to combat the U-boat menace, some of which were in sharp contrast to those advocated by the Prime Minister.'

'Not really, sir,' Stirling tentatively replied. 'With respect to Winston, he suggests the escorts should cavort miles away from the convoy seeking out the enemy like a nautical cavalry charge. In my opinion this is wrong. This should be done only if there is Asdic contact relatively close to the convoy. I realise this is taking a chance, but so far, the U-boats have proved almost immune to surface or airborne search. They like to do their work on the surface at night, trimmed down so as to make a poor silhouette. Reports tell us that after torpedoing a ship, the U-boats usually remained close to the stricken vessel to capture her captain or speed away thus escaping from the slower escorts. If the escorts do dash around before making contact with the enemy, they leave the convoy open to attack.'

'What would you propose, then?' enquired the admiral and giving Stirling a searching look.

'I should use one group to protect the convoy,' answered Stirling, 'and another to seek out the enemy when contacts are made.' Stirling paused, stubbed out his cigarette then continued,

'When one of them got through and attacked, I would then plaster the area around the torpedoed ship with depth charges forcing the blighters to dive and illuminate the most likely direction they would make their escape. Once submerged, it should be easier for the escorts to sink the buggers.'

The admiral leaned forward and picked up the secret report. Suddenly, his pleasant manner became serious. He narrowed his grey eyes and his jaw line became even firmer than normal.

'Hmm...' mused the admiral, studying the paper again. 'Your ideas leave a lot to chance. Using star shells to illuminate the area could expose the rest of the convoy. And even if you guessed correctly the escape route of the enemy, the U-boats can outrun any of our present escorts.'

'With respect, sir,' Stirling replied cagily. 'It wouldn't be guesswork. Experience shows the U-boats invariably make away from the rear of the convoys.'

'I see what you mean,' the admiral said, sitting back and folding his arms. 'However, the only problem is the paucity of escorts. In 1939 we only had a handful of sloops whose endurance made them ideal for escort work. But they are still thin on the ground. The Americans have sent us those fifty old destroyers. Of course they will help, but it will take time for the British crews to become used to them, so at present we must make do with what we've got. Nevertheless,' the admiral said, rising slowly from his chair, 'your ideas do seem rather unorthodox,' he added as they shook hands. 'I'll speak to you again when you return from sea. In the meantime be guided by Winston. It'll make him happy and keep him off my back. Good luck to you and your crew, my boy.'

Stirling thanked him, unhooked his overcoat, gas mask and steel helmet and left the room. His meeting with the admiral had left him somewhat frustrated. Seeking U-boats in a wide area around a convoy as advocated by the Prime Minister would, in his opinion, be like looking for a needle in a haystack. 'He's wrong,' muttered Stirling, 'and one day I shall prove it.'

With a feeling of relief Stirling made his way to the exit. Outside the cold February air attacked his face. Thank God, Stirling thought, as he drew back the door of the tilly and climbed inside. At long last I can get to sea and come to grips with those bloody U-boats.

# CHAPTER FIVE

Onboard *Sandpiper,* QM Able Seaman Jackson, watched as the tilly came along the wharf and stopped at the bottom of the gangway.

'Captain coming onboard,' cried Jackson.

Bob Shilling, the tall, sandy-haired Duty PO, turned and in a thick North Country accent, repeated the information by shouting down a nearby hatchway to the wardroom. A few seconds later the First Lieutenant appeared in time to salute Stirling as he stepped onto the ship's steel plated deck.

'Good morning, Number One,' Stirling said, returning the salutes of Manley and PO Shilling. 'We sail on Wednesday, at 0800. Leave will finish at 2300 on Tuesday. Make sure this is on tomorrow's Daily Orders.'

'Very good, sir,' replied Manley, as Stirling turned and made his way down a hatchway to his cabin.

PO Shilling gave Manley an all-knowing look, grinned and whispered, 'No need to put it on Orders, sir, it'll be all around the ship in next to no time.'

The time was a little after 1000. Stand Easy had been piped and several senior ratings were in the mess enjoying a mug of tea. Most of them were smoking and the warm atmosphere was heavy and sticky. The door opened and in came Bob Shilling grinning like a Cheshire cat.

'Well lads,' he said, rubbing his hands together and looking around. 'You'll all be 'appy to know we're going to sea on Wednesday at 0800.'

'How d'yer know that?' The speaker was Chief Stoker Digger Barnes, a medium sized, dark-haired Yorkshireman whose pale blue watery eyes matched his pallid complexion. Barnes was married with a son in the army. He had been in the navy for over twenty-one years and was due for his pension. The outbreak of war had put that on hold adding to his already poor disposition.

'I 'eard him tell the Jimmy when he came onboard just before,' Bob smugly replied. 'Now where's the char?'

'What's the new captain like?' Digger enquired, taking a sip from his mug. 'I hear he's tall and is a stickler for discipline.'

'He certainly is a big bugger,' Bob answered, raising his eyebrows. 'He's like a beanpole and glares down at you when he speaks. If you ask me he's a man who'll take no nonsense from anybody.'

'A mate of mine in *Osprey* told me he's a specialist in anti-submarine warfare,' added Percy Bradley, a tall, rangy thirty something Chief ERA with dark hair, well lined features and baggy grey eyes, 'and his lad's a midshipman in submarines.'

Two other men holding mugs of steaming hot tea joined them.

'What 'ave you 'eard, Pony?' Bob asked the taller of the two, a small stocky grey-haired Coxswain Petty Officer named Daniel Moore.

'Search me, lad,' replied Moore in a thick Liverpool accent. Moore was a brawny six-foot, three-badge man with sharp, penetrating grey eyes. He was divorced and when in port was living "tally" with Hilda, a buxom blonde barmaid working in the *Nag's Head*, an old Edwardian pub situated in Bootle. As he spoke his heavily tanned face creased into a wide grin as he watched the steam rising from his mug. 'I only 'ope he speaks better than the last skipper. I could hardly understand his orders when I was on the wheel,' he added, carefully taking a sip of tea. 'Some of these officers talk so posh I don't fuckin' well know wot they're sayin'.'

'Hark who's talking, my 'andsome,' interrupted Chief Gunnery Instructor Miller, his pale blue eyes glancing enquiringly over his mug. "Dusty", as he was known, was from Truro in Cornwall. 'I can never savy anything you say.'

'Only when yer want ter borrow a few quid on blank week, yer miserable bugger,' Pony sarcastically replied.

At that moment in came a medium sized, white-haired, wizened-faced chief petty officer, blowing into his hands. 'I hopes you lot have saved me some char,' he said, picking up a large aluminium teapot. 'If it gets any colder me balls will drop off.'

'They might as well, Ben,' Dusty Miller replied, tossing his head back and laughing. 'At your age it's a wonder they haven't wasted away through lack of use.'

Seaman Chief Petty Officer Ben Lyon was serving his fifth five (twenty-five years) when the war prevented him retiring. He was from Newcastle and like his oppo, Digger Barnes, he was non-too happy with Hitler.

'Cheeky bugger,' Ben angrily replied, 'now pass me the sugar and pipe down.'

As Ben stirred his tea Bob told him about the ship sailing.

'Bloody good job, too, if you ask me lovely lad,' replied Ben, 'too much time in port makes some of them soft. Ain't that right, Spud?'

His question was aimed at Henry Murphy, nicknamed "Spud". He was a medium sized, well-built three-badge Seaman Petty Officer, with dark curly hair, bloodshot blue eyes and a typical Bass drinker's rubicund complexion.

'Quite right, boyo,' said Spud in a deep accent straight from the Welsh Valleys. 'Most of the depth charge party have just joined the ship. Just wait till I get 'em on the quarterdeck. Anyways,' he added with a toothy grin, 'I expect most of the buggers will be poxed up.'

Meanwhile Able Seaman Jackson was also quick to spread the word about the ship sailing. He was sitting at a well-scrubbed table in the for'd seamen's mess enjoying a mug of tea. With him were several ratings. Those off duty wore a vest and underpants; the rest were dressed in overalls, faded pale blue from constant scrubbing. Bits of clothing hung from steel rails next to lashed up hammocks. The air was warm and heavy with the smell of sweat, tobacco and bodily odours. Swirling clouds of cigarette smoke lay close to the deck head that were covered with boxed-in cables, wires and punkah-louvres. (These were movable air vents that could be altered to re-direct or close off the air.)

Everyone stopped talking and listened to what Jackson had to say.

'How long do you think we'll be at sea, Jacko?' asked Ordinary Seaman "Nipper" Morris, a young fresh-faced lad with dark hair and pale blue eyes. 'I have a date tomorrow with a party I met at the Grafton.' (This was a popular ballroom close to the city centre.)

One or two ratings gave each other all-knowing looks and grinned. 'To be sure, if you mean that ugly bitch I saw you dancing with,' remarked Patrick Duffy, a burly Able Seaman from Belfast. 'Drop her like hot cakes. She's poxed up to the hilt.'

'How do you know that, Paddy?' Nipper asked, with an air of innocence.

'Why d'yer think the doc stopped me tot,' Paddy replied, shrugging his shoulders and grinning, 'and I'm under stoppage of leave.'

'Me too, Nipper,' came a gruff voice from the stoker's mess deck. This area was separated from the seamen by a row of metal lockers. 'I had a short time with her last week. Best stay onboard and toss yerself off.'

'Come on, Jacko,' said another rating, 'answer Nipper's question. How long will we be at sea?'

'How the hell do I know,' retorted Jacko, finishing his tea and standing up. 'I'm only a simple gunnery rating. Now bugger off.'

The same questions were being asked in the Supply and Secretariat Mess. This was where cooks, stewards, stores and medical personnel lived. It was situated right aft near the sick bay which lay almost directly under X gun turret.

'From what I hear, we're sailing at 0800 on Wednesday,' said Sick Berth Attendant "Brum" Appleby, a big, athletically built lad from Birmingham with an untidy mop of light brown wavy hair. As he stared around at the anxious faces of his messmates, his dark blue eyes set in a round fleshy face, wrinkled into an all-knowing grin. 'My boss told me a few minutes ago.'

'More bloody evolutions, I suppose,' growled Stores Assistant "Dixie" Dean, a tall, gangly, dark-haired lad from Doncaster. Along with Steward "Smudge" Smith and Writer "Chats" Harris, he was a member of the first aid party. 'Up and down ladder carrying bodies in Neil Robertson stretchers, makes me bloody sick it does.'

'Maybe you'd be better off being a casualty,' remarked Dixie rubbing his hands together and grinning wildly, 'then we could throw you overboard.'

Just then 'Out Pipes, Hands Turn To' echoed around the ship.

'Oh well,' said Brum, smiling slyly, 'no rest for the wicked. Must away and get out those lovely big syringes with big round ends that I use for sticking down the dicks of those of you who've caught the boat up. Judging by what I've heard, I'll need them.'

'You're all the same,' Dixie muttered sarcastically, 'bloody sadists, the lot of you.'

An hour later 'Up Spirits, Cooks To The Galley' was piped. In the Spirit Room, the ship's Tanky, Able Seaman Buster Brown, a small, portly two-badge man from Manchester, had just finished checking his mess list. The contents of this small, claustrophobic space were considered sacrosanct. It was here that the supply of rum was kept. The door was made of steel and Tanky had the only key.

Using a shiny brass jug Tanky transferred the requite amount of rum from a large jar into a stout, highly polished oaken barrel. Around the middle of the barrel embossed in a wide, shiny brass plate, were the words, THE KING. GOD BLESS HIM. Nearby was another, smaller barrel containing water. Next to this, resting on a table was another jug, larger than the one Tanky had used. At that moment the rangy figure of Duty CPO Dusty Miller entered the room.

'Got the water measured out, Tanky, my bird?' Dusty asked while sniffing the air.

'That I 'ave,' replied Tanky. 'The senior rates' rum is in that big jug on the table.'

'Right, let's do the junior rates,' Dusty said, 'how much water?'

'Four jugs' worth,' replied Tanky. 'Two in one it is.'

Dusty dipped his jug into the barrel of water and measured out four lots of water then poured them into the barrel containing the rum. Using the empty jug he then mixed up the water and rum.

'I wish we could have neaters like you lot,' Tanky moaned as he tenderly placed a wooden lid on the barrel. Tanky was referring to the fact that ratings below the rank of petty officer had their issue weakened by adding two parts of water to one of rum. Senior ratings were allowed to have theirs neat.

'Ah, stop complaining,' replied Dusty. 'After the officer of the watch and meself have dished it out to the duty mess rum bosuns, you can come round and I'll give you a sip of mine.'

Taking hold of the handles on each side they carried the barrel up a flight of ladders onto the canteen flat. It was here under the auspices of the Officer of the Watch, that the duty CPO, using a jug and Tanky's checklist, issued the rum to the duty rating from each mess. Except in the naval hospitals it was a daily ritual that was carried out in every ship and shore establishment in the navy throughout the world.

Shortly after secure at midday, 'Mail is ready for collection' came over the tannoy. In the wardroom everyone except for OOW Sub Lieutenant Amery was standing around talking and smoking while enjoying a gin and tonic. However, Peter Graves, the Navigating Officer, stood apart from them, his heart racing, hoping he would receive a letter from his wife before the ship sailed in the morning.

'Here we are, gentlemen,' cried Slinger Wood, the wardroom PO as he came in cheerfully clutching a bundle of letters. 'Mail from your wives, sweethearts and bank managers.' He placed the letters on a table and was immediately surrounded by officers.

'One for you, Peter,' shouted Surgeon Lieutenant Colin Coburn handing Graves a buff-coloured envelope. During the past weeks he and the other officers couldn't help but notice the dispirited expression in Graves' eyes and face at not receiving any mail. With a look of relief Sub Lieutenant Jock Weir watched as the doctor handed the letter to Graves.

'Thank you, Colin,' Graves replied, almost snatching the envelope from his colleague. He immediately recognised Dorothy's small, neat handwriting. Tearing open the letter he felt his hand shake. Turning away from the others, Graves withdrew a single folded piece of cream writing paper. As he read the opening paragraph he felt the blood drain from his face. He blinked several times to ensure himself he was reading properly. The letter ran...

*"Dear Peter,*

*I am writing to tell you that I have met someone else and have decided to leave you. I know this will come as a shock, but I have felt for some time that physically and emotionally our marriage wasn't going to work out. Please don't blame yourself, the fault, I can assure you, lies entirely with me."*

Graves paused to allow the words to sink in. He turned and knocked into Colin.

'Are you all right, Peter?' said Colin, staring at Graves. 'You look a little pale.'

Graves ignored him and as if in a trance, slowly lowered himself into an armchair. As he did so he felt a sickening emptiness in the pit of his stomach and for a moment he thought he would faint. He then looked down and continued reading the letter.

*"I realise we haven't been married long, but from the beginning I knew I was wrong to marry you. Perhaps it was an excuse to get away from my father. I am sorry if this hurts you, but as I've already mentioned, I have become very close to another person. If you wish a divorce I will only be too glad to agree to whatever you want. Please don't come to the flat, it would only make matters worse. Try to forget me, and I hope one day you will find happiness with another woman.*

*Yours affectionately,*
*Dorothy"*

Graves hardly heard the ribald comments of his fellow officers as they read their mail. Staring vacantly at the carpet-covered deck, Graves slowly folded the letter and placed it in the envelope. He suddenly felt a hand on his shoulder. He looked up and saw the heavily lined face of Jock Weir.

'What's the matter, laddo?' he said, grinning while holding a gin and tonic. 'Don't tell me she's run of with the milkman?'

Graves felt something snap inside him. He stood up and knocking Jock's drink out of his hand, shouted, 'Why don't you mind your own bloody business?' And under the surprised gaze of the other officers, stood up and stormed out of the mess.

After Graves had left, Jock Weir turned to Coburn. 'Och man,' he said, shaking his head in disbelief, 'Peter must have received some bad news. It's not like him to be so bad tempered.'

'Mmm... yes, you're right, Jock,' Coburn replied ponderously. 'As far as I know he hasn't had a letter from his wife for some time now. If that was from her, I hope it wasn't bad news.'

Graves reached his cabin which was situated below the after deck house next to those of the other officers. He went inside and slammed the door. Without switching on the small electric light, he slumped on a chair near his desk. His head was spinning and he felt a mixture of anger and jealousy raging through him.

'How could she do this to me?' he cried, placing both elbows on the desk and holding his head in his hands. 'And who is this man she has met? I'll kill the bastard and her with him.'

# CHAPTER SIX

'Special Sea Duty men fall in. Close all screen doors and hatches,' echoed around the ship. The time was 0730 on Wednesday 4 September.

Lieutenant Commander Bill Manley knocked sharply on Stirling's door and entered. He was wearing a dark brown duffle coat and a muffler.

'Port and starboard lookouts closed up. Ship's ready for sea, sir,' Manley reported, adding, 'a strong nor-westerly wind is blowing down river and the barometer's dropping.'

'Thank you, Number One,' Stirling replied, standing up and reaching for his cap. 'I'll be up right away.'

Manley left the cabin as Stirling struggled into his duffle coat and tucked a white towel around his neck. After making sure his cigarettes and lighter were in his pocket he left and made his way up top. The canvas awning attached around the bridge did little to protect Stirling as a bitterly cold wind invaded his face.

'Good morning, gentlemen,' Stirling said, in a stern but pleasant manner, acknowledging Manley and "Harry" Tate a stocky, red-faced two-badge Petty Officer Yeoman from Doncaster. Next to him standing by the binnacle was Gunnery Officer Lieutenant Anderson, nervously shuffling his feet. In a small compartment aft of the bridge, Lieutenant Graves was bent over a table on which rested a chart of the Irish and North Seas. He had spent a sleepless night and felt heavy eyed. Standing in the port wing was Able Seaman Jackson, the duty QM and his runner,

Junior Seaman Nipper Clark a tall, thin-faced lad, who, three months ago, earned five shillings a week delivering groceries. When Stirling arrived, nobody shouted, "captain on the bridge", a ritual reserved for those serving onboard larger ships. Nevertheless, the tension felt by everyone was evident not only on the bridge, but throughout the ship. Many, especially the officers, realised their futures depended on how they performed. The "buzz" had spread around the ship that their new captain was a stickler for efficient drill and routine. They would all soon find out how true that was.

'Coxswain on the wheel, ser, everyone closes up,' came the sharp Scouse voice of Pony Moore in the wheelhouse.'

'Thank you, coxswain,' replied Stirling heaving himself up into his chair. 'Ring on engines, Number One, and stand by to single up. I'll use the head spring.'

(When the engines are put to 'Ahead' this will cause the ship's stern to slowly swing out.)

'Let go head rope.' Using a loudhailer, this order was passed to Sub Lieutenant Amery and his party on the fo'c'sle.

'Head rope gone, sir,' Amery signalled as a seaman on the wharf removed the rope from the for'd bollard.

Stirling left his chair and moved to the port wing.

'In fenders,' he added. 'Let go aft,' he shouted. His order was quickly related to Sub Lieutenant Harper-Smyth on the quarterdeck. The order was obeyed and Harper-Smyth raised a white flag to show the rope was inboard and clear of the propellers.

Still leaning over the port wing Stirling shouted, 'Slow ahead, Number one.'

The order was passed below to Jock Weir who rang the speed on the revolution telegraph. Everyone felt the deck vibrate as the engines suddenly sprang into action.

'Half ahead, revolutions one hundred.'

PO Coxswain Moore below repeated the order.

Half an hour later, after passing through two locks, *Sandpiper* entered the calm, dark green waters of the River Mersey. Away to their left, New Brighton Pier, jutting out into the river like a man-made peninsula, looked deserted and forlorn. Opposite Bootle and the Liverpool docks lay the Forth Perch Rock. Constructed in 1826, this imposing edifice was built to protect the port against the French. However, its guns never fired a shot in real anger. That is, until 1940 when the Royal Artillery was stationed there, adding its firepower against the Luftwaffe.

'Increase revolutions one two, steer green ten oh,' Stirling calmly said. Once again, Coxswain PO Moore repeated the order.

Some two hundred yards away on the ship's starboard bow the mast, yardarm and rusting funnel showed above the water. With his binoculars clamped to his eyes Stirling asked, 'What's the name of that wreck, Pilot?'

From his compartment, Graves replied, 'According to my chart, sir, it's the remains of an Irish ferryboat called the *Tacoma Star*, sunk during an air raid in May.'

'Thank you, Pilot,' Stirling answered, silently hoping her crew got off safely, but doubting it. 'Fall out sea duty men. Number One. Steer One One Zero. Best to keep well clear of it.' Giving Manley an approving glance, he added, 'The ship seems to handle quite well, Number One.'

'So far, sir,' Manley replied with a slight air of scepticism.

Passing the Bar lighthouse, *Sandpiper* sailed into Liverpool Bay. Directly ahead the horizon was a blurred grey as angry rollers charging in from the Irish Sea hit the ship bow on. Huge waves of white spray cascaded over the fo'c'sle as the ship reared up before flopping back into the sea. The wind increased and a thin mist of rain began to fall from the angry, dark, low-lying clouds.

'What was that you said, sir?' yelled Manley as he grasped hold of a stanchion.

Stirling didn't reply. Instead he reached forward and pressed the alarm bell. He then bent into the voice-pipe and shouted, 'Hands to action stations. Unidentified planes approaching,' repeating the order again. The time was just after 0900.

With a startled expression Lieutenant Anderson quickly donned his steel helmet and climbed up above the bridge to his small gun director station. He then put on headphones that would connect with all turrets including the twin pom-poms and 20 mm Oerlikons. Engineer Lieutenant Jock Weir disappeared below. PO Yeoman Harry Tate and the others pulled on their anti-flash gear and donned their steel helmets. The two lookouts did the same, glancing anxiously at the sky.

The heavy trample of boots as men rushed to their stations could be heard over the sound of the sea beating against the ship. Some lost their footing and slipped on the watery deck. Others stumbled as they climbed up ladders while those already closed up looked at one another and shook their heads in disbelief.

'Aircraft me arse, Pincher,' yelled Leading Seaman, Bungy Williams, captain of A Gun, to Able Seaman Pincher Martin, his opposite number on B turret. 'If he can see a bloody plane in this weather I'm a fuckin' Dutchman.'

'Yer right there, Bungy,' came Pincher's surly reply from the platform below. 'I wouldn't mind, but we haven't even got radar.'

'All guns closed up, sir,' reported Anderson via his headphone to the bridge. Shortly afterwards all departments followed suit.

'Eight minutes, Number One,' commented Stirling, wiping water from his face and looking at his watch. 'Not good enough, far too slow,' he added solemnly, 'especially the depth charge party.'

Stirling unhooked the voice-pipe. 'This is the captain speaking,' he said in a sharp, stern voice. 'That was a drill. If an enemy plane had attacked us, in all probability we'd be sunk. All departments must act quicker. Be prepared to close up at action stations at any time, day or night. Only speedy and efficient drill will enable us to defeat the enemy. That is all. Secure from actions stations.'

'What does he think we've doing since we commissioned last year,' Able Seaman "Jumper" Cross sarcastically remarked as he secured the starboard Oerlikon, 'playin' bloody uckers?'

'Aye,' said Bud Abbott, his number one ammunition feeder, a small, ruddy-faced Able Seaman from Bury. 'But don't forget, we've had a load of HOs join us since then who are as green as grass.'

The force of the wind increased and the rain, fine at first, turned into slanting lines of icy water. Visibility decreased, blotting out what little daylight there was.

On the bridge the wind and rain rattled against the canvas awning offering scant protection to those on duty. Looking like miniature eruptions, the rain spread over the sea as far as the eyes could see. The ship began to dip and roll as they ploughed through the heaving seas. In the mess decks, men clung to anything at hand. Passageways became dangerously slippery. Loose gear rattled in lockers like an orchestra tuning up. Hammocks, lashed up, swayed in unison as if pushed by an unseen hand while those men, unused to the motions of the sea, vomited into buckets and aluminium spittoons.

'What's our course, and speed, Number One?' Stirling shouted, his voice carrying above the wind.

'Course one, one two, speed ten knots, sir,' Manley cried, wiping his eyes while bending towards the compass bearing.

'And our position, Pilot?' Stirling asked using his binoculars to study the bleak outline of the Lancashire coastline.

'Thirty miles due north, sir, latitude fifty degrees, longitude eighty,' Graves quickly replied after using his dividers to check the map.

'Thank you,' said Stirling. 'Increase revolutions ten, steer one, one oh.'

'Revolutions increased. Steer one, one oh, sir,' shouted Able Seaman Wiggy Bennett from the wheelhouse.

Just before 'Up Spirits' at 1130, Stirling smiled slyly at Manley. 'This will make me the most unpopular man in the ship,' he said as he pressed the alarm bell. 'Hands to action stations,' he yelled down the voice-pipe. 'Submarine contact ten miles away on the port bow. Set depth at two hundred feet.' Once again the sound of men running to their stations could be heard throughout the ship.

On the quarterdeck the black, drum-shaped depth charges were laid on runners over the stern. At one end of each depth charge was a special nut. The nut is attached to a mechanism leading inside the drum to the depth charge adjuster. Using a special wrench, a rating can set the various explosive depths. As the ship moves ahead, a depth charge is launched to port, then another to starboard; finally one is dropped astern to complete a diamond pattern. The rate of which each formation is dropped depends on the efficiency of the depth charge crew.

Stirling sat back in his chair, studied his wristwatch and pursed his lips. Five minutes elapsed before all departments reported in.

'Still too bloody slow, Number One,' Stirling grunted, 'especially Amery and his depth charge team.'

'At least the gunnery department have improved, sir,' Manley replied, glancing approvingly at Lieutenant Anderson above on the gun director platform.

'Quite so, Number One,' Stirling flatly replied, 'but it's depth charges that sink U-boats.'

'The weather may have something to do with it, sir,' Manley replied tersely.

'Tell that to Admiral Doenitz,' Stirling answered, frowning while shaking his head. 'It won't stop him attacking the convoys.'

During the afternoon, when the crew least expected it, the crew went through every drill Stirling could think of from "man overboard" to "silent running". But he was still far from satisfied.

Despite the heavy seas, Stirling wanted to see how the ship would handle.

Bending down to the engine room voice-pipe, he said, 'Captain here. Let me speak to the engineer officer.'

'Yes, sir,' came the unmistakable voice of Jock Weir, 'what canna do fer yer?'

'I intend seeing how fast she can go and don't worry, I'll accept responsibility for any damages.'

'Damages, you say, sir,' Weir harshly replied. He, like all ship's engineers had a special affection for his engines, something that "landlubbers" couldn't understand. Weir considered his mass of gauges, cable and pipes the most important part of any vessel. If they broke down, the ship would be a sitting duck for any U-boat that happened to be in the vicinity. 'But remember, sir,' Weir emphasised, 'we've just had the engines overhauled.'

'Then let's see if the dockyard have done a good job, eh?' Stirling cautiously replied. Turning to Manley he went on, 'Increase revolutions twenty. Steady as she goes.'

As if stung by a sea monster, *Sandpiper* sprung forward, sending a huge white bow wave curling over the fo'c'sle. For the next half hour Stirling ordered the ship to alter course twice. On each occasion, the ship heeled precariously to port and starboard.

'What's he tryin' to do?' yelled one of the gun crew, grabbing a stanchion. 'Every rivet in the ship is rattling. At this rate we'll fuckin' capsize.'

'Ah stop moanin',' shouted his opposite number. 'If you fall overboard can I 'ave your tot?'

'Fuck off,' came the disgruntled reply.

The ship continued to dip, dive and plough through the high rolling sea. Everyone on the bridge was continually being drenched with stinging cold spray. In the boiler and engine rooms stokers looked ponderously at one another while gripping anything to prevent sliding on the slippery metal plating. Half an hour later, Stirling, wiping water from his face with the back of his hand, ordered a reduction in speed and revolutions.

'There,' he said, smiling smugly while looking at Manley's shiny wet features, 'that wasn't too bad, was it, Number One? Fifteen knots in this weather was excellent, don't you think?'

'Indeed it was, sir,' Manley replied, 'but can she outrun a U-boat?'

'I intend to find out one day,' Stirling answered confidently.

Throughout the rest of the day more evolutions were carried out.

Under the critical eye of Chief Buffer, Sammy Taylor, 'Away sea boat's crew,' was piped and practised until he got an appreciative nod from Stirling. Brum Appleby's first aid team puffed and panted as they hauled "injured" men cocooned in Neil Robertson stretchers from mess decks and the engine room. Gun crews met with fierce criticism from Chief GI Dusty Miller for failing to improve on their previous time. But Stirling was still far from happy with the speed of the depth charge party.

'Ask Amery to come and see me, will you, Number One,' said Stirling easing himself off his chair. 'I'll be in my cabin.'

The time was 1600. A few minutes later a knock came at Stirling's door and in came the slightly built, figure of Sub Lieutenant Amery. His normally heavily tanned complexion looked paler than usual. Stirling was sat at his desk still wearing his duffle coat.

'You sent for me, sir,' he said, nervously licking his lips while removing his cap. He had a good idea what his captain wanted and took a deep breath. For a fleeting moment Amery recalled his father's suggestion of him obtaining a cushy shore job but quickly dismissed the idea. He was determined to succeed, no matter what the cost. But he new that if he and his depth charge team didn't improve Stirling was liable to have him removed from the ship. The disgrace this would bring made him come out in a cold sweat.

'Yes, Amery,' Stirling replied, sitting back and folding his arms. 'I'm far from happy with your depth charge team,' he said in a measured, but stern voice. 'Five minutes is far too long, don't you agree?' he added, making a questionable gesture by raising his eyebrows.

'Er... yes, I do, sir,' Amery timidly answered, biting his lower lip.

Stirling was only too aware of Amery's inexperience. He was also aware that to rant and rave would prove unproductive. He felt that the important approach would be to encourage Amery, and for that matter all officers, to do their best and instil pride in themselves, the ship and the service.

'You do realise how important your job is, don't you?' said Stirling, noting the expression of apprehension on the face of the young officer.

'Yes, sir,' Amery replied. Regaining his composure he added, 'I certainly do.'

'It's not that you and your team are not performing well,' Stirling replied. 'It's just that you're not quick enough. Now,' he went on, sitting forward and placing both hands flatly on the desk, 'what do you intend doing about it?'

'More practice, sir,' Amery firmly answered, 'until we get it right.'

At that moment Manley's strident tones over the tannoy interrupted him.

'Submarine contact ten miles away. Hands to action stations!'

'Looks like you'll get a chance to do just that,' Stirling cried, giving Amery a confident smile while reaching for his steel helmet.

# CHAPTER SEVEN

In the Asdic compartment situated below the bridge, "Wacker" Payne, a tall, red headed two-badge Leading Seaman from Tooting was sat, earphones clamped to his head. The impulses coming through his transmitter-receiver were becoming stronger by the second. The TS, as it was known, was a delicate instrument encased in a metal dome projected from the bottom of the ship. When these impulses hit an object they came back as a series of metallic "pinging" sounds. By manipulating the sound waves sent by the transmitter-receiver with the compass receiver, an efficient operator was able to tell which direction the impulses were coming from. Also, by noting the interval between the transmission and return of the "echo" he could fairly accurately tell the range of the object.

'What's our position, Pilot?' Stirling snapped, peering though his binoculars. The time was 1700. 'Darken ship' had just been piped. *Sandpiper* was now cutting its way through the inky black waters of the Irish Sea. The bitterly cold northerly wind suddenly increased. Once again the halyards and rattling rigging threatened to break loose. The thin hazy line of light stretching across the horizon had given way to darkness. An anaemic moon flitting between low-lying grey clouds failed to penetrate the wide bank of swirling grey mist approaching from the north.

'Fifty miles off the Fylde coast, sir,' Graves cried over his shoulder, 'latitude fifty degrees west.'

A dull overhead blue light showed clearly the details on Graves' charts. On the table was a signal log labelled *Admiralty Notices to Mariners*. This provided mariners with an up-to-date position of wrecks and alteration of marker buoys. Every time the ship altered course, Graves, using a slide rule and pencil, marked this on his chart. Graves stood up and looked up at the night sky and with a forlorn sigh, wondered what Dorothy was doing. Picturing her in another man's arms made him feel physically sick. He angrily threw down his pencil and waited to mark down the next change of course on his chart.

'How far is the contact now, Number One?' Stirling asked.

'According to Payne, about eight miles and moving northwards at fifteen knots, sir.'

'What's our speed?'

'Eighteen knots, sir.'

Stirling pensively stroked his chin. He knew that the sound of the ship's engines could distort the echo coming from the submarine. Suddenly he was faced with a dilemma; if he increased speed he might make it difficult for the operator to keep track of his prey; alternatively, by slowing down, the submarine might escape. He was also faced with the sudden change in the weather.

'Damn this mist, Number One,' cursed Stirling, his binoculars pressed to his eyes. 'Visibility can't be more than a few hundred yards. Reduce revolutions one-third, Steer green one, one oh.'

Graves also noted the change in position on his chart.

'You'd better put someone on the fo'c'sle, Number One' Stirling went on, 'and put the Asdic on the loudspeaker.'

Almost immediately the intermittent, soporific sound of the "pinging" could be heard over the ship's tannoy. Throughout the ship, men listened, staring nervously up at the loudspeaker and wondering what would happen next. On the bridge, the dull throbbing of the engineers and the constant hissing of the sea added to the tension. Despite being protected by mufflers and towels, the mist seeped down necks and penetrated thick clothing. Some stamped their feet to relieve nervousness. Others like Stirling silently watched and waited.

'How close are we inshore and what's our depth, Pilot?' Stirling asked bending close to the voice-pipe.

'Twenty miles, sir, depth ten fathoms,' came Graves' muffled reply.

'Any contact?' Stirling impatiently snapped.

'Echo bearing red, five, five,' cried Payne, 'moving right to left. Echo weak.'

Meanwhile the monotonous "pinging" added an extra dimension to what was a nerve-racking situation.

'I don't want to go any closer to shore,' Stirling said cautiously, 'got a fix, Pilot?'

'Yes, sir,' replied Graves, marking down the ship's position.

'Echo seems to be fading, sir,' cried Payne.

'Steady in course red four five,' Stirling calmly replied.

Once again Graves plotted the course on his chart.

'How far can I alter to port, Pilot?' Stirling asked cautiously.

Using his slide rule, Graves measured the distance from the coast, then replied, 'Thirty degrees, sir, that's safe for ten miles.'

'Echo now very weak, sir,' said Payne.

The blighter's getting away, Stirling inwardly cursed, staring thoughtfully into the gloomy mist. With an exasperated sigh, he bent close to the compass repeater. 'Course oh six one, Number One. Port twenty.'

'Twenty a port wheel on,' came the reply from the coxswain below.

'Midships, sir, port twenty.'

Suddenly the "pinging" increased.

'Echo much louder, sir,' Payne reported, his voice slightly raised.

With a worried expression on his face, Stirling looked at Graves who had come onto the bridge.

The sound of the echo continued even louder than before. What on earth is it? Stirling asked himself. If it were a submarine surely it would be moving away from us. Turning to Graves, he asked, 'Anything marked on the chart, Pilot?'

'No, sir,' Graves nervously replied, listening as the echo impulses became shorter, indicating the presence of something. 'Maybe the sub has …'

Graves' remark was abruptly interrupted by the foc's'le lookout yelling, *'Bridge, wreck dead ahead, sir!'*

Pushing Graves out of the way, Stirling shouted down the voice-pipe, *'Hard a port!'* The ship instantly heeled to the left. Glancing upwards, Stirling saw *Sandpiper*'s mast and yardarm together with the funnel appear to lean over. A huge wave of icy water bounded over the port side, drenching A and B gun crews and everyone on the bridge. Men were sent stumbling, grabbing anything to prevent falling over.

'I only hopes Tanky has got the rum well secured,' cried a gunnery rating to his oppo gripping a stanchion on A gun platform.

'Much more of this,' cried Tanky, vomiting a foul smelling mess onto the steel deck, 'and I'll go T.' ("T" was marked in his pay book and showed he didn't take his rum and was "Temperate".)

In the engine room and boiler rooms, stokers slipped on the slippery metal plating. Mess decks suddenly became awash with anything left loose. The contents of lockers rattled and hammocks lurched sideways as if pushed by an unseen hand.

SBA Brum Appleby and Surgeon Lieutenant Coburn clung onto the sides of the sick bay cots as cabinets, and everything else tilted over at an acute angle.

On the bridge Stirling and the others, watched in horror as the remains of what was once a tanker came at them. It loomed so close they could see the ragged remains of the red duster, flying raggedly from its mast.

'Christ almighty, Pilot,' Stirling raged staring wide-eyed at Graves. 'Was this wreck plotted on your chart?'

With a sudden sinking feeling, Graves nervously replied, 'I... I don't think so, sir.'

'*You don't think so, man!*' shouted Stirling. '*Go and check the signal log.*'

Graves turned and stumbled into the chart compartment. As he opened the *Mariners'* log, his mouth felt dry and his hands shook. To his horror the signal received before they sailed, read, *Wreck of SS Langley, tanker sunk on 1 September 1942, latitude 5 6 degrees longitude 5 degrees. Insert on all charts.*

My God! He inwardly cried, how on earth could I have missed it? The implications of his negligence immediately flashed through his mind. This surely would mean a court martial or even worse, dismissal from the service. He could never face his parents and friends again. Clutching the signal log, he came and stood next to Stirling who was too busy trying to save his ship to talk to him.

With baited breath everyone braced themselves, mentally and physically, waiting for what they thought would be a life threatening collision. For what seemed like an eternity they watched, half hypnotised with fear as the dark, rusticated shape of the sunken ship's hull came closer and closer. Everyone froze as if resigned to his fate.

Everyone, that is except Stirling.

With his heart racing Stirling managed to grab the voice-pipe and yell, '*Starboard ten, full speed!*'

*Sandpiper* heeled over to the right and increased speed sending a wall of water surging high in the air between the two vessels. By this time the chasm between the ships was a so narrow the edge of the tanker's yardarm almost hit the men on the bridge. In a matter of seconds *Sandpiper* pulled away and the danger had passed.

The sudden cant of the ship caught Stirling off balance. He was about to fall when Graves, who was himself holding onto a nearby stanchion, grabbed hold of Stirling's arm.

'Thank you, Pilot,' said Stirling, beads of sweat running down the side of his face. 'That was too close for comfort,' glancing enquiringly at Graves,' he added, 'was the wreck reported to us?'

'Yes, sir, I did receive it,' he murmured, slightly nodding his head, 'I... I don't know how I could have missed it.' A mixture of embarrassment, shock and contrition was written over his normally clean-cut, handsome features.

'I see,' said Stirling, furrowing his brow, 'we'll discuss this when we get back. It looks like we've lost the sub, so I suggest you set a course for Liverpool.'

Despite the howling wind, Manley couldn't help overhearing the conversation between Stirling and Graves. Since the incident in the mess with Jock Weir, Graves had been unusually withdrawn. At dinner Graves had sat in silence toying with his food, before abruptly standing up and leaving the mess.

'Och, that letter Peter received must have contained bad news,' Manley remembered Jock Weir saying, 'I've never known the laddie t' be so quiet.'

'You're right there, Jock,' Harper-Smyth had added, nodding in agreement. 'He's in the cabin next to mine and I'm sure I heard him crying.'

'Maybe you could have a quiet word with the Doc, Number One,' Sub Lieutenant Amery offered as he took a sip of tea. 'There's certainly something upsetting him.'

Manley decided to speak to Stirling as soon as possible.

# CHAPTER EIGHT

Shortly after midnight, *Sandpiper* passed the Bar Lighthouse and cruised down the Mersey. The harsh northerly wind continued to blow downriver and flurries of dark clouds raced across the night sky. Half an hour later the ship was berthed alongside Gladstone Wharf.

'Ring off engines please, Number One,' Stirling said, 'who's officer of the day?' he asked while easing himself off his chair. Only Manley and the duty PO were on the bridge. Graves had left as soon as the ship was secure.

'Lieutenant Anderson, sir,' Manley replied. 'By the way, sir,' he went on, unconsciously biting his lip. 'May I have a private word with you?'

Stirling raised his eyebrows. 'Of course, Number One,' he replied cautiously, 'Sounds very ominous, nothing serious I hope? Follow me below,' he added, giving Manley a searching glance.

A few minutes later the two officers were in Stirling's cabin. With a tired sigh Stirling removed his duffle coat and cap, then sat down behind his desk.

'Please sit down, Number One,' Stirling said, indicating a chair, 'and tell me what the problem is.'

'Well, sir,' replied Manley leaning forward and accepting a cigarette and a light from Stirling, 'I'm certain Lieutenant Graves is in some sort of trouble.'

'Hmm... I should say he is,' Stirling answered lighting a cigarette. 'I'm sure you're aware of what happened.'

'Yes, sir,' Manley replied, 'but there is something you should know.' He then explained Graves' behaviour in the wardroom after receiving a letter.

With a look of concern etched in his tired grey eyes, Stirling sat back in his chair, allowing a thin trail of smoke to eddy upwards from his cigarette. 'I see,' he said pensively. 'He's only been married less than a year. Did he say who the letter was from?'

'No, sir,' Manley answered, flicking ash into an ashtray. 'But everyone was amazed at his reaction. He didn't touch his dinner, just played with his food then left the wardroom without speaking. He's normally a pleasant fellow. Maybe there's something wrong at home.'

Stirling stood up and stubbed his cigarette out. 'Tell him to see me tomorrow directly after breakfast,' Stirling said, doing his best to stifle a yawn. 'Now I think it's time we both turned in.'

Meanwhile, Graves returned to his cabin and angrily flung down the *Mariner's* signal log onto his bunk. He then sat at his desk and held his head in both hands. Tomorrow Stirling would be sending for him. Yet again he asked himself what excuse could he possibly give for such a blunder.

'Heavo, heavo, heavo, lash up and stow, cooks to the galley,' came the strident voice of the QM over the tannoy. The time was 0600. Graves woke from a fitful sleep, rubbed his tired eyes and switched on his overhead light. His mouth felt dry and raw from smoking cigarettes. The first thing that came into his mind was the contents of Dorothy's letter. He was immediately gripped by a sickening feeling of emptiness. Filled with pent-up anger and jealousy he flung back the bedclothes and for a few minutes sat on the edge of his bunk staring blankly at the deck. With a weary sigh he ran his fingers through his unruly fair hair remembering the events of the previous night. For the life of him he couldn't remember receiving the signal in the Admiralty log, let alone reading it. With mounting anguish he knew such negligence couldn't be countenanced by Stirling or any commanding officer. With an effort he washed, shaved and dressed then made his way to the wardroom. It was still dark and a bitterly cold wind blew downriver biting against his face.

Everyone looked up as Graves drew back the door curtain and entered the wardroom. At first nobody spoke. The gentle clattering of cutlery and the dull throbbing of the generator filled the air. Feeling very self-conscious Graves sat down next to Sub Lieutenant Jock Weir.

'Sorry about last...' Graves mumbled giving Jock a contrite glance.

'Och. Forget it laddie,' Jock cheerfully replied, 'and pass me the sauce, these bloody sausages are tasteless.'

His outburst relaxed the tension that had built up.

'How are you feeling, old boy,' ventured Harper-Smyth, 'you seemed a bit...'

Manley quickly interrupted Harper-Smyth's tasteless remark. 'Mail will close in an hour,' he said, cutting through a piece of bacon, 'and leave will be granted from 1200.'

'Does that include the officers, sir?' asked Sub Lieutenant Amery in his usual plummy voice.

'Why?' replied Manley grinning, 'are you on a promise?'

'Hardly, sir,' Harper-Smyth said, giving his friend a playful dig with his elbow. 'He wouldn't know what to do with it if he had. Anyway, I do believe you're Officer of the Day and Colours is in five minutes' time, so you'd better get yourself to the quarterdeck.'

'Gosh, Andrew!' Amery exclaimed, hurriedly putting down his knife and fork, 'so I am,' and grabbing his cap rushed out of the room.

During this friendly banter Graves felt too nervous to eat. All he managed was a cup of coffee after which he sat and smoked a cigarette lost in thought. Shortly before 0800, Colours was piped. In harbour this was the ritual raising of the white ensign on the quarterdeck. The pipe 'Duty watch fall in, hands turn too,' followed this. A similar ceremony was conducted in the evening when the flag was lowered.

A few minutes later everyone except Jock Weir and Manley left the mess.

'Now dunna look so downhearted, Peter,' he said, trying his best to cheer Graves up. 'We've all made mistakes. God knows I've made plenty and I'm still here. Believe me, everything will work out.' He then stood up, and after giving Graves a consoling pat on the shoulder, added, 'See you later, my friend.'

No sooner had Weir gone than Manley, having finished his breakfast and after dabbing his mouth on a serviette, stood up. 'The captain will see you whenever you want, old boy,' he said, glancing at Graves. His voice quiet and full of concern. 'If there's anything he should know, don't hesitate to tell him. I think you'll find he has a sympathetic ear.'

'Maybe, sir,' Graves replied, standing up and looking warily up at the wardroom clock. 'I'll know in a few minutes.' He stubbed his cigarette out and feeling his heart rate increase, left the room.

Shortly before 0815 Graves knocked on the captain's door and went inside.

Stirling was sitting behind his desk reading a signal from Sir Percy Noble requesting his presence at Derby House at 1300. He looked up as Graves entered.

'Ah, Pilot,' he said in a quiet but stern manner. Noticing Graves' pale, drawn features, he went on, 'Do come in. I'm sure you know why I've sent for you.'

'Yes, sir,' Graves replied, penitently glancing at the linoleum covered deck. 'I... I don't know what to say. I did receive the signal but...' His voice wavered slightly as he bit his lip. 'I'm sorry, sir, I realise I endangered the crew and the ship.'

Stirling pensively furrowed his brow and sat back in his chair. 'Tell me, Peter,' he said, purposely using Graves' Christian name hoping to lessen the strain he knew the young officer was under. 'Is there anything worrying you? I heard you had a difference of opinion with the engineer officer.'

Stirling watched as Graves swallowed nervously and took a deep breath. 'It was nothing, sir,' he replied, 'just a minor disagreement.'

'I see,' said Stirling, indicating a chair, 'I think you'd better sit down.'

'Thank you, sir,' Graves muttered and did as Stirling suggested.

'I believe you received a letter just before we sailed, is that right?' Stirling asked, passing him a cigarette and lighting both with a small silver lighter.

'Yes, sir,' Graves answered, taking a welcome, deep drag.

'May I ask who it was from?' Stirling asked, pushing a brass ashtray towards Graves.

Graves exhaled a steady stream of smoke, then in a faltering voice, said, 'My, er... wife, sir.'

'How are things between you?' Stirling asked, noticing Graves' hand tremble slightly as he took another puff of his cigarette.

Graves didn't answer. Instead he clenched his teeth lowered his head and stared blankly at the deck.

Sensing something was wrong, Stirling leaned forward, and adopting a consolatory tone, said, 'Look here, old boy, if there's trouble at home or whatever, remember I'm here to help you. Now,' he went on straightening up, 'tell me what the problem is.'

At first Graves didn't answer. Then, still looking at the deck, he replied, 'She's met someone else.' Graves' faltering voice was barely audible over the hum of the generator. He took a nervous pull of his cigarette then added, 'And doesn't want to see me any more.'

'Have you had a row or something?' Stirling asked raising his eyebrows and suddenly feeling uneasy.

Shaking his head slightly Graves replied, 'Nothing like that, sir. We've only been married a year.'

'You say she's met someone else?' Stirling asked, stubbing his cigarette out. 'Any idea who the fellow is?'

Fighting back tears, Graves replied tersely, 'No, sir, she didn't say.'

Stirling sat back in his chair. 'Hmm…' he said, pursing his lips. 'I suggest you go home and sort this out. You live in London, don't you?'

'Yes, sir,' Graves replied. 'We have a flat in Bayswater.'

'Right then,' said Stirling, standing up and placing both hands flatly on his desk. 'See the coxswain and get a railway warrant. Take a few days off, more if necessary. I have to see the admiral today and if we have to sail, the First Lieutenant can do your duties.'

'Thank you, sir,' Graves muttered, 'that's very decent of you. But,' he went on avoiding Stirling's steady gaze, 'what about…'

Stirling quickly interrupted him. 'We'll deal with that when you return, now off you go. I'll order a tilly to pick you up in, say, half an hour.'

An hour later Graves arrived at Lime Street Station. Under his Burberry he wore his best uniform. Over his left shoulder he carried a small canvas gas mask satchel and in his left hand was a holdall. Shortly afterwards he boarded the 1100 train. Sliding open the door of a first class compartment he found it was occupied by an Army lieutenant captain and two RAF officers. He was not in the mood for small talk and settled down in a corner and closed his eyes. During the five hour journey to Euston his mind was in a whirl. Whenever he thought of Dorothy in another man's arms, doing to her the things he had lain in his bunk dreaming about made him distraught. But what was he going to say to her, he asked himself? Even though she had told him not to see her, he decided to ask her to reconsider her intention to leave him. It seemed the only thing he could do. But what if she was determined to finish their marriage and go off with this other man? Thinking about this filled him with rage and jealousy. But, he told himself forlornly, there was little he could do... or was there?

Graves finally dozed off but was woken up by the strident voice of the ticket collector. A few hours later after a dreamless sleep he felt someone shaking his shoulder.

'Euston, old boy,' said the voice. Graves was slumped in a corner resting his head against the damp window. He opened his eyes and saw the young face of the army officer staring at him. 'Thought you'd appreciate a shake.'

'Er... thank you,' muttered Graves, feeling stiff and tired. The time by his wristwatch was a little after 1600. He stood up, stretched his arms then took his grip down from the rack. He then followed the three officers out of the compartment onto the crowded platform. The acrid smell of steam and dust attacked the back of his throat as he made his way out of the station where, after waiting a few minutes, he hailed a taxi.

Three hours earlier Stirling had sat in Derby House, staring into the keen grey eyes of Admiral Percy Noble.

'Coffee, or something stronger?' the admiral asked in his usual pleasant manner. His dark thinning hair was, as usual, well groomed and his aquiline features set in a welcoming smile.

'How was your work up, Bob?' the admiral asked, 'I believe you chased a sub.'

'Yes, sir,' Stirling replied as he accepted a cigarette from the admiral who lit them both with a small silver lighter. 'Sorry to say we lost the blighter.'

'Indeed,' said the admiral taking a deep draw of his cigarette. 'Why was that?'

Stirling thought before answering. 'We almost hit a wreck, sir,' Stirling answered, sitting back in his chair and exhaling a steady stream of smoke. 'The damn thing wasn't marked too clearly on the chart and we missed it.'

'Hmm...' the admiral muttered giving Stirling a searching look. 'A cock-up somewhere I suppose,' and took another drag on his cigarette.

Stirling gave an inward sigh of relief. But he suspected the admiral knew a little more than he was prepared to let on.

'Now,' the admiral said, raising the tone of his voice. 'Tobruk is still holding out but the navy is having difficulty getting through with supplies due to the presence of U-boats and the Luftwaffe. Auckinleck's Eighth Army is preparing to attack Rommel but is badly in need of ammunition and tanks. As usual, Stalin is demanding a second front to take some of the pressure off his armies, but Winston considers this impossible at present.' The admiral paused, took a final puff of his cigarette, stubbed it out then continued. 'Our main worry at the moment is the presence of U-boats operating in the area off Gibraltar. Based at St Nazaire and Lorient, they are in easy striking distance to attack convoys bound for Malta and Tobruk. These blasted U-boats have to be dealt with at all costs,' he emphasised, raising his voice. He paused, took a deep breath and sat back in his chair, then went on. 'On Monday the 12 September *Redshank* and *Curlew* will arrive in Liverpool from Scapa Flow. The next day *Petrel* and *Shearwater* will join them. These, as you already know, will form the 15th Escort Group. You will be senior officer. The group will sail on the 20th for Gibraltar. Here, you and your group will patrol the approaches to the Straits of Gibraltar, hunt down the enemy and await further convoy duties. Now, old boy, do you have anything to ask me?'

Stirling was about to mention the problem with Graves, but changed his mind. His wife threatening to leave him had clearly affected his pilot's actions. He had already made up his mind to give Graves a severe reprimand and leave it at that. Graves was a good officer and a first-class navigator and, as such, deserved a second chance.

'No, sir,' Stirling replied, 'that'll give me time to meet the captains of the other ships and outline my plans.'

'Splendid,' the admiral heartily replied. 'Now,' he added glancing at the wall clock. 'The sun is well over the yardarm, how about a gin and tonic?'

# CHAPTER NINE

Five hours after Stirling left the admiral, Graves flagged down a taxi outside Euston Station.

'Sussex Place, Bayswater, please,' Graves said climbing inside.

'Better get indoors quick, guv'nor,' said the driver in a gruff Cockney accent. 'The Jerries come over at six o'clock, so they do. Dead on time most nights. The East End Docks have taken a bloody awful pounding.'

After driving along the Edgware Road they turned right into Sussex Place, a small, quiet cull-de-sac. Blackout curtains were drawn across the windows of the red-bricked Edwardian houses that were also criss-crossed with white tape. The area was deserted and a damp mist was beginning to fall giving the area an air of eerie gloom.

'What number, guv?' asked the driver.

'Just here will be fine,' Graves replied. 'How much do I owe you?'

'Five bob to you, mate,' replied the driver, 'and good luck to yer.'

Graves handed the driver five shillings and climbed out of the taxi.

The ground floor flat he and Dorothy had briefly shared was half way down the road on the left side. Feeling his heart pounding against his ribs Graves walked along the pavement and stopped outside an oak-panelled door. For a few minutes he stood remembering the day Dorothy and he had first viewed the flat. He remembered the lounge decorated in pale green wallpaper embossed with flowers. The chinz-covered sofas and armchairs, the shiny glass cabinet and sideboard complete with bottles of whiskey and gin; and the bedroom with its king-sized bed.

He nervously fumbled in his pocket and took out a small Yale key. His hand shook so much he only just managed to insert it into the lock. Feeling the blood pound inside his head he opened the door.

The warmth and tangy smell of alcohol mingled with perfume met him as he slowly walked down the small, narrow lobby. He walked past the door leading into the lounge. On the right side of the lobby was the bedroom. Graves stopped outside the door and heard the muted sound of sighs and gasps. Blurred images of Dorothy and the man she left him for making love flashed through his mind. Consumed with anger and jealousy he flung open the bedroom door.

For what seemed like an eternity, Graves stood hardly believing what he was seeing. The light was on and Dorothy was lying naked on the bed. Her knees were spread and her eyes were closed. Crouching between them he saw the back of a dark-haired woman. She was completely naked except for a short black slip that had moved up her body revealing a pair of pale buttocks and the pink, fleshy folds of her vagina. Her arms were tightly clasped around Dorothy's hips. Dorothy had one arm across her face with the other one clutching the bedclothes. With each jerky movement of the woman's head Dorothy moaned as if in pain. Both women were in the throngs of sexual excitement and hadn't heard Graves enter.

With sickening horror, Graves realised what they were doing and felt his stomach retch. He dropped his holdall and yelled, *'What the hell's going on here?'*

Dorothy opened her eyes, removed her arm and saw him. Her face was flushed and her blonde shoulder-length hair a tangled mess.

*'My God, Peter!'* she screamed, wide-eyed while pushing herself up from the bed. *'What are you doing here?'*

Graves hardly noticed her red, pointed nipples and her firm breasts. At the same time the woman turned around and with a surprised expression on her pale face, looked up at Graves.

'Who the bloody hell are you?' she cried, glaring at Graves while pushing herself off the bed and standing up.

Graves didn't reply. Instead he gave her a cold, passionless stare. She was a little over five feet with short black hair, narrow hips, tiny pink nipples and a flat chest.

'Well may you ask,' Graves replied, gritting his teeth. Clenching his fists he turned and with eyes aflame, looked down at Dorothy, who was sat up clutching a sheet around her body. He then glanced first at the woman then at Dorothy and cried, 'Who the hell is she, and what the bloody hell's happening here?'

It was a stupid question. While at university he had heard of homosexual practices between women, but had dismissed them as wild rumours. After all this was 1942 and such activities were hardly, if ever, discussed in polite society. But now standing in the room he was faced with the reality of the situation. If Dorothy had betrayed him with a man, he might be able to understand, even if he couldn't accept it. But to do so with a woman left him feeling bewildered, confused and helpless.

'What does it look like, you idiot?' Dorothy replied, climbing out of bed and reaching down for a white robe that was lying in a

93

wrinkled mess on the floor. 'Janet and I are in love, so there.' She defiantly went on, angrily tying the belt, 'And there's nothing you can do about it. Isn't that right, Jan?'

Janet stood, naked with both hands on her hips. 'Absolutely,' she replied with a confident sneer, 'so tell him to fuck off.'

With a look of contempt Dorothy glared at Graves, and said, 'I told you I had met someone else and didn't want to see you again. Now please go and leave us alone,' Dorothy moved close to Janet and after placing her arms around Janet's naked waist, went on, 'besides, we love each other, don't we?'

Hearing Dorothy refer to her friend as "darling" an endearment she had never used to him, angered Graves even more. For a fleeting moment he was tempted to wipe the smirk off her face with his fist. *'Love! Love!'* he seethed, 'how on earth could you love someone like this?' he cried, glowering at Janet.

'What do you mean, someone like this?' Janet cried indignantly, as she pushed Graves in the chest, 'just who the fuck do you think you are? Can't you see Dot doesn't want you any more, she has me.'

'*You, you bloody pervert,*' Graves shouted. Using the back of his hand he hit Janet full in the face. With a loud cry she fell over, legs akimbo and with a dull *thud* hit the back of her head on the floor. Her naked body gave a series of twitches and then, lay still.

'*Janet, Janet darling!*' screamed Dorothy kneeling by her friend. Reaching down and touching Janet's ashen face, she cried frantically, 'How *are you, are you all right? Please, please speak to me!*' It was then she saw Janet's lifeless eyes staring up at the ceiling. *'My God, she's dead. You've killed her!'* she screamed, staring wildly up at Graves. She then cradled Janet's head in her arms. With tears streaming down her face, Dorothy glowered up at

Graves. *'How could you, you brute,'* she sobbed, *'I'll tell the police what you've done and you'll hang, war or no war!'*

*'I don't care what you do,'* Graves bellowed, *'damn the pair of you,'* he then turned around and stormed out of the room and left the house.

Graves thrust his hands in his Burberry pockets and as if in a trance, turned and left the house, leaving the door open. The time was a little before 1800. For nearly an hour he walked aimlessly, ignoring passers-by and oblivious to what little traffic there was. By this time darkness had fallen and high above a full moon shone down from a clear sky showing the white rings painted around trees and lampposts. He found a seat near a bus stop and sat down. Gradually the events of the last half hour filtered into his head. Images of Dorothy and Janet naked in bed came into his mind. He could still hear Dorothy moaning and see the back of Janet's head doing something he had only read in racy magazines at university. He stood up and with head bowed leaned against a tree praying the mental picture of his wife and Janet would go away, but sadly they didn't.

With his mind still in a whirl Graves reached Bayswater Road. On the opposite side of the road was Kensington Gardens. With the exception of the main gate, all the railings had been removed. Like those throughout the land they would be melted down to help with the war effort.

He appeared to be totally oblivious to the wail of the air raid siren. He was even unaware of the drone of aircraft high in the sky. Suddenly the night came alive with dazzling white cones of searchlights, criss-crossing each other, eagerly seeking out the enemy. The dull *thud, thud, thud* of bombs exploding didn't seem to affect him. He paid no attention to the ear-splitting barrage as hundreds of anti-aircraft ack-ack guns opened up. Suddenly mushrooms of red and yellow explosions pockmarked the darkness. He stared blankly as ambulances and fire engines roared down the road heading towards the scarlet haze that appeared over the East End of London. The ground around him shook as crunching detonations became closer.

He never heard the voice of an air raid warden yelling at him to take cover. If he did, it was too late. A huge flash followed by a wall of flame suddenly engulfed him. Propelled by an unseen force Graves' body was lifted up high in the air. He felt no pain, only a vague sensation of weightlessness. By the time his body hit the ground he was dead.

# CHAPTER TEN

After leaving the admiral Stirling arrived onboard *Sandpiper* and immediately sent for Manley. The time was just before 1100. A knock came at Stirling's cabin door and in came the tall, broad shouldered figure of his First Lieutenant.

'Good morning, Number One, please take a seat,' said Stirling, relaxing back in his chair.

'Thank you, sir,' replied Manley, removing his cap. 'Good news, I hope?'

'I think so,' said Stirling with a cheerful smile. 'The rest of the group will arrive in five days. On the 20th we will sail for Gibraltar and await instructions. You may tell the officers but keep it from the crew until we leave. I shall want to ammunition and take on fuel and stores as soon as possible and I'll be sending for the commanding officers of the other ships as soon as they arrive.' Stirling went on to explain the increase in U-boat activity in that region and the importance of their mission. 'Is all that clear?'

'Perfectly, sir,' Manley answered, 'I'm sure the crew will welcome a bit of Meddy sunshine after the weather we've had recently.'

'It may get hotter than they hope for,' Stirling answered ominously.

Three days later Stirling received a signal from Admiralty informing him Graves had been killed in an air raid, ending with, *"his next of kin have been informed. Lieutenant AP Evans, RANVR will join as relief 11 September."*

For a while Stirling sat staring at the white paper too shocked to speak.

The voice of Leading Signalman Tansey Lee brought him back to reality. 'Will that be all, sir?' asked Lee.

'Er... yes, thank you,' muttered Stirling, furrowing his brow as he glanced up. 'Would you ask the First Lieutenant to see me right away.'

A few minutes later Manley entered. Stirling took a deep breath and said, 'You'd better sit down, Number One,' and handed him the signal.

With a curious expression on his face Manley sat down and read the signal. 'Good Lord!' gasped Manley, 'what bloody awful bad luck, the poor chap.'

'Yes, it is,' Stirling replied, taking out a cigarette from an open packet and sliding it to Manley. 'You'd better have his kit sent to his wife,' he said leaning across and lighting Manley's cigarette, 'and I'll write her a letter. His relief is an Australian lieutenant. He'll arrive on Wednesday.'

'Wasn't Graves having some sort of trouble with his wife?' Manley asked, turning his head slightly and exhaling a stream of smoke in the air.

'Maybe,' Stirling replied, 'we'll never know, will we?'

'I don't expect we will, sir,' Manley quietly replied. 'Peter was a decent chap, perhaps a mention of Graves' death on Daily Orders?'

'Of course,' said Stirling giving Manley an appreciative glance. 'Kindly see to it.'

Thanks to Leading Signalman Lee the news about Graves and the ship's patrol duty around Gibraltar spread around the ship like an electric current.

At tot time in the seaman's mess Able Seaman Jackson's reaction was typical of the his mess mates. He turned to Able Seaman Dinga Bell, rubbed his hands gleefully together and said, 'That's just what we need, a run ashore down Strait Street in Gib. I wonder if sweaty Betty is still dancing at the Grand.'

'Don't make me laugh,' said Able Seaman Darby Allen. 'All them dark-eyed beauties disappear over the border into Spain at midnight, so you might as well stay onboard. As for Lieutenant Graves, he was decent feller, as officers go. Now pass me the glass,' he went on sardonically, 'and remember, it's my turn for the Kings.' (Any spare run left after issue was referred to as the "Kings".)

The reaction in the senior ratings mess was similar.

'Dear old Gib,' remarked CGI Dusty Miller, before taking a sip of his rum. 'A bit of bronzy bronzy will make me look handsome, like Errol Flynn.'

'Ha!' laughed CERA Percy Bradley, 'I doubt it, matey,' he said in a thick, Yorkshire accent, 'you'd still look like the back of a horse.'

'Tansey Lee told me the old man's face turned white as a sheet when he read the signal about Graves' death,' said PO Yeoman Harry Tate, to Chief Stoker Digger Barnes.

'I'm not surprised,' Barnes replied as he stirred his mug with a dirty pencil, 'perhaps he felt guilty for letting him go on leave.'

'Very sad,' added Chief Shipwright Harry Tweedle, a small, stocky, red-faced man from Manchester. 'I liked him. He was a quiet pleasant sort, unlike some of 'em I've met.'

'A cryin' shame,' said PO Coxswain Pony Moore. 'He was a real gent. At least I could understand wot he said. I wonder who his relief will be?'

'Some ninety-day wonder, I suppose,' Digger Barnes replied sarcastically. Then in an obvious reference to Graves' recent navigating error added, 'I don't care who he is as long as he bloody-well knows his job.'

The conversation in the wardroom during lunch was subdued. Graves was not only a colleague, but also a close friend to many of the officers.

'Rumour had it Peter's wife left him,' Gunnery Officer Lieutenant Anderson said quietly while sipping a coffee.

'Steady on, old boy,' Sub Lieutenant Oliver replied, who was sat opposite Anderson, 'how on earth do you know that?' he added, indignantly putting down his newspaper.

'Potts, the captain's steward, overheard the conversation between him and Peter,' Anderson replied. Glancing furtively first at Manley, then across at Sub Lieutenant Jock Weir, he went on, 'What do you two think?'

'Och, whatever the problem was,' Jock Weir replied, lighting a cigarette, 'I only hope he patched it up before...' His voice trailed away as he exhaled a stream of smoke.

With a shake of his head, Surgeon Lieutenant Coburn said, 'Maybe if he'd come to me I might have been able to help.'

'I doubt it, Doc,' answered Jock Weir, 'anyway we'd all better get our minds on Gib. From what I've heard we're losing quite a lot of ships in the Med.'

Manley stood up, carefully folded his napkin and placed it on the table. With a disconsolate expression he looked at them and in what seemed to some a callous comment, said, 'Graves is gone but we still have a ship to run. I've a feeling Gib will not be a picnic. The ammunition barge and fuel tender will arrive tomorrow, so let's make sure every department is top line,' he added reaching for his cap.

The next day, just as the officers off duty were finishing lunch, the wardroom door opened and in came a very tall, broad-shouldered officer in his mid twenties.

'G'day gentlemen,' he said, placing his large canvas grip on the deck. The sharp inflexion in his voice was unmistakably Australian.

'Who the hell are you, laddie?' Jock Weir asked, who, like the other officers stared up at this blond-haired monster that had suddenly appeared among them.

'Allan Prospero Evans,' he added, removing his cap to allow a mass of untidy fair hair to tumble over his broad forehead. 'But my friends call me Ape, can't think why,' he added, allowing his pale blue eyes and clear-cut features to wrinkle into a wide grin. 'Any chance of a beer, I've a mouth like a dingo's crutch-piece?'

Sub Lieutenant Harper-Smyth mockingly rolled his eyes up and together with his friend Sub Lieutenant Oliver Amery, burst out laughing.

'Bill Manley, First Lieutenant,' said Manley, disguising a smile while standing up and offering his hand. 'And what part of the Antipodes are you from, may I ask?'

'Dear old Sydney, sport,' Ape replied as they shook hands. 'Late of HMS *Perryworth*, a lovely old minesweeper now lying at the bottom of the English Channel.'

'Thank you, er... Ape,' Manley answered with a wry grin, 'and please refer to me as Number One. I can't remember when I indulged in any kind of sport.'

'You look familiar,' Colin Coburn said, narrowing his eyes and staring intensely at the newcomer. 'Did you ever play rugby?'

'Too right, sport,' Ape replied, flashing a set of white teeth. 'Prop forward for Oz against England in 1939. We beat you 18-12. But this bloody war's soon put paid to all that,' he added with an air of disgust, 'especially after I got a pier head jump to join you lot. Now,' he went on as he shook hands with the others, 'how about that beer?'

Shortly after 1200 on the 13 September the last of the ships forming the 15th Escort Group arrived in Liverpool and secured alongside Branch Number Two Berth in Gladstone Dock. The next morning Stirling summoned the commanding officers of the four vessels to report onboard *Sandpiper* at 0900.

The first to arrive was Jeremy Gifford, the captain of HMS *Curlew*, a tall, fair-haired officer with sharp features and deep-set blue eyes. Close behind him came Henry Parker-Grace. He was a small, broad-shouldered man whose bull neck and lantern jaw made him look more like an all-in wrestler than the commanding officer of HMS *Redshank*.

Peter Parsons, RNR, *Petrel*'s captain, was a sturdily built man with sharp features and keen pale blue eyes. However his long brownish hair evident under his cap suggested he was strongly in need of a barber. *Shearwater*'s captain, Graham Hastings, was the last to arrive. His six feet plus frame was disguised slightly by a pronounced stoop. Returning the Duty PO's salute as he stepped onboard, his inquisitive dark brown eyes darted inquisitively around as if expecting a more formal greeting. Like his three colleagues, his weather-beaten features were the result of many hours spent on the open bridge of his ship. With the exception of Peter Parsons, who was a commander and regular navy, but junior to Stirling, the rest wore the wavy stripes of RNVR, Lieutenant Commanders.

Each knew one another and the atmosphere was relaxed and friendly. The door opened and the tall figure of Stirling came in. Every officer stopped what he was doing and looked at him.

Stirling greeted them with a 'Good morning, gentlemen,' smiling while glancing quickly at their faces. 'I do believe I've met all of you at *Osprey.*' His voice, sharp and firm carried the unmistakable air of authority. He moved forward and warmly shook their hands.

PO Steward Knocker White appeared and handed Stirling a cup of coffee then disappeared into the pantry leaving the door slightly open.

Each officer reciprocated Stirling's greeting, found an armchair and sat down.

Stirling remained standing. His tall, athletic frame seemed to dominate the room. He finished his coffee and placed the cup on a table. With both hands thrust in his jacket pockets he surveyed his small audience.

'Some of you may remember in *Osprey* I insisted that as in the last war, the U-boat menace would become Britain's main adversary.' His voice was resonate, clear and concise. As he spoke his sharp dark brown, eyes looked into those of each officer pressing home his message. 'That was five years ago and everything that has happened since then has confirmed what I said.' Stirling paused momentarily, took out a packet of cigarettes and lit it using a small silver Ronson. A few officers followed suit, sat back and waited. Stirling took a deep drag and breathed out a steady stream of smoke. 'The key to success,' he went on, 'is to become a well-knit team,' he paused and gave a wry smile, 'with me it's player manager.' This comment brought a ripple of muted laughter. 'I am not joking, gentlemen, as you will soon find out. Unfortunately, we don't have much time to practise drills, because in six days we sail for Gibraltar.' He then gave details of the mission. 'I don't have to tell you what our main objective is. If a U-boat is sighted or detected it is to be attacked continuously without orders, with guns, depth charges or ram. Although I will be in charge, I want you to use your initiative. Only in dire emergencies should I expect to receive signals from commanding officers, "requesting instructions" or "action proposed" or "intended" by men on the spot, especially if I am not aware of a situation. I will blame no officer for getting on with the job even if he fails. From now on gentlemen, we are to be the hunters instead of the hunted.' Stirling stopped talking and weighed up what he had said. Then looking inquisitively at the four officers he asked, 'Any questions?'

'Do you advocate the use of star shells sir,' asked Commander Parker. 'Reports inform me that the flash of the guns almost blinds those on the bridge. I'm told that their night-vision can also be affected.'

'Good point, Peter,' Stirling replied, taking a final puff of his cigarette then stubbing it out. 'This question was raised by Admiral Noble at a meeting last week. I prefer to use rockets as their illuminant, or snowflakes as they are called, are more effective. If star shells are to be used, please remember to tell those on the bridge to close their eyes until the guns have fired. The signal for firing star shells will be called "Operation Buttercup". The admiral suggested the use of this might illuminate other ships thus putting them in danger. I took his point and suggested I deal with any problems as they arise.' Stirling paused, allowing his words to be taken in, then continued. 'Remember, the enemy always like to attack the convoys at night. They will either stay close to the torpedoed ship or leave on the surface at high speed to avoid the slower escorts. Therefore we must plaster the area around the wreck with depth charges. This is when "Buttercup" might be used. By illuminating the area we can determine the enemy's escape route. Once they are submerged we must nail the blighters. Now,' he said with a sly grin, 'if that is all, as the sun is almost over the yardarm, I suggest a gin and tonic is in order.'

## CHAPTER ELEVEN

Being berthed in Liverpool suited the crews of the escort group, especially those who lived locally. Merseyside's population was renowned for the warm welcome given to seafarers, particularly in wartime. They regularly witnessed convoys, low in the water, sometimes damaged and covered in red rust sailing down river. They also heard of the losses suffered en route from Canada, America and South Africa. Wrecks of torpedoed ships in the Mersey estuary, their yardarms poking up from the sea like nautical grave markers, were a constant reminder of the sacrifices made by the men of the Merchant and Royal Navies.

Situated on the Strand, facing the river, St Nicholas's Church, dedicated to all mariners, was regularly attended by families and sweethearts praying for the safe return of their loved ones. But for many, their prayers were not answered.

Shortly before 2359 on Tuesday 19 September the last rating came onboard *Sandpiper*. The ship was under sailing orders and leave finished at midnight. Among them was PO Coxswain Pony Moore. Looking pale, bleary-eyed and smelling strongly of beer he staggered slightly and saluted the quarterdeck Bob Shilling, the duty PO shrugged his shoulders and grinned at Sub Lieutenant Amery who was OOW.

'Had a good night, Swain?' Bob said, 'you look knackered, so you do.'

'I'm fine, ta,' Pony slurred, putting a fatherly arm around Bob's shoulder, while beaming like a Cheshire cat. 'You're looking at a man whose just got engaged to the sweetest girl in all the world.'

'Bloody hell!' Bob exclaimed, raising his eyebrows in surprise. 'You don't mean that bint from the Nag's Head, do you?'

'That's right,' Pony replied staring angrily at Bob. Removing his hand, he muttered, 'And don't you or anyone else call the future Missus Moore a bint. She's the most beautiful judy in Liverpool.'

'And the best fuck,' muttered Bob to himself watching Pony staggering along the passageway to his mess.

Next morning in the senior rates everyone congratulated Pony when he told them the good news.

'When's the happy day, then Pony?' asked Chief PO Sammy Taylor, pouring out a mug of tea.

Giving Pony a sideways grin, Chief GI Dusty Miller, quipped, 'Don't tell us you've put her up the duff, Pony, if you have you can always put in for a draft.'

'Cheeky bugger,' Pony replied contemptuously, 'we'll probably get hitched when we come back from this next trip, and what's more, Dusty me old gash bucket, you're gonna be me best man!'

'Cheers, mate,' said Dusty. 'You can have my tot, but don't expect any fancy speeches after the wedding.'

'Where will you have your honeymoon, then, Pony, New Brighton?' Chief ERA Percy Bradley asked, doing his best not to laugh.

'Mind yer own business, ' Pony replied, 'and if yer must know, we're gunna have a do in the Nag's Head when we come back from this trip, and any more lip from you and you won't be invited.'

'Can I come as well, Swain?' asked the mess man, Ordinary Seaman Nipper Morris, who was busily collecting the empty mugs.

'Of course, and tell the lads,' Pony answered, as he finished his drink. 'They're all welcome.'

At 0700 the next morning *Sandpiper* pulled away from Number One berth and slowly nosed her way into the Mersey. Dawn was gradually breaking. A pale, sorrowful moon, flitting between the dark, low-lying cumulonimbus clouds cast an anaemic glow on the inky black waters. Near the Bar Lighthouse *Sandpiper* was joined by the four other sloops. They had sailed earlier and waited line ahead rolling with the high running tide. Despite the bitterly cold easterly wind, the ship's companies were fallen in for leaving harbour. Each rating wore shiny black oilskins with their cap secured by chinstraps.

'Attention on the upper deck,' was piped as *Sandpiper* took station some fifty yards ahead of the group.

'Pipe hands fall out, Number One,' said Stirling sitting in his chair. Like Manley and those on duty, he wore woollen gloves, a duffle coat and muffler. 'And increase revolution ten and steer port twenty.'

'Port ten wheel on, sir,' came the voice of Pony More from below.

'Midships.'

'Midships ... wheel's amidships, sir.'

'Steady.'

'Steady... Course eighty west, sir.'

Through his binoculars Stirling watched the docks and Liver buildings become a grey blur on the horizon as the group entered the Irish Sea.

'Starboard ten. Steer south, eighty-five west,' Stirling snapped, feeling the harsh wind bellow against his face.

Dawn finally broke. One moment the sea was awash with silvery phosphorescence then suddenly it became a vast expanse of dull, undulating dark blue water. The outlines of the vessels became clearer and the bridge personnel changed imperceptibly from blurred shadows into tired, pale faces. The only things that didn't alter were the steady, monotonous throbbing of the engines and the unmistakable hiss of the sea.

'What's our position, Pilot,' Stirling snapped, his binoculars clamped to his eyes, staring at the yardarm of a wreck a mile away on the starboard beam.

'Ten miles off Holyhead, spor... er... sir,' replied Ape from his tiny compartment behind the bridge personnel. 'Latitude fifty-three degrees west, longitude ninety north.'

Apes's reply made Stirling smile. Shortly after Ape arrived he spoke with him in his cabin. Like Manley and the others he was impressed by Ape's cheerful personality and physique.

'Welcome onboard, Pilot,' Stirling said as they shook hands. He went on to explain the circumstances of his appointment. 'I'm only sorry we had to meet this way. You're not married I see?'

'No sir,' Ape replied, adding with a grin, 'maybe one day, if I'm unlucky.'

'According to your documents you completed a navigation course at *King Alfred* before being appointed First Lieutenant onboard your last ship. I suggest you familiarise yourself with the charts in your compartment,' said Stirling, offering Ape a cigarette, taking one himself and lighting both. 'As you know we sail in nine days' time on convoy duty. Please ensure you have charts of Gibraltar and the Mediterranean.'

'So it's not to be Halifax, Nova Scotia, sir?'

Stirling gave him a non-committal shake of his head.

'It's all the same to me, sir,' Ape replied with a wide grin. 'The sooner this war's over the sooner I'll be back home sipping some decent beer.'

During the morning the wind increased to gale force.

'The barometer's dropping, sir,' remarked Manley, glancing ruefully at the black clouds and feeling the sudden force of the wind. 'Looks like we're in for a storm.'

'Better rig lifelines and pipe hands to keep clear of the upper deck, Number One,' Stirling answered as he also gazed upwards.

Half an hour later gigantic banks of dark greeny-blue sea started hitting them beam-on. *Sandpiper* and the four sloops rose in the air as if in a lift. After hovering uneasily on the crest of a wave with a wicked sideways roll, they settled into a trough and were immediately met by another massive wave. Tons of seething white water thundered along the upper deck crashing onto the bridge. Daggers of icy cold spray attacked the faces of those on duty. The wind howled like a frenzied banshee as the ships beat their way through the turbulent waters.

In the mess decks the clatter of loose gear rent the air. Hammocks swayed eerily in perfect unison. Some men chose to sleep on the deck oblivious to the wetness and damp. Gas buckets and round aluminium rubbish bins became filled with foul smelling vomit. Those in the boiler and engine room clutched onto anything while carefully watching gauges and dials hoping the hull wouldn't burst.

'What's our speed, Number One?' yelled Stirling his voice barely audible above the clamour of the wind.

'Fifteen knots, sir,' Manley shouted, 'with a bit of luck the group should clear Land's End by 0900 tomorrow. With a bit of luck we should enter the Bay of Biscay sometime during the next twenty-four hours.'

'You hope,' cried Stirling, wiping water away from his face with the back of his gloved hand.

# CHAPTER TWELVE

Wednesday 23 September dawned overcast with clusters of dark, low-lying clouds and a febrile sun. A damp grey swirling mist reduced visibility to less than a mile. Two days later, sailing line abreast, the 15th Escort Group felt the angry swell of the Atlantic Ocean. Once again a high rolling sea battered and bounced against the bulkheads. Each ship began to corkscrew in and out of the angry waves. Streaks of lightning on the horizon were followed by crashes of thunder as the heavens opened up. A monsoon deluge that splattered against oilskins and attacked faces quickly followed.

'This is nowt, sir,' PO Yeoman Harry Tate, cried to the OOW Sub Lieutenant Amery. 'When we get into the Bay of Biscay tomorrow, you'll really see what rough weather is like.'

'I can hardly wait,' Amery muttered sarcastically while using the back of his hand to wipe away water from his face.

Much to the surprise of the older hands the Bay, notorious for its inclement weather, was remarkably calm.

In the wheelhouse, Coxswain Pony Moore shot Able Seaman Jackson a suspicious glance. 'This weather certainly is strange, Jacko,' he remarked, closely watching the movement of the gyro repeater markers while clutching the wheel. 'I've never know the Bay to be like this. It ain't natural, I tell yer.'

'You're right, there, Swain,' replied Jackson. 'It's even stopped raining. Maybe the sun will come out.'

'The only sodden thing that'll come out will be a fuckin' periscope,' Moore ominously replied.

The small flotilla was sailing line abreast with *Sandpiper* in the centre. On *Sandpiper*'s bridge Stirling placed his binoculars to his eyes and swept the immediate vicinity around the group.

'What's our position, Pilot?' he asked without moving his head.

'Latitude forty-six, longitude seven, sir,' replied Ape, 'we're about a hundred miles off the coast off La Rochelle.'

'I don't like it, Number One,' remarked Stirling, lowering his binoculars, 'better double the lookouts.'

Stirling's suspicions proved correct. A few minutes later Leading Signalman Bungy Williams, who had relieved PO Yeoman Tate, reported, 'Signal from *Petrel*, sir, "Asdic contact green three oh, three mile off port bow. Intend investigating."'

'Signal the rest of the group, "Starboard ten, increase revolutions one third. All ships follow *Petrel*."' Stirling glanced at Manley. 'Pipe hands to action stations,' he said, rubbing his hands together excitedly, 'here's hoping it's a sub and not a school of damn whales.'

Stirling watched as *Petrel* heeled to starboard and broke away. The chase was on as the rest of the flotilla turned in unison. The warm southerly wind caressing their faces was a welcome relief from the cold westerlies. By this time, *Petrel* was about a mile in front of the others. Onboard *Sandpiper* all eyes watched for the small, V-shaped telltale wash of a periscope.

'Anything on Asdic, Number One?' shouted Stirling.

'Leading Seaman Payne reports contact is slowly moving north, sir,' replied Manley.

'Yeoman,' Stirling shouted. This could be the first time he could put into practice a few of his ideas and he could hardly contain his excitement. 'Make to the group, "turn ten degrees to starboard. Increase revolutions two oh. If contact made with enemy, attack at will."'

Throughout *Sandpiper* men sweated as the tension mounted. The deck shook and every rivet threatened to burst as the ship bounded through the sea. But it was all to no avail.

'Signal from *Petrel*, sir,' yelled Williams. 'False alarm. Three whales surfaced half a mile ahead.'

'Bastard!' Stirling cursed, angrily thumping the side of his chair. He turned and glanced frustratingly at Manley. 'Mark my words, Number One,' he went on defiantly, 'the swine are out here somewhere. This is their stomping ground and one of these days we'll catch up with them. Make to the group, "Resume station".'

Even though it was September the sea was like a millpond. High in the sky the sun broke though a fleece of white clouds bathing everyone and everything in rays of welcome sunshine.

*Curlew* and *Redshank* were on *Sandpiper*'s port bow. Then came *Petrel* and *Shearwater* away to starboard. Each vessel sent up a small curl of white water over their respective fo'c'sles as they dipped gently in and out of the clear blue sea. Feeling the gentle roll of *Sandpiper*'s deck and the warm wind bathe his face, Stirling glanced approvingly at Manley, and with a touch of pride, said, 'Those exercises we did a month ago are paying off.' He glanced at Leading Signalman Williams and added, 'Make to the rest of the flotilla, "Well done to each of you. Every ship is in perfect station. Keep it up."'

'Aye, aye, sir,' replied Lee, and with a cheeky grin, added, 'makes you want to sign on, don't it sir.'

Stirling didn't reply. Instead he said, 'What's our position, Pilot?'

'That thin black line on the port horizon is Spain, sir,' came the voice of Ape, 'and at present we're sailing close to Cape

Trafalgar. Wasn't it here where old Horatio beat up the Dagos and Frogs?'

'Hmm… quite so,' replied Stirling, not overly impressed with his pilot's reference to Lord Nelson's victory over the French and Spanish in 1805. 'Better make a signal to Gib, requesting berthing instructions.'

Sub Lieutenant Oliver opened his mouth and gave a tired yawn. He had the middle watch and had just left a warm bed. Sipping a welcome mug of kye brought to him by Able Seaman Darby Allen, the duty QM, he said, 'Cape Spartel is on our starboard bow and the lights you can see close by is Tangiers. Looks quite lively, eh?'

'Never mind, sir,' Darby replied, 'we'll soon be in Gib. A run ashore down Main Street is just what we need.'


Dawn on the 26 September broke early. One moment it was quite dark, then in what appeared to be a blink of an eyelid the sun came up spreading a patina of yellow on an otherwise dark blue sea. At 0700 Stirling and Ape appeared on the bridge. Manley, lookout Able Seaman Buster Brown and PO Yeoman Tate joined them. As it grew lighter, Tarifa, a small port in Spain near the entrance to the Straits, could be seen on the port bow. The aromatic aroma of burnt grass combined with the hint of spices hung in the air reminding everyone that Africa was not far away.

'Hmm…' muttered Buster Brown wrinkling his nose, 'that smell reminds me of Big Bertha, a tart I met in Gib in '39 when I was onboard the *Prince of Wales*.'

'Oh I remember her,' replied Tate with a smirk on his face. 'She gave me and the crew of the *Dido* the pox. Best to avoid the Jippo Queen if we get ashore.'

PO Yeoman Tate threw back his head and laughed. 'Keep it in your trousers, then, or the doc'll have is work cut out.'

Half an hour later, 'Close all screen doors and scuttles. Hands fall in for entering harbour,' came over the tannoy.

Suddenly, Gibraltar's mighty Rock came into view. Jutting out against the dazzling blue of the Mediterranean sky, this magnificent monolith was an awesome sight. It hovered over the port like a guardian angel casting a protective shadow across the entrance to *Mare Nostrum*. (The name Gibraltar is derived from the word "Calpe" given to the peninsula by the Phoenicians in circa 950BC.) A mass of red terracotta roofs swept upwards from the base of the harbour. These formed a backdrop to several warships secured to buoys or alongside wharves. A forest of masts and funnels reflected in the blue waters, and huge cranes towered in the air like giant predators.

With *Sandpiper* in the van, the five ships entered harbour. By 1000 they were tied up alongside Ragged Staff Wharf.

No sooner had Stirling ordered all engines to be wrung off, than PO Yeoman Tate handed him a signal.

'It's from Rear Admiral Maitland-Smyth, C in C Gib, sir,' said PO Tate, 'It reads, "15th Escort Group to accompany convoy HG 46 en route from Malta to England. Convoy will pass through the Straits 0300 28 September accompanied by the carrier *Audacity* plus destroyers, *Blankey, Stanley* and *Exmoor*. Your group are to meet the convoy outside Gibraltar at 0400. Fuel tender will arrive today at 1300."' Tate glanced up from his signal pad and with a sly grin, said, 'Just enough time for a good run ashore, eh, sir?'

Tate's words were overhead by Able Seaman Buster Brown. With a salacious expression on his face he looked at Able Seaman Darby Allen and said, 'Bloody great! Me right hand is getting tired from doing you know what, so roll on Big Bertha.'

Stirling handed the signal to Manley. With a slight shake of his head and a wry smile he said, 'No rest for the wicked, eh, Number One? You'd better tell Engines and the Chief ERA and the Chief Stoker to expect the tender. And ask Sub Lieutenant Hailey to ensure we have enough food and stores. I expect we'll be away for some time.'

'Very good, sir,' replied Manley, adding, 'normal leave for both watches?'

'Yes, and make sure the signal is circulated to the commanding officers of the other ships and mark it secret.'

By 1130 the "buzz" had swept around the crew telling them of the ship's movements.

'What time do you think we'll meet the convoy, sir?' said "Bagsy" Baker, a tall, stocky Seaman Petty Officer, who was overseeing the rum issue. He was standing next to Manley who was OOD.

'So much for secrecy,' Manley replied, shaking his head, 'it wouldn't surprise me if the Fifth Column on the Rock and Jerry spies across the harbour in Spain also knew when we were sailing.'

# CHAPTER THIRTEEN

'D'yer hear there! Leave! Leave to the First Part of Starboard and Second of Port watches from 1600 to 0600. Rig of the day, Number Ones. Mail is now ready for collection,' echoed over the tannoy.

The time was 1530. Throughout the ship, men were getting ready to go ashore, everyone, that is, except SBA Brum Appleby.

'Just our bloody luck to be medical Guard first night, eh sir,' moaned Brum. He and Surgeon Lieutenant Coburn were in the sick bay having a mug of tea.

'Apparently,' replied the doctor, 'the names of the group were put in a hat and ours came out first. Anyway,' he added tentatively, 'maybe we'll have a quiet night.'

'Ha!' cried Brum, throwing his head back and spilling his drink, 'with all the off duty lads from the other ships ashore, not bloody likely, sir.'

In the after seaman's those off duty were getting ready to go ashore. The warm atmosphere was filled with tobacco smoke and the smell of sweaty bodies. A few ratings were using the mess table to iron a white front. Others were engrossed arranging their white lanyards around the bow of their black silks. One or two were shining their shoes while those in their full blues jostled in front on the solitary mirror ensuring their well Brylcreemed hair was in place.

'That means us, Tanky, my son,' said Able Seaman Darby Allen, straightening the collar of his messmate then pulling down his own uniform top. Darby's remark was aimed at Able Seaman Buster Brown, who was busy ensuring his cap was on straight.

'I say, Tanky, ' Darby enquired, 'what's on the end of that string you've got tucked down your neck?'

'As you buggers know I'm in charge of the rum store,' he paused and touched the string barely visible under his white front, 'and this is the key to the store. It never leaves me, even when I'm in bed with a bint.'

'Hope you've got a few Frenchies, then Tanky,' Darby replied, standing behind Buster and pulling down his collar. 'You never know your luck.'

'Chance would be fine thing,' replied Tanky, checking to see he had enough duty-free cigarettes. 'The most I've ever got was a quick wank in the alley behind the *Blue Parrot*.'

'What did it cost you?' asked Able Seaman Dinga Bell, preening himself in front of the mirror.

'Why d'you think he's stuffin' an extra packet of fags down his jumper,' Able Seaman Jackson said with a salacious grin. 'I only 'ope she washes her 'ands afterwards.'

Half an hour later Darby Allen, Tanky, Dinga Bell and Jacko in company with several others left the ship. In doing so they were joined by a stream of ratings leaving from the other four ships. Underfoot, the cobbled-stoned road felt oddly still after the steady roll of the ship. The sun was still warm and a tropical breeze, balmy and scented, caressed their faces. Relaxed and full of joviality, they could hardly wait to reach town.

As soon as they left the dockyard many ratings scrambled into the *Trafalgar Arms*, a pub outside Ragged Staff Steps.

'Let's give it a miss,' said Darby Allen. 'It's only a small pub and it'll be so crowded you won't be able to see the bar. The best places are further down.'

'All with dancin' girls, as I recall,' said Dinga Bell, gleefully rubbing his hands together.

'Your right there, Dinga, me old gash bucket,' Darby joyfully replied. 'Even though there's blackout, the place still comes alive. It'll be like Boom town later on.'

After passing the Governor's Residence, an imposing, red-bricked Victorian building, Darby suggested big eats in a nearby restaurant. For the next hour or so they enjoyed steak, egg and chips, the matelots' favourite meal, washed down with bottles of cool local beer. By the time they left, it was just after 1800 and almost dark.

'Come on lads,' said Darby, giving the pretty dark-haired waitress a lecherous wink, 'let's see if the *Jippo Queen* is still open.'

Main Street was jam-packed with servicemen. Music from gramophones blaring from cafes and bars filled the night air. Free French sailors wearing distinctive red, white and blue berets mingled with British and Commonwealth soldiers, some wearing colourful, swaying kilts. To this bustling crowd was added a spattering of RAF in pale blue, but the majority of men wore the distinctive round caps of the Royal Navy.

On either side of the wide cobbled street, carpets and bedding were draped over iron balconies. Strung across limp washing lines festooned with clothing hung limply in the warm night air. Stout women wearing drab black dresses sat on chairs seemingly unconcerned with the hustle and noise below. Darby and the others bustled passed *The Texas Bar, The Blue Peter, Harry's Bar* and others, blasting out an assortment of popular music. Lounging in each darkened doorway heavily made-up women in tight dresses beckoned passers-by.

'Big eats, clean sheets, Jack,' one cooed enticingly.

Darby Allen saw Tanky flashing a packet of cigarettes. 'Keep it in your trousers, mate, remember what happened to Harry Tate.'

'What the fuck,' Tanky cheerfully replied. 'I might as well enjoy ourselves while I can. This time next year we might be shark bait.'

Darby and the other two stopped outside a set of tall, wooden swing doors. A sign painted gaudily in peeling paint, read "The Egyptian Queen. Gibraltar's Finest Ales and Spirits". On either side was a painting of a scantily dressed dancing girl playing a tambourine.

'Well, me lads,' Darby said, ignoring the enticing smile of a pretty dark-haired girl. 'Let's get inside. The first round's on me.'

The crisp clatter of castanets and Spanish music attacked their senses as they entered. The place was full and the atmosphere was hot and sticky. The sour smell of sweaty bodies, alcohol and cheap perfume hung in the air like a libidinous fog. A blue haze of tobacco smoke almost blocked out the light from a cheap glass chandelier. Servicemen were busy chatting up swarthy, dark-haired girls dressed in tight-fitting skirts and colourful blouses. One or two sat with a girl on their knee drinking while attempting in vain to slide a hand up her thigh.

On a small round stage in the centre of the room, a girl with long jet-black hair wearing a swirling red dress was dancing the Flamenco. Her legs were encased in black stockings and she wore red shoes with reinforced high heels. Frowning as if in anger, she stamped noisily on the floor then throwing her head back, clicked her tiny castanets while glaring seductively at the wide-eyed expressions on the faces below. Everyone clapped and cheered madly each time she twirled, each man straining to catch a glimpse of white thighs, red suspender belt and lacy black underwear. It was brash, bawdy and licentious, and the men loved every minute of it.

'Get 'em off,' shouted a sailor, trying to reach up to her.

'Put yer laughing gear around this,' yelled a marine while grabbing his crutch.

Suddenly the music stopped. With a defiant toss of her head the girl gave a swish of her skirt and hurried off the stage. She then vanished through a side door leaving in her wake a cacophony of boos and ribald catcalls.

Darby and the others pushed their way onto the bar and ordered three pints of beer. A few of the *Sandpiper*'s crew, including one or two senior ratings had managed to find a table. Among them were Chief ERA Percy Bradley and fifty-year-old Buffer, Sammy Taylor, who was sitting with one leg stretched out.

The beer arrived. Darby and the other two took a deep gulp, leaned against the bar, lit cigarettes and looked around. The gramophone music had restarted and a few couples were moving sluggishly around the dance floor.

'Look out lads and keep your hands on your wallets,' warned Dinga, as two girls with swaying hips and flashing smiles sidled up alongside them. The taller of the two, a dusky skinned beauty wearing a tight fitting black skirt and a vivid red sweater rested an arm on Dinga's shoulder. Her friend was smaller, slightly fairer and similarly dressed.

''Ello Jack,' she said, flashing a set of tobacco-stained teeth. 'My name is Maria,' she glanced at her friend and added, 'and this is Rita. You buy us a drink, yes?'

'OK,' replied Dinga staring at the two enticing bulges in her sweater, 'but it'll cost you a dance.' As he spoke she allowed his hand to slowly creep down the side of her skirt.

'All right, big man,' the girl replied, retrieving his hand, 'Rita and me will 'ave a rum and coke, but no hank panky, yes?'

An innocent expression spread over Dinga's face. 'Just as if I would,' he answered, playfully patting her bottom. The barman gave an all-knowing wink at the girls and quickly served them.

Meanwhile, Rita had her arm around Tanky's waist and was whispering something in his ear. Tanky looked away, his fleshy features fixed in a broad smile. 'No problem,' he said giving her a hug.

'I hope you buggers know what you're doing,' remarked Darby finishing his drink, 'now get 'em in, it's your round Tanky.'

At that moment Darby heard a loud yell coming from where the Buffer and the CERA Percy Bradley were sitting.

A tall, broad-shouldered marine with ginger hair was lying on the floor close to where the Buffer was sitting.

'You stupid old bastard,' cried the marine, picking himself up and glaring angrily at the Buffer, 'you ought to be in an old people's 'ome instead of in the fuckin' navy.' He then pulled one of the legs of the Buffer's chair. The Buffer immediately toppled over grabbing the table as he did so. The table overturned. Beer glasses and liquid ran everywhere. Darby and the others gathered around the table.

'Who the bloody 'ell are you calling an old bastard, you cheeky young whippersnapper,' yelled the Buffer, his wizened face red with anger. 'I was in the *Andrew* before you was born.' CERA Bradley immediately helped the Buffer up and straightened the table.

'Why don't you fuck off, Grandpa,' replied the marine, pushing the Buffer in the chest. 'Before I teach you a lesson you'll never forget.'

The Buffer's dark eyes narrowed. He took a deep breath and with the full force of his medium-sized frame, clenched his fist and hit the marine full on the chin. With a wild cry the marine staggered back and fell against a table. Girls screamed. Bottles and glasses crashed onto the floor. Beer mingled with bits of broken glass. Another marine, a stocky corporal with a ruddy complexion, came at the Buffer. CERA Percy Bradley intervened and caught the marine with a right cross to the side of the face. With an anguished yell the marine charged at Percy, who dodged out of the way allowing the marine to crash into another table. Pandemonium immediately broke out. With a hideous scratching noise the man playing the gramophone removed the record and hurried away. More girlish screams along with yells as tables and chairs tumbled over. Drunken marines, soldiers and sailors joined in the fray. A small, broad-shouldered marine appeared and took a swing at the Buffer and missed.

'Come on lads,' shouted Darby Allen, 'let's give the Buffer a hand.'

He and Dinga Bell left the girls and hurried across the floor. In doing so, Dinga caught sight of Rita dragging Tanky through the crowd towards a side door. This distraction cost him a heavy blow to the side of his head delivered by a marine. As Dinga hit the floor he didn't see Darby retaliate by kicking the marine in the groin. By this time marines along with soldiers and sailors were yelling and trading punches. Someone threw a bottle shattering the mirror behind the bar. Girls holding their hands to their faces continued to scream doing their best to avoid the brawlers. The barman grabbed the till and quickly placed it under the counter. It was a scene reminiscent of a brawl in a western film.

Suddenly the main door opened and in came the naval shore patrol. This consisted of half a dozen matelots and a stout, red-faced petty officer. All of them wore white belts and gaiters. The piercing sound of whistles rent the air as the patrolmen, wielding wooden batons, waded into the fray in an attempt to break up the fighting. One of them was hit and fell over. Military MPs wearing their distinctive red caps then arrived. These were tall, tough-looking men who immediately dragged the brawlers apart. In a matter of minutes the fray was over. Everyone stopped and with expressions of bewilderment and shock stared wildly at one another. Battledresses and shirts and collars were torn. The white fronts of several sailors were ripped and splattered with blood. Caps, berets and sailors' hats, soaked in beer, were strewn around the floor. Girls, whimpering and cuddling together, cowered against the walls.

The Petty Officer saw the Buffer who was sitting down holding his head.

'What started all this, chief?' he asked. 'And what ship are you from?'

The Buffer, half dazed, looked up at the PO and said, 'Buggered if I can remember.'

The next day at 0900, defaulters onboard *Sandpiper* were a sad sight. Earlier, Stirling had sent for the Buffer and CERA Bradley. He and Manley were in his cabin.

'My goodness, Chief,' said Stirling staring at the Buffer, 'your left eye looks half closed,' he paused and glanced at Bradley. 'And the side of your face is badly bruised. I take it you have both seen the MO?'

'Yes, sir,' replied the Buffer, his voice quiet and full of contrition. 'We saw him last night along with several others from our ship.'

'Yes, he and the SBA had quite a night,' replied Stirling. 'Now tell me. What happened?'

The Buffer sighed wearily and was about to speak when CERA Bradley intervened. 'A marine insulted Chief Taylor, sir,' said Bradley, 'and aimed a punch at him. I saw it all.'

'Hmm... I see,' murmured Stirling, pensively stroking his chin, 'so the Buffer was defending himself?'

'Yes, sir,' replied Bradley. 'And some of our lads joined in to defend the Buffer. And that's how it all started.'

'The report given to the PO of the shore patrol by the pub manager states differently,' Stirling replied shaking his head. 'He maintains the navy started fighting with the marines over a women and is claiming damages.'

'A likely story, if I may say so, sir,' said the Buffer.

With a weary sigh, Stirling stood up. 'I'll see you both at defaulters. I suppose you will both plead self defence?'

'Yes, sir,' the Buffer replied confidently, 'that it was.'

After they left Stirling, looked at Manley and said, 'Anyone adrift last night, Number One?'

'Yes sir, only one, sir, Able Seaman Brown.'

'Good Lord!' Stirling replied, raising his eyebrows in concern. 'Isn't he in charge of the rum store?'

'He is indeed, sir,' replied Manley. 'So far he hasn't returned onboard.' And, Manley paused and, with a look of concern, added, 'He's got the key of the rum store with him.'

## CHAPTER FOURTEEN

An expression of surprise spread across Stirling's face. 'I take it we have a spare?' he asked Manley standing up and walking towards the door.

With a hint of despair, Manley replied, 'No sir, we seem to have lost it!'

'Can the door be broken down?'

'Er... no sir,' Manley answered hesitatingly. 'The door's one of the strongest in the ship. It's made of solid steel and you can only get in with the key.'

Stirling gave a short laugh. 'The builders got their priorities right then, but what are we going to do about rum issue?'

'I thought we could borrow some from *Rooke*,' replied Manley. 'The shore base should have plenty in stock.'

'Mmm... all right,' muttered Stirling warily. 'And let me know when Brown returns. I shall have a few choice words to say to him.'

HMS *Rooke* was a shore base named after Admiral Sir George Rooke, who, in 1704, during the War of the Spanish Succession, captured Gibraltar from the Spanish. Up to the present day, this has remained a bone of political contention between Spain and Great Britain.

The news of Tanky's absence soon spread around the ship.

'You two went ashore with Tanky,' Coxswain Pony Moore said staring accusingly at Darby Allen and Dinga Bell. 'What the bloody 'ell happened to 'im?'

The time was 1000. Darby Allen, and Dinga Bell, along with several others, were standing outside the coxswain's office prior to defaulters at 1015.

'Search me, Swain,' replied Dinga, gingerly touching the large blue-black bruise under his left eye. 'The last I saw of 'im he were with some tart.'

'Bloody marvellous!' cried Pony, glancing menacingly first at Dinga Bell then Darby Allen. 'You two would lose your own mothers in a bingo hall.'

Defaulters were held in the wardroom flat. Stirling's first offender was the Buffer, CPO Sammy Taylor. With an embarrassed expression written over his wrinkled, weather-beaten features, Taylor pleaded self-defence and was given seven days' stoppage of leave. CERA Percy Bradley was next. Like several ratings he nursed a black eye and bruised face. All of them received similar sentences.

During the day, ratings working on the upper deck kept looking to see if there was any signs of Tanky.

Able Seaman Jackson, who was duty QM, glanced enquiringly at the burly figure of Able Seaman Patrick Duffy, and said, 'I wonder how much rum we got from *Rooke*, Paddy? The buzz is we're running short.'

'To be sure,' replied Duffy. 'If Tanky doesn't arrive soon there'll be a fuckin' mutiny, so there will.'

Tanky finally arrived at 1600. All eyes watched as he walked up the gangway, escorted by two burly naval patrolmen. His uniform was clean and he appeared to have had a shave. Stepping over the brow he grinned, lifted both arms to show a pair of handcuffs to Sub Lieutenant Weir who was OOD, and said, 'Sorry to be adrift, sir. I sort of lost me way.' His remark brought a peel of laughter from the ratings working on the quarterdeck.

Sniffing the air, the officer looked suspiciously at Tanky, shook his head and said, 'What rubbish. You smell like a lady's boudoir.' He looked at the two escorts and with a weary sigh, added, 'Take the handcuffs off, we'll deal with him.'

'OK, sir,' replied the biggest of the two patrolmen, handing the officer a piece of paper. 'If you'll sign this you can 'ave 'im, smell an' all.' He bent down and using a small key undid Tanky's handcuffs. Tanky immediately grinned and did a few wrist exercises. At that moment the ringing of the quarterdeck phone interrupted the proceedings.

QM Able Seaman Jackson unhooked the receiver. 'It's the captain, sir,' he said handing the phone to Weir, 'he wants to speak to you.'

Stirling happened to be on the bridge and along with Manley watched Tanky come onboard. With a frown Sub Lieutenant Weir accepted the phone from Jackson. A few seconds later he said, 'Very good, sir,' and handed the phone back to Jackson. He turned, glared ominously at Tanky and said, 'The captain will deal with you after you've been examined by the MO.'

For the second time that morning defaulters was convened. Peering across his tall, narrow slanted table, Stirling watched as Coxswain Pony Moore, using his best parade-ground voice, marched Tanky before him.

'Off caps,' shouted Pony. In his left hand he held a clipboard containing Tanky's charge sheet. 'Leading Seaman Brown, sir. Twelve hours adrift contrary to ship's standing order one zero two.'

'What have you to say for yourself, Brown,' Stirling asked, noticing Brown's blood shot eyes and tired features.

'I er... got lost, sir,' Brown meekly replied, 'there was a fight and I had a knock on the 'ead and lost track of time.'

Furrowing his brow Stirling glared at Brown. 'You did realise you had the key of the run store?'

'Yes, sir,' Tanky answered carefully touching his white front. 'It's right here, safe and sound.'

'That's just as well for you,' replied Stirling, giving Brown a withering look. 'Not only have you caused a great deal of embarrassment, but you smell as if you've been in the company of women.'

With a hurt expression written all over his face, Tanky cried, '*Me, sir? Never! Like I say, I was lost.*'

Glancing pensively at Manley who was Buster's Divisional Officer, Stirling asked, 'Anything in mitigation, Number One?'

'Ahem,' Manley replied, clearing his throat, 'only to say Brown is a competent gunnery rating and looks after the rum store very efficiently, sir.'

'You don't say,' snapped Stirling glaring angrily at Tanky. 'A week's stoppage of rum and leave and the loss of one good conduct badge. If we were in Nelson's navy, I'd have you flogged, so think yourself lucky.'

'On, cap, left turn, quick march!' yelled Pony Moore.

Tanky put his cap on, and as he turned to go, he looked at Stirling and with a startled expression on his face, said, 'Would you *really* have had me flogged, sir?'

Stirling raised his eyebrows and doing his best to suppress a smile, shouted, '*Get him out of here Coxswain, before I change my mind!*'

## CHAPTER FIFTEEN

At precisely 0200 on the morning of 28 September the 15th Escort Group, sailing in line ahead, slipped their moorings and left Gibraltar. After the relative warmth ashore a chilly wind blew from the north sending shivers through those on duty. The sea was calm and a pale moon lighted up the grey clouds scurrying across the sky. A myriad of stars turned the calm sea into rippling daggers of twinkling light.

On the afternoon prior to sailing, Stirling and the commanding officers of the other four sloops had held a meeting in *Rooke* with the C in C, Admiral Maitland-Smyth, a dour, sharp-eyed man with short, greying hair who, as a young sub-lieutenant had won a Victoria Cross at Jutland. Sitting behind a sturdy leather topped desk, puffing gently on a well-stained meerschaum pipe, he welcomed the officers and beckoned them to sit down.

'Nice to see you, gentlemen,' he said in a throaty voice while waving his hand through a cloud of tobacco smoke. He stood up and shook their hands then resumed his seat. 'Do smoke if you want. I know how busy you are so I'll come straight to the point. Intelligence from Bletchley informs us that Doenitz is concentrating his wolf pack in and around Gibraltar and the Bay of Biscay. He now has sufficient co-operation from the Luftwaffe to enable the Focke-Wulf bombers to either attack or send wireless reports to give our convoy's positions.' The admiral paused and placed his smouldering pipe in an ashtray thick with black ash then went on. 'These damn wolf packs are playing havoc with us.

Unfortunately, shore-based Coastal Command planes don't have the range to combat the U-boat tactics. To counteract this we have decided to include an aircraft carrier with the convoys.' With an air of finality he stood up and added, 'Be prepared to meet stiff opposition. Good luck and Godspeed.'

Now, sitting on his chair on *Sandpiper*'s bridge, the admiral's words echoed in Stirling's ear. He turned around and could clearly see the frothy wake of *Petrel* and the swaying masts of the other three ships silhouetted against the sky. Standing close by Manley were Leading Signalman Tansey Lee and the bulky figure of Lieutenant 'Ape' Prospero, who was OOW.

'Signal *Petrel* and repeat to the others, "double the lookouts and increase revolutions one third, I expect to sight the convoy pretty soon and I don't want us to be adrift".'

Shortly after 0300 lookout Able Seaman Lofty Day with the frosty glare of the horizon in the background, reported masts approximately five miles away.

'Looks to be about thirty ships in five columns, sir, heading in a northerly course,' he shouted through his intercom. 'There's an aircraft carrier in the middle and a destroyer on either flank.'

Half an hour later, with dawn slowly breaking, the escorts met the convoy. Using their binoculars, Stirling, Manley and Ape watched the lumbering shape of the aircraft carrier HMS *Audacity*, accompanied by the destroyers *Blankey, Stanley* and *Exmoor* cut through the high rolling sea.

'I do believe *Audacity* is one of those converted merchant ships,' Manley thoughtfully remarked.

'That's right, Number One,' muttered Stirling, 'notice her small flight deck. She can only carry about half a dozen Martlet fighters. Their job is to patrol around the convoy searching for U-boats and chase off any Focke-Wulfs before they can report our position to their bases.'

'No bloody use if the sea is rough and visibility lousy,' added Ape. With a tired sigh he added, 'I don't know about you lot, but I could do with mug of kye.'

By dawn the escorts had spread themselves around the convoy in two protective screens – one close to the convoy and the other further away to act as scouts. *Sandpiper* led the way a mile ahead of the convoy.

At dusk on the 29 September, *Shearwater* signalled *Sandpiper* saying her lookouts had sighted two aircraft.

'Does it say approximately how high the blighters are?' Stirling asked, warming his hands around a mug of kye.

'No sir,' replied Leading Signalman Buck Taylor.

'Repeat the signal to *Audacity* and add "request Martlet be launched to investigate".'

A few minutes later Taylor received *Audacity*'s reply: "Request denied. If it were enemy aircraft, they are well away."

'Dammit,' muttered Stirling, 'by now the bloody Focke-Wulfs have passed our full particulars to every U-boat for miles.'


Surrounded by members of his staff at his headquarters in Lorient, forty-nine-year-old Admiral Karl Doenitz stood pouring over a large map of the Atlantic Ocean. At forty-nine Doenitz was Commander of all German submarines. (Befehlshaber der Unterseebote B.d.U.) He stood a little over six feet with a narrow, intelligent face, aquiline nose and dark brown hair receding over a high forehead. His sharp blue eyes were focussed on a series of small markers indicating the position of convoy HG76. Standing close by, a tall, fair-haired Oberleutnant lent across a table and moved the tiny red flags on their operations map. Another officer plotted the probable position, course and speed of the convoy.

With an air of confidence, the officer snapped to attention and reported, 'Our U-boats should be in a position to attack within the next twenty-four hours, mein Admiral.'

Admiral Doenitz straightened up and took out a packet *Players,* his favourite cigarettes, recently captured from a British cargo ship. He then carefully fitted a cigarette into the end of a long-stemmed black holder. Straight away an officer, standing nearby, clicked his heels and lit it. After taking a deep drag and allowing smoke to dribble from both nostrils, Doenitz smiled smugly and in a sharp, clear voice, replied, 'Very good. I will in inform all wolf packs in the area.'

Doenitz's habit of personally contacting his U-boats irritated the submarine commanders. Up to seventy times a day he would ask for details of fuel consumption, stores and torpedoes spent. It would eventually prove to be his undoing as, unknown to him, the Allies were monitoring all transmissions.

Using HF/DF Direction Finding nicknamed "Huff Duff" they were able to track the U-boats' radio signals. By mid-day the enemy's movements were confirmed by the code-breakers at Bletchley who immediately informed the Admiralty. Two hours later, *Audacity* was informed and passed the information to the convoy commodore and the escorts.

'As if we couldn't have guessed,' Stirling sarcastically remarked after reading the signal telling him U-boats were in the area. 'Better double the lookouts, Number One, and tell Leading Seaman Payne to keep a sharp ear on his Asdic set.'

At 0400, a signal flashed from *Redshank* to *Sandpiper* reported contact with a U-boat twenty miles on the port side of the convoy. Stirling knew that U-boats shadowing a convoy usually stayed on the surface at visibility distance, submerging only when there was a danger of being detected. The submarines were low in the water and could keep watch on the convoy's mastheads while their flat silhouettes made it difficult for them to be seen by the escort lookouts.

Once again, Stirling signalled *Audacity* reporting the position of the U-boat and requesting an aircraft be launched. With a hint of optimism in his voice he turned to Manley and said, 'With a bit of luck, in this grey light the plane might be able to spot the blighter before it can submerge.'

Shortly after 0900 the Martlet reported, 'U-boat on surface, twenty-two miles on convoy's port beam.'

Stirling was now faced with a dilemma. Should he ignore the C in C's instructions and remain with the convoy, or follow his instinct and order his group plus the three destroyers to detach from the convoy and search for the enemy. To do so would leave the merchantmen protected only by the corvettes *Penstemon, Blankey* and *Exmoor* and the carrier *Audacity*. If the U-boat got amongst the convoy they could cause havoc! Stirling clenched his teeth and with a look of determination, glanced at Ape and said, 'Sound action stations. Signal all ships. I intend going to attack the enemy. Relay signal to *Audacity* and the convoy's commodore.'

'Is this wise, sir,' Manley warned, giving Stirling a searching look. 'If we lose the U-boat and it...'

'Yes, yes, Number One,' Stirling interrupted impatiently, 'I'm perfectly aware what would happen.'

'But is it worth risking the convoy, sir,' Manley said, a dubious expression in his eyes.

'It's a risk I am willing to take, Number One,' Stirling replied defiantly. 'We'll just have to wait and see. If I'm wrong then it's my responsibility. Increase revolutions one-third. Better make an announcement over the tannoy. Now get on with it.'

Surgeon Lieutenant Coburn was sitting in his cabin writing a letter to Fiona. Suddenly the ear-splitting jangling of the alarm bell brought him back to earth. This is it, he thought as he grabbed his steel helmet and medical valise, action at last. In a matter of seconds, breathless and sweating he reached the sick bay in time to hear the First Lieutenant's voice telling the crew what was happening. Appleby was there sitting at his desk engrossed in a dog-eared copy of *Tit Bits*.

'Looks like we'll see a bit of fun at last, sir,' said Appleby, putting his magazine down, and grinning.

'Yes it does,' Coburn nervously replied. The noise of the X gun's shell hoist only served to increase his anxiety. Accepting a mug of tea from Appleby he felt his heart rate increase as he waited for hammer-like blows against the bulkheads when the first salvo was fired. At that moment the door opened and in came PO Steward Slinger Wood, Steward Potts and Writer Chats Harris.

'First aid team all present and correct, sir,' beamed Slinger, 'any chance of a cuppa?'

On the bridge a bitterly cold north-westerly wind played havoc with the halyards. Stirling watched as the escorts cut through the sea, one mile apart formed line abreast.

'How far away is the convoy, Number One?' Stirling asked, glancing apprehensively at Manley.

'Roughly five miles on our port bow, sir,' Manley replied. With a look of concern, he added, 'Do you want any of our ships to return in case the blighter dives and makes for the convoy, sir?'

'No, I do not, thank you, Number One,' Stirling snapped. 'I intend nailing the bastard.'

Shortly after 1100 on 30 September a signal from *Curlew* relayed to the rest of the escorts including *Audacity,* reported, "U-boat sighted two miles on port bow and moving northwards at about fifteen knots".

Stirling felt his stomach tighten and his pulse rate increase. 'Yeoman,' he shouted, 'flash a signal along the line, say "open fire independently when in range" also send a signal to *Audacity*, say, "request Martlet to be launched to attack the sub". With a bit of luck,' he added glancing hopefully at Manley, 'it'll slow the bastard down.'

Five minutes after sending the signal to the aircraft everyone on *Sandpiper'* s bridge watched as a fighter took off. In a matter of seconds it screamed over the convoy and spotted the U-boat – a tiny target on a dark blue, heaving sea. The pilot immediately banked his plane and came in low towards the sub. In doing so both his wing guns flickered into life as the pilot opened fire. Smoky explosions accompanied by yellow sparks littered the deck and conning tower of the U-boat.

'The number on her conning tower is U131,' said Stirling, his binoculars clamped to his eyes, 'and the pilot seems determined to sink her.'

'Good luck to him,' Manley soberly replied, his binoculars glued to his eyes. 'But I would have liked to have got the...'

Manley stopped talking as he saw the two 20mm guns mounted on the U-boat's conning tower and 8.8cm gun on the upper deck, open up. Arcs of coloured tracers and shells streaked towards the oncoming plane. The barrage hit home. The front section of the Martlet's fuselage burst into a mass of flames and smoke. Tiny bits of metal were flung into the air. One wing caught fire as the plane dipped and headed downwards.

'*My God!*' Manley cried, 'the poor blighter's going to crash onto the sub.'

Dazed by the speed of events, everyone on the five ships watched as the Martlet, bellowing a stream of smoke and flames, crashed in a cloud of spray almost alongside the U-boat.

'What's our range now, Pilot?' shouted Stirling, his binoculars clamped onto his eyes.

'Less than seven miles, sir,' replied Ape.

'Commence firing,' yelled Stirling.

As if reading Stirling's mind, *Curlew, Redshank, Shearwater, Stanley* and *Petrel* also joined in the barrage.

'Great minds think alike, eh, sir,' shouted Manley, his voice hardly audible against the wind.

'Not really, Number One,' cried Stirling, with an air of satisfaction. 'They're doing exactly what I would have expected them to do.'

Coburn had heard and felt the guns firing during the workup, but somehow they sounded louder and fiercer. Even so, the retort of X gun made him jump out of his seat. Appleby, who was sitting nearby on the deck quietly smoking just managed to save him from tumbling over. Slinger Wood and his fellow first aiders were also sat on the deck clutching mugs of tea.

'Always seems worse when it's the real thing, eh sir?' said Slinger, delicately sniffing the air which by now smelt strongly of cordite. 'I only 'ope it don't sour the milk in me tea.'

The barrage lasted for about twenty minutes.

'Fancy another cuppa, sir?' said Appleby, smoking a cigarette while watching the doctor sitting, pale-faced holding his head in his hands. 'The other one's cold by now.'

Coburn released his hand and looked down at Appleby. With a relieved sigh, he sat back in his chair. For the first time he had heard the guns fire in anger and felt somewhat relieved. Accepting a mug of steaming hot tea from Appleby, he said, 'At least there's been no casualties.'

Meanwhile, on the bridge, Leading Signalman Tansey Lee glanced sharply at Stirling and shouted, 'Signal from *Curlew,* sir, "Submarine badly damaged and is abandoning ship".'

Stirling's weather-beaten features broke into a wide grin. 'Hoist "cease fire", Number One.'

As the smoke surrounding the U-boat cleared, everyone on *Sandpiper'*s bridge watched as figures could be seen leaping from the conning tower into the choppy sea.

'Signal *Curlew* to pick up survivors.' Just as Stirling finished speaking, everyone saw the U-boat suddenly upturn and point her black, snub-nosed bow to the sky and slide stern first below the waves, leaving behind a swirling mass of frothy bubbles. A huge explosion rumbling from below followed this. A thick pall of water flew into the air. For a few seconds it hung in the air like a vaporous shroud before collapsing into the sea in concentric rings of dark oily water.

Stirling turned and gave Manley an all-knowing look. 'Nothing ventured, nothing gained, eh, Number One?'

'Yes, sir,' Manley replied cautiously, 'but if the sub had got away…'

'But it didn't,' Stirling quickly interrupted. 'And it proves that attacking the enemy before he gets to you pays off. Send a signal to the Admiralty and the C in C, Western Approaches. Give the location and number of the U-boat and say survivors being picked up.' Inwardly he gave a huge sigh of relief. His tactics introduced for the first time into the Atlantic war had not only succeeded, but had demonstrated to the captains of the other ships in the group, his courage and leadership. However, Stirling's assumption of success was in grave danger. Some ten miles away lying on the surface U131 lurked ominously waiting for an opportunity to attack the convoy.

# CHAPTER SIXTEEN

Shortly after midnight on 1 October U434 was on the surface checking the position of the nearest escorts. Normally her captain, Kapitanleutnant Karl Heyda, would have received a "homing" report from his colleague in U131. Having received no message her captain decided to attack the convoy.

The time was 0400. Dawn was slowly breaking. From the east the crescent-shaped orange moon cast a pale yellow sheen across the choppy sea. High above a blustery northerly wind sent the dark clouds racing across the sky.

*Shearwater*'s lookout, Soapy Waters, a one-badge Able Seaman, had the morning watch. He gave a tired yawn feeling the cold wind attack his leathery features. After ensuring his muffler was firmly tucked inside his duffle coat, he began scanning the horizon with his binoculars. It was monotonous work, but Waters had been the service long enough to know how important his job was. At first the glint of the morning sun distorted his view. When this had cleared he moved his binoculars in a slow arc from left to right. Suddenly he gave a quick intake of breath. Some six miles away from the convoy on the port beam was the unmistakable flat shape of a squat conning tower. Waters immediately reported this to the OOW in the bridge. He in turn informed *Shearwater*'s captain, Lieutenant Commander Graham Hastings, who was in his sea cabin.

'Break radio silence,' he yelled though his voice-pipe. 'Inform *Sandpiper* that I intend to attack.' Fully clothed, he leapt out of his bunk and seconds later was on the bridge.

'Increase revolutions two-thirds, hard a starboard,' ordered Hastings.

*Curlew, Redshank, Petrel, Sandpiper* and *Stanley* received the signal and joined in the hunt.

Onboard *Sandpiper* Stirling nervously licked his lips and looked at Manley. 'Another U-boat has been sighted, sound action stations, Number One. We're going in for an attack.'

The rumour soon spread around the ship that Stirling had previously taken a risk leaving the convoy.

'The old man's certainly pushin' his luck, again, ain't he Swain,' said Able Seaman Wiggie Bennett. He and Chief Coxwsain Pony Moore were closed up in the wheelhouse. 'There's only the escorts and the carrier protecting the convoy.'

'Shut up will, you,' retorted Moore, 'the old man knows what he's doin', anyways three of our ships should be enough to deal with any emergencies.'

'I bloody hope so,' murmured Bennett, his hand on the telegraph.

In the sick bay SBA Appleby's round, fleshy face wrinkled into an all-knowing grin. Looking pensively at the doctor, he said, 'Maybe you spoke too soon about not getting any casualties, sir.'

Coburn didn't answer. Instead he looked at the faces of the first aid team and wondered if they were as nervous as he was.

On the bridge Stirling's heart was pounding a cadence against his ribs. The soft metallic sound of the Asdic, now being piped over the tannoy, told him the submarine was close by. He shot an apprehensive glance at Manley and said, 'If that bastard gets among the convoy, God knows what will happen. Better send another signal to the C in C. Give the position of the sub.'

Meanwhile, *Shearwater* was roughly three miles away and closing fast in on the enemy. However the U-boat's captain who had seen her approach, immediately ordered the submarine to crash dive.

'*Blast it!*' cried Stirling, who, due to his experience was able to imagine what was happening in the U-boat. He knew that to make an 1100-ton submarine dive, a series of complex orders must unfold with precise timing. First, the order, *"alarm, alarm"*, would be shouted by the sub's captain. The hand on the telegraph is then turned to *"Dive"*. There would be no panic. Two weeks' intensive training at Wilhelmshaven had ensured that each man was well trained. Next, the main watertight hatchways leading to the upper deck are tightly secured. Men off duty in various states of undress would be tumbling out of their bunks hurrying to their stations. Those on duty would be closed up sweating profusely; eyes and ears alert awaiting orders. Speed and concentration were essential to avoid a watery death.

Stirling imagined men frantically turning off the diesel oil and closing the air intakes. This allowed the electric motors to take over moving the sub. He could almost hear the captain's strident voice ordering, *"flood all tanks"* allowing seawater into ballast tanks. Men not on duty would be ducking through hatchways hurrying along the narrow, claustrophobic passageways leading to the front part of the sub. Here, there combined weight would help to point the submarine downwards. Stirling was well aware that an emergency dive is the most critical test a U-boat crew can face. He also knew it could take thirty seconds for the submarine to disappear under the water. Stirling smiled ruefully knowing that this very short passage of time would seem the longest in the lives of each of the U-boat's crew.

With the rest of the group still a mile away, *Shearwater*'s captain ordered single depth charges to be dropped around the area. *Curlew* arrived and her captain, Lieutenant Commander Jeremy Giffon, immediately joined in the fray.

'Set the depth charges to explode at 300 feet,' he yelled down the voice-pipe to the young sub lieutenant on the quarterdeck. 'I intend to drop a pattern of five around where she dived.'

By this time the other four warships had arrived in the area. Lieutenant Commander Giffon in *Curlew* passed on the range and bearing to them.

Onboard *Sandpiper*'s bridge all eyes watched anxiously as *Curlew*'s depth charges, each containing 1290lbs (189kg) of amatol flew in the air and with a small splash, disappeared into the sea. A series of explosions rumbled from deep down in the sea. These were quickly followed by several tall, geyser-like eruptions of white foamy water. In a matter of seconds each watery spout settled down into a fizzy mass of bubbles and spray. But there was no sign of a tell-tale oil slick or debris.

Stirling grasped the sides of his chair, his knuckles white with tension. 'Tell Harper-Smyth to set his charges at 150 and 300 feet. I intend to drop fourteen close to those of *Curlew.*' Listening to the "pinging" of the Asdic becoming louder he quickly ordered the depth charges to be released. A cluster of cylindrical shaped depth charges, rolled from the quarterdeck and splashed into the sea. Once again the sea was churned into a seething mass of foam as they exploded.

By this time *Redshank* and *Petrel* had arrived and joined in the attack. A series of loud paroxysms of water leaping high into the air quickly followed this.

'*Submarine breaking surface, sir!*' *Redshank*'s lookout yelled excitedly, '*about half a mile away to starboard.*'

All eyes onboard *Redshank*'s bridge immediately turned to the right. Using binoculars, they clearly saw the black, rounded shape of U-434's bows breaking the surface. Many of the U-boat's crew could be seen jumping into the water. Some already in the sea were waving frantically.

'They're abandoning ship, Number One,' yelled the stocky figure of Parker-Grace, *Redshank*'s captain.

'Great Scott!' exploded *Redshank*'s First Lieutenant. '*Petrel* is heading towards the blighter. I think she's going to ram her!'

Onboard *Sandpiper* Stirling, bareheaded, had climbed on top the bridge '*Go on, Petrel!*' he shouted, waving his cap wildly in the air. His keen brown eyes shone with excitement and several strands of his thick wiry hair wavered in the wind. '*Nail the bugger!*' Even though his voice was barely audible in the strong northerly wind his animated actions brought smiles on the faces of those on the bridge. The effect of Stirling's enthusiasm was infectious and was slowly spreading throughout the group.

PO Yeoman Tate turned to Leading Signalman Lee and said, 'The old man really is determined to sink the bugger no matter what, ain't he Tansey?'

'That he is,' Lee replied rubbing his hands excitedly and grinning, 'and with a bit of luck *Petrel* will do just that.'

Stirling climbed down from the bridge and along with everyone else watched as *Petrel,* sending a huge bow wave in the air, closed in on her prey. But before she could reach the enemy, the U-boat, covered in smoke and flames, like its predecessor, capsized and spewing a mass of black, oily bubbles, disappeared under the sea.

'That's a second one the group has sunk, sir,' said Manley, with a touch of pride. 'It looks like you were right to leave the convoy and attack the buggers.'

'Perhaps, Number One,' Stirling replied reflectively staring out to sea, 'but I've a feeling there's still a few more out there, waiting to pounce on us. Signal *Petrel* and the others. Say, "Well done all. Pick up survivors and rejoin the convoy, then Splice the Mainbrace."'

Stirling's words of caution were confirmed when two Focke-Wulf spotter planes appeared low on the horizon. *Audacity* flew off two of her Martlets to engage them, but the enemy planes quickly retreated into the denseness of the clouds and vanished.

'To be sure, I bet every fuckin' U-boat knows exactly where we are by now,' retorted Able Seaman Patrick Duffy to Able Seaman Jackson, his opposite number on the port Oerlikon gun.

'Aye, and that bastard probably radioed our position before she sank,' replied Jacko gazing cautiously at the sky.

Both men were right.

Shortly after midday *Petrel* flashed an alarming signal to *Sandpiper*. Stirling was on the bridge, sitting in his chair when PO Yeoman Tate, handed it to him. It read: *"Have learned from prisoners that position, course and speed of convoy are known to the enemy, together with name of aircraft-carrier."*

'Can't say I'm overly surprised,' muttered Stirling dryly as he handed the signal to Manley. 'Repeat it to *Audacity,* and request a dawn patrol. With a bit of luck the Martlets might catch one of the sods recharging their batteries.'

In late afternoon, Stirling watched as a Martlet took off from *Audacity*'s flight deck, dipping slightly before soaring into the evening sky. An hour later as darkness approached the plane returned from a fruitless search. That evening the corvette

*Convolvulus* joined the group. Almost immediately her commanding officer, Lieutenant Commander David Budding, RNVR, ordered R/T silence to be broken when a U-boat was sighted on the surface ten miles off the convoy's port beam.

Budding's signal brought a devil-may-care gleam into Stirling's eyes. He shot a hopeful glance at Manley. 'Signal the rest of the group,' he ordered, 'say, "I intend to join *Convolvulus* to attack U-boat. Remain on station."' With a wry smile he shouted, 'Hard a port. Increase revolutions two-thirds and sound action stations, Number One. This could be our lucky day.'

Like a hare being chased by hounds, *Sandpiper* leapt through the sea. By the time they joined *Convolvulus* the U-boat had dived. Both warships attacked. Suddenly the sea was studded with mountainous walls of water as their depth charges exploded. At first the "pinging" over the tannoy was slightly faint. Suddenly it became loud and clear.

'*Two torpedoes approaching to port!*' cried Lofty Day from the crow's nest.

'*Hard a starboard!*' Stirling yelled, feeling the blood drain from his face. '*Full speed ahead.*'

Painfully and slowly *Sandpiper*'s bows began to swing to the right. Ape, PO Yeoman Tate, and the lookouts held tightly onto anything at hand, anxiously gritting their teeth. Stirling and Manley rushed to the port side of the bridge in time to see two white, bubbly wakes of the torpedoes streak past the ship.

'Cor blimey!' exclaimed one of the lookout to his oppo, 'if the bugger had come any closer, I could've pissed on it.'

'If it had of been,' replied his mate nervously wiping his brow with the back of his hand, 'you wouldn't have had a dick to piss with.'

With a huge sigh of relief, Stirling glanced ominously at Manley and said, 'That was too close for comfort, eh Number One?'

'What was that you said about this being our lucky day, sir?' said Manley, his mouth dry and beads of sweat running down the sides of his face.

For the next two hours both ships attacked the U-boat. By 1900 the "pinging" had faded away.

'Submarine on the surface about three miles way, sir,' yelled Able Seaman Day. 'Doin' roughly eighteen or more knots, sir.'

'*Bastard!*' exploded Stirling, thumping the side of his chair. 'The buggers can really shift. We'll never catch her now. Better signal *Convolvulus* to rejoin the convoy, Number One,' said Stirling. 'If the sod gets among the merchantmen they'll need all the protection they can get.'

Stirling was reluctant to admit it but this time he had been outwitted.

## CHAPTER SEVENTEEN

During the rest of the afternoon the convoy HG76 continued without interruption. Two miles away on the starboard quarter, the convoy commodore signalled all ships to zig-zag. As if moved by some unseen hand the three columns of the convoy would slowly alter course. Then, at varying times they would turn again before continuing their journey.

Meanwhile in the depths of the sea the U-boat that escaped was watching and waiting...

The planning of an attack by a U-boat was a complicated affair. The captains had to plot the course and speed of the merchant ship to be attacked. The depth and running speed had to be accurate in order to coincide with that of their prey. These factors plus the weather and the danger of being detected by the adversaries' Asdic made matters even more difficult. Therefore the zig-zagging performed by the merchant ships was designed to make the planning of an attack as difficult as possible.

'I don't want to take any chances,' Stirling cautiously remarked to Manley, 'I have a feeling that bugger that got away could be part of one of Doenitz's so-called wolf pack.'

Away to port *Petrel* and *Redshank* covered the rear of the convoy roughly six miles dead astern. *Curlew* and *Shearwater* patrolled a few miles on the starboard side. The remainder of the warships including *Stanley* surrounded the convoy. Each warship had a code name to be used whenever R/T contact was made. The weather was surprisingly calm with a light but bitterly cold northerly wind. A pale moon appearing from breaks in the dark clouds cast a bleak veneer on the choppy sea.

At 0345 on 2 October, Stirling was in his sea cabin dozing on his bunk. Suddenly the squeaky noise of the voice-pipe above his head disturbed his reverie.

'*Shearwater* reports, submarine in sight, sir,' came the excited voice of OOW Sub Lieutenant Amery.

'On what bearing?' cried Stirling as he leapt fully dressed from his bunk.

'The signal doesn't say, sir.'

'Bugger it!' raged Stirling, 'sound action stations.'

During most of the trip he had retired to his cabin only to shave and collapse wearily and grab an occasional hour or two during the day. His tired eyes were slightly bloodshot and his face looked pale and drawn. It was too dark to see *Shearwater*. Stirling arrived on the bridge and sat fulminating at *Shearwater*'s lack of information that would enable him to steer his ship to support the attack. Grabbing the R/T phone he shouted *Shearwater*'s code name and ordered, 'Fire a star shell to indicate your position.'

He had just replaced the telephone when he heard a terrific explosion coming from the direction of *Stanley*. The time was a little after 0400. All of a sudden a sheet of yellow flames billowing mercilessly some hundred feet into the air lighted the sky. Balls of fire raged along the sloop's deck. The water surrounding the stricken vessel turned from dense black to a mass of shiny orange speckles.

For a few seconds everyone on *Sandpiper*'s bridge was too stunned to speak. A mere six miles away men they all knew were being incinerated.

'*Christ almighty!*' shouted Manley. '*It's Stanley. She's been torpedoed!*'

Stirling left his chair and in strident tones, shouted, 'Signal all escorts to turn away from the convoy, Number One, and fire star shells, it may illuminate the sub as she gets away. Port ten and increase revolutions one-third. I intend to drop a pattern of depth charges in case the blighter is lurking nearby.'

'That'll bring us dangerously close to *Stanley,* sir,' Manley said warily, 'if there is a sub nearby we'll be sitting ducks.'

'That's the chance we'll have to take,' came Stirling's stoic reply.

The remaining three sloops plus the corvette *Convolvulus* arrived and began to pick up men from the water. By this time *Stanley* was perilously low in the water. A concentration of dense smoke and flickering flames stretched from her stern to bow. Suddenly, an explosion sent her bows high in the air. As she settled down, the once proud vessel slowly sank stern first, her white ensign still flying defiantly from her quarterdeck. Out of her complement of 125 officers and men only eighty survived.

Stirling ordered Sub Lieutenant Harper-Smyth to set his depth charges to 100 and 200 feet. All gun crews, including Able Seaman Dinga Bell manning a Lewis gun on the port wing, were closed up. During the next quarter of an hour *Sandpiper, Curlew, Petrel, Redshank* and *Shearwater* turned the sea into a seething mass of foam as patterns of depth charges exploded a mile or so from where the destroyer was last seen. Finally their efforts bore fruit. During one attack Asdic operator Leading Seaman Wacker Payne reported to the bridge.

'Submarine contact, sir,' he cried, in his inimitable cockney accent. 'Dead ahead, one mile away.'

'All guns ready, sir,' came the voice of Lieutenant Anderson from the Director platform above the bridge.

'Thank you, Guns,' answered Stirling, straining his eyes though his binoculars hoping to see the wake of a periscope. 'I'll need you shortly.' Turning to Manley he went on, 'Increase revolutions two thirds, and set depth charges at 200 and 150 feet.'

The "pinging" became louder. Stirling gripped the sides of his chair and clenched his teeth. 'This time, you bastard, you won't get away,' he muttered to himself.

Once more underwater explosions were followed by tumultuous watery masses reaching high into the air. But the telltale sound of the Asdic continued louder than ever.

'Hard a starboard, Number One,' snapped Stirling, 'I'm going to turn and have another go at the blighter.'

'No need, sir,' Manley yelled excitedly, his binoculars clamped to his eyes while pointing directly ahead. 'The sub's surfaced.'

Stirling quickly focussed on the slender black object and squat conning tower a hundred yards away.

'*Got you, you bugger!*' He shouted hoarsely while standing up. '*Tell engines to give me all he's got. Full speed ahead.*'

A few seconds later *Sandpiper* bounded forward. Huge bow waves spurted over her fo'c'sle as the ship dipped in and out of the sea. Everyone on the bridge braced himself as the elongated shape of the U-boat loomed closer. Sensing Stirling's intention, the sub's captain ordered an increase in speed.

'The sub's pulling away, sir,' yelled Ape, shooting an anxious glance at his captain.

'Order *Petrel* and *Shearwater* to fire rockets, Number One,' cried Stirling feeling the deck shudder under his feet. 'I want to keep her well in our sights.'

A few seconds later the 4-inch guns of the two sloops opened up. The rockets zoomed upwards and burst into the night sky.

Directly after this a shower of tiny glittering snowflakes illuminated the dark shape of the U-boat and the surrounding sea.

'She's increasing speed and turning to port, sir,' shouted Ape.

By this time the U-boat, still clearly visible, was a mere hundred yards away.

Keeping his binoculars in place, Stirling shouted, 'All guns open fire!'

Immediately all *Sandpiper's* guns spurted flame. The ship shuddered as salvo after salvo pierced the night air. Fountains of water erupted around the submarine and for a moment vanished in a wall of white water. A sailor on the U-boat's conning tower started firing a machine gun. Moments later the deadly rattle of bullets ricocheted around the sides of the bridge.

'We're too close, sir,' yelled Anderson from the GDP, 'the guns can't depress enough to be effective.'

Clenching both fists Stirling cried, 'Keep firing with the Lewis and Oerlikons.'

The twang and rattle of bullets from the U-boat's machine gun hitting the ship's hull echoed around the bridge. Just then Dinga Bell, who had begun firing the port Lewis gun suddenly clutched his left arm and fell against the side of the port wing. Lines of blood oozed from between his fingers and trickled down his hand onto the sleeve of his duffle coat. His Lewis gun fell silent and tilted forward on it small tripod.

'For Chrissake, someone help me!' he yelled and slumped to the deck.

Ordinary Seaman Nipper Morris who was Dinga's ammunition provider looked wide-eyed at Sub Lieutenant Amery and shouted, 'Bell's been hit, send for the doc!' Nipper dropped the ammunition drum and knelt down beside his injured friend whose face was contorted in pain. Blood continued to run between

Bell's fingers. He looked up at Nipper and muttered, 'It's me arm, Nipper, me fuckin' arm.'

'Take it easy, mate,' said Nipper, supporting Bell's head with his hands, 'the doc'll be here soon.'

'That's if I don't fuckin' well bleed to death,' Bell whimpered before closing his eyes and passing out.

Stirling along with Manley was taking cover behind the bridge screen. Manley moved away and quickly took a shell dressing from the first aid bag hanging behind the wing screen. He ripped it open and applied the yellow pad of lint over the bloody area on Bell's duffle coat and tightly bandaged it.

'How is he, Number One?' Stirling shouted.

'Bleeding badly, sir,' replied Manley, 'but otherwise all right.'

Stirling then saw Amery grab the butt of the Lewis gun. He watched as the young officer curled his finger around the trigger and tilted the weapon towards the U-boat. He then began to rake the conning tower with a tirade of fire. Stirling saw Amery's young face gleaming with sweat. His brow was deeply furrowed and his eyes, peering through the sight of the Lewis gun were full of defiance. Lines of small flashes flickering from the end of the tubular-shaped Lewis gun barrel raked the conning tower and fo'c'sle of the U-Boat. Several of her crew crumpled up and tumbled headlong into the water. In quick succession those in the conning tower suffered a similar fate as Amery's torrent of fire hit home. A few lucky ones managed to jump, unharmed into the sea, hoping to be picked up by a kindly foe. The enemy's guns were now silent. Amery, pale and shaking, let go of the gun and leaned against the side of the bridge. His hands were shaking, sweat poured down his face and he felt weak.

But U-434, lying about fifty yards in front of *Sandpiper*, remained afloat.

Nervously licking his lips Stirling picked up the ship's intercom and in a voice devoid of emotion, quickly said, '*Captain here. Grab anything you can. Stand by to ram!*'

He needn't have bothered. As if pushed by an unkind hand, the submarine suddenly toppled over, and with an eerie groan, disappeared under the water in a tumultuous rumble of oily bubbles.

At that moment everyone's attention was diverted from witnessing the demise of the U-boat to a loud explosion and a large yellow flash coming from the convoy.

'A merchant ship's been hit, sir,' reported Lofty Day from the crow's nest. 'And from what I can make out it's a big 'un.'

In fact it was the cargo vessel SS *Ruckijnge*. Her captain had managed to send out her name on the radio before the crew abandoned ship. Stirling ordered *Curlew* to stay and pick up survivors. Clearly, more than one U-boat had attacked the convoy.

By this time Surgeon Lieutenant Coburn and SBA Appleby had arrived. Appleby removed the duffle coat off Bell's uninjured arm allowing the doctor to administer a shot of morphia.

'You'll be OK, Dinga, he said, applying another shell dressing over the first one. 'It's only a flesh wound.'

'Any chance of me bein' sent 'ome,' Bell asked hopefully.

'Not a hope, mate,' Appleby replied, adding jokingly, 'I might have to stop your tot, though!'

'Signal *Shearwater* and *Petrel*,' shouted Stirling, 'and tell them to pick up any German survivors. Then ask *Convolvulus* to rescue those from *Stanley*.'

He then noticed Amery leaning against the side of the bridge, wiping his brow with a handkerchief. His face was ashen and he still looked shaken up. He took out a packet of cigarettes, placed one to his lips and tried to light it with a small lighter. But his hand trembled so much he almost dropped the cigarette.

'Here,' said Stirling, taking out his lighter, 'let me help you. By the way,' he went on as he lit Amery's cigarette. 'You did a damn good job with that Lewis gun. Where did you learn to shoot like that?'

'Nowhere, sir,' Amery tamely replied. 'I've never fired a gun in my life!'

'Indeed,' said Stirling, raising his eyebrows in surprise. 'You amaze me. You did very well. Well done old boy.'

Suddenly Amery felt everything spinning around him. 'Thank you, sir,' he managed to say before clutching hold of a stanchion.

Stirling immediately reached out and grabbed hold of Amery's arm. 'Better sit down,' he said, 'and I'll send for the Doc.'

'No need, sir, I'll be all right...' Amery muttered before slumping against Stirling in a dead faint.

That evening Stirling reported the night's events to the C-in-C, Western Approaches and the Admiralty. Despite this, losing a sloop and cargo ship, they had sunk two submarines, a feat no other escort group could claim for such a relatively small loss.

However, this small victory was soon forgotten when Stirling received a copy of a signal marked "urgent" from Commander D W MacKendrick, RN captain of *Audacity* informing him that six U-boats had been reported in the vicinity. Stirling ordered his now depleted group to return to the convoy.

The enemy was far from finished with convoy HG46.

# CHAPTER EIGHTEEN

The 3rd October dawned miserably overcast and bitterly cold. A fierce northerly wind continued to churn the choppy sea into high waves topped with angry white horses. In the afternoon, Able Seaman Duffy, one of *Sandpiper*'s lookouts, reported an unidentified plane high to starboard. A few seconds later, after carefully concentrating his binoculars on the aircraft, he added, 'To be sure, sir, it's a Focke-Wulf Condor, so it is.'

'*Audacity* must have seen it also, sir,' said Manley. 'She's just sent off two Martlets.'

Everyone craned their neck and watched as the Martlets climbed upwards. Cheers rang out as one of them levelled out then dived towards the Focke-Wulf, whose pilot, sensing danger, tried to take cover in the clouds. But he was too late. The clear rattle of machine-gun fire echoed over the steady throb of the ship's engines. Suddenly, another cheer went up as a trail of smoke and flame belched from the enemy's fuselage. For a few seconds the Focke-Wulf hung limply in the sky, then, twisted awkwardly and, with a huge splash, plunged into the sea.

'Ten to one the bugger's reported our position, Number One,' muttered Stirling, listening to the steady, soft, metallic sound of the Asdic "pinging" coming from the ship's loudspeaker.

'I wouldn't be at all surprised, sir,' Manley replied wryly. 'Keep everyone closed up just in case.'

At varying intervals during the day *Audacity* launched her Martlets in response to Asdic reports of U-boats shadowing the convoy. Unfortunately their searching proved unproductive and the planes returned to the carrier.

Onboard *Sandpiper*'s bridge Manley turned to Stirling and, in a cautious manner, said, 'I'm sure the blighters are out there but I wonder why they don't attack, sir?'

At first Stirling didn't reply. Instead he stared out to sea feeling the steady roll of the ship and listening to the monotonous hum of the engines. Then, narrowing his eyes, he took a deep breath and with a quiet air of predictability replied, 'Don't worry, Number One, they will...'

But Stirling was about to make an uncharacteristic costly error.

That night the moon disappeared behind a dense layer of overcast clouds. *Sandpiper,* like the other escorts, had darkened ship. Deadlights were secured over scuttles, canvas awnings drawn across hatchways and passageways dimmed with dull blue lighting. The dark silhouettes of the merchant ships appeared to move ghostlike through the inky black sea.

On *Sandpiper*'s bridge, those on duty stood around cold and damp, stamping their feet and blowing into mitten-clad hands. At 2300, Stirling ordered PO Yeoman Tate to send a signal to the commanding office of *Audacity* recommending that the convoy should alter course and head straight for the Western Approaches. He ended the signal by saying, "I will take the escort group and patrol an area in a north-westerly direction. *Convolvulus, Penstemom* and *Redshank* to remain with you."

'Excuse me, sir,' Manley said, glancing apprehensively at Stirling, 'is this wise? We've been warned there are U-boats shadowing the convoy.'

'Thank you, Number One,' Stirling abruptly replied. 'I'm well aware of that, but I have a trick or two that might surprise them.'

'And what might those be, sir?' Manley asked guardedly.

'You'll find out,' Stirling replied, 'signal the escorts to turn to starboard and increase revolutions one-third. I want to draw away from the convoy as soon as possible.'

'Very good, sir,' Manley replied, raising his eyebrows in surprise.

An hour later *Curlew, Petrel* and *Shearwater* were closed up nine cables, (roughly a mile) apart on *Sandpiper*'s starboard beam. Keeping good station, the silhouettes of the four sloops were barely visible in the darkness.

By 0100 *Sandpiper* and the escorts were well away from the convoy. Stirling was ensconced in his chair, apparently lost in thought, his chin resting on his chest. Like the rest of those on watch he was listening to the Asdic echoing from the ship's loudspeaker. Unfortunately, the quiet, regular "pinging" indicated no contact with the enemy. Suddenly Stirling lifted his head and looked across at the huddled figure of PO Yeoman Tate.

'Flash signals to the group, Yeoman, say, "Carry out Operation Buttercup. Fire five rounds of star shell and rockets. A and B guns only."'

Yeoman PO Tate thought this rather odd, especially as the escorts were all alone. Nevertheless he put the Aldis lamp in the crook of his left arm and carried out the order.

'Great Scott, sir!' exclaimed OOW Lieutenant Anderson. 'If there's any U-boats around,' he added glancing warily at Stirling, 'surely that'll make us a sitting target!'

'That's precisely what I hope will happen, Guns,' Stirling answered smugly. 'That'll draw them away from the convoy and we'll be able to get after them.'

With a look of incredulity hidden from his captain, Anderson nervously replied, 'I hope you're right, sir.'

In A and B turrets situated on the fo'c'sle directly below the bridge, gun crews loaded each of the 4 inch barrels with star shell.

'Why the hell are we doing this if there's no bloody U-boats around,' said Able Seaman Darby Allen to the portly figure of Able Seaman Bud Abbott as he closed the breach and waited for the order to fire.

'Maybe it's just an exercise to keep us on our toes,' grumbled Abbott, 'but if you ask me it's a bloody waste of time, I'd sooner be in me mick 'aving a wank.'

Abbott's salacious remark was abruptly interrupted by the strident voice of Chief GI Miller over the GDP's intercom. 'Elevate all guns sixty degrees,' he cried. A few seconds later he cried, 'Stand by... *fire*.'

Short barrages of flame flickered from each barrel as the shells roared into the night sky. Seconds later, explosions followed by particles bursting in arcs of glittering light. Those men on the *Sandpiper*'s bridge momentarily closed their eyes, their faces shining under the reflected light. When they open their eyes they saw umbrellas of shimmering particles turning the sea into a carpet of shiny silver paper.

'Cor blimey,' cried PO Yeoman Tate, 'it looks just like Piccadilly Circus afore the war, so it does.'

'Quite right, Yeoman,' said Stirling, craning his head upwards, 'that's exactly what I wanted.'

At that moment Manley's attention was directed to a series of rockets exploding on the horizon away to port.

'Look, sir,' yelled Manley, 'I think the convoy's in trouble.'

Watching the snowflakes fired by the merchantmen flicker and burn, Stirling suddenly realised he had made a terrible mistake. 'Damn and blast,' he yelled, thumping the sides of his chair. 'I should have warned them. They probably think they're being attacked and are warning their escorts and us. If there is a U-boat around, they certainly know the exact position of the convoy now, Number One,' Stirling muttered uneasily. 'Better signal the escorts to return to the convoy and resume their station. *Sandpiper* will patrol astern of the convoy.'

Shortly after 0300, a sudden explosion lighted up the night sky as a merchant ship, the 3,000-ton tanker SS *Annavore* burst into an incandescent ball of flame.

'That merchantman is the last one in line of the centre column, sir,' said Manley, using his binoculars. '*Convolvulus* and *Penstemon* are closing in to pick up survivors.'

Stirling switched on the ship's radio transmitter and said, '*Sandpiper* to escorts. Fire star shells and snowflakes away to starboard and search for the enemy.'

Once again the snowflakes exploded into arcs of glittering light highlighting the position of the convoy.

'*Hell's teeth!*' Stirling uttered angrily. He suddenly realised he should have ordered the search to be astern of the convoy, the position Manley had reported where the stricken vessel was.

'Signal from Commander MacKendrick in *Audacity,* sir,' shouted PO Yeoman Tate. 'It reads "propose operating starboard side of the convoy. Request a sloop to be detached and protect the starboard side of the convoys."'

Stirling was aware that for the past three nights the carrier had been independently zig-zagging well away from the convoy.

Manley gave Stirling a look of deep concern. 'But sir,' he stressed, 'we'll need the escorts and destroyers to protect the convoy.'

Stirling gave a tired sigh. 'Yes, Number One, you're right.' Turning to Tate he said, 'Reply "regret cannot spare any escorts. Suggest you take station to port of the convoy."'

A few minutes later the reply came. Once again PO Yeoman Tate read it out to Stirling. '"Alteration of course would be inconvenient. Intend to take station on starboard side."'

MacKendrick was senior to Stirling, therefore he could give him a direct order. He could only diplomatically "suggest" to the commander what the best course of action might be.

Manley's eyes narrowed. 'Is that wise, sir?' he cried alarmingly, 'without protection the carrier will be vulnerable to attack.'

'Hmm... yes, you're right,' muttered Stirling, furrowing his brow. 'Better pipe action stations just in case...'

However, Stirling was worried. He told himself it would have been wiser to have warned MacKendrick of the dangers of going off almost alone. He should have strongly suggested *Audacity* to take station either in the middle of the convoy or on its port side away from where he had anticipated the enemy might attack.

Four hours later, just after 0700, *Audacity* was torpedoed.

'Signal from Commander MacKendrick, sir,' shouted PO Yeoman Tate, 'it says, *"listing badly. Intend abandoning ship"*.'

'My God, Number One!' Stirling exploded, glancing ruefully at Manly. 'A bloody U-boat must have been shadowing her. Signal *Curlew* and *Convolvlus* to pick up survivors. Inform *Shearwater* and tell her to take station a mile on the convoy's port beam. *Petrel* to bring up the rear. Now that we've lost *Audacity,* they'll need all the protection we can give them.'

*Sandpiper'*s crew had been closed up at action stations on and off for the past three days. All of them were tired. Some grumbled about anything they could think of, but their faith in Stirling was absolute. Thanks to the cooks, hard tack (ship's biscuits), hot soup and sandwiches had become their staple diet.

'Dinga my son,' growled Able Seaman Jackson, leaning against the barrel of his 20 mm Oerlikon, while holding a corn beef sandwich, 'when this fuckin' war is over I 'ope I never set eyes on a bleedin' cow.'

'Ah, stop moanin' will you,' replied Able Seaman Bell, holding his banged arm, 'I bet the old man's not complainin' and if you don't want your sarnie, give it to me. As for the cows, you'll see plenty of them down Union Street in Plymouth.'

During the afternoon nearly all of *Audacity*'s crew were rescued. Unfortunately, Commander MacKendrick was not among them.

For the rest of the day the convoy continued on their way unmolested. Low-lying dark cumulonimbus clouds threatened rain and the bitterly cold north-westerly wind churned the sea into masses of angry white-topped waves. However, this period of relative safety was about to end.

Shortly after 1800, *Shearwater* sent signals to *Sandpiper* and *Petrel* reporting, *"Submarine on the surface a mile on the port beam between ourself and the convoy. Intend attacking."* 'I bet that'll be the bastard that torpedoed *Audacity*,' Stirling said, giving Manley a suspicious glance. 'Signal *Shearwater*, say, *"Will join you. Fire star shell"*.' Using his binoculars he scanned the horizon away to port and saw the dark outline of the U-boat about half a mile away. Manley, Lieutenant Anderson and the others on the bridge did the same. Just then the ship's gun opened fire. Moments later the sky exploded in a crescendo of bursting shells. Suddenly, the snub shape of the U-boat's bows and squat conning tower stood out starkly against the inky black sea.

'Damn and blast, Number One,' Stirling shouted, 'the bugger's diving.'

The intervals between the Asdic "pinging" shortened as the two sloops arrived in the area where the submarine had dived.

'*Fire four diamond patterns,*' Stirling shouted, his voice barely audible over the sound of the wind and the roar of the engines. '*I want to splatter the whole area with depth charges.*'

*Shearwater* joined in the attack, dropping salvo after salvo into the sea. Each sloop rocked as mountain after mountain of white seawater erupted all around. The strong wind sent walls of effervescent spray over everything and everyone. After each explosion eyes became strained searching for telltale black oil, bits of clothing or bodies floating on the surface, evidence of a kill.

After two hours and several runs, Stirling, turned to Manley and slowly shook his head. 'The sod's either gone very deep or is too damaged to surface. At least we've stopped the blighter attacking the merchantmen.'

The submarine they had attacked was in fact the U-567 commanded by Kapitanleutnam Muller, which was later reported by the Germans as having been destroyed.

At 0100 Stirling reluctantly ended the attack and ordered the escorts to return to the convoy. For a while all was quiet. The monotonous "pinging" of escort's Asdic sets indicated the absence of the enemy. Meanwhile a wall of fine icy mist had descended on everyone seeping into the thick clothing and reducing all-round visibility to a mere fifty yards. Cloaked in darkness the escorts took station around the convoy. Then came disaster…

# CHAPTER NINETEEN

At 0300 *Sandpiper's* crew stood down and resumed normal watch keeping stations. Stirling was in his sea cabin lying on his bunk, fully dressed, dozing and feeling the steady hub of the engines vibrating under him. On the bridge, the burly figure of OOW Lieutenant Allan Prospero Evans was slumped in the captain's chair. A towel was tucked into the neck of his duffle coat and he was quietly smoking a cigarette. Both lookouts were closed up, their eyes straining in the darkness for any sudden danger. Sheltering in the navigator's caboose, Leading Signalman Tansey Lee blew into his hands and stamped his feet against the cold night air.

Suddenly, Ape's reverie was ended by the port lookout yelling, *'Ship closing to port, sir. Christ almighty, she's gunna...'* His words were quickly interrupted by an almighty *bang*.

Ape immediately felt the ship shudder violently. He turned and for a fleeting second couldn't believe his eyes. Looming in the mist and larger than life was the unmistakable sharp bows of a destroyer wedged into the port side of *Sandpiper's* quarterdeck. With the reflexes of a trained athlete he grabbed the wheelhouse intercom and yelled, *'Slow astern both engines!'*

The noise of the collision brought Stirling to his senses. Without waiting to be informed of what had happened, he leapt from his bunk. In a few seconds he arrived on the bridge. Manley and Lieutenant Anderson quickly joined him.

'*Great Scott, what the hell happened!*' exclaimed Stirling as he and the two officers stared unbelievingly at the destroyer's bows lying unnervingly against *Sandpiper*'s quarterdeck. '*How on earth...*' He was about to finish when the destroyer began to move backwards. '*Call the Doc, Number One,*' he shouted. '*Tell him to go aft and see if anyone's hurt and let me know. You'd better go as well. Keep me informed.*'

In the wheelhouse the sudden, grating jolt sent QM Able Seaman Jackson and his assistant Ordinary Seaman Nipper Morris tumbling against one another.

'Fuck me,' Jacko cried grabbing hold of Nipper, 'I think we've been hit!'

Nipper quickly disentangled himself from Jacko, reached across and changed the engine room telegraph to STOP. This order was automatically relayed to the engine room where the force of the collision had sent Chief Stoker Digger Barnes and his stokers falling against the bulkhead and slipping over the steel deck. Clutching a stanchion Barnes looked up and saw the hand on the glass-covered dial housing the engine room repeater move to STOP. His reaction was similar to that of Nipper Morris.

'Christ almighty!' he yelled at Leading Stoker Bill Martin who was clutching a guardrail. 'It sounds as if we've been fuckin' torpedoed!'

'I bloody-well hope not, Chief,' replied Martin, an anxious expression written over his face. Unlike the men on the upper deck who could dive overboard if the ship was abandoned, the chances of those in the engine and boiler rooms were precarious, to say the least.

On the bridge everyone held on to anything at hand. Below decks everything rattled. Cries of anger and surprise echoed around as men woke up and instinctively stumbled from their hammocks.

In the sick bay SBA Appleby, almost fully dressed, couldn't sleep. The light above his head was on and he was curled up reading his western. He felt the ship shudder violently rattling medicine bottles and cabinet doors. Realising something had happened he dropped his paperback, jumped out of his bunk and grabbed his shoes. At that moment the door opened and in came Surgeon Lieutenant Coburn. His normally well-groomed dark hair was a tousled mess and he wore a duffle coat over his trousers and shirt.

'What the hell was that, Appleby?' enquired the doctor, stifling a yawn.

'Search me, sir, but I...' Appleby's reply was abruptly interrupted by the ringing of the telephone. He quickly unhooked the receiver. 'Sick bay,' he said, paused, and in a voice fraught with anxiety, added, 'yes, sir, right away, sir.' Replacing the receiver, Appleby turned and stared wide-eyed at the doctor. 'Quick, sir,' he cried gabbing the medical valise. 'There's been a collision. We're to go to after mess deck, the first lieutenant says some of the crew might be injured.'

Directly behind the sick bay a steel ladder behind X gun led down into the after seamen and stokers' mess deck. Arriving at the top of the hatchway, Appleby and the doctor had to stand back as several sailors, some half dressed, others wearing overalls rushed up.

'Anyone hurt down there?' the doctor shouted.

'Don't know sir,' a sailor stuttered, 'but there's water coming in from one of the bulkheads.'

Appleby and the doctor managed to push their way down. Two strips of dull blue neon lights lighted the mess deck. At a glance the doctor and Appleby saw thin lines of seawater seeping through a series of spidery cracks in the port bulkhead. A tall leading seaman wearing overalls and boots stood nearby and looked alarmingly at the doctor.

'Better get out of here, sir,' he said warily. 'If that lot bursts,' he added, nodding at the leaky bulkhead, 'half the oggin will hit us.'

'Is anyone injured?' asked the doctor anxiously looking around at the empty hammocks and loose bedding on the tables and deck.

'No, sir,' the sailor answered nervously licking his lips. 'I'm the killick of the mess. I've made sure everyone got away.'

At the moment Manley arrived, red-faced and out of breath. He immediately noticed the leaking bulkhead.

'My God!' he exclaimed, 'you lot had better leave.' He then hurried and unhooked a telephone from the nearby bulkhead. 'Hello, sir, nobody appears to be hurt. But get the damage control party down here chop chop. The port bulkhead's damaged and likely to burst any minute.'

The doctor and Appleby hurriedly left. At the top of the ladder Chief Petty Officer Sammy Taylor stood, beads of sweat running down his wizened face. Close by, holding planks of wood, were several ratings and Harry Tweedle, the Chief Shipwright carrying a large canvas bag of tools.

'Hope you lot have brought fishing rods with you, Buffer,' quipped Appleby, grinning at Sammy Taylor and his team, 'you'll need it if that bugger bursts.'

'Bugger off and take one of yer pills,' came the Buffer's caustic reply as he and the others clambered down the ladder into the mess.

Meanwhile Ape had left the bridge and discovered the Asdic dome was full of water. He quickly returned to the bridge and reported this to Stirling.

'Well,' Stirling muttered, removing his cap and scratching his head in resigned dismay. 'It looks like a spell in dockyard hands when we return home.'

'And maybe a spot of leave, sir,' Ape replied hopefully.

'Quite possible, Pilot,' Stirling mused, giving Ape a cautious smile, 'quite possible.'

The destroyer involved in the collision was identified as HMS *Exmoor*. Stirling shook his head in disbelief as he watched the dark shape of *Exmoor*'s mangled bows slide away from *Sandpiper*. The destroyer slowly faded away in the dank mist and rain like a grey monster having eaten its prey.

'Signal flashing from *Exmoor*'s bridge, sir,' said PO Yeoman Tate. 'It's from her captain. It reads:

*"Sorry about that, Bob, Officer of the Watch thought you was a U-boat. Four German prisoners in the for'd mess killed. Hope your lads are OK."*'

After a weary sigh, Stirling said, 'Thank you, Yeoman, reply: *"Suggest your OOW sees the eye specialist in Plymouth. Sorry about your Germans. Must blow main ballast tanks and rejoin the convoy!"*'

On a dull, overcast morning of the 7th October the group cruised into Plymouth Sound looking somewhat battle-weary. With her after mess deck flooded and Asdic useless, *Sandpiper* was low in the water and reduced to five knots. *Exmouth*'s bows were a mangled mess and could only muster a similar speed.

A cold, blustery northern wind attacked the faces of the men fallen in for entering harbour, flapping their collars and bellbottoms. Away to starboard the lush green mounds of the Hoe swept up into the city. Anti-aircraft batteries draped with camouflage netting lay on the bowling green, where, four centuries ago, Francis Drake paused before attacking the Spanish. A mile or so on the escort's port bow lay the island named after him, its dense woodland hiding the antennae of early warning systems, while away to the left the rolling hills of Cornwall poked through the grey morning mist.

'To be sure, Dinga,' remarked Able Seaman Patrick Duffy, gazing upwards at a flock of squawking seagulls circling above the ship, 'they say that those bloody shite-hawks crowing in the sky are supposed to be the souls of dead sailors.' He was standing next to Able Seaman Bell, who, like several others was fallen in on the fo'c'sle.

'You could be right, there, Paddy, me son,' replied Able Seaman Bell, who was also looking skywards. 'And the big bastard that's just shit on me is my Uncle Silas. He was a chief petty officer and died last year. I hated the bugger, so I did.'

By 1000, the convoy and escorts sailed down the River Tamar towards the docks. *Sandpiper* and *Exmoor* were in front. *Curlew, Redshank, Petrel* and *Shearwater* drew up the rear. *Convolvulus* and *Penstemon* had earlier detached from the group and after a "good luck" signal continued down the English Channel to Portsmouth.

Onboard *Sandpiper*, Stirling sat on his chair watching as one by one the merchantmen, aided by tugs, were ushered into various docks where cranes and teams of stevedores waited to unload their precious cargo.

'Signal from the convoy commodore, sir,' said PO Yeoman Tate, 'It reads, *"On behalf of the convoy, many thanks for your excellent help. God bless and good luck."*'

With a relaxed smile playing around his lips, Stirling said, 'Thank you, Yeoman, reply, *"Glad to be of service. Look forward to seeing you next time."*'

During the first part of the afternoon *Sandpiper* passed through two locks before finally arriving at Number Two Dry Dock. As the water drained from the horseshoe-shaped dock, cranes, with the aid of workers wearing yellow waders, lowered stout oaken beams against the ship's side. When in place they kept the ship upright and secure.

'Better arrange for a skeleton crew of local men to remain onboard, Number One,' said Stirling standing on the bridge watching as the last beam was put in place. 'The rest can go on seven days' leave, including yourself and other officers. I expect Patricia and your son will be glad to see you.'

'What about you, sir?' Manley asked, looking at the gaunt, drawn features of the tall man next to him. Stirling had been almost constantly on the bridge and had more than earned a rest. 'Don't you think you should take a few days' leave?'

'Oh, don't worry about me, Number One,' Stirling replied giving his shoulders a quick, nonchalant shrug, 'I'll stay here and keep an eye on things. Maybe Pamela could come up from Emsworth for a few days.'

He was about to say something about finding accommodation ashore when PO Yeoman Tate interrupted him.

'Signal from Admiralty, sir,' he said, handing Stirling a small sheet of paper. After reading it he raised his eyebrows and turning to Manley, said, 'I've been summoned to attend a meeting at the Admiralty in three days' time.'

'Sounds ominous, eh, sir,' Manley replied, giving Stirling a searching look. 'Something to do with your tactics, maybe?'

'It wouldn't surprise me in the least, Number One,' Stirling replied with a wry smile.

# CHAPTER TWENTY

As soon as Stirling had handed *Sandpiper* over to the dockyard superintendent, a small, officious man called Mason, he went ashore, found a telephone booth and called Pamela.

'Oh darling, I've missed you as always,' Pamela replied in that soft clear voice he remembered so well. Stirling closed his eyes and pictured her standing in the lounge with its yellow and brown chinz-covered sofa and armchairs; her lovely turquoise blue eyes radiant with excitement, casually flicking strands of loose blonde hair from her face

'And I've missed you also,' Stirling replied, ready with a sixpenny piece to put into slot B in case he ran out of time. 'Have you heard from Mark?' He added anxiously, 'if you know where he is, better not say so over the phone.'

'I had a letter two weeks ago, dear,' she replied. 'He wrote saying he is well and sends you his love,' she paused and gave a short, throaty laugh. 'Naturally he didn't say exactly but he mentioned something about "smelly camels".'

'Ha,' laughed Stirling, 'I think I know where he is,' Stirling replied realising his son was probably in the Royal Navy's base at Alexandria. He went on to ask if she could come to Plymouth for a few days. He also mentioned the meeting he had to attend in London.

'Of course I'll come down, darling,' she gushed. 'But I can only stay overnight. I have joined the WVS and expect to be sent to London sometime next week. If I catch the train from Portsmouth this evening, I should arrive about eight o'clock.'

'I don't like the idea of you being in London, the East End is taking a terrible battering,' he replied furrowing his brow, 'so please take care.'

'Don't worry about me, darling,' she answered, knowing full well she was wasting her breath, 'all I'll be doing is handing out cups of tea and sticky buns to tired firemen.'

'I expect you'll look very smart in those bottle-green uniforms and felt hats they wear.'

'Nonsense,' Pamela replied, 'when we meet I intend to wear something more fetching, just for you.'

'Splendid,' Stirling answered with a short laugh. 'I'll check with the train times and be on the platform to meet you. I'll book us in at the Grand. It's on the Hoe. I'm it told has a great view of the sea.'

'It's not the view I'm interested in my love,' she replied coyly.

Her hidden message wasn't lost on him. Even though they had been married for over twenty years, the thought of seeing his wife again and feeling her body close to his still sent a warm sense of anticipation running through him.

At 1930 a tilly took Stirling to North Road Station. The small brown leather case he carried contained a clean shirt, toilet gear, a carton of *Players* and a few bars of Cadbury's chocolate. The blackout was in force and the platforms were barely visible in the dimmed blue lighting. Not surprisingly the concourse was crowded with servicemen and civilians. Many were sailors, their dark blue bellbottomed uniforms and collars unmistakable amongst the khaki of the army and RAF pale blue. Some sailors had bulky, light brown kit bags slung over their shoulders. Many soldiers wore webbing and carried rifles. On the far side of the station one platform was a heap of rubble, evidence of the recent air raids that had devastated the city.

Bellowing steam and smoke the train shunted to the platform just after eight o'clock. Stirling waited anxiously staring as each door opened allowing passengers to leave. Suddenly, he saw her five feet plus frame alighting from a first-class compartment. He waved a hand and hurried towards her.

Over the left shoulder of her beige cashmere coat hung a light brown shoulder bag and cardboard box containing a gas mask. A smart dark green Robin Hood style hat covered most of her short blonde hair and in one of her brown patent leather gloved hands she carried a black, overnight suitcase. On her small feet were stylish cream coloured court shoes with tiny gold buckles. Upon seeing Stirling she smiled broadly and hurried towards him.

Ignoring the wolf whistle from several servicemen he took her in his arms. She dropped her suitcase and as they kissed he smelt her freshly applied make-up and Evening in Paris perfume.

'Oh, darling,' she gasped smiling coquettishly as they broke away, 'I couldn't sleep last night thinking of you, even after all these years… silly aren't I?'

'Not at all, dear,' Stirling replied, staring fondly into her slightly moist eyes. 'I know exactly what you mean.' Picking up her suitcase he added, 'There's taxis outside. If we hurry, we'll just be in time for gin and tonic before dinner.'

The journey to the Grand Hotel took ten minutes. Stirling paid the driver and helped Pamela out of the taxi. Picking up her suitcase they walked up three flights of steps, through a set of revolving doors, parted a thick black curtain and entered a well-lit lounge. Standing behind a desk was a pretty, dark-haired receptionist. Stirling introduced himself and signed the register.

'Room twenty-seven on the third floor, sir, the lift is there on your left,' she said handing him a heavy iron key. 'The curtains are drawn and the maid has lit the gas fire.'

The room was tastefully furnished with a wide, oaken dressing table and mirror, two comfortable-looking brown leather armchairs and a highly polished wardrobe. A large, double bed occupied one end of the room. On either side was a small bedside table. On one rested a black telephone and a glass ashtray. A plush thick brown carpet covered the floor and a solitary electric light surrounded by a pale cream lampshade bathed the room in a clear white light. The walls were decorated in pale green damask embossed with flowers and an open door led into a bathroom tiled in yellow.

Pamela put down her case and removed her hat and coat and placed them over one of the armchairs. She then took a quick peek through the side of the curtains. Darkness had fallen and high above an anaemic moon flitting between grey clouds cast a pale glow onto the sparkling waters of Plymouth Sound. The black shapes of two destroyers slowly cutting through the water on their way into port, reminded her that soon, Stirling's ship would soon be sailing in the opposite direction.

'You were right, darling,' she said quickly closing the curtains, 'the view is lovely.'

From where he sat on the bed's elaborately patterned fleecy eiderdown, Stirling looked admiringly at Pamela's back. Over a pale brown twin set she wore a dark green woollen pleated skirt that looked new.

'Yes, I know, dear,' Stirling replied, standing up and raising both arms. 'Now come here and let me kiss you, it's been ages since…'

With her heart beating a cadence against her ribs, she flung her arms around him. They kissed passionately, so hard each could feel the other's teeth pressing through the membranes of their lips. When they parted, she looked up and gazed longingly into his eyes. 'Even after all these partings over the years,' she gasped, 'when we meet I still feel like a schoolgirl.'

That night their lovemaking was prolonged, tender and passionate. Over the years they had come to know and feel every delicate nuance of their bodies. Nevertheless, each gentle touch and caress of their hands sent a shiver of delight running through both of them. He felt like a conductor of an orchestra knowing exactly how to obtain the most satisfying sound from each instrument. In turn, she felt and heard every ecstatic shiver he uttered as she moved her body against his. And after they climaxed together they lay, cocooned in each other's arms knowing each had give the other total sexual and emotional satisfaction.

Just after two o'clock Stirling gently withdrew his arm from around Pamela's warm naked waist. He then reached across and managed to remove a cigarette from a packet resting on the bedside table.

'Light one for me, darling,' Pamela murmured, looking up and cuddling closer to him. Like a scene from a Hollywood film Stirling put two cigarettes in his mouth and using a small silver lighter lighted them both.

'Thank you,' said Pamela, reaching up and accepting the cigarette. After taking a deep drag she looked up at Stirling and said, 'What time do you have to leave in the morning, darling?'

'Six,' he replied, turning his head away while exhaling a steady stream of smoke. 'I've asked the operator for a call. Breakfast is at seven.'

'And I don't suppose you know when you'll be sailing?'

'I'm afraid not,' Stirling replied, kissing the top of her head and giving her a gentle squeeze, 'I'll know more about that after my meeting with the admiral tomorrow.'

'Sorry, I shouldn't have asked,' she said, then looking coyly at him, added, 'now let's put these cigarettes out. We still have four hours left.'

At 1000 on 10 October Stirling caught a train from Plymouth and arrived at Paddington at 1300. Two hours later, after lunching at the Officer's Club in Mayfair, he caught a taxi to the Admiralty Buildings. At precisely 1500 he entered the office of the Director of Anti-Submarine Warfare.

Admiral Sir Percy Noble, Captain George Creasy and other senior officers were sitting at a round shiny oak table lying in the middle of a long room. In front of each officer was a leather-bound blotting pad, a small inkstand and pen, a carafe of water and a tumbler. As Stirling entered they stopped talking and looked up expectantly at the tall, lean, heavily tanned man who had just come in.

'Good afternoon, Robert,' said Admiral Noble, easing his thickset frame from his chair and offering his hand. 'Hang your coat and gas mask up then take a seat. Smoke if you want to. I think you know Captain Creasy,' he added before introducing Stirling to the others.

'Yes thank you, sir,' Stirling replied. 'Good to see you again, George.'

'And you, Bob,' replied Creasy, smiling warmly as they shook hands. 'I trust Pamela and Mark are well?'

'Pamela's joined the WVS,' replied Stirling with a grin. 'And as far as I know, Mark is in a submarine somewhere in the Med, I expect.'

Stirling took a chair next to Captain Creasy. In doing so he glanced quickly around the room. At the far end a wide bay window, criss-crossed with white tape when opened, gave a panoramic view of Horse Guards Parade. A blue haze of tobacco smoke eddied around an ornate crystal chandelier hanging from a high cream-coloured ceiling. An expensive looking blue carpet embossed with tiny gold anchors filled the floor. However, it was the leather-bound book along with framed photographs of battleships past and present that gave the place a distinctly naval appearance.

'I've asked you here today, Commander,' said the admiral, adopting a more formal manner, 'to discuss the strategic and tactical approach you carried out with convoy HG76.' As he spoke his grey eyes framed by thick white eyebrows stared expectantly at Stirling. 'From your reports I gather some of your methods were, er... slightly unorthodox.'

'And from what I understand you went against the standard procedure as laid down by the Prime Minister.' The speaker was a stocky, pallid-featured captain with pale blue eyes sitting opposite Stirling. His manner was abrupt and his attitude surprisingly hostile. 'You also ordered most of the escorts to leave the convoy and search for the enemy.'

'And your use of star shells exposed the convoy,' said another officer, a heavy-set captain with a ruddy complexion and baggy brown eyes. 'In doing so it enabled a U-boat to get close to the convoy and sink the carrier *Audacity* and a merchant ship, is that not so, Commander?'

So far, Stirling hadn't spoken. Listening to what was tantamount to dereliction of duty, he sat back in his chair, lighted a cigarette and exhaled a stream of smoke into the air.

Suddenly, the admiral, glancing disapprovingly at the officers who had spoken, stood up. 'Gentlemen, gentlemen,' he retorted, splaying both hands on his desk. 'Please allow Commander Stirling to give his version of events,' and after another wary glance, sat down.

Stirling stubbed out his cigarette in a round, brass ashtray and stood up. He cleared his throat and with a slight frown stared defiantly at the faces sitting around the table.

'The loss of *Audacity* and *Stanley* was regrettable and I take full responsibility,' he said, pursing his lips. 'From the convoy commodore's report we now know that on seeing the escort's star shells, he thought the convoy was about to be attacked and ordered the merchant ships and his escorts to fire their rockets and tar shells,' he paused and weighed his words, then went on, 'the commodore admits this was a mistake.'

'Are you saying the loss of the carrier was the commodore's fault?' asked the baggy-eyed captain aggressively.

Stirling stared at the officer, wondering when he was last in command of a ship at sea. 'An error of judgement any of those who have been at sea on convoy duty could make,' he replied with a hint of sarcasm.

'But surely you must have been aware of the perilous position you put the convoy in by leaving and chasing around the sea willy-nilly?' remarked another captain, a portly, tired-looking officer with strands of dark hair plastered over a shiny bald scalp.

By this time Stirling was doing his best to control his temper. After glancing indignantly first at the admiral, then at the speaker, he clenched his fists and using a strong tone of voice, replied, 'With respect, sir, my sloops were not chasing around willy-nilly, as you indelicately put it. We were doing so in response to strong Asdic contacts. If you read the report properly you'll note I left three warships to guard the convoy,' he added with a slight touch of irony. He then glanced expectantly at Captain Creasy, who was sat back, doing his best to hide a smile, and went on, 'Furthermore, gentlemen I would remind you that despite the loss of the two warships, convoy HG76 arrived home having lost only two merchantmen out of thirty-two. I would also remind you that two U-boats were sunk.'

Captain Creasy looked up at Stirling and lighted a cigarette. 'Commander Stirling,' he said, his voice conciliatory and calm, 'are you quite certain the actions you took were justified?'

'I am, sir,' Stirling replied, somewhat relieved to hear a friendly voice.

'Indeed,' remarked the portly officer, shrugging his shoulders mockingly. 'Despite colliding with another warship?'

'Again, sir,' Stirling replied sharply. 'If you read the report you'll see that the weather was poor and visibility down to less than fifty yards. These things do happen at sea as I'm sure you are aware.'

'Quite frankly, Commander,' Baggy-eyes added in pompous tones, 'I think blaming the weather is a poor excuse. The fact is, you put your ship and crew in mortal danger.'

This latest remark really annoyed Stirling. He leant forward, placed both hands on the table and stared defiantly first at the portly officer, then around the table. 'Sometimes the sea and weather can be a greater danger than the enemy. Surely you must know that.' He paused for a few seconds then continued. 'The Prime Minister has admitted winning the war in the Atlantic is paramount and that's what I and my colleagues intend to do.'

'Thank you, Commander,' said the admiral, a wry smile playing around his lips. 'You may be pleased to learn that the DSO you recommended for Sub Lieutenant Amery has been approved and will be gazetted in *The Times*. Now,' he said easing his stocky frame up and offering his hand, 'thank you for attending. I hope,' he added glancing furtively around, 'we haven't been too hard on you. The results of this meeting will be conveyed to you in due course.'

After a withering glance at the portly officer, Stirling, shook the hands of the admiral and then Creasy.

'Don't forget to mention me to Pamela,' Creasy said, smiling while giving Stirling a sly wink.

'I'll do that, George,' Stirling replied. 'It was a pleasure seeing you again.' After a cursory nod to the others, he took his coat, gas mask and cap and left the room.

# CHAPTER TWENTY-ONE

'Great Scott, come in my boy!' exclaimed Sir Charles Amery, putting down his copy of *The Times* and rising from his black leather Chesterfield. As he did so a white lace antimacassar slipped down into the chair. 'My dear chap,' he went on extending his hand. 'Why on earth didn't you tell us you were coming home, he really ought to have shouldn't he Helen?' His question, spoken in a deep, clear, plummy voice was addressed first to his son, then his wife, Helen, who was sitting opposite him in a matching armchair.

The time was a little after nine o'clock and outside darkness had fallen. A glittering crystal chandelier hanging from a high white, stuccoed ceiling cast its clear light on a room tastefully furnished in solid Victorian oak. The wallpaper embossed with flowers on a pale green background added a touch of freshness to the surroundings.

In one corner rested a Sheraton sideboard complete with family photographs and an assortment of bric-a-brac. Behind where Amery's parents sat rested a shiny rosewood coffee table. Nearby, a mahogany drinks cabinet lay snug against the wall. Below a high white Adam mantelpiece logs crackled sharply in an open iron fire grate At the far end of the room black curtains were drawn across a set of French windows that led onto a spacious, well-kept lawn edged with rose bushes and surrounded by a high, evergreen hedge. At the bottom of the lawn a garage housing the family Bentley, opened onto a narrow road that wound along the banks of the River Thames. Like the remainder of the house, the room, expensively furnished, reflected the status of its owner.

The small figure of Sub Lieutenant Oliver Amery, their only child, was standing in the doorway, his well-polished black shoes sinking into the lush pile of the dark green, Axminster carpet. Under his blue naval Burberry he wore his best uniform. His normally well-groomed wavy dark brown hair was a tousled mess and his heavily tanned face ran with nervous perspiration. In his left hand he carried a green standard issue, "Pussers" suitcase. The other held his cap. His mother put down her knitting, stood up and with a wide smile spreading across her face hurried towards him and kissed him lovingly on his cheek.

Eight hours earlier Amery had left *Sandpiper* and caught an early morning train to London arriving at Richmond Station shortly after four o'clock. He then took a taxi to the family home, a large, white, detached, Edwardian house situated in leafy Petersham Road.

In a plummy voice, similar to his father's, he said, 'I thought I'd surprise you.' Placing an arm tightly around his mother's waist, he added, 'I do hope you don't mind?'

'Mind!' gushed Helen, kissing him again, 'we're so pleased to see you, aren't we Charles?'

'We certainly are,' replied Charles, warmly shaking his hand. 'And we're damn well proud of your DSC.'

A curious expression spread into Amery's brown eyes. 'What DSC is that?' he asked, frowning slightly. 'I don't know what you're talking about.'

'It's here in the *The Times,* old boy,' Sir Charles replied, raising his voice slightly. He hurriedly found the relevant page and column, then, stabbing a finger at it, went on, 'The citation reads, "Nineteen-year-old Sub Lieutenant Oliver Amery, of HMS

*Sandpiper* and son of Sir Charles Amery, MP for Chiswick, has been awarded the Distinguished Service Cross for conspicuous gallantry under fire". Here,' Charles continued excitedly waving the newspaper across to his son, 'read it for yourself.'

At first Amery couldn't believe his eyes. But there it was, just as his father had said. He was now the proud owner of a one of the most prestigious medals a man can receive in wartime.

Charles stood back his arm around his wife's waist, both beaming with pride.

'How wonderful, dear,' said Helen. Then dabbing her eyes with a handkerchief, went on, 'It sounds as if you did something very brave. We really are proud of you.'

'Yes indeed, old boy,' Charles said, his grey eyes shining with pride, 'you must tell us in great detail exactly what you did. I can't wait to tell them at the club.'

Feeling his face redden, he looked at his father and gave his shoulder a nonchalant shrug. 'Sorry, Father,' he said modestly, 'I really can't remember much about it. Just the sound of machine gun fire and a few explosions.'

Helen's hand shot to her mouth. 'Oh my God, Oliver!' she cried, 'you could have been killed.' Then reaching out with a trembling hand, she grabbed his arm and added, 'Please dear, promise me you'll take more care.'

'Oh don't take on so,' said Charles, the earlier suggestion of a desk job due to his son's weak disposition suddenly forgotten. Giving his wife a comforting hug, he added breezily, 'Oliver will be all right, he's as brave as a lion. Now let's open a bottle of bubbly. It's not everyday we have a hero in the family.'

About the same time that Amery was enjoying a glass of champagne with his parents, Surgeon Lieutenant Colin Coburn was on his way to meet Fiona Barrington, his erstwhile fiancée.

From a telephone booth at North Road railway station, he had managed to telephone her at her flat. Before his pennies ran out they arranged to meet that evening at seven o'clock at her flat. He arrived at Paddington at six o'clock. Outside it was almost dark. In the distance the steady hub of the city could be heard. The blackout was in progress. Lights on cars and buses were dimmed blue. Trees, postboxes and road curbs were painted white. People finishing work hurried home expecting to hear the mournful wail of the air raid siren warning heralding yet another attack by Goering's Lufwaffe.

Under a blue Burberry Coburn wore his uniform and over his left shoulder hung a canvas bag containing his gas mask. His right hand held a brown grip containing his toilet gear, a clean shirt and a pair of nylons he had managed to obtain from a colleague who knew a black marketer. He turned left outside the station and a few minutes later arrived outside number twenty-four. A small, rusting wrought iron gate led down a small flight of steps to the front door. Close by was a window criss-crossed with white tape and drawn by black curtains. He was about to knock when Fiona opened the door.

He removed his cap and for a few seconds they stood staring longingly at one another; she at his heavily-tanned handsome face and he at her soft, porcelain features and beguiling violet eyes he had seen so often in his dreams.

Suddenly, her hand went to her mouth and she burst out crying. Seeing her weep startled Coburn. Normally she greeted him with a huge smile and hug.

'What's wrong, Fiona,' he asked, his voice full of concern. 'You're not ill or anything, are you?'

'No... no darling, it's not that,' she replied hesitatingly. Taking out a handkerchief from her pocket she quickly dabbed her eyes. Then standing on tiptoe she threw her arms around him, and said, 'It's just because I've missed you so. How long has it been, three months?'

'Three months too long,' Coburn muttered, dropping his grip on the floor. Her unexpected reaction was instantly forgotten as their lips met with such passion each thought their hearts would burst with excitement. Slightly breathless, they broke away. Picking up his grip he could still feel the pliable softness of her warm lips. The dark blue, double-breasted uniform she wore fitted her well-formed figure perfectly. She had removed her tricorn cap allowing her jet-dark hair to curl loosely around her shoulders.

With a dazzling smile she squeezed his hand led him along a short narrow lobby passed a flight of stairs into a well lit lounge which he knew from previous visits was surprisingly large, but had the same well used look about it. The floor was covered in a frayed brownish carpet and coloured prints of country scenes failed to add to the walls decorated in a sickly pale yellow. At one end a gas fire flicked brightly under an old iron mantelpiece, above which hung a good size mirror. A comfortable looking dark leather armchair lay close to a settee whose sagginess was disguised by two large floral cushions. Two wooden chairs were tucked under a round oak table on which lay a pristine white tablecloth. An open door next to a sideboard led into a small kitchen. The bedroom with a large double bed was further down the hallway.

'I wanted to change into something nice for you,' she said apologetically, 'but I didn't get away until five. I'm afraid I've used up my ration of sugar and butter,' she added apologetically, 'but there's come eggs and bacon in the ice-box.' She paused, taking hold of his hand. '*But,*' she emphatically cried, 'I did manage to get a decent bottle of red wine from the mess steward.'

'I shouldn't worry too much about food, darling,' he replied, kissing her quickly, 'later on we can always go down the road to that café we went to last time. As for wearing your uniform, we can soon take care of that,' he added with a mischievous grin while unbuttoning her jacket.

'All in good time,' she replied lowering her arms and stepping slightly away from him. 'But first,' she added almost as an excuse, 'why don't you go and unpack while I put the kettle on. Then we'll see...'

An hour later they lay naked in bed cocooned in the warmth of each other's body. Even though their lovemaking had for him been emotionally fulfilling, she in turn had lain, hardly making a sound feeling him quickly climax inside her.

'I'm sorry, darling,' he said, breathing heavily and feeling beads of warm sweat running down his face. 'It's just that...'

'Don't worry, darling,' she whispered consolingly. She was lying under him and could hear his heart pounding against her chest. 'It really doesn't matter,' she added dismissively before cuddling closer to him.

'I did bring some of those, you know... things,' he said slightly embarrassed, 'but I forgot to use one.'

'Forget it,' she flatly replied, nonchalantly shrugging her shoulders, 'I'm sure it'll be all right. Now,' she added, giving him a quick kiss, 'how about going to the kitchen and fetching the wine. You'll find some glasses in a cupboard over the ice-box.'

At that moment the undulating wail of the air raid siren rent the air.

'Eight o'clock, dead on time,' said Fiona, glancing quickly at her wristwatch. 'I expect the East End and the docks will get it again.'

'Do you want to go to that air raid shelter down the road?' asked Coburn, standing up and reaching for his clothes.

'No,' Fiona replied, wrapping her woollen dressing gown around her, 'under the stairs as before. I've read they're just as safe, even if we get a direct hit.'

For the next half hour they sat in the dark stuffy confined space feeling the ground shake and hearing the dull *thud, thud* of bombs exploding. To the cacophony was added the almost non-stop barrage of the anti-aircraft guns. Occasionally the piercing clanging of ambulance bells could be heard, loud at first before fading in the distance. Half an hour later the welcome moan of the 'All Clear' echoed around.

'Thank God that's over,' Coburn said, giving her a kiss as she unwound herself and opened the small door leading into the lobby. 'Are you all right, darling?' he added compassionately.

'Yes, darling, I'm fine,' Fiona replied, running her fingers through her tousled hair, 'after a while we get used to it. Now I don't know about you, but I could do with a drink of that wine.'

During the rest of the week Coburn sensed something was wrong. Since he arrived her behaviour had been completely out of context to the cheerful, bubbly person he knew. More significantly, when they made love she seemed tense and unresponsive. Occasionally, she had diplomatically rebuffed his advances giving him a consoling kiss saying she was too tired and hoping he would understand. And blamed pressure of work. On one occasion he woke up and found her sitting on the edge of the bed smoking a cigarette. When he asked her why she couldn't sleep, she quickly shrugged her shoulders and blamed pressure of work.

While Fiona was at the Admiralty he sat in the lounge racking his brain wondering what it could be. Maybe she had met someone else; after all, he told himself, there were plenty of desk-bound johnnies who must have found her as attractive as he did. The thought sent an acute feeling of jealousy running through him.

The night before he was due to return to his ship there was a particularly fierce air raid. Once again they sat, huddled under the stairs listening to the all-too-familiar sounds of bombs exploding and feeling the ground shake. When the raid was over Coburn helped her out of the closet.

'I'll put the kettle on, darling,' he said as they switched on the light and went into the lounge.

With a tired sigh, she stood up and replied, 'Good idea,' brushing specks of dust from behind her skirt.

Shortly afterwards he entered the lounge carrying a tray with two mugs and a teapot. Fiona was standing close to the mantelpiece. Her back was turned to him and she was smoking.

'Here you are, darling,' he said cheerfully, placing the tray on the table. 'I found a few Digestives. Thought you'd like one.'

At first she didn't reply. Then, with tears streaming down her pale face, she slowly turned around. After taking a quick, nervous puff of her cigarette, she stared worryingly at him and in a strained voice, said, 'Darling, I think I may be pregnant.'

For a few seconds Coburn stood transfixed, holding a mug while staring wide-eyed at her. Gradually her words sunk in. '*Pregnant!*' he blurted, spilling some tea on the carpet. Suddenly, the reason for her unusual behaviour became clear. He quickly placed his mug on a table and hurried to her. 'Darling, that's wonderful,' he said, taking Fiona in his arms and holding her close. 'I knew something was worrying you, but *pregnant*,' he cried, smiling as he spoke, 'how long... I mean when was your last...?'

She looked up at him, her eyes still wet with tears, and hesitatingly replied, 'Oh darling, I've been at my wits' end. I've missed my last two periods.'

'Why didn't you tell me?' he asked, using a finger to gently wipe away a tear. 'You know I would have understood.'

'I didn't want to spoil your leave,' Fiona replied, blinking nervously, 'besides,' she paused and stared painfully up at him, 'I wasn't sure how you'd react. And anyway, you'll be going away again and God knows when we'll meet again.'

'How I would react, you ask,' he cried, holding her close, 'I'm overjoyed. But,' he went on, kissing the top of her head, 'two months isn't conclusive. Would you like me to take a look at you, after all I am a doctor?'

Fiona glanced pensively up at him, then looking away, said, 'No, darling, I'm seeing the surgeon commander next week.' She gave a worrying sigh and with a pained expression in her eyes, added, 'If I am pregnant, what a world to bring a child into. Wars, millions dying and if anything should happen to you, my love, I should die too.'

Coburn took her face in his hands and gazed lovingly into her tearful eyes.

'You must try not to worry about me,' he said tenderly. 'And please, as soon as you know for certain, write and let me know. Promise?'

'Of course, darling,' she replied, then turning her head to one side, murmured sombrely, 'but how will I tell father…'

Coburn hurriedly interrupted her by placing a finger across her lips.

'To hell with your father,' he cried dismissively, 'and to hell with the war and Hitler. I'll marry you, pregnant or not. Now let's see if there's any wine left.'

# CHAPTER TWENTY-TWO

On Monday 16 October *Sandpiper*'s crew returned from leave. By this time the damage to her Asdic and bows had been repaired. While most of the crew were on away, she had been moved from dry dock and was now alongside Gunner's Wharf, ready for sea.

In the mess decks the repartee between the men was jovial and good-natured.

'Had a good leave, Jacko?' Able Seaman Dinga Bell enquired cheerfully as they unpacked their kit.

'Not bad,' Able Seaman Jackson answered surly. 'Me missus is up the duff again. She's three months overdue.'

'That's odd,' Bell replied frowning curiously, 'our last leave was only two months ago, and before that we were away for almost a year.'

'Maybe it'll be a grudge baby,' quipped Able Seaman Buster Brown, giving Bell a crafty wink.

'What the hell d'yer mean by that?' blurted Jacko, glaring inquisitively at Buster.

'Someone's had it in fer you while you've been away,' Buster replied throwing his head back and giving a throaty laugh.

'*Bollocks,*' cried Jacko, hurtling a boot at him.

In the senior rates' mess all eyes were focused on the badly bruised face of PO Coxswain Pony Moore. It was tot time and each one was waiting to draw his daily ration of neat rum.

'Bloody hell, Pony!' exclaimed Chief GI Dusty Miller, 'what happened to you?'

Pony didn't reply. Instead he glared angrily at Dusty, placed a three fluid ounce Bakelite measure into the aluminium rum fanny, withdrew it and carefully poured the contents into a brown stained tumbler. Then, in his thick Scouse accent, he said succinctly, 'Fuck off,' and quickly downed his drink.

'Awe common, Pony,' joined in CPO Sammy Taylor, his wizened features breaking into a wide, suspicious grin. 'Don't tell us you got pissed and walked into a lamppost?'

'Or maybe she closed her legs on you,' added CERA Percy Bradley, his baggy brown eyes smiling as he leisurely took a sip of his rum.

'Common, mate,' said Chief Stoker Digger Barnes, his rich Yorkshire voice full of curiosity, 'don't keep us in suspense. Tell us what happened.'

Pony drew his six-foot plus frame up and put his tumbler on the table. With a sheepish expression on his weather-beaten face he looked around at the others and said, 'I caught the cow with another feller.'

'Bloody hell, Pony!' Exclaimed PO Yeoman Tate, his tumbler poised precariously near his mouth, 'did you catch them in bed or summat?'

'No,' Pony replied pensively, lighting a cigarette. 'It were like this.'

Everyone suddenly stopped what he was doing. Only the steady hub of the generators disturbed the quietness of the tension-ridden atmosphere.

'When I got to Liverpool, I went 'ome, kissed me ma, then caught a tram to the *Nag's Head* which as yer know is in Bootle.' He paused. All eyes watched as he slowly took a deep drag of his cigarette. 'It were packed with lads off some of the ships in port.'

'Yea! Yea! Go one,' came the squeaky voice of Chief Shipwright Harry Tweed, his rheumy brown eyes agog with anticipation. 'What did you do?'

'Hilda was standing behind the bar,' Pony went on, angrily exhaling a steady stream of smoke. 'She didn't see me because she was too busy leaning forward with her arms around the neck of a chief stoker.' Pony stopped talking, angrily stubbed out his cigarette in a round brass ashtray, then lit another one.

'For fuck's sake,' cried CERA Bradley, 'don't stop now. What did you do?'

'What d'yer think I did, you daft bugger?' Pony replied fiercely. 'I went over and asked her what the 'ell she was doin'. She nearly shit herself when she saw me. Her face turned red and she took her arms away from the chief.'

'And then what happened?' PO Yeoman Tate asked eagerly while taking a sip of his rum.

'When I told him I was Hilda's fiancé he just laughed. "No he's not, 'arry," I heard Hilda cry. "I've finished wiv 'im." Since when?' I asked.

'"Since now," she yelled, and told me to piss off.

'Then the chief stood up. He was a big bugger, over six feet. "Yea, bugger off or I'll make yer," he said.

'That's when the fight started,' said Pony. 'I gave the chief a right hook on the point of his jaw. He fell backwards knocked over a table of drinks. Then all bleedin' hell broke loose. Hilda and some women started screaming. The chief got up and I went to belt 'im again, but 'e got me first with a few good uns. Before I knew it I wuz on the deck seein' stars. When I came round I wuz bein' 'elped outside by two coppers. Bert Parker, the landlord, must 'ave called them.'

'What happened to the chief stoker?'

'I dunno,' Pony replied surly. 'I spent the night in clink. The coppers were OK though, they gave me a mug of tea and even shared their corn dog sarnies with me.'

'I suppose the wedding is off then?' said PO Yeoman Tate, doing his best not to laugh.

'Get stuffed,' grunted Pony glaring contemptuously at Tate, then stormed out of the mess.

Stirling was sat at his desk studying a batch of signals when a knock came at the door and Manley came in.

'Hello, Number One' Stirling said, smiling cheerfully while closing the green covered signal log. 'Do sit down. How are Patricia and your boy? Well I hope.'

'Fine thank you, sir,' Manley replied, 'luckily Redditch was spared the bombing, but Coventry will take ages to recover. I take it your family are all right.'

(The air raids on Coventry in November 1940 had claimed the lives of 800 people. More than 2,000 men and women were injured and over 20,000 made homeless.)

With a worried frown Stirling said, 'Pamela has joined the WVS and is in London. What with the Blitz and all, I expect she's kept pretty busy.' He paused, opened a packet of *Players,* took one out and passed one to Manley then lit both with a small, silver lighter. 'As for Mark, he's in a submarine, somewhere in the Med, I think.'

Manley sat back in his chair and said, 'According to the BBC, the Jerries have sunk an American battleship, the USS *Reubin James.* Apparently she was escorting a convoy to Iceland. As you know they have a base there. Luckily most of her crew were rescued.'

'That'll prove to the doubters in Congress that America should be in the war,' Stirling replied soberly. 'And with the Wehrmacht near the gates of Moscow, the sooner the better.'

'I agree, sir,' Manley said nodding slowly while leaning forward and flicking ash into a solid brass ashtray. 'Those fifty destroyers they sent were a godsend, but we're still short of escorts.'

'Talking of escorts,' Stirling said, opening his signal log, 'in a week's time, on the 23rd, after we have stored and ammunitioned the group are to sail for Liverpool. Then on Wednesday 25,' he added firmly, 'Admiral Sir Percy Noble, no less, is to pay *Sandpiper* a visit. According to the signal he is only coming to address the ship's company, but you can bet he'll be giving the ship the once-over.'

'Oh gawd!' moaned Manley, grinning while shaking his head, 'extra spit and polish. The crew will love that.'

'That'll be up to you, dear boy,' Stirling breezily replied. 'One day when you have your own command, you'll be able to sit back and let your First Lieutenant get on with it.'

The mention of him receiving his own ship sent a surge of excitement running through Manley. His questioning Stirling's decision to leave the convoy to attack the U-boat had not gone against him. In a perverse way it may have helped him as Stirling had no time for "yes men" and encouraged his officers to speak their mind.

Throughout the following seven days *Sandpiper* buzzed with activity. Lower deck was cleared and all hands had to turn to. Wooden platforms were lowered over the side and under the eagle eye of the Buffer, ratings hastily repainted the ship's battleship grey and green and black camouflage.

'And make sure you do a good job with the pennant number,' CPO Sammy Taylor, shouted, leaning over the ship's side.

'Why doesn't the old bugger get a brush and join us,' muttered Able Seaman Soapy Waters to Ordinary Seaman Nipper Morris, who, like him, was standing on the platform slapping paint on the ship's bulkhead.

'What was that you said, Waters?' the Buffer growled defiantly. 'I may be old but I'm not bloody-well deaf.'

'Er… nowt, Chief,' Soapy hastily replied, glancing upwards and allowing spots of white paint to drip from his brush onto his pale blue overalls. 'All I said was why all the rush.'

Using long-handled scrubbers ratings worked like beavers to make the wooden deck sandy white. Chains, and anchors hitherto heavily coated with rust were chipped and painted. Gun turret and gun barrels were lovingly attended too as were the masts, yardarms and cables.

'Better make sure the brasswork and silverware are polished,' Wardroom PO Steward Knocker White warned his staff.

'But they're cleaned every day, PO,' replied Steward Potts, glancing apprehensively at the three other stewards.

'Then do 'em twice a day,' the PO snapped angrily, 'now take that fag out of your mouths and get crackin'.'

In the engine and boiler rooms the daily routine never changed. The silver footplates, pipes, clocks and dials were constantly wiped, cleaned and polished.

The daily cleaning routine in the sick bay remained the same as cleanliness and hygiene was of paramount importance. The day after everyone returned from leave SBA Appleby was sat as the desk writing yet another letter to some barmaid he had met ashore. The door opened and in came the Surgeon Lieutenant Coburn.

'Don't get up,' he said seeing Appleby about to rise, 'finish your letter. Any idea when the mail will be coming onboard?'

'Let's see, sir,' Appleby replied, detecting a note of anxiety in the doctor's voice, 'it's just after 1000 now, mail should arrive sometime after 1300,' he paused, then with a sly smile, went on, 'why sir, expecting a letter from your lady friend?'

'Something like that,' Coburn replied curtly, 'now mind your own business and make some tea.'

Coburn sat on one of the cots, lit a cigarette and with a worried expression, wondered how he would react if Fiona was pregnant. He told himself perhaps it would be better for all concerned if she were wrong. For the umpteenth time the same unanswered questions ran through his mind. If she left the service where would they live, and more important, what would they live on? And then there was her father…

'Don't look so worried, sir,' said Appleby handing Coburn a steaming hot mug of tea. 'It may never happen.'

'Perhaps you're right,' Coburn replied with a half-hearted laugh. However, as he was having lunch, the wardroom steward arrived carrying a small bundle if letters. Alas, the only one he received was a bill from Grieves Naval Tailors in Portsmouth.

# CHAPTER TWENTY-THREE

'I am very much impressed with the efficiency of this ship,' Admiral Sir Percy Noble started in a well-modulated clear voice. Standing on a wooden platform on *Sandpiper*'s recently painted fo'c'sle his six-foot plus frame hovered over Stirling and the ship's officers standing behind him. The thumbs of both hands poked out from inside both jacket pockets and as he spoke the firm jaw of his narrow, pallid features jutted out defiantly. The time was shortly after 0900. Facing the admiral was the senior ratings and behind them came the crew. All wore their number one uniforms and were standing at ease. 'We can win this battle against the U-boat by constant drilling and training,' the admiral continued, his keen eyes sweeping over the faces of his captivated audience. 'You are all very well trained, your recent actions have demonstrated this in no uncertain measure,' he paused and raising his voice slightly, went on, 'and I am proud of you and all your colleagues in the fifteenth escort group.'

Two days later the group left Plymouth. *Exmoor,* which was still in dockyard hands, had been replaced by HMS *Milton.*

'We seem to be scraping the barrel, sir,' Manley remarked sarcastically, upon hearing which ship would be replacing *Exmoor.* 'Isn't *Milton* an old First World War destroyer?'

'That's right, Number One,' Stirling replied giving Manley a reassuring smile, 'but her three sets of 4.5 anti-aircraft guns might come in handy, and she's been converted to carry depth charges. Her captain Steve Sharp is an old friend of mine. He's a gunnery specialist. I had a drink with him before we sailed and he assures me his ship, despite its age, is ready for anything.'

*Sandpiper* was moored alongside Gladstone Wharf. *Curlew, Redshank, Shearwater* and *Petrel* were lying further along the quayside. Promptly at 0845 on Wednesday 25 a black staff car, flying the admiral's gold and green pennant, arrived at the base of *Sandpiper*'s recently painted prow. Bending his tall, gangly frame slightly, Admiral Noble climbed out of the car followed by a small, pale-faced lieutenant. The gold braided aiguillette hanging decoratively around the lieutenant's left shoulder indicated his position as the admiral's aid-de-camp. The shrill whistle of the bosun's pipe greeted them as they walked up the gangway and stepped onboard the ship. The admiral stiffly returned the salutes of Stirling and the rest of the ship's officers.

'Welcome onboard, sir,' said Stirling, 'the ship's company are fallen on the fo'c'sle' ready for your inspection.' Stirling then introduced him to the officers, and after a friendly word to each he shook their hands.

'No need for an inspection, Bob, 'the admiral cheerfully replied. 'I just want to say a few words before you give me a large Horse's Neck in the wardroom.'

An hour later the admiral's address was over and just as Stand Easy was piped Stirling escorted the admiral and his aid-de-camp to the wardroom.

'I suppose you're all wondering what your next job will be,' the admiral said, after downing his Horse's Neck (brandy and dry ginger.) 'Well I can tell you,' he paused, finished his drink and gave Stirling a wry smile, 'I hope you'll forgive me for announcing this before telling you privately, but as you know there are precious few secrets onboard small ships.'

Stirling gave a short but understanding nod and replied, 'I quite understand, another drink, sir?'

'I'm afraid it's another trip to Gib,' said the admiral, accepting another Horse's Neck from PO Steward Knocker White. A few frustrated sideways glances by the officers told their own story.

'Now don't look so disappointed,' the admiral said, accepting a cigarette and a light from Stirling. 'Be grateful you're not going on an Arctic convoy,' he added, staring warily at them, 'at least it's a darn sight warmer in the Med.'

'I can't say I'm surprised, sir,' Stirling said, taking a good gulp of his drink. 'When do we sail?'

'A week from today at 0800,' the admiral replied sternly, 'the group will leave for Gibraltar and rendezvous with a convoy consisting of twenty merchant ships code-named HG 84, and escort them as far as Liverpool. You and the escorts will then join the convoy and berth alongside Gladstone Wharf. The convoy, plus the destroyer *Convolvulus* will continue to the Clyde. In the meantime,' he paused and gave Stirling a thoughtful glance, 'I expect your captain will want to go to sea and put the group through their paces.'

At 0800 the next morning, with *Sandpiper* in the van, the ships slipped their moorings and left Liverpool.

On *Sandpiper*'s bridge, Stirling was firmly encamped in his chair. Like everyone else on duty, under his dark brown duffle coat he wore a thick, blue woollen sweater. A cream coloured muffler was wrapped warmly around his neck. Even so, he felt the harsh north-westerly wind gradually seep through his clothing and make his eyes water. Glancing apprehensively at Manley, at the low-lying clouds racing across the sky, he said, 'Looks like being a bit rough, eh, Number One?

'Yes indeed, sir,' Manley replied, steadying himself as the ship cut through the choppy, dark green sea. 'Ape tells me the barometers is dropping and the wind is expected to increase to Force eight.' (Wind velocity thirty-five knots.)

'At least it'll allow the crew to find their sea-legs again after all that boozing ashore,' Stirling replied with a rueful smile.

With the twin towers of the Liver Buildings fading in the grey morning mist, the small flotilla passed the Mersey Bar and into the angry waters of the Irish Sea. Almost immediately the high rollers hit the ships sending bursts of while water curling over their bows. The searing wind whipped the cables and rigging into a wild frenzy as each vessel cut through the sea.

'Here we go again,' moaned PO Yeoman Tate, using the back of his hand to wipe away the icy spray. 'Back to bloody normal.'

'Stop complaining, Yeoman,' said Stirling, smiling thinly, 'flash signals to *Curlew* who is directly in our rear, say: "In half an hour all ships are to go to actions stations, then turn to port in hunting formation." Repeat to other ships.'

'It'll be a bit tricky in this weather, sir,' replied Manley giving Stirling a cautionary glance.

'That's exactly why I want it done,' Stirling answered dryly. 'U-boats tend to stay submerged in this weather, if we contact one, rough sea or not, we'll have to sink the bugger.'

With the heavy, rolling sea hitting each vessel beam on, the group slowly changed direction. Manoeuvring each ship was slow and difficult. One or two struggled to achieve formation but eventually a semblance of a straight line was achieved.

'Not bad, Number One,' Stirling remarked, a satisfied smile written on his weather-beaten features, 'signal "Well Done" and add, all ships to carry out depth charge exercises.'

Later that day the weather and visibility deteriorated. The skies darkened and walls of rain slanted down turning the sea into millions of mini watery eruptions. Despite the inclement conditions Stirling ordered gunnery exercises, sea-boat lowering and as dusk began to fall, a star shell shoot. During the next two hours the crew were closed up at action stations. Those men on the upper deck were soaked to the skin and numb with cold.

'What's the old man trying to do?' moaned SBA Appleby as he and his first aid team struggled along *Sandpiper*'s slippery upper deck holding the rope handles of a Neil Robertson. Strapped inside was the bulky figure of lookout Able Seaman Dinga Bell. The wound on his arm had healed but he had been detailed as a "casualty" and had been lowered, albeit very precariously, from the bridge onto the deck below.

'Much more of this,' cried Brum Appleby, straining to keep hold of his handle, 'and we'll all be too knackered to do anything if we meet a U-boat.'

At that moment they were enveloped in an icy spray as a huge wave sent the ship rolling dangerously to port. Suddenly, Appleby and the others slipped, but managed to cling onto the stretcher. Struggling against the constant pitching of the ship, the first aiders only just managed to keep their feet.

'Chuck the sod overboard,' yelled Darby Allen looking down from the after port Oerlikon gun platform.

'Don't do that, Doc,' yelled Able Seaman Jackson, poking his hooded head from around the gun barrel, 'the bugger owes me a tot.'

By 1800 the escorts had returned to Liverpool. Very few of *Sandpiper*'s crew, and those of the other escorts went ashore. Instead they flopped on their bunks or in their hammocks, too tired even to eat. But there was little or no respite. The next morning the escorts sailed again. Stirling ordered more evolutions including "man overboard" exercises, and "silent running".

Manley summed up the reaction of the crew. Turning to Stirling he said tersely, 'Well, sir, after the last four days, meeting the enemy will be a relief.'

On 2 November the group left Liverpool bound for Gibraltar. A Force 9 gale met them as they turned to port and headed down the Irish Sea into the English Channel. For the next three days the small flotilla battled against the elements. High sea tossed the ships about like corks in a bottle. Once again conditions below decks became damp, cold and miserable. On day five a grey rainy squall aided by a fierce head wind reduced visibility to a mere hundred yards.

'At least this weather will keep the damn U-boats away, Number One,' Stirling commented, squinting as icy rain attacked his face, 'so we must be grateful for small mercies.'

Six days later the flotilla entered the Bay of Biscay. Much to everyone's surprise and relief the harsh gales subsided and were replaced by the warmer breezes flowing from Spain and Africa. Dark clouds gradually gave way to clear cerulean blue skies and life became tolerable. Thick woollen jerseys were removed. Overalls were rolled down and tied around waists as those off duty lay anywhere and soaked up the warmth of the sun.

'This is the life, eh Jumper?' Tanky said to Dave Cross, a thickset Able Seaman. They and a few others were on *Sandpiper*'s quarterdeck lounging about, bare-chested against the base of X gun turret. 'Just think,' he went on casually flicking a dog-end overboard, 'before the war, toffs used to pay a fortune for this.'

Cross who was engrossed reading a dog-eared copy of *Tit Bits,* sighed peacefully and muttered, 'Aye, your right there, Tanky, when this fuckin' war's over I'll…' He was abruptly cut short by the ear-splitting noise of the alarm bell ringing around the ship. This was quickly followed by, 'Hands to action stations. Submarine contact two miles on the port bow.'

In a matter of minutes everyone was closed up at their appropriate station. On the bridge Stirling, sitting in his chair was carefully studying his wristwatch. With an air of satisfaction he looked up, turned to Manley and said, 'Four minutes, Number One, the fastest yet,' with a wry smile he added, 'better tell the crew it was a school of porpoises, and stand them down.'

On 10 November the rugged coastline of Spain shrouded in grey mist appeared on the port bow. The time was 0600. Dawn was breaking over a relatively calm sea and the darkness of night was quickly giving way to a new day. A few hours later the peak of the Rock could be seen poking though a thin layer of cotton wool clouds.

'Convoy on the starboard bow two miles away, sir,' reported Able Seaman Lofty Day from the crow's nest, 'about twenty of them I'd say.'

Using a voice-pipe OOW Lieutenant Anderson relayed the message to Stirling in his sea cabin sitting at his desk. In front of him was a signal from Admiralty giving him the details of the convoy.

'Thank, you I'll be up immediately,' Stirling replied, 'flash a signal to Commodore Hudson in the SS *Pelavo,* and say, "Good to see you. Will deploy my escorts both sides of you. *Sandpiper* will take up position in your stern. Hope we have a quiet trip."' He noticed that a C.A.M. ship, (Catapult Aircraft Merchantman) was in the port outer column. The SS *Copeland,* a rescue ship responsible for picking up survivors should any ships be sunk, had taken station half a mile away on *Sandpiper*'s port beam.

By the time Stirling reached the bridge the message had been sent. Five minutes later PO Yeoman Tate received *Pelavo*'s reply. It read, "Glad to see you, Focke-Wulf sighted yesterday. U-boats reported in the vicinity."

'Can't say I'm surprised, Number One,' Stirling remarked warily to Manley who had joined him on the bridge. 'Better double the lookouts and switch the Asdic on over the tannoy. That'll keep everyone on their toes.'

There was a harsh westerly wind, and the heavy, undulating swell was strong enough to cause several ships to swing dangerously close to each other.

During the next twenty-four hours the Focke-Wulf spotter planes were never far away. On one occasion, Stirling, shielding his eyes from the sun, said, 'The cargo ship *Empire Sun* carries a hurricane. I'm tempted to order it to be launched. That'll chase the sod away.'

Manley replied dubiously, 'Maybe, sir, they've already reported our position. May I suggest you use the plane for a more urgent mission.'

Nodding in agreement, Stirling said, 'Yes, Number One, I think you're right.'

'Signal from *Copeland*, sir,' said PO Yeoman Tate, 'it says, "Message intercepted on our HF/DF from U-boat somewhere on our port quarter, giving accurate position of convoy".' (HF/DF or Huff-Duff As it was known is an instrument for intercepting U-boat wireless signals.)

Stirling was now faced with a dilemma. He was aware that most commanding officers would take the safer, and in many ways the sounder course, of staying with the convoy in the hope of beating off any attack. But should he stay or go after the U-boat?

Manley was only too aware of his captain's obsessive determination to destroy the enemy. As if reading Stirling's mind he said, 'If you leave the convoy you'll be putting them at risk the same as last time.'

'I'm well aware of that, Number One,' came Stirling's ponderous reply. 'But we can't just wait here and allow the sod to escape.' With a determined look in his tired brown eyes, he said, 'Signal *Curlew* to join me. Then signal the rest of the group to patrol a mile or so around the convoy. *Convlvulus* and *Copeland* are to remain on station. Hard a port Number One, we're going after the bugger!'

Stirling was only too aware he was throwing away the rule book. Once again his career was in the hands of fate.

# CHAPTER TWENTY-FOUR

*Sandpiper* and *Curlew* broke away from the rest of the escort group. The two ships heeled to port and cut through the high, rolling sea for almost fifteen minutes. However, an early evening mist had begun to fall hampering visibility. The force of the wind was now reduced, but low-lying dark clouds set in a grey sky threatened rain.

Shortly after 1700 Able Seaman Jackson in *Sandpiper*'s crow's nest reported, 'Submarine on the surface dead ahead, sir.'

Stirling immediately focused his binoculars on an area of dark blue ocean, directly ahead. Manley, Ape, who was OOW, PO Yeoman Tate and the lookouts did the same.

'There she is!' cried Ape, pointing with his free hand, 'about ten miles ahead of us.'

'Better pass this on to *Curlew* in case she hasn't spotted the blighter,' snapped Stirling.

'A bit lucky, eh, sir,' Manley commented laconically.

'Luck had nothing to do with it, Number One,' Stirling replied ruefully. 'That's the result of good training. The lookout could have easily missed it in this haze.'

'I think the sub's seen us, sir,' yelled Jackson. 'She's turning to port and gathering speed.'

A brief look at the sub's squat conning tower moving through the water confirmed this.

'Hard a port, Number One,' he cried, hearing the blood pound in his head. 'Let's see if we can catch the bugger. Hands to action stations, full speed ahead and tell the crew what's happening.'

Sensing the imminence of action the gun's crew were already closed up.

'It'll make a bloody change from all the practice shoots we've been doing, eh chief,' said Able Seaman Darby Allen, placing a heavy shell in X gun's breech. His face, like those of the four other gunners, was streaked with sweat.

'Pipe down, and concentrate on your job,' growled CGI Dusty Miller, 'and maybe we'll hit the bastard.'

'How far away is the sod?' asked Able Seaman Dixie Dean wiping his brow with the back of his grimy hand.

'You'll soon find out,' admonished the chief dryly, 'now close the breech and keep your wits about you.'

'*Curlew* is losing speed, sir,' Lofty Day reported from the crow's nest, 'and she's falling behind.'

Stirling was sat on his chair, his binoculars still trained on the sub. 'Then we'll just have to go on alone,' he caustically replied. 'What's the range, Guns?'

'Eighteen thousand yards and closing, sir,' Lieutenant Anderson's sharp voice replied in the Range Finder's intercom situated above on the GDP. (One nautical mile is equal to 2,000 yards.)

Stirling knew that at eight miles his guns were slightly out of range. At six they could possibly score a hit. He listened intently, gripping the handles of his chair as Anderson called out as the gap narrowed.

'Fourteen thousand yards, sir.'

The minute that passed seemed like an hour. The tension on the bridge and throughout the ship was gut-wrenching. The quick throbbing of the engines, the steady in and out dipping as the ship bounded through the sea told those below decks that the enemy wasn't far away.

'Thirteen thousand yards, sir.'

Another agonising minute passed.

'Twelve thousand yards, sir.'

'The sub's crash diving, sir,' yelled Lofty Day, ignoring the wind whipping against his face.

'*Bastard!*' Stirling exploded. 'Stand by depth charge, crews.' But he knew it would take *Sandpiper* nearly twenty minutes to reach the diving point. In that time the sub could be about two miles away in any direction.

'She's gone, sir,' said Manley, watching pensively as their prey disappeared under the sea in a swirl of frothy bubbles.

Once again Stirling was faced with a momentous problem. He had to decide the direction he must steer his ship in order to intercept the sub and pick her up on his Asdic. It was a decision that could not only cost him his command but also his career.

'What was her course when she dived, Pilot?' Stirling asked, feeling beads of warm perspiration running down his back.

'North-westerly, sir.'

Stirling's mind went into overdrive. Logically, the sub might be expected to continue on that course. This would enable her to keep up with the convoy and carry on shadowing if Stirling gave up the chase. But, he told himself U-boat commanders do not deal in logic. In a flash he decided to gamble on the enemy doing the opposite to what Stirling might expect him to do. If it failed and the U-boat escaped, the convoy would be in grave danger.

'Alter course ten degrees south, Number One,' he said, 'and signal *Curlew* to follow suit.' Even though his manner was quiet and confident his heart was pounding like a hammer.

Manley was only too aware that his captain was taking a major risk. Last time he was lucky because he knew where the U-boat was. This time, however, the enemy could be anywhere, and the ocean was the perfect place to hide in.

'Reduce revolutions one-third, Number One,' Stirling grunted, surveying the sea for the telltale wash of a periscope. 'And tell the Asdic operator to begin their sweep.'

'What if the blighter torpedoes us?' Manley asked, giving Stirling a cautionary glance.

'Hmm, I suppose that's possible, Number One,' Stirling replied, pursing his lips. 'Better double the lookouts, just in case.'

News of the U-boat's disappearance soon spread throughout the ship and tension remained high. In the sick bay Appleby glanced apprehensively at his boss, and said, 'I wonder why we're slowing down, sir. Suppose we are attacked by one of them Focke-Wulf Condors?'

Coburn noticed the pale faces of his first aid team and smiled. All three were sitting on the deck, grim-faced while nervously smoking cigarettes. 'If that happens, Appleby,' Coburn answered laconically, 'it'll all be over in seconds. Now stop worrying and make some tea.'

Meanwhile, Able Seaman Buster Brown and Darby Allen manning the port Oerlikon moved to the guardrail scanning the ocean searching for the foamy wake of a periscope. Their vigil was abruptly interrupted by the stern voice of Chief GI Barnes.

'All of you buggers get back to your posts,' he yelled, 'or I'll have your guts for garters.'

'Makes you feel cheated somehow,' muttered Buster as he and Darby returned to their gun.

On the bridge Stirling sat hunched in his chair. Glancing down at the gyrocompass, he bent slightly towards the wheelhouse voice-pipe and said, 'Steady as she goes, Chief, and keep one ear on reports from the Asdic team.'

For the next ten minutes the two sloops slowly cut through the relatively calm sea. The metallic sound of the steady "pinging" of the Asdic echoing around the ship served to increase the tension.

With an exasperated sigh, Stirling thumped the arm of his chair and cried, '*Where the devil is the blighter? I'm sure he must...*'

Suddenly Asdic operator Leading Seaman Wacker Payne reported, '*Echo bearing three hundred and forty degrees, sir.*'

Stirling gave an audible deep sigh of relief – his gamble had paid off.

'Can you be more specific?' he shouted down to the Asdic operator.

'Yes, sir,' Payne replied confidently, 'the sub's slightly on our starboard bow.'

'Increase revolutions two-thirds,' snapped Stirling, then smiling broadly he looked at Manley, and added, 'depth charge party stand by.'

*Sandpiper* shuddered and increased speed. Gradually the interval between each Asdic "ping" decreased.

'Range six hundred yards, and closing,' came Payne's excited voice over the Asdic voice-pipe.

'Three hundred yards,' yelled Payne.

'She must be almost underneath us now, sir,' Manley said, feeling his pulse quicken. 'Shall I...'

'*Release depth charges!*' Stirling said, trying his best to sound calm.

Manley immediately pressed the bell warning the depth charge crews on the quarterdeck to release their deadly missiles.

Immediately depth charges tumbled from their racks and splashed into the water.

'Reduce revolutions one-third,' Stirling cried, 'turn five degree to port.'

For nearly a minute Sub Lieutenant Harper-Smyth and his team waited tensely as *Sandpiper* slowed down and turned. Seconds later the rumble of detonations echoed ominously from below the sea. Mountains of foamy water cascading skywards quickly followed this.

On the bridge, Stirling sat grim-faced, doing his best to contain his excitement.

'Starboard ten,' he shouted down the wheelhouse voice-pipe.

The watery explosions settled and spread into foamy concentric circles. Everyone on the bridge and men manning the guns strained their eyes hoping to see signs of an oil slick. But to their dismay nothing could be seen. The quick "pinging" over the tannoy told its own story. The attack had failed.

'Our man is trickier than I thought, Number One,' Stirling remarked bitterly. 'He's damn well gone deep.' With a determined expression in his eyes, he added, 'Tell Harper-Smyth to set his charges at one-fifty and three hundred feet. Let's try again.'

By this time *Curlew* was in the hunt. For the next hour both ships conducted more attacks. Once again explosion after explosion transformed the sea into palls of turbulent water.

With a feeling of unease, Stirling glanced apprehensively at Manley. 'Looks like her captain is varying his depths after every attack. How many depth charges have we left?'

'Just ten, I'm afraid, sir,' Manley grimly replied. 'Enough for another run at the bugger.'

Just as he spoke an explosion a hundred yards away on *Sandpiper*'s port beam sent a huge jet of black water surging upwards. A few seconds later came a sickening rumble followed by another cascade, higher and louder than its predecessor. A pool of black oil oozed onto the surface. Jagged pieces of metal and broken bits of wood quickly followed this. To this flotsam was added a few arms and legs and a headless corpse still wearing the uniform of Doenitz's Kreigsmarine.

'We've got her at last, Number One,' Stirling cried excitedly as he moved quickly to the port wing. Gradually a mixture of sadness and compassion suddenly replaced the excited expression in his eyes. He immediately thought of his son. God forbid, he muttered to himself, that the enemy would ever subject Mark to such horrific treatment.

'A terrible way to die, eh, Number One,' Stirling muttered frowning at Manley.

'Indeed, sir,' Manley replied sombrely. 'But remember, it could easily have been us in the water. And if your instincts had been wrong, then what?'

'A barge on the Thames, probably,' Stirling replied half-heartedly. With a weary sigh, he added, 'Better return to the convoy. Signal *Curlew* and inform Admiralty. Give the location of the U-boat and report no survivors.'

From the wireless room directly below the bridge came the strident voice of Able Seaman Williams. '*Redshank* has broken radio silence, sir,' he cried in a sharp Welsh accent. 'Morse code message reads, "Have taken position four miles port side of convoy. U-boat reported fifteen miles on starboard bow. Am investigating."'

'Breaking radio silence doesn't matter,' Stirling casually remarked. 'The bastards know where we are anyway. Reply, "Good luck. Keep me informed."' Casting an uneasy glance at the darkening sky, he looked at Manley, and said, 'It'll be dark soon, that's when the U-boats like to attack. I only hope the bugger doesn't infiltrate the convoy.'

'And remember there's only *Convolvulus* and *Copeland* protecting the convoy,' warned Manley.

'I'm well aware of that, Number One,' Stirling replied sternly, 'that's why we'd better get back quickly.'

'*Redshank* reports she is in contact with the sub and is attacking, sir,' cried Williams.

During the next hour everyone, especially Stirling, anxiously waited to hear from *Redshank*. Shortly before 2300 the signal they had been waiting for arrived. It read, "Have attacked three times without success. Breaking away and expect to rejoin convoy at 0100."

'By this time, Number One,' Stirling said, somewhat annoyed with himself, 'the U-boat captain will have radioed every sub in the area giving them our position.'

'Well, at least we've managed to sink one of them and keep the others from attacking the convoy,' Manley replied in a conciliatory voice.

'So far, you mean,' muttered Stirling cautiously.

With *Curlew* gradually falling behind *Sandpiper* the two sloops headed due west and by midnight they reached the convoy.

'Signal *Curlew* to take station a mile on the starboard side of the convoy, Number One. Meanwhile we will bring up the rear,' Stirling said, adding confidently, 'that's where we can expect an attack to come from. How far away are the others?'

'*Shearwater,* and *Petrel* are conducting a search about twenty miles from the convoy, sir,' Manley replied. '*Milton* is about forty miles ahead of the convoy.'

'Better break radio silence and signal *Shearwater* and *Petrel* to close in around the convoy, *Milton* can remain where she is,'

Stirling said pensively rubbing the bristles on his chin. 'I have a gut feeling...'

Almost immediately, a report from the Asdic operator Leading Seaman Wacker Payne interrupted him.

'Contacts in front of the convoy, sir,' he cried, 'looks like quite a few of them as well.'

'Jesus Christ!' Stirling blasphemed, shooting an alarming glance at Manley, 'the buggers have changed their tactics. Sound action stations.'

Suddenly an ear-splitting explosion rent the air. From *Sandpiper*'s position well astern of the convoy clouds of yellow smoke and flames could be seen billowing into the air like a miniature volcano. For a while the darkness was tinged with a reddish hue turning the surrounding sea into a dappled mass of flickering yellow flames.

'It's the *Pelavo* in the centre column, sir,' shouted one of the lookouts, 'and she's sinking fast!'

'Good Lord, Number One,' gasped Stirling, his binoculars hard against his eyes. 'That's Commodore Hudson's ship.'

(According to one of *Pelavo*'s crew who was later rescued, the explosion threw Commodore Hudson off the bridge into the sea and he was never seen again.)

Another yellow and red detonation lit the sky as a ship, later identified as the cargo vessel SS *Strib* was struck amidships. On the far side of the convoy a third ship suffered a similar fate.

'*Copeland*'s in for a busy night, Number One,' Stirling said wearily. 'Better order *Curlew* to fire a star shell.'

'But sir,' Manley hurriedly replied, '*Curlew*'s too far behind and you just said the blighters are coming from ahead of the convoy. It would be pointless...'

'Of course, you're quite right,' Stirling answered, quickly realising his mistake. 'You'd better signal *Curlew* to leave her position and help *Copeland* pick up survivors. Signal the other escorts to drop depth charges within a two-mile radius in front of the convoy. Wishful thinking, Number One, but maybe that'll scare the buggers away.'

But would it?

# CHAPTER TWENTY-FIVE

The U-boats continued to press home their attack. Their presence over the Asdic became louder with each passing hour. Dusk began to fall. A pale blue hue lay across the horizon and a pallid moon, moving imperceptibly through clusters of dark clouds, cast an eerie glow on the inky black sea.

*Sandpiper* had taken a position a mile away on the port side of the convoy. Stirling, who was sharing the middle watch with Ape, was crouched in his chair, muffled in scarves and sweater, scanning the eastern horizon with his binoculars. He sat in silence while Ape conned the ship.

'It's far too quiet,' he finally said to Ape, adding ominously, 'the silhouettes of the ships will make perfect targets.'

Now that the commodore was missing it was incumbent upon Stirling to take command of the convoy. 'The SS *Brisbane* is now senior ship. Signal her to tell the convoy to commence zig-zagging.'

At 0430, the U-boats struck.

A sudden flash of scarlet lighted the sky as a ship in the middle of the convoy disintegrated into a white, blazing ball of fire.

'The attacks are coming from the convoy's starboard beam, sir,' Manley cried, noticing the worried frown on Stirling's brow.

'*Sod it!*' Stirling exploded. If he had ordered *Curlew* to remain on the starboard side of the convoy, she might have picked up the

U-boats on her radar. Her captain could have informed him and the convoy could have taken evasive action.

'Yes, Number One,' Stirling replied giving an exasperated sigh, 'I can see that.'

'Bloody hell, sir,' interrupted PO Yeoman Tate, 'the *Thurso*'s been hit and she's going down fast.

Squinting their eyes against the glare of the flames, Stirling and Ape watched helplessly as tiny figures leapt from the *Thurso* into the sea. Just then another explosion echoed from a cargo vessel about fifty yards behind *Thurso*.

Ape was able to identify her as the *City of Oxford*. 'It looks as if a torpedo has hit her amidships, sir,' Ape cried, 'and she's low in the water.'

For the first time since the attack began, Stirling felt close to panic. Feeling sweat trickled down his spine he watched as *Copeland* and *Curlew*, slowed down in order to pick up survivors from the two stricken merchantmen.

'Good Lord,' he finally said, 'the glow from the *City of Oxford* will make them easy targets.'

'I'm sure the poor buggers are aware of that, sir,' Manley sombrely replied.

Meanwhile the foreboding sound of the Asdic "pinging" became quicker and louder.

Suddenly the chaos became complete when every ship in the convoy began firing snowflake rockets wildly and indiscriminately

'Stone the crows!' Ape yelled almost hysterically, 'the place is lit up like Bonzi Beach on a Saturday night. Every ship in the bloody convoy is standing out like a sore thumb.'

The sight set Stirling fuming with rage.

'Who the hell gave that order, I wonder,' Stirling growled angrily.

'Whoever it was needs their arses kicking,' Manley added, shaking his head in disbelief. 'Some of the ships are even firing tracers thinking there is an air attack. They must be crazy.'

'Or just shit-scared,' Ape added sombrely.

'Order all escorts to proceed at full speed around the convoy out of the glare of the snowflakes,' he snapped, angrily. 'With a bit of luck we'll catch one of the U-boats on the surface.'

Unfortunately, their search, however, proved fruitless.

Dawn gradually broke and by 0800 the convoy, still in remarkably good order could be seen rolling and pitching in the choppy dark green, sea. Black clouds threatened rain and an icy wind, blowing in strong gusts, filtered through the warmest clothing.

At 0830 Stirling left the bridge, washed and shaved and reappeared half an hour later, tired and bleary eyed.

'Anything happening, Guns?' Stirling asked, stifling a yawn while tucking a woollen scarf down the neck of his duffle coat.

'It's pretty quiet sir. *Curlew* and *Copeland* are on our port beam,' reported OOW Lieutenant Anderson, shivering slightly while holding his binoculars to his eyes. 'They're both crammed with survivors. The rest of the escorts are deployed around the convoy as you ordered.'

But the quietness was not to last long.

Shortly before 'Up Spirits' at 1100, wireless operator Able Seaman Williams reported a signal from *Convolvulus* that read, *"U-boat sighted two miles starboard side of convoy. Am altering course to attack"*.

'Splendid, sound action stations!' cried Stirling, his eyes shining with boyish excitement. 'Give the sub's position to the other escorts and say, "follow me and attack at will".'

In the for'd seaman's mess, Able Seaman Patrick Duffy, reaching for his life jacket cried angrily, 'To be sure, I thought it was too bloody good to be true.'

Groans, moans and curses echoed around the mess. The crew had been closed up at action stations on and off for the last four days. Hard tack, soup and thick, corn beef wedges had been their staple diet, and the rum issue had to be taken in-between lulls in the action. Sleep had been almost impossible. Now, for the first time in days, the rum issue was to be taken at the normal time. However, the ear-splitting jangle of the alarm bell was once again ruining the precious ritual.

'I'm sure the fuckin' Jerries do this on purpose,' yelled Able Seaman Darby Allen, pulling his anti-flash hood over his head, 'maybe they've got a spy onboard with a secret radio or summat.'

'Ah, stop complainin' will yer,' bellowed Able Seaman Jumper Cross hurrying towards the ladder. 'If we manage to sink another of the buggers, maybe we'll get an extra tot.'

Sub Lieutenant Harper-Smyth left the bridge where he was sharing the watch with Lieutenant Anderson and made his way to the quarterdeck. His depth charge team were already closed up. Tiny Woods, a tall, stout Able Seaman and four other ratings were busy clearing away the release gear on the depth charges.

On the bridge, PO Yeoman Tate shouted, 'Signal from *Convolvulus,* sir, *"Sub dived, a mile way on port bow".'*

'Steer one one oh, increase revolutions one-third,' Stirling ordered.

On the quarterdeck the ringing of the telephone blared out over the noise of the ship's engines. Harper-Smyth immediately unhooked the receiver from its attachment against the port bulkhead. 'Depth charge party,' he said smartly. After a slight pause, he added, 'Very good, sir,' and replaced the receiver.

Turning to Woods he snapped, 'Set five charges at one hundred feet and five at fifty.'

Stirling gripped the sides of his chair and felt the grating rise and fall as the ship bounded through the water. By this time the "pinging" coming from the tannoy was pronounced and quicker.

*'Fire a pattern of ten, Number One,'* he shouted excitedly, 'the bastard's close to us.'

Straight away Harper-Smyth ordered ten missiles to be rolled off *Sandpiper*'s stern. With the wind whipping against their faces everyone on the upper deck anxiously waited, watched and listened. Seconds later, one after another ten, tumultuous mountains of foamy sea soared in the air.

With an air of finality Manley said, 'Well, sir, that's the last of our depth charges. I hope the others have plenty left.'

By this time *Shearwater, Petrel* and *Curlew* had arrived and launched their depth charges. Once again the sea became seething mountains of white water and once again everyone throughout the ships held his breath. Gun crews licked their lips nervously. Men below in boiler and engine rooms sweated more than usual. In the sick bay Appleby, in his usual flippant manner, shrugged his shoulders and with a weak smile glanced at Coburn and said, 'Much more of this, sir, and it'll curdle the milk in the ice box.'

Their anxiety was allayed by the sound of the "pinging" gradually becoming weak and almost inaudible.

'Sounds as if we've nailed the bastard,' said Appleby grinning like a Cheshire cat. 'If the milk hasn't gone off we can have ourselves a brew.'

Stirling wasn't so convinced. Hunched in his chair he gave Manley a cautious look. 'She's either playing possum or has gone deep,' he muttered grudgingly. 'What do you think, Number One?'

'Let's wait and see,' Manley replied cagily. 'The sod can't stay down forever. She has to come up to recharge her batteries. If she does we'll have to use our guns.'

'Message from *Milton,* sir,' reported Leading Signalman Tansey Lee. '"Six enemy bombers approaching from the west flying towards the convoy, approximately fifteen thousand feet. Am engaging."'

'Signal *Brisbane* to alter convoy twenty degrees north, Number One,' said Stirling scanning the sky. '*Curlew* to remain and continue dropping her depth charges. If the blighter isn't sunk, it'll at least keep her away from the convoy. Now,' he added with a touch of sarcasm, 'full speed ahead and tell Lieutenant Anderson he's about to get a chance to see how good his gunnery lads are.'

Meanwhile *Milton* was cutting through the water almost directly under the path of the enemy planes. Action stations had already been sounded and gun crews closed up. On the Gun Director's platform the gunnery officer peered through his angle sight and called out the elevation angle for his twin sets of 4.5 guns.

'They're peeling off, sir,' cried one of the lookouts straining his eyes through his binoculars. 'Three to the port the rest on our starboard beam.'

'*All guns open fire!*' shouted her captain, Commander Peter William R.N., a tall, dark-haired man with sharp features and keen grey eyes. 'Signal *Sandpiper, "am under attack. Will try to divert them from convoy".*'

A minute later Stirling received William's message. Looking sternly at Manley, he said, 'I wish we could go and help him, but the safety of the convoy is paramount,' with a deep sigh he added solemnly, 'if anyone can stop the bastards, Peter can.'

'And if he doesn't, sir?' Manley asked ruefully.

'Then we'll just have to manage ourselves,' Stirling replied dryly.

Another message from *Milton* arrived. "Three planes hit and crashed. Others have fled. Have sustained severe damage. Four dead. Sinking slowly by the stern. Request assistance."

Stirling received Slater's message with equanimity.

'Good old Peter,' he cried, pounding the sides of his chair. 'Reply, "Well done. Will send *Copeland* to you."' He paused and with a wide grin, looked at Manley and added, 'What price an old World War One destroyer now, eh, Number One?'

This was the last skirmish with the enemy. *Copeland* picked up all of *Milton's* crew before the gallant ship sank. Three days later on 18 November they reached the mouth of the Mersey. After a few farewells and good luck signals, *Convolvulus* and the convoy left for the Clyde. *Copeland* was the first to dock in order to transfer her injured survivors ashore into a fleet of ambulances. Battered and tired, the escort group followed on and by 0800 the following morning all four ships were secured alongside Gladstone Wharf.

Stirling looked across at Manley who had just returned from the fo'c'sle having ensured the ship was tied up alongside the wharf. His weather-beaten face was streaked with sweat and he was slightly out of breath. 'Well, Number One,' he said, his forehead creased with a worrying frown, 'on the balance of things convoy H.G. 84 wasn't particularly successful was it? Five merchantmen sunk, a Hurricane lost, one U-boat destroyed and maybe another one.' He paused, took out a packet of *Players*, gave one to Manley and lit both with a match. He took a deep sullen drag of his cigarette allowing a thin line of smoke to trickle down each nostril then added, 'What do you think?'

'It's not what I think, sir,' Manley replied staring at the haggard features of his captain, 'it's what his nibs the admiral will have to say.'

## CHAPTER TWENTY-SIX

Two hours after *Sandpiper* had docked the pipe that everyone had been eagerly waiting for, echoed around the ship – 'Mail is ready for collection.' Stirling was in his cabin writing his Report of Proceedings of the Group to be submitted to Admiral Noble.

Upon hearing the pipe Stirling sat upright. Even after all the years at sea the thought of receiving a letter from Pamela still excited him. And maybe, he told himself as he lit a cigarette, there might be news of Mark.

In the sick bay, Coburn was sitting at his desk writing up a patient's medical card. He put down his fountain pen and stood up. Since the ship sailed Fiona's possible pregnancy had constantly been on his mind. Surely by now she must know one way or the other. Without speaking to Appleby who was filing a few medical folders away in a drawer, he reached for his cap and quickly left.

By the time he entered the wardroom his mouth was dry with anticipation. He immediately focussed on an assortment of letters resting in a line on a small table under the arms cabinet. Feeling his hand tremble he disturbed them silently praying to see Dorothy's small, neat handwriting on one of them, but there was none. Overcome with disappointment he inclined his head and using both hands leant on the table. He was so positive there would be a letter from Dorothy. The time was a little after 1300. He knew Dorothy wouldn't return to the flat in Gloucester Road before 1800. Telephoning her at work was impossible as she wasn't allowed personal calls, and besides she hadn't told him which department she worked. He decided to wait and call her later on. He hardly heard the comments from a few other officers who had received letters.

'What's the matter, Doc, you look a bit peaky. Are you all right?' Coburn recognised the familiar voice of his captain.

Coburn stood back and straightened up. Taking a deep breath he replied, 'Yes thank you, sir, it's just that I was expecting an important letter and…' as he spoke his voice became almost inaudible.

The pained expression in Coburn's eyes told Stirling something was wrong.

'Are you sure?' Stirling asked thoughtfully. 'You look a bit upset.'

'I… I'm fine sir,' Coburn replied hesitatingly then added, 'it's just that I haven't heard from my fiancée for some time.'

'Isn't that the Wren in London?' asked Stirling.

'Yes, sir,' Coburn replied, his voice filled with emotion. 'She works in the Admiralty.'

'Try not to worry, old boy,' Stirling said, giving Coburn a conciliatory smile, 'I'm sure there's a perfectly good reason for her not writing. It happens to all of us. As you know the mail is very erratic. Why don't you give her a ring, there's a telephone box at the end of the wharf?'

'Thank you, sir,' answered Coburn. 'I intend doing just that.' He paused then hesitatingly added, 'Er… do you have any idea how long the group will be in Liverpool?'

'We'll know for certain after I meet the admiral,' Stirling replied, 'but if there's anything I can do please don't hesitate to come and see me.'

'That's very considerate of you, sir,' Coburn replied, and left.

Making sure he had plenty of change Coburn hurried down the gangway and left the ship. The time was a little after 1830.

'*Blimey!*' exclaimed, duty PO Dusty Miller to QM Able Seaman Patrick Duffy, 'there must be some sort of emergency. The doc didn't even return our salutes.'

'A heavy date more likely,' Duffy sarcastically replied.

Coburn arrived at the telephone booth and took out a handful of coins and placed them on the top of the black box. Feeling a trickle of nervous sweat run down his back, he placed a sixpenny piece in slot B and dialled Fiona's number. A few seconds later, to his consternation, a high-pitched sound met his ears. After what seemed like an eternity, the operator finally answered. 'I'm sorry, sir,' she said, 'that number is unobtainable. The line appears to be down.'

Coburn felt his stomach lurch and his heart rate increase. Why was the telephone line down? Destroyed in the Blitz maybe, or simply a technical fault. Perhaps Fiona had been appointed to another job, or was staying with a friend. But these would not account for her not writing. These thoughts failed to calm his nervous state that was verging on panic. Somehow or other, he told himself as he hurried from the telephone booth, he must find out.

Stirling received three letters, two from Pamela and one from Mark. He placed Pamela's letters to one side and with undue haste ripped open his son's noting it was two weeks old. Because of strict censorship there was very little concrete information Mark could write. However, a smile broke over Stirling's weather-beaten features as he read of Mark's promotion to sub lieutenant. *"Also,"* the letter went on, *"this includes myself undergoing a two-week navigation course in you know where, but I'll be glad to get back to sea again as this place gives me the 'dromedary' hump!"*

Camels again grinned Stirling, staring at the letter; he must still be based in Alexandria.

Pamela's letters were short and dealt with the day-to-day work of her and her colleagues in the WVS. Stirling was quick to notice she failed to mention the long hours handing out welcome mugs of tea and sandwiches to exhausted firemen, policemen and dockyard workers and the dangers from the constant air raids. She also had a letter from Mark, and sounded quite proud of his promotion. *"How well I remember how smart you looked when you were a sub lieutenant,"* and ended by writing, *"I love and worry about you both constantly. God bless you darling."*

In his written report to Admiral Sir Max Horton, who was now Commander-in-Chief Western Approaches, Stirling accepted the blame for his mistakes. (Sir Percy Noble had been sent to Washington on liaison duties.) He stressed how well his sloops had performed and recommended that HMS *Milton*'s captain and crew should be granted some form of recognition for their bravery. Privately he was proud of the way the group had carried out his orders. He ended his report by writing *"As for Sandpiper, it is inspiring to command such a magnificent body of men. Especially my First Lieutenant, Lieutenant Commander Manley, who, one day will make a fine commanding officer."* He ended by saying, *"I adopted an offensive policy in the belief that the best defence is to attack the enemy and sink as many U-boats as I could."*

A week after submitting his report Stirling was summoned to Derby House.

# CHAPTER TWENTY-SEVEN

The buzzer on the admiral's desk was followed by a female voice announcing Stirling's arrival.

'Send him in,' replied the admiral who was engrossed reading a report on the latest convoy losses. Born on Anglesey in North Wales, his closeness to the coast resulted in a love of the sea. Aged fifty-one, Admiral Max Kennedy Horton, DSO, and two bars, was a veteran submariner having served with distinction in the First World War. Prior to taking up his present position he was Commander-in-Chief, Naval Planning.

Stirling entered and noted that the room hadn't changed since his interview with Sir Percy Noble. He removed his cap displaying streaks of grey amongst a mass of dark wiry hair.

'Ah Commander Stirling,' said the admiral, looking up and fixing Stirling with a pair of keen grey eyes. The tall, spare figure with a gaunt, weather-tanned face that stood before him looked very tired. 'Do come in a take a seat and smoke if you want.' His voice, with a slight Welsh inflexion was warm and welcoming. He stood up and they shook hands.

Stirling and the admiral had never met. The man shaking his hand was a medium-sized, highly decorated officer with a round, pale, fleshy face and dark bushy eyebrows.

'Can I offer you some tea, Commander?' said the admiral slowly lowering his heavy-set frame into his chair.

'No thank you, sir,' Stirling replied. 'I had lunch before I came.'

'Right then,' said the admiral, leaning forward. 'I read your report with great interest. As a matter of fact your tactics of leaving the convoy and searching for the enemy coincide with my thinking.'

Stirling's reputation as a fighting captain was by this time well known to him and others. Before leaving for Washington he and Admiral Noble had discussed Stirling's offensive tactics. Admiral Horton smiled inwardly, remembering the look of approval on Noble's face as he said, 'Stirling is inclined to be a little headstrong but he commands great loyalty from the men in the fifteenth escort group. I wish we had more commanding officers like him.'

The admiral's remarks came as a complete surprise to Stirling who was sure he was about to be reprimanded for once again disobeying orders. For a few seconds he sat, staring incredulously at the admiral. The officer speaking to him was someone who was directly responsible to the Prime Minister for the tactical policies adopted by the convoy escorts. Raising his eyebrows in surprise, Stirling, replied, 'If you'll excuse me, sir,' Stirling replied nervously, 'there are those in, er... high places who disagree with my ideas.'

The admiral's face wrinkled into a wry smile. 'I'm well aware of that, Commander,' he said, sitting back in his chair, 'and I can see their point. Leaving a convoy almost unattended as you did can result in losses. However,' he went on placing both hands flat on the desk, 'the job I'm going to give you and your team will enable you to put your theories into practice.'

Stirling sat forward his eyes focussed on the admiral. 'With respect, sir, what may that be?' he asked, trying his best to control his curiosity.

The admiral opened a small wooden box of cigarettes, took one out then slid it across to Stirling. Using a lighter, he leaned forward and lit Stirling's cigarette and then his own. Relaxing back in his chair, the admiral allowed thin lines of smoke trickle from each nostril.

'What do you know about U-boat tankers?' the admiral asked, lifting his chin and bayoneting Stirling with a pair of keen grey eyes.

'U-boat tankers, sir,' Stirling repeated, giving the admiral a searching look. 'When I was in *Osprey* it was rumoured that the Germans might be building some sort of large submarines to act as supply ships to their smaller U-boats,' Stirling paused and took a deep puff of his cigarette, then with a slight frown went on, 'Milk Cows I believe they were called, however,' he added quickly, 'I don't know if any were ever built.'

'Well,' the admiral replied flicking ash into a round brass ashtray, 'recent information from Bletchley informs us that Doenitz has done just that. What I have to tell you is of course, classified information. Is that quite clear?'

'Of course, sir,' Stirling replied with a quick nod. 'I understand perfectly.'

'Because Doenitz now controls the ports along the French coast,' replied the admiral, stubbing his cigarette out, 'he is able to send his U-boats deeper into the Atlantic. As you know there is a vast area of sea some twenty degrees west of Ireland that is out of range of coastal command and many of our escorts.'

'Yes, sir,' Stirling answered dryly, 'that's where the Wolf packs are having a field day. Two hundred and fifty thousand tons of shipping lost in the last two months, I believe.'

'That's correct,' the admiral replied. 'And the U-boats are able to remain at sea longer because they are being replenished by these so called Milk Cows.'

Stirling gave a wry smile and said, 'And that's where the Fifteenth Escort group comes in, isn't it sir?'

'Quite so, Commander,' the admiral flatly replied, 'but it won't be an easy task. Let me explain. We know that two Type XIV U tankers, U 459 and U 460, have been built at Deutsche Werke at Kiel. These are now operating somewhere in the Atlantic.'

'Can't we track them, sir?' Stirling said, stubbing out his cigarette. 'I know Bletchley are able to intercept their wireless signals.'

'It's not that easy,' the admiral answered pensively. 'The tankers carry fuel, which as you know is lighter than water. And,' the admiral paused and gave Stirling a cautious glance, 'their hulls are constructed using a stronger and heavier grade of steel. They are also capable of diving deeper than conventional U-boats making them difficult to sink and harder to detect.' The admiral reached across and depressed a small switch on his intercom. 'Ah, Janet,' he said in a slightly lighter tone of voice, 'please be kind enough to send in a pot of tea and two cups. And, if there's any left, a few of those lovely Digestive biscuits. Thank you so much.'

Stirling realised the request for tea was a polite way of the admiral telling him the meeting still had a long way to go. A few minutes later a tall, attractive Third Officer Wren came in carrying a tray containing a teapot, two cups, saucers a small jug of milk a glass jar of sugar and a plate of biscuits. The admiral gave her a warm smile and moved his leather blotter aside allowing her to place the tray on his desk. She returned his smile then left the room.

'Allow me,' said the admiral as he poured out the tea. 'Help yourself to the sugar,' adding with a grin, 'what there is of it and do have a biscuit.'

'I'll forgo the biscuit, sir,' Stirling said accepting a cup and saucer. After taking a sip he asked, 'What else do we know about these tankers?'

The admiral put his cup and saucer down and opened a brown coloured folder and pushed it towards Stirling. Stirling rested his saucer on the desk and leaned forward. Lying in front of him was an enlarged photograph of an unusually long and big submarine.

'This was taken by coastal command a few weeks ago,' said the admiral. 'As you can see it is much larger than a conventional U-boat. Its displacement on the surface is 1,688 tons compared with a 1,200 of a normal sub, and has a cruising radius of 12,350 miles. They carry 432 tons of oil that could be made available to other U-boats.' The admiral paused, picked up a biscuit, dunked it in his tea and leaning forward managed to put it in his mouth before it fell apart. 'The bulges you can see either side of the hull not only carry extra fuel, but also spare torpedoes and replacement parts, lubricating oil, provisions, but very little armament. Also, they don't have torpedo tubes therefore have no attack capability.'

'How do we know all this, sir?' Stirling asked while examining the photographs.

'Through the French Resistance,' the admiral replied dunking another biscuit. 'Apparently, they managed to pose as workers and sent the information to us by carrier pigeon,' he added wiping a few crumbs from the corner of his mouth.

'Indeed,' Stirling answered suitably impressed. Still studying the photographs, he added, 'they must have taken a terrible risk.'

'They did,' the admiral said, furrowing his brow. 'Two of them were caught by the Gestapo and executed.'

Stirling didn't reply. Instead he finished his tea and lit another of the admiral's cigarettes. He sat back in his chair, took a deep drag then exhaling a steady flow of smoke, went on, 'How are we going to find them, sir?' he asked closing the folder. 'The Atlantic is a vast place?'

'Good question, Commander,' the admiral answered, as he emptied his cup. 'We've learned that the German Naval Command has divided all the seas of the world into a large number of quadrants. I'm happy to say British Intelligence captured one of these maps and have managed to decipher them – more tea?'

'No thank you, sir,' Stirling replied, anxious to hear the reply to his question.

The admiral poured himself another cup of tea and muttering something about the shortage of sugar, stirred his cup and went on. 'The U boat Command would name a certain square to rendezvous with the U-boats giving dates and approximate times.'

'What is the area of these quadrants, sir?'

'Twenty square miles,' replied the admiral. 'If it was dark the tanker would usually fire a recognition rocket hoping the U-boat will see it.'

'Rather hit and miss if you ask me, sir,' said Stirling.

'I agree,' the admiral answered, nodding his head.

'So how are we to find these elusive beggars?' Stirling asked, furtively narrowing his eyes. 'It'll be like looking for a piece of seaweed in the ocean.'

'Quite so,' replied the admiral. 'However spies have told us the tankers have been seen off the coast of Tarrafa, one of northern islands forming the Cape Verde Group. This is where your group will be going. As you are aware these islands belong to Portugal and are surrounded by a five-mile neutral zone. Under no circumstances are you to enter it. Portugal are neutral and we don't wish to offend them.' The admiral stopped talking and poured himself another cup of tea, then continued. 'Doenitz communicates with his U-boats by wireless codes. Bletchley, I'm happy to say, have broken these. We know that the Germans have prepared grid charts of the world's oceans and seas. We also know that in three weeks' time on or around December 16 a tanker, U-459, is due to meet up with a U-boat in quadrant seven marked on the chart you'll be given. The area is close to St Antoa, the most northerly tip of the Cape Verde Islands. Intelligence informs us U-459 always enters the rendezvous area submerged and surfaces for an hour or so before sunset to establish contact with the U-boat. If you're lucky that will be an ideal time to attack her.

'What about coastal command?' replied Stirling, 'surely they can handle it.'

'That can be tricky,' said the admiral. 'As soon as the beggars dive, the RAF can't touch them. Besides the Cape Verde Islands are slightly out of range of their planes.' He stopped talking then, with a wry smile added, 'So you see old boy, it's up to you. If you succeed it may force Doenitz to reduce the time his U-boats can stay at sea. Winston hopes this will lessen the attacks on the convoys.'

'*Churchill*!' exclaimed Stirling, allowing ash to fall from his cigarette onto the floor. 'Is this his idea?'

'It certainly is,' the admiral replied, beaming like a Cheshire cat, 'the whole thing is his brainchild. And by the way,' the admiral went on, 'Bletchley have informed us that the pocket battleship *Graf Spee* has been reported in the South Atlantic, not that you're likely to meet her.'

'I certainly hope not,' Stirling replied giving a short, nervous laugh.

'Good,' said the admiral, laying his hands palm down on his desk, now, tell me, how soon can your escort group sail?'

'*Shearwater, Curlew* and *Redshank* need their boilers cleaned plus routine maintenance of guns,' Stirling answered, stubbing his cigarette out. '*Petrel* has a problem with her condenser and my engineer officer tells me *Sandpiper* could do with an engine overhaul. I'd say,' he mused, 'about ten days.'

'Hmm… I see,' muttered the admiral pensively stroking his chin. 'I would like you and the group to leave Liverpool on Sunday 7 December. That'll give you eight or nine days to reach the area. Try to avoid engaging other U-boats, remember your mission is to sink the tanker. HMS *Plover* a destroyer equipped with 4.5 anti-aircraft guns will accompany you. I must warn you that after you reach the Bay of Biscay you'll have to observe radio silence, so if I hear any news about Mark I'm afraid I won't be able to let you know. You will have to refuel at Gib on the way back. All the details concerning the mission will be in a report I'll send to you by special courier. All right, so far?'

'Yes, sir,' Stirling answered confidently.

'Good,' the admiral replied before finishing his drink. 'Each escort will carry three new Mark VI depth charges. These contain Torpex, a new explosive that's fifty percent stronger than amatol. They're still in the experimental stage but the boffins assure me they are quite safe. *Sandpiper* will carry an extra one to test it to gauge its strength and any adverse reaction. They are painted bright green in order to distinguish them from dark blue Mark VIIs. I'm informed they are so powerful they should breach the steel hulls of the submarine.'

'And if they don't?' Stirling asked, giving the admiral an expectant glance.

The admiral gave a quick non-committal shrug of his shoulders then said calmly, 'Play cat and mouse with the blighter until she's forced up to surface to recharge her batteries, then sink her with gunfire. If you're successful, and I'm confident you will be,' said the admiral, sitting back in his chair, 'break radio silence and simply send "Mission Complete".' He then looked enquiringly at Stirling and asked, 'Any questions?'

'Just one, sir,' Stirling answered, 'I'd like to take the group to sea for two days to practise a few drills before we leave.'

'Of course,' replied the admiral, standing up and offering his hand indicating the meeting was over. 'And good luck to you and your ships.'

They shook hands and Stirling left, excited at the prospect of taking on a new challenge but wondering what the commanding officers of the group would make of it all.

# CHAPTER TWENTY-EIGHT

Immediately Stirling returned to *Sandpiper* he sent for his First Lieutenant. A few minutes later Manley knocked and came into the captain's cabin.

'Come in, Number One,' said Stirling, glancing up from his desk and smiling, 'and have a seat.'

'Thank you, sir,' Manley replied taking off his cap and pulling up a chair. 'You seem cheerful enough. Good meeting with his nibs, I trust?'

Stirling sat back in his chair and told Manley about the meeting with the admiral.

'Don't look so surprised, Number One,' grinned Stirling, 'just think. Before the war the Cape Verde Islands were a popular place for rich tourists. Now you can see them for nothing.'

Manley grinned, noticing the excited glint in the eyes of his captain.

'A damn sight better than being given that barge on the Thames you mentioned, eh, sir?' he replied with a wry smile, 'but it'll be like looking for a needle in a haystack.'

'My sentiments entirely,' Stirling answered dryly, 'however, I intend calling a meeting of the other commanding officers at 1600. Meanwhile, Jock Weir and the Chief ERA will have to work overtime on the engines. Give both parts of the watch four days' leave and also any officer that can be spared. I'm afraid that won't include you and I.'

Surgeon Lieutenant Coburn greeted the news of four days' leave with relief. Since they had sailed he had hardly slept wondering if Fiona was pregnant. But there was still no word from her. He had tried three times to telephone her, but the result was the same: the line was still down.

'Could I possibly leave this evening, sir,' he had asked Stirling, 'it... it's rather important,' he added anxiously.

Remembering the captain's offer of help Coburn had decided to speak to him. Stirling was in his cabin writing a letter to his wife when Coburn knocked and came in. The anxious expression on the doctor's face told him something was bothering him. He was also aware Coburn was usually a quiet, laid-back person who rarely complained or asked favours.

'Yes, I suppose so,' Stirling replied leaning back in his chair. 'I'm sure Appleby can cope for a few days. Is anything wrong?'

'Just a slight problem,' Coburn answered nervously, 'nothing I can't sort out.'

'Good,' Stirling replied firmly. 'Inform the First Lieutenant then tell Able Seaman Jackson to drive you to the station in the ship's tilly.'

'Thank you, sir,' Coburn quietly replied and left the cabin.

Coburn left the ship at 1800. Dark clouds threatened rain and a cold northerly wind blew downriver. Wearing a Burberry over his uniform and carrying a canvas grip containing a clean shirt, underwear and shaving kit, Coburn arrived at Lime Street in time to board the 1845 train to London. As the train left the station it began to rain. Very soon the windows fogged up and the first-class compartment he shared with three army officers became warm and muggy. He was in no mood for idle chitchat and simply gave his companions a brief nod, stowed his grip in the rack then settled into a corner space close to a window. Two officers became engrossed in their newspapers while the other fell asleep. Coburn stared, tight lipped, into the gloom of the night and for the umpteenth time, racked his brain wondering why he hadn't heard from Fiona. Once again his mind went into overdrive imagining her lying in a hospital bed sick or even dying. With a tired sigh he leant back listening to the steady rumble of the train and feeling the occasional jolt of the compartment. His worries slowly receded as the somnolent atmosphere overcame him. By the time the train arrived in Crewe he was sound asleep.

Coburn woke up feeling someone shaking his arm.

'Euston, old boy,' said a voice. 'Better wake up and get your things.'

Coburn looked up and saw the young face of an army lieutenant grinning down at him.

'Er... thank you,' mumbled Coburn, blinking his eyes and yawning. 'I must have dropped off.'

'I'll say so,' laughed the lieutenant, opening the compartment door, 'you've been snoring almost continually for the last four hours.'

The time was just after midnight. He took down his grip from the rack and stepped onto the platform. As he made his way through the crowd towards the exit he was met by a cold wind attacking his face. He quickly left the station and hailed a taxi.

'Home for a spot of leave, guv'nor,' said the driver as Coburn climbed in the taxi.

'Yes, you could say that,' Coburn replied, feeling his heartbeat increase. 'Gloucester Road, please.'

The drive across London took over fifteen minutes. Darkness had fallen and the blackout was in force. The time was shortly after 0100. High above a pale moon flitted between dark clouds. Pedestrians bent against the cold November wind hurried about like automatons. Cars with their lights dimmed and buses with darkened interiors moved slowly along the roads. The bases of trees, lampposts, postboxes and the edges of pavements were painted white and were barely visible in the gloom. Driving down Cromwell Road Coburn noticed the ruins of several shops and houses. An ironic smile spread over Coburn's face as he saw a sign over a shop door, which, despite having most of its windows smashed, proclaimed defiantly, "Still Open For Business".

The taxi driver was about to turn right into Gloucester Road but was waved down by a policeman wearing white gloves. Coburn looked out of the window and to his horror saw a red wooden barrier blocking off the entrance to the road. He leapt out of the taxi and stared dumbfounded at the smouldering remains of a row of houses, one of which was where Fiona lived. The acrid smell of wood burning and the sharp odour of dust hung in the night air. Bricks, broken tables and chairs were scattered everywhere. Among a mass of rubble a child's wooden rocking horse told its own sad story. Whole front sections of houses lay open. Floors, fire grates and furniture lay suspended by gravity. Strips of wallpaper flapped eerily from walls along with lopsided framed pictures. ARP men and workers in shirtsleeves searching in the dark moved heavy pieces of masonry listening and searching, hoping to hear or find survivors.

'Sorry, mate,' Coburn heard the policeman say, 'the road was bombed in a raid five nights ago and there's an unexploded bomb in one of the houses.'

'But my fiancée lives in one of those houses,' Coburn cried desperately moving towards the barrier. 'How many were…' His voice trailed away as he saw a team of St John's men carrying a stretcher with someone covered by a blanket into an ambulance.

'It were a direct hit,' said the policemen, his face covered in black dust. 'All of them in the 'ouses must 'ave been killed outright. Sorry, sir,' he added compassionately.

For a few seconds Coburn stood still, unable to take in the enormity of the devastation strewn before his eyes.

His heart sank as he imagined Fiona lying unconscious and trapped beneath some masonry or bleeding to death covered by a mass of masonry. 'She must be somewhere,' he cried, wide-eyed and panic-stricken. 'I… I must find her!'

'I'm sorry, sir,' said the policeman, raising his arm to stop Coburn moving towards the barrier. 'It's far too dangerous and I must ask you and the driver to move away. If that bomb goes off we might all be killed.'

'Come on, matey,' said the driver, 'best if I take you and get a cuppa tea or summat.'

Too dazed to resist Coburn felt the driver's arm on his shoulder leading him towards the taxi.

Coburn gave a painful glance at men sorting through the wreckage and rubble of the houses then in a hoarse whisper, muttered, 'Just take me to Euston.'

The driver took Coburn's grip and helped him into the taxi. Looking quickly over his shoulder he noticed the ashen expression on Coburn's face. Realising his passenger was still in shock, he said, 'Are you sure yer all right, guv'nor? A drop of whisky might do you the world of good.'

Coburn didn't reply. Instead he slowly shook his heads and slumped back in his seat. The thought that Fiona was probably lying on a cold slab in a mortuary, her beautiful face, bloodstained and covered in dust made him feel physically sick. He clenched his fists and bit his lip in despair. Why God! Why? He muttered to himself. And as the taxi moved away he felt hot tears well up in his eyes.

They arrived at Euston shortly before midnight.

'How much do I owe you?' Coburn asked wearily after he climbed from the taxi.

'Forget it, guv'nor,' the taxi driver replied noticing a bit of colour had returned to Coburn's face. 'How far are you going?'

Ignoring the need for national security, Coburn simply replied, 'Liverpool.'

From the inside pocket of his jacket the driver took out a small, silver hip flask. 'Here,' he said, handing it to Coburn. 'It aint full but it'll keep you warm. I was in your lot in the last war and it's a five-hour journey to the "Pool".'

'No, no,' mumbled Coburn, raising a hand. 'It's very kind of you but...'

'Go on, take it,' the driver insisted, thrusting the flask at Coburn. 'I've got another one handy. And besides there's nowt open at this time of night.'

Coburn took a deep sigh. 'Thank you again,' he said solemnly. He accepted the flask and slipped it in his Burberry pocket. He picked up his grip, gave a grateful nod to the driver and went inside the station.

The train left Euston at 0200 and arrived in Lime Street five hours later. Coburn shared a first class compartment with an Army priest and his wife. At first Coburn found sleep impossible. Every time he closed his eyes he saw Fiona's lovely violet eyes staring at him. It was then he remembered the taxi driver's hip flask. The compartment lights were dimmed and his two companions were asleep. He sneaked his hand into his pocket and took it out. Against the rocking of the train he managed to unscrew the top and take a deep gulp. The whisky did the trick and he soon fell into a deep, dreamless sleep. When he woke up the compartment was empty and the train was slowly shunting into Lime Street Station. The first thing that he thought about when he opened his eyes was Fiona. The realisation that she was gone gave him a sickly sinking feeling in the pit of his stomach. He promptly reached inside his pocket for the flask and finished the remains of the whisky.

The time was 0715. Bellowing clouds of steamy vapour, the train slowly ground to a noisy halt. The compartment door opened allowing passengers to leave. Among the few civilians were many members of the three services. All carried gas masks and steel helmets, others heaving kitbags and cases.

Outside the station a bitterly cold westerly wind made Coburn's eyes water. Suddenly the greyness of the day looked greyer and the vast umbrella of black cumulonimbus clouds seemed unusually bleaker. With a jaded sigh Coburn pulled his collar up around his neck and despite the early hour managed to find a taxi. Fifteen minutes later the taxi arrived at the large double wrought iron gates of Gladstone Dock. Coburn showed his pay book to a policeman and they drove to the wharf where *Sandpiper,* along with the other ships of the group, was moored. As the taxi approached the wharf Coburn could hear the high-pitched shrill of the bosun's pipes coming from the rest of the ships. The time was just after 0800 and morning "Colours" had just finished.

Coburn paid the driver, looked up, hesitated momentarily then clutching his holdall, walked slowly towards the gangway.

'Back early, Doc.' Stirling, who with OOW Sub Lieutenant Wier, had watched Coburn come onboard. Coburn reached the brow, straightened up and saluted the flag. In doing so Stirling immediately noticed Coburn's unshaven, drawn features and immediately felt uneasy. 'Is everything all right?' he asked.

Coburn frowned and shook his head. 'Not really, sir,' was his curt reply before turning away and walking towards the after deckhouse.

'That's odd, sir,' remarked Weir glancing uneasily at Stirling, 'the Doc wasn't due back for another two days, I hope nothing's wrong.'

The same thought struck Stirling as he watched Coburn disappear down a hatchway to his cabin.

Coburn opened the cabin door, switched on the light, flung his holdall on the deck then sat down at his small desk. He then placed his head in his hands and tried not to think of Fiona. But it was impossible. Her face kept on appearing before his eyes. A knock at his door brought him temporary relief. He looked up and saw the tall figure of Stirling outlined against the dimness of the passageway. In his left hand he held two letters.

'Sorry to disturb you, Doc,' he said apologetically, 'but a letter arrived for you today. I thought you'd like it.' Stirling knew it was a weak excuse but the doctor's uncharacteristic behaviour worried him. He moved forward and placed the letter on Coburn's desk.

Coburn glanced up but didn't speak. With a tired sigh he looked down at the letter expecting to see another bill from Gieves. Suddenly, he felt his stomach contract. The small neat handwriting belonged to Fiona. Dear God, he thought as he picked the letter up, she must have written it before... It was then he noticed the postmark dated 27 November, one day after her flat was bombed. In a flash he stood up and ripped the letter open. With his heart beating a cadence in his chest he read the first page.

*"My Darling,*

*A bit of bad news – I've been bombed out! While I was on night duty the houses on one side of the road were flattened. It was dreadful."*

Coburn paused, finished the first page and with a look of shear relief grabbed Stirling's arm and cried, '*She's alive, I tell you, she's alive!*'

Coburn's reaction caught Stirling unawares. He stepped back and with Coburn still holding his arm said, 'What do you mean, old boy. What the devil's happened?'

As best he could Coburn explained the events of the past twenty-four hours.

'I really did think she had been killed,' Coburn said shaking his head.

'And where is she now?' Stirling asked.

Coburn let go of Stirling's arm and, slightly out of breath, said, 'Just a second, sir, let me read the rest of the letter.' Coburn nervously licked his lips, sat down and read the second page.

*"The four elderly people living above me and many neighbours were all killed. I couldn't tell you as you were at sea. I am now staying with a girlfriend at Balham. Luckily, we're almost the same size so I can borrow her things. Her phone number is Balham 2369. I am glad to say that the tests came through and I'm not pregnant. The doctor told me the problem was due to the strain of work etc, so you won't be a father after all. Maybe one day when this damn war is over. Must close now and catch the post.*

*All my deepest love*
*Yours forever,*
*Fiona."*

'My God, sir, I can't tell you how relieved I am,' Coburn said, looking at Stirling, his face wreathed in smiles. 'She's staying with a colleague from work and has given me her phone number.'

'Good,' Stirling replied, placing a comforting hand Coburn's shoulder. 'You must ring her as soon as possible then take a few more days' leave and go and see her.'

'Thank you, sir,' Coburn replied, smiling happily, 'but not until I've had something to eat. I'm absolutely famished.'

On his way to the wardroom the daylight seemed brighter and even the anaemic sun racing across the overcast November sky felt warm.

# CHAPTER TWENTY-NINE

'Good afternoon gentlemen, thank you for coming so promptly,' said Stirling who's tall, imposing presence dominated the wardroom. Manley sat discretely behind him, sitting awkwardly on the edge of table.

With both hands thrust businesslike into his jacket pocket Stirling scanned the faces of the five officers seated before him. 'I've met most of you before,' he added with a warm smile, 'and may I say how pleased I am to see you again.' Stirling suddenly fixed his penetrating brown eyes on a broad-shouldered, dark-haired lieutenant commander. 'I don't believe we've met,' he said, moving forward and proffering his hand, 'I believe you're Lieutenant Commander Richard Valentine, *Plover*'s captain.'

'A pleasure to meet you, sir,' replied the officer standing up. He spoke with a distinct north-country accent and as they shook hands his dark blue eyes wrinkled into a suspicious grin. 'Everything's very hush-hush, so I believe?'

'That's right,' Stirling replied noticing the puzzled expression on the faces of the other officers, 'but rest assured,' he added with a wry smile, 'all will be revealed in due course.'

Except for the five officers sat facing him, *Sandpiper*'s wardroom was empty. The time was 1000 on 30 November. At 1530 Stirling had ordered PO Steward Slinger Wood to ensure there was an urn of tea water along with cups, saucers, milk, sugar and biscuits on a nearby table. He then dismissed the PO with a warning to make sure nobody was loitering outside listening to what was going on.

'As if we'd do a thing like that, sir,' Wood sarcastically replied and left the room. However, Stirling couldn't know Junior Seaman Nipper Clark was on his hands and knees busily scrubbing the wardroom flat.

'Please smoke if you want to and help yourselves to tea,' Stirling said smiling broadly. Suddenly, the atmosphere from being slightly tense and uncomfortable became relaxed.

None of the officers accepted his offer of tea but most lit cigarettes. Stirling followed suit. In a matter of minutes a cloud of pale blue smoke hovered above their heads, curling slowly up to the deck head.

'Right, gentlemen,' said Stirling, taking a deep drag of his cigarette, 'let's get down to business.' Suddenly, he had a captivated audience.

'On Sunday 7 December the group, in company with *Plover,* are to sail for the South Atlantic.' Stirling paused momentarily noticing the surprised expression on their faces. He gave a quick smile then in a calm, serious voice, continued. 'I thought this might come as a shock to you, no doubt you expected another trip to Gib.'

'Well at least it's better than the Russian run,' Commander David Graham, RNR, *Shearwater'*s six-foot plus captain, remarked with a wide grin.

'Indeed,' Stirling said. 'Our destination is the Cape Verde Island. As some of you may know this is a group of ten small islands in the Atlantic roughly five hundred miles off the west coast of Africa. The capital of the group is Tarrafa, in the northern section. They belong to Portugal and are therefore neutral. The reason we are going there is this.' For the next twenty minutes

Stirling gave them the details of the mission and the new depth charges, then paused to answer questions.

*Curlew*'s captain, Lieutenant Commander Gifford, a tall, fair-haired RNVR officer raised a hand. 'How powerful do you think these new depth charges are, sir?' he asked staring at Stirling with deep-set blue eyes.

'I'm not sure, Jeremy,' Stirling replied pensively. 'But they are more than double the strength of conventional ones. I intend to test one after we clear the Bay of Biscay.'

'Sounds a bit dodgy to me, sir,' said Lieutenant Commander Parker-Grace, RN, the small, stocky dark-haired officer commanding *Redshank*. 'I take it we'll still be carrying our usual twelve conventional depth charges, just in case the others don't do the trick?'

'Indeed we shall,' Stirling replied while stubbing his cigarette out in an ashtray, 'and thank you Henry, for mentioning it.'

Lieutenant Commander Peter Parsons, RNR, the tall captain of *Petrel* whose ginger hair was tinged with grey, then asked, 'Will we have any air support, sir?'

Stirling shook his head. 'I'm afraid not, old boy,' he replied, 'the islands are out of range of the RAF.'

'You mentioned avoiding U-boats, sir,' said Lieutenant Commander Valentine. '*Plover* carries torpedoes. If we meet any U-boats on the surface, maybe we could use them.'

'Indeed so,' Stirling replied with a slight smile, 'but you'd have to catch the blighters first. As you know they move pretty fast on the surface.'

'How will each ship keep in contact, sir,' asked Lieutenant Commander Henry Jarvis, RNVR, *Sparrow*'s captain, a tall man with light brown, well-groomed hair.

'By Aldis lamp or ship-to-ship telephone,' Stirling answered curtly.

'How long will we be at sea tomorrow undergoing exercises, sir?' enquired Lieutenant Commander Graham, staring keenly at Stirling. 'Many of the ships' companies live in Liverpool.'

'As long as I think fit,' Stirling flatly replied. 'Now, gentlemen, all this talking has made me thirsty. I therefore suggest a few Horse's Necks are in order.'

Once again the lower deck "tom-toms" echoed around the ship. Junior Seaman Nipper Clark made sure of that.

'Cape Verde Islands, eh?' remarked Able Seaman Jackson, a cigarette dangling from his mouth. The time was 1830 and as cook of the mess he was in the process of clearing up after supper. 'I wonder if we'll get a run ashore,' he pondered, allowing cigarette ash to fall into one of the aluminium trays that had once contained Manchester Tart. (Jam topped up with custard.)

'Don't be a prick all your life,' interrupted Leading Seaman Wacker Payne. 'You heard what Nipper said. We're going there to sink some bloody big U-boat with depth charges that's never been used before.'

'At least we'll all get bronzy-bronzy for when we come back,' said Able Seaman Darby Allen, mopping his plate with a piece of bread. 'Maybe it'll make me look like Clark Gable.'

'In your dreams, you ugly bugger,' grunted Able Seaman Bungy Williams. 'Anyways, if it gets too hot maybe the Jimmy will order hands to bathe.'

'In that case,' grinned Able Seaman Soapy Waters, 'you can be the first over the side. There's bloody sharks in the South Atlantic.'

The only note of caution was echoed in the senior-rates' mess.

'I don't like the idea of carting a dozen or so untested depth charges half way across the ocean,' remarked the CPO Sammy Taylor, 'it makes me feel uncomfortable, so it does.'

'You worry too much, yer silly old bugger,' CGI Dusty Miller curtly replied.

'Let's wait and see,' replied Sammy, then raising his voice, added, 'and less of the "old".'

In the sick bay SBA Brum Appleby greeted the news with alacrity.

'Just think,' he said grinning at Coburn who was sitting at his desk writing up a medical card. 'Swaying palm trees and dancing girls in grass skirts. Just a holiday eh, sir?'

'I doubt it,' Coburn, answered cautiously, 'I have a feeling this will anything but a holiday.'

At 0800 the next morning the six warships slipped their moorings and sailed, line ahead, down the Mersey. *Sandpiper* led the way with *Plover* bringing up the rear. A strong north-westerly wind churned up the murky waters and the sun, a pale yellow orb, was half hidden behind a layer of dark clouds. No sooner had the small armada cleared the mouth of the river than they were hit by the surging swell of the Irish Sea.

On *Sandpiper*'s bridge Stirling sat in his chair watching the smoke from his cigarette quickly dissipate in the wind.

'Tell Harper-Smyth to make sure those new depth charges are secure in their racks,' Stirling said, glancing warily at Manley. 'If any break loose, there's no telling what may happen.'

'Very good, sir,' Manley replied, then added, 'naturally they're not primed so they're quite safe.'

'I'm aware of that, Number One,' Stirling replied curtly. 'But do it all the same.'

'Aye, aye, sir,' replied Manley, who then left the bridge, returning five minutes later.

'All secured, sir,' said Manley, taken aback by Stirling's caustic order. 'I expect the rest of the squadron have taken the same precautions.'

'Hmm...' muttered Stirling. 'Yeoman,' he shouted above the wind, 'signal all sloops, say, "Ensure all depth charges are secure".' Glancing furtively at Manley, he added, 'Better to be safe than sorry.'

Half an hour later, Stirling grinned at Manley and snapped, 'Increase revolutions two-thirds. Port ten. Signal this to the escorts, add, *Plover* to remain in the rear.'

From the wheelhouse voice-pipe came the sharp, Scouse accent of PO Coxswain Pony Moore. 'Port ten then, ten 'o port wheel on, sir.'

'Midships,' ordered Striling.

'Midships... Wheel's amidships, sir.'

'Steady.'

'Steady... course south, eighty west, sir.'

'Very good, coxswain.'

Fighting against the unrelenting force of the sea *Sandpiper* heeled to port. Twisting in his chair Stirling watched as the other four ships followed suit. In a matter of minutes angry bow waves were curling over the bows of the other four ships as they turned to form a straggly line abreast.

A satisfied smile played around Stirling lips. 'Not bad, Number One,' he said, peering through his binoculars, 'considering the time we've been in harbour.' Stirling waited about twenty seconds then said, 'Starboard ten. Steer north, eighty-five west. That'll keep the rest of them on their toes.'

One by one the four ships, bucking like wild-west horses, slowly turned right allowing the howling wind and rolling waves to hit them bow-on.

'Reduce revolutions, one-third, slow ahead,' said Manley, cupping his hands in an effort to light a cigarette. 'Signal *Redshank* and *Petrel,* "Turn to port. Leave the group and sail for two miles and drop a depth charge and remain there until recalled".'

'But, sir is this wise?' cautioned Manley, 'we'll be moving perilously slow.'

'I know that, Number One,' Stirling grunted angrily. 'Just do as I ordered.'

'Of course, sir,' Manley replied, feeling his face redden.

'Do you remember the creeping barrage I mentioned at the meeting with the commanding officers?' Stirling asked, gripping the sides of his chair.

'Yes, sir,' Manley hastily replied. 'They seemed quite surprised by it.'

'Well,' said Stirling, raising his voice slightly, 'now's the time to try it out. So let's see how they shape up.'

Using his binoculars Stirling watched as *Redshank* and *Petrel* left the group and hauled to port and almost vanished under the high rolling waves. Ten minutes later the muffled sound of depth charges exploding brought a sly smile to Stirling's face.

'Signal *Redshank* and *Petrel* to rejoin us, Yeoman,' Stirling shouted, satisfied the first part of his tactical plan had been carried out successfully. 'And add, "Well done".'

Shortly afterward the two sloops took up their previous stations. For the next half an hour the remaining five sloops struggled against the high wind and sea to keep in line abreast. Ugly dark green waves splashed high over the bows as each vessel fought against the turbulent sea. In a matter of minutes the duffle coats of those on the bridges became heavy with seawater. The black oilskins of the lookout and those closed up on open gun platforms glistened like coal, while in the mess decks and engine and boiler rooms men held on to anything at hand.

'What the fuck's the old man tryin' to do,' shouted a stoker to his oppo, 'much more of this and we'll bloody well capsize.'

The reply was lost in the booming sound as another wave bounced against the outer bulkhead.

'Signal, "All depth charge crews set new charges at 300 feet",' Stirling shouted above the howling wind.

Using his Aldis lamp, PO Yeoman Tate flashed the signal to the other ships.

Shortly afterwards Sub Lieutenant Harper-Smyth reported all depth charges primed and ready.

'Three minutes, very good, Sub,' Stirling barked down the voice-pipe. 'I only hope the rest of the ships are as efficient.'

The group remained at sea for the next two days practising various drills and ensuring any defects were repaired. At 0800 on Friday 4 December, with *Sandpiper* in the van, the ships returned to Gladstone Wharf. Stirling moved to *Sandpiper*'s port wing and watched as the dockyard workers waited to receive the heavy lines.

'Stop engines,' Stirling ordered as the ship bounced slightly against the quayside.

He was about to turn away when he saw a black staff car arrive a few yards away from where the ship was about to berth.

'Stone the crows, sir,' remarked Ape who was OOW. 'Looks like a bloody reception committee.'

Stirling was about to reply when a tall, three-badge petty officer got out and walked around and helped Pamela, his wife, out of the car. She wore a dark ankle-length coat with the collar turned up and a headscarf. A handbag and gas mask valise hung loosely over her left shoulder. She immediately looked up and upon seeing Stirling, gave a quick wave.

For a few seconds Stirling was too surprised to move. What on earth is she doing here, he asked himself. In her last letter she never mentioned coming to see him, so why the sudden visit? It was only when she didn't smile when he returned her wave that he sensed something was wrong.

'The gangway is being put out, sir,' said Ape with a jovial smile. 'You'd better get down there and meet her before she changes her mind and leaves.'

Without replying Stirling left the bridge and made his way aft. He reached the quarterdeck in time to see Petty Officer Spud Murphy help his wife step down from the top of the gangway onto the deck.

As soon as Stirling saw her face he knew she had been crying. She looked pale and drawn and her eyes looked slightly bloodshot.

Aware that many of the crew were watching them, he merely took her elbow, kissed her demurely on the cheek and said, 'Pamela, dear, what a lovely surprise. Why didn't you tell me you were…'

'Oh, Robert,' she murmured, grasping his arm, 'let's go to your cabin. There's something I must tell you.'

Pamela's words sent a stab of apprehension running though him. Keeping hold of her arm he escorted her to an open hatchway leading into the citadel. Before entering, he stopped and looked down at her tear-filled eyes and said, 'It's Mark, isn't it?'

'Yes, darling,' she sobbed, burying her head in chest. 'He's been reported missing.'

# CHAPTER THIRTY

On their way along through the citadel several ratings stood aside allowing Stirling and Pamela to pass. Keeping her head slightly bowed Pamela did her best to avoid their well-meaning smiles and glances.

Watching the couple disappeared up the ladder onto the wardroom flat, a rating turned to his oppo and said, 'I say, Nobby, the old man's missus looked as if they'd add a tiff or summat.'

Nobby grinned and casually shrugged his shoulders. 'Wrong time of the month, I expect' he replied sarcastically, 'women get like that y'know.'

As soon as Stirling closed the cabin door they held each other in a desperate embrace.

'How did you find out, darling?' Stirling managed to ask, looking down at Pamela's tear-stained eyes.

'Admiral Horton telephoned me personally and provided the car,' she replied, her words coming in fits and starts. 'I asked him not to send you the news as I wanted to speak to you personally,' she said, opening her handbag and handing him a telegram.

This was the moment, Stirling knew, all parents and wives prayed would never happen. Feeling his heart beating a cadence in his chest, he opened the telegram. Its contents were succinct, cold and impersonal. His eyes burned as he read, *"His Majesty's government regrets to announce that your son, Lieutenant Mark Stirling, has been reported missing. Further information will follow when more is known. Signed J. Barry, First Sea Lord."*

Suddenly Stirling felt his heart lift slightly. 'But darling,' cried Stirling, looking at Pamela's pale face, still surrounded by her headscarf. 'It just says he is missing. It doesn't say he… he's been…' he hesitated then in a slightly positive tone, added, 'so you see there's still hope.'

'That's what the admiral said,' Pamela replied. 'Do you *really* think he might be alive,' she added pleadingly, 'or are you just…'

'No, darling,' Stirling replied, 'for all we know he could be wallowing in some dinghy somewhere in the Med.'

'Oh, Robert,' Pamela replied, putting her arms around his waist and pulling him close, 'I do hope you're right.'

At that moment they heard someone give a cough. Stirling turned and saw the rangy, pasty-face-figure of Steward Potts.

'Sorry to interrupt, sir,' he muttered, feeling embarrassed at interrupting what was obviously a very private and personal conversation, 'but can I get you and madam coffee or anything, sir?'

'Er… yes, thank you, Potts,' Stirling replied. Taken aback by the sudden appearance of his steward he gave a nervous cough and moved slightly away from Pamela. 'I know it's only nine thirty, dear,' Stirling said, glancing gingerly at the cabin clock, 'but I think we could both do with a large pink gin.'

'Yes, I agree,' Pamela answered, removing her headscarf and sitting down in an armchair. Stirling took out a silver case and gave her a cigarette, removed one himself and lit them both.

'The admiral has booked us a room at the Adelphi,' she said, taking a deep puff and exhaling a long stream of smoke. 'I've left my overnight suitcase there.'

Stirling sat down and placed a comforting hand over hers. 'That was very considerate of him, but we sail on the seventh, dear,' he said sombrely. 'I can only stay with you tonight as I'll be required onboard.'

'And I'm on duty tomorrow night,' Pamela whispered. 'I'm in charge of the tea wagon. I expect we'll be sent to the East Docks again.'

Potts arrived and placed the two drinks on a table in front of them.

'Thank you,' said Pamela giving Potts a weak smile. She took a deep sip then with a sigh, sank back in the chair. 'I think you should send the car away, don't you, darling?'

Stirling picked up his drink and downed it in one swift gulp. 'Yes, you're right,' Stirling replied. He looked up at Potts, who was standing nearby and said, 'Go and ask the QM to tell the driver of the car waiting on the wharf to leave and return at sixteen hundred.'

The news about Mark spread around the ship like wildfire. A small warship is like a family. Living in such close proximity with one another breeds a deep bond of comradeship. Not only does each man rely on each other, they share one another's problems. Many of the crew had relatives in the services. Some of the older ones had sons and daughters in uniform. Therefore each felt a mixture of concern and sympathy for their captain and his wife.

'Reported missing, eh,' Manley remarked to Ape, taking a sip of tea. It was "stand easy" and they and a few other officers were in the wardroom. 'I only hope he learns more before we sail.'

'Too bloody true, mate,' Ape answered, nodding in agreement. 'As if he hasn't enough on his plate running the ship.'

'Aye, yer right there,' interrupted Jock Weir, 'especially as we'll be out of radio contact after we reach the Bay. He won't know if his boy's alive or not until we return to Liverpool.'

Shortly after 1030, the telephone on Stirling's desk rang. Pamela was lying down on his cot, exhausted after a tiring overnight journey from London. However, she couldn't sleep. Every time she closed her eyes she thought about Mark and prayed he was safe. In less than forty-eight hours her husband would be going to sea and God only knew when he would be back. She heard the ringing of the telephone and hoped it might be news of Mark. But as she listened her hopes were dashed.

'Thank you, sir,' she overheard Stirling say, adding, 'it's very kind of you to ring. I'll pass on your good wishes to her. All we can do now is hope and pray. Goodbye, sir,' then came a sharp "click" as he put the receiver down.

Stirling turned and saw Pamela's pale, anxious face staring at him.

'That was Admiral Horton, darling,' he said wearily then with a sigh added, 'I'm sorry, there's no news. A car will be at the Adelphi at eight in the morning to take you to the station. Your train leaves at eight thirty.' He stood up and walked to the side of his cot then bent down and kissed her softly on the forehead. 'Now I must leave you,' he said tenderly, 'do try and get some rest. I'll tell Potts you're not to be disturbed.'

'Please, darling,' she sighed, 'don't worry about me, I'll be all right but I feel so tired,' she added almost incoherently and closed her eyes.

For a few seconds Stirling stood and looked lovingly down at his wife's face. He gently took her hand and felt her give it a tight squeeze. He then turned and quietly closed the door as he left. He saw Steward Potts standing outside the wardroom.

'Mrs Stirling is not to be disturbed, understand?' he said, adjusting his cap.

'Yes, sir,' Potts quietly replied, 'and sir…' he added, about to say how sorry he was to hear about his son, but quickly changed his mind.

Making his way along the main passageway Stirling passed several ratings busy polishing the bright work and mopping the deck. Normally, the talk between them was loud and raucous. Now it was muted. One or two ratings shot him concerned glances while others quickly stood aside allowing him to pass. It was the same when he reached the quarterdeck. Manley was talking to OOD Lieutenant Anderson, Ape and Engineer Sub Lieutenant Weir. All four were smiling as if sharing a joke. Upon seeing Stirling approach their demeanour changed. They stopped talking and trying their best to disguise their concern, looked at him.

'Good morning, gentlemen,' Stirling said, returning their salutes and glancing casually around, 'any problems?'

'No, sir, 'Manley replied. 'Terribly sorry to hear about your son,' he added in a sympathetic tone, 'and I'm sure that goes for all the officers and men.'

'Thank you, Number One,' said Stirling, 'that's very kind of you.' Turning to Weir, he asked, 'How did your engines bear up, Jock?' In retrospect it was an unnecessary question, as he would have been informed earlier if the problem with the engine hadn't been solved, but it seemed to break the tension of the moment.

'No problems, sir,' replied Weir, 'they bore up well, I'm glad to say.'

'Good,' Stirling answered flatly. Looking at Ape he added, 'I take it you have received the charts for the South Atlantic?'

'Yes, sir,' Ape replied forcing a smile. 'All ready to go.'

'Fine,' said Stirling. 'Mrs Stirling and myself will be leaving the ship at sixteen hundred,' he said, addressing Manley.

'Very good, sir,' Manley answered. 'Leave to the first and second parts of starboard and first part of port watch?'

'And to those who live locally,' Stirling replied.

'Yes,' said Stirling. 'I'll be in my cabin if required.' He turned and walked along the port side of the ship and up a steel ladder that led into the wardroom flat.

As ordered, Steward Potts was keeping vigil outside his cabin. Stirling opened the door and entered. Pamela was still on his cot and appeared to be sleeping.

In an effort to take his mind off Mark, Stirling wrote up the ship's log, then buried himself in a myriad of reports, signals and request chits. At noon a gentle tap came at the door and Potts entered.

'Do you and Mrs Stirling want lunch, sir,' he whispered, glancing enquiringly at Pamela, still curled up on Stirling's cot then at him.

'Just a few sandwiches and coffee would be appreciated, thank you, Potts,' he replied, 'and I'd like a pot of coffee now, please.'

'Right away, sir,' said Potts and tiptoed into the galley. Five minutes later he appeared holding a silver tray, a matching pot and two cups and saucers. After laying them down on a nearby table, he turned and quietly left.

For the next hour Stirling continued to wade through the paper work. The pipe, 'Up Spirits, cooks to the galley,' made him realise it was almost midday. He turned around and saw his wife sitting up stretching her arms and yawning.

'What time is it, dear,' she said, glancing at her wrist. 'My watch seems a bit slow.'

'Near twelve, darling,' Stirling answered, adding tenderly, 'I see you managed to get some sleep. Coffee?'

'Oh yes please,' she said, levering herself off the cot. Running a hand through her short dark hair, she added, 'I must look a sight. I think I'd better use your bathroom first.'

'Through there, dear,' Stirling replied, nodding towards an oak door next to the galley.

Pamela eased herself onto the deck and gathering her handbag, disappeared into the bathroom. Fifteen minutes later she emerged, refreshed with her hair well groomed; but her make-up failed to disguise the dark circles under her red-rimmed eyes.

'Ah, coffee,' she sighed, sitting down in an armchair and accepting a cup and saucer from Stirling. 'Just what I need, and sandwiches too.'

'At that moment a gentle knock came at the door.

'Yes,' grunted Stirling, taking a sip of coffee.

The door opened and in came Manley.

'Sorry to disturb you, sir,' he said feeling awkward at interrupting what he knew was a delicate meeting. Removing his cap he added, 'Just thought I'd remind you that you have request men at thirteen hundred.'

'Ahem, of course,' Stirling replied, doing his best to disguise the fact that he had forgotten, 'anything untoward?'

'Not really, sir,' Manley replied, 'just two ratings to be promoted to leading seamen.'

'Very good, sir,' Manley said, then smiling weakly at Pamela he added, 'good afternoon Mrs Stirling, I'm sorry to hear about…'

'Yes, yes,' Stirling quickly interrupted, 'thank you, Number One, I'll be up shortly.'

With a slow shake of her head Pamela looked forlornly at Stirling. 'News certainly travels fast, doesn't it darling?'

'Yes it does,' he replied, pursing his lips. 'But they're a damn good lot and I'm proud of them.'

# CHAPTER THIRTY-ONE

During the next two hours Stirling visited the captains of the five other ships charting the course the flotilla would take when they sailed in two days. After every meeting he shook their hand and said, 'Good luck and remember, the area we are making for is some twenty miles north of Mindello.'

At 1530 he returned to his cabin. Pamela was sitting in an armchair lying back with her eyes closed. Stirling bent down and kissed her lightly on the forehead. She opened her eyes, smiled and quietly asked, 'What time is it, darling?'

'Fifteen thirty, dear,' he replied standing up, 'the car will be here soon.'

'Any news, dear?' she asked hopefully.

'I'm afraid not, dear,' he replied. 'I'm sure the admiral will phone when he hears anything.'

'Oh Robert,' she said pleadingly, 'if you hear anything before you sail, please try and telephone me, won't you?'

'Of course I will, darling,' he answered quietly, and kissed her gently on the cheek.

Shortly after 1600 Manley knocked on the door, came in and announced the arrival of the staff car. Stirling wore a Burberry over his uniform and carried a small brown canvas grip. A gas mask and steel helmet hung from his left shoulder. Wearing her dark coat, red headscarf and shoulder bag Pamela followed Stirling out of the cabin.

'I'll be at the Adelphi should you need me, Manley,' Stirling said as the walked along the passageway.

'Very good, sir,' Manley answered dryly, 'but I hope that won't be necessary.'

'Captain leaving the ship,' shouted Yeoman Tate, the duty PO, 'attention on the quarterdeck.'

Manley and OOD Sub Lieutenant Amery snapped to attention and saluted.

Stirling saluted and allowing Pamela to walk in front, they made their way down the gangway. The staff car was on the wharf close to the end of the gangway. A Wren driver stood with the passenger door open.

'The Adelphi, sir?' asked the driver turning her head slightly, noticing Stirling and Pamela were holding hands.

'Yes, thank you,' replied Stirling as they climbed inside the car.

Neither spoke as the car sped along the dock road and into the city centre. The many ruins of bombed houses and shops they passed only served to remind them of the war and Mark.

By the time they stopped outside the Adelphi it was almost dark. All the windows of the hotel were protected by tape, and sand bags blocked out the view of those rooms on the ground floor.

'Oh eight hundred tomorrow, sir,' the Wren said as she opened the passenger door.

'Yes and thank you,' Stirling replied taking hold of his grip. Pamela gave her a warm smile as Stirling helped her out of the car.

They walked up a small flight of steps and acknowledged the salute of a tall, elderly commissionaire. After pushing the revolving doors they entered a spacious foyer bathed in a dull blue light. Except for one or two army officers and a few couples sitting in armchairs smoking and chatting, the place looked deserted. On the left a few small steps led into a bar. Directly opposite where Stirling and Pamela entered a row of steps led to a set of French doors behind which was a highly decorative lounge.

Stirling introduced himself to an elderly, grey-haired receptionist and signed the register.

'Room number eighty on the fourth floor, sir,' she said smiling benignly and handing him a heavy iron key. 'We've been expecting you. Breakfast is at seven.'

'Thank you,' Stirling replied. 'We'd like a call at six thirty please.' He picked up his grip and they made their way across the foyer to the lift.

The room was reached along a well-lit oak-panelled corridor. A pair of thick, dark green curtains was drawn across the large window overlooking Ranlagh Street. Nearby stood Lewis's Store, once the biggest in Liverpool, now a gutted shell after being heavily bombed seven months previously.

The room was quite spacious. Ornately framed watercolours of local scenes hung on the wall decorated in pale green. Dark brown Axminster carpet covered the floor and a miniature glass chandelier bathed the room in a clear yellow, light. A shiny pale green eiderdown lay over a king-size bed flanked on either side by a marble-topped table and brass lampshade. A small Bakelite wireless and black telephone rested on one of them. Next to a highly polished wardrobe was a dressing table and wide mirror and in one corner an open door led into a bathroom tiled in pink.

'Tired, darling?' Stirling asked dropping his grip and placing his arms around Pamela.

'Weary more than tired, dear,' she replied, resting her head gently against his chest. 'Every time I close my eyes I think of…'

'Yes,' Stirling quietly replied, holding her close. 'I know exactly what you mean.'

Pamela looked up at him, smiled weakly and said, 'Perhaps a bath will make me feel a bit better.'

'Splendid idea,' Stirling answered. In a weak attempt to cheer her up, he kissed her quickly on the lips and attempting to make a joke, added, 'But I'd take your coat and scarf off first.'

Shortly after 1900 Stirling suggested they go down for dinner.

Pamela had changed from her earlier clothes into a black skirt and a white, long-sleeved blouse with a ruffle collar. Stirling was in uniform having showered and put on a clean shirt.

'Oh, Robert,' Pamela said resignedly, 'I'm really not very hungry. Perhaps a drink might help.'

'Any excuse,' Stirling replied with a grin, 'but I know what you mean.'

Suddenly the undulating wail of the air raid siren filled the room. For a few seconds they stood and looked warily at one another.

'Looks like dinner and that drink will have to be postponed,' Stirling remarked. 'We'd better grab our gas masks and go downstairs.'

'What about your steel helmet?' Pamela asked as Stirling helped her on with her coat.

'You can have it, darling,' Stirling replied with a grin. 'It'll look better on you than me!'

Along with a young army lieutenant and a dark, attractive WAAF, they caught the lift. The same elderly commissionaire who met them earlier directed them down a set of well-lit stairs into a wide, musty-smelling room with a cold, concrete floor. Bare electric lights hung from a low slung ceiling and a long wooden table lay in the middle. Straight-backed wooden chairs looking like cast-offs from a jumble sale, lined the drab, whitewashed walls. As everyone entered the room the crack of gunfire could be heard.

This was followed by the *thud, thud, thud,* of bombs exploding some distance away.

'The docks and Bootle again, Charles,' commented a portly woman to a tall, thin-faced man who was sitting next to them. Her pink, low-cut chiffon dress exaggerating her ample proportions was slightly crumpled contrasting sharply with his immaculate dark blue pinstriped suit.

'Yes, Aida, dear, you're probably right,' he replied meekly, giving her a nervous smile while clutching her chubby hand.

Pamela glanced apprehensively at Stirling. 'Isn't that where your ship is?' she whispered.

'Yes, it is, darling, but it would be pointless trying to get back there. By the time I arrived, the raid would be over,' Stirling replied, taking out a cigarette from a packet of *Players,* handing her one and lighting both. 'Anyway,' he added, taking a deep drag, 'there's very little I can do now.'

For the next fifteen minutes they sat holding hands listening with the others as dull explosions and gunfire echoed close by. After one loud bang a woman became hysterical as the ceiling shook sending thin lines of dust floating down onto the floor. In a perverse way the air raid served to distract Stirling and Pamela from their personal problems. This was reflected in the consolatory glances they gave each other after each detonation. Just after eight o'clock the welcome sound of the "All Clear" heralded the end of the raid. Returning to the restaurant Pamela smiled at Stirling and said, 'Oh Robert dear, I really have lost my appetite. Let's forget dinner and adjourn to the bar.'

'Damn good idea, darling,' Stirling replied, giving her hand an agreeable squeeze.

The bar was quite crowded with a mixture of service personnel and civilians. In a matter of minutes the atmosphere was warm and heavy with tobacco smoke. Stirling ordered two gin and tonics and despite not being in the mood for idle chitchat, they were quickly engaged in conversation by Charles and Aida, the two people from the air raid shelter. Charles was smoking a large, expensive cigar.

'I heard on the wireless that Roosevelt has appealed to the Japanese Emperor to avoid war with America,' said Charles, 'what do you think, old boy?' he asked, wafting a cloud of smoke away with his hand.

'The sooner they come into the war, the better,' Stirling replied thoughtfully before finishing his drink.

'Terrible about the *Ark Royal* being sunk a few weeks ago,' chimed in Aida, 'thank God our son Harold was rescued. He was an officer like yourself,' she added haughtily.

'I'm glad to hear it,' Stirling replied, feeling Pamela dig him slyly in the back.

'Do let me get you and your good lady a drink,' said Charles, waving his cigar about wildly.

Sensing they might be in for a long, boring night, Pamela shot a quick warning glance at her husband and replied, 'Er... that's very kind of you but we have an early call in the morning, but thank you all the same.'

'Very pleasant meeting you,' said Stirling, shaking their hands, 'and I wish your son the best of luck.'

'That was quick thinking, darling,' Stirling said, kissing her on the cheek after they left the bar.

'Wasn't it just?' she replied glancing affectionately at him while giving him a hug.

Neither of them slept very well. The possible loss of Mark weighed heavily on their minds. Both lay quietly smoking a cigarette. Despite having experienced frequent partings over the years this time it was different. Now, the three of them were in uniform, she with the WVS, he captaining his ship and Mark missing at sea. The feeling she might lose one or both of them hung over her like a heavy shroud.

'Oh, Robert, darling,' she cried softly, turning her head and staring lovingly into his eyes, 'if anything happened to you and Mark, life wouldn't be worth living.'

'How do you think I feel about you, dear,' he replied, reaching across and stubbing his cigarette out in an ashtray, 'dashing about during air raids in a van, handing out tea and sandwiches, you're probably in more danger than me.'

'I'll pray night and day for you both,' she murmured, pulling him closer to her.

'So will I, my darling,' he softly replied, kissing her wet eyes, 'so will I...'

Eventually, cocooned in each other's arms they fell into a fitful sleep. Several hours later the sharp ringing of the telephone woke them up. Stirling opened his eyes, yawned then reached across and switched on the bedside light and picked up the receiver.

'Your six o'clock call, sir,' came a clear female voice. Stirling thanked her then sank back onto his pillow. 'Time to make a move, sleepy head,' he said, putting his arms around Pamela's warm, pyjama-clad body and kissing her gently on the forehead.

She opened her eyes, looked up and gave him a sleepy smile and muttered, 'Mm... I suppose so, darling, but give me another kiss first,' she muttered.

He pulled her close and kissed her lovingly on the lips, smelling the faint odour of her talc and lavender soap.

Suddenly, they both felt a dull, heavy knotted feeling descend into the pits of their stomachs. Both had felt it in the past but this time the feeling was more acute. In two hours they would say goodbye and God only knew when, or if, they might meet again.

Neither spoke as they dressed and packed their few belongings. The atmosphere suddenly became strained.

'It's just after seven, dear,' Stirling said, nervously running his tongue along his lips. 'Breakfast?'

'Just coffee for me,' Pamela replied, folding her coat over her arm. 'What about you?'

'The same,' he replied.

The restaurant was almost empty. Stirling placed Pamela's overnight case alongside his grip as they sat down at a table. He took out a packet of *Players* and passed her one, then lit them both. Stirling ordered a pot of coffee, but even after the second cup it seemed tasteless. In a perverse way it was almost a relief when Stirling glanced tactfully at his watch and almost in a whisper, said, 'Better leave now dear, I expect the car will be outside.'

Pamela gave a quick nod of her head and pushing her empty cup and saucer away stood up. 'Right, darling,' she managed to say picking up her hand bag, 'I'm ready.'

The dark low-lying clouds promised rain and as they left the hotel the cold December wind bit into them. The black staff car was parked at the edge of the pavement. The same Wren driver who brought them immediately got out and opened the passenger door.

'Good morning, sir,' she said, sounding very chirpy, 'a bit parky if I may say so. The station, isn't it, sir?' she added giving Stirling a smart salute.

'Yes, thank you,' Stirling replied allowing Pamela to enter first. 'Then take me to Gladstone Dock.'

'Very good, sir,' replied the driver and started the car. 'The station is just down the road, we'll be there in a jiffy.'

The car moved off and in a matter of seconds the driver stopped at the foot of a pavement opposite two sets of wide steps leading into the station. This was the moment Stirling and Pamela had been dreading. For a few seconds they sat in silence tightly holding hands, looking at each other.

Choking back tears, Pamela finally said, 'I... I'd better go darling, the train...'

'Yes, yes,' Stirling muttered, 'I'll come to the platform with you.'

'No, no, darling,' cried Pamela. Uncoupling their hands she tenderly touched the side of his face. 'We've said too many goodbyes on too many railway stations, just hold me tight and kiss me.'

Stirling took her in his arms and feeing her warm tears trickling against his face, kissed her so hard his lips hurt. Then with a painful gasp she broke away and cried, 'Goodbye my love. God's speed and come back safe.' She grabbed her overnight case, climbed from the car and without looking back, hurried up the steps and into the station.

For a few minutes Stirling was tempted to run after her. Instead, he sat forward listening to the racing rhythm of his heart thumping against his ribs. The sound of the Wren driver's voice startled him. 'Back to your ship, sir,' he heard her say.

'Yes please, miss,' he replied, struggling to light a cigarette. 'And thank you for being so...'

'That's all right, sir, I understand,' she replied. 'I said goodbye to my fiancé here yesterday.'

# CHAPTER THIRTY-TWO

'*D'yer hear there. Heavo, heavo, heavo. Lash up and stow. Cooks to the galley. Special sea duty men will be required at 0630.*' The time was 0500 on Sunday 7 December.

The first thoughts that entered Stirling's head when he woke up were of Pamela and Mark. Maybe, he hoped, reaching up and switching on his overhead light, there might be news of Mark before they sailed. Poor Pamela, he mused, must be asking herself the same thing. A sharp knock on the door brought him back to reality.

The door opened and Potts came in holding a mug of steaming hot tea.

'Mornin', sir,' he said quietly, placing the drink on the small bedside table. He then proceeded to give Stirling his usual early report. 'Strong wind blowin' down river, sir,' he said, thoughtfully rubbing his chin, 'and it looks like a drop of rain.'

'Thank you, Potts,' replied Stirling lighting a cigarette and enjoying the first drag of the day. 'Breakfast in half an hour.'

Promptly at 0600 Manley knocked and came in. Stirling was sitting at his desk glancing through the signal log.

'Good morning, Number One,' he said, noticing the red flush on Manley face. 'I see the weather report isn't too friendly, and you look as cold as ice.'

'It is a bit nippy outside, sir,' Manley answered rubbing his hands together, 'the ship's ready for sea, but the barometer's dropping.'

'Better pipe wet weather routine for leaving harbour and rig life lines,' Stirling replied, stubbing out his cigarette. 'Anyone adrift?'

'No, sir, I'm happy to say,' Manley replied with a wry smile. 'Maybe the beer ashore has gone off.'

'Right then,' Stirling sighed, closing the signal log and standing up. 'I'll address the ship's company about our little jaunt as soon as we pass the Bar Lighthouse.'

'Just as well, sir,' said Manley doing his best to disguise a smile, 'the buzz is we're off to the Meddy, or even America,' he paused then added sombrely, 'by the way, sir, any news…?'

'No, nothing,' Stirling quietly replied reaching for his cap and duffle coat.

Upon reaching the bridge both men felt the vibrations of the engines and blinked as a blast of icy wind invaded their faces.

'Good morning, everyone' he said nodding casually at Ape, who was OOW, Sub Lieutenant Amery and PO Yeoman Tate.

''Morning, sir,' they replied in unison.

Stirling heaved himself into his chair and looped the straps of his binoculars over his neck.

'What was that you said about the barometer dropping, Number One?' Stirling remarked, glancing apprehensively at the black cumulonimbus clouds, 'it wouldn't surprise me if it snowed.'

From his chair Stirling could see the line of seamen lined up on the fo'c'sle ready for leaving harbour. All of them wore shiny black oilskins with their chinstraps around their chins keeping their caps from flying off.

'Time to slip, Number One,' Stirling said, giving Manley a quick nod, 'single up to the breast and spring.'

Manley went to port wing and using a loud hailer repeated the order to Sub Lieutenant Harper-Smyth standing on the fo'c'sle. All lines except the single breast and spring rope running from aft to a shore bollard amidships securing the ship to the wharf were released. Dockyard workers on the quayside unhitched these allowing the ropes to be hauled in by the men on the fo'c'sle.

'Let go head rope,' snapped Stirling.

'Let go head rope, sir,' repeated Harper-Smyth.

'Head rope gone, sir,' reported Seaman PO Dusty Miller.

'Screw flags white, sir,' said Manley, leaning over the side of the wing. (These are flags shown by ratings on both sides of the ship indicating that the screws were clear of the ropes thus avoiding fouling the propellers.)

'Slow ahead,' said Stirling. The order was repeated from PO Coxswain Moore below in the wheelhouse.

'Recover fenders and all hawsers please, Number One,' said Stirling, feeling the ship slowly move from the quayside.

'Half ahead, port.' Stirling snapped, followed by, 'Stop, starboard, slow ahead both engines.'

By 0900 *Sandpiper* was lying in the middle of the river waiting to be joined by the remaining five sloops and HMS *Plover.*

'Increase revolutions one third, Number One,' said Stirling, lighting a cigarette and watching the smoke disperse. The order was passed to the engine room and almost immediately the ship increased speed.

'Fall out special sea duty men, Number One,' Stirling shouted making himself heard against the fierce wind, 'and tell the Buffer to make sure everything is secure.'

No sooner had the flotilla passed the Mersey Lighthouse and into the estuary than each vessel was hit by the surging rollers sweeping in from the Irish Sea. Like the other ships behind, *Sandpiper* performed her usual nautical acrobatics as each wave crashed over her bow in a fury of white angry foam.

Stirling adjusted his white woollen muffler around his neck, switched on the ship's tannoy and picked up the handset. 'This is the captain speaking,' he said, clutching the side of his chair with his free hand. 'I'm sure you are all anxious to know exactly where we are going and why,' he paused momentarily to wipe a cold wash of spray from his face, then continued, 'well I'm happy to say we're not going to the Arctic or into the Atlantic, we are in fact bound for an area around the Cape Verde Islands, in the South Atlantic about five hundred miles off the coast of West Africa.' He paused again and smiled imagining the reaction throughout the ship. 'Our task is to sink an unusual type of U-boat. These are larger than normal submarines and act as supply ships to the enemy. The Germans call them Milch Cows or Milk Cows, a fitting name considering their task. Their hulls are constructed of stronger steel than a conventional submarine and they can also go deeper. That's the reason we are carrying depth charges containing special explosives.' He stopped talking and allowed the importance of this to sink in, then taking a deep breath, continued. 'If we can destroy the blighter it will reduce the time the enemy can spend at sea and therefore protect the convoys. So you see, our mission is of vital importance. It will be no picnic. On our way we will only attack U-boats if we ourselves are attacked but I expect our main danger will come from those damn Focke-Wulf Condors, so the lookouts will be doubled,' he paused then added, 'I intend that we shall test one new depth charge when we leave the Bay of Biscay. Good luck, I'm sure we'll succeed. That is all.'

He replaced the handset and noticed the broad satisfied grin on PO Tate's face. 'I shouldn't be too pleased, if I were you, Yeoman,' Stirling said gravely, 'as I said, this will be no picnic.'

The crew greeted the news of the mission with a mixture of relief and alacrity.

During "stand easy" in the seamen's mess Able Seaman Darby Allen grinned at Able Seaman Buster Brown. 'What was that about cows!' he exclaimed gripping his mug of tea with both hands, 'no need to go these 'ere Verde Islands, Tanky, old son, I've met one or two of 'em in the Long Bar in Plymouth.'

'Aye, that's right, Darby,' Tanky answered shaking his head and grinning, 'Big Bertha certainly milked me all right, the bitch stole me wallet.'

'To be sure,' chimed in Able Seaman Patrick Duffy spilling tea down the front of his overalls, 'does anyone know what "Verde" means?'

'It's French or Spanish for "green" ain't it Nipper?' replied Leading Seaman Wacker Payne, winking slyly at Ordinary Seaman Nipper Morris. 'The same colour as them new depth charges.'

'Yea, that's right,' cried Nipper, giving Wacker a surprised look, 'everyone knows that, even me.'

'Bollocks,' Duffy replied curtly. Then with a quizzical expression on his face he muttered, 'They don't call Ireland the Verde Isle, do they, so you're both bloody wrong,' and with a supercilious grin left the mess.

For the next eight hours the flotilla battled their way through the heavy seas and by 2000 they were some twenty miles off Land's End. Lifelines had been rigged and nobody was allowed on the upper deck. Stirling was in his sea cabin writing up the ship's log when a sharp knock came at the door.

'Come,' snapped Stirling curtly.

Ape came in holding a signal. A wide grin had spread across his rugged features and he looked flushed. *'The Japs have bombed Pearl Harbour!'* he cried, waving a signal frantically in the air, *'without any warning as well, it says so here.'*

'Calm down, Pilot,' said Stirling, 'and give the signal to me,' he added reaching out his hand.

As Stirling read the signal he felt the hairs on the back of his neck stand up.

It read: "Today at approximately 0700, Southern Pacific Time, Japanese planes bombed Pearl Harbour. Many ships have been sunk and there are said to be many casualties. President Roosevelt has declared a state of emergency and is expected to announce America is at war with Japan forthwith. Tomorrow, 8 December GMT, Great Britain is to declare war on Finland, Rumania and Hungry."

'Thank God, Pilot!' Stirling exploded, 'with their industrial muscle and manpower we'll really give it to Jerry.'

'Well,' replied Ape his face wreathed in smiles. 'It's similar to the last war when it took the sinking of the *Lusitania* to bring them into the show, still,' he added philosophically, 'better, late than never, I suppose.'

'Be that as it may, Pilot,' Stirling replied gravely, 'the way things are going the Americans will be more than welcome. But I expect the cost in lives will be high,' he added solemnly, thinking of Mark. He stood up, glanced at the signal and said, 'I'd better announce this to the ship's company.'

The news brought instant cheering from many members of the crew. Nevertheless, some reacted with pessimism.

'Bloody "Dough Boys" they called 'em in the last war,' remarked Chief Bosun's Mate Sammy Taylor. Despite the bad weather he was on the well deck keeping an eye on Leading Seaman Wiggy Bennett making sure the port lifeboat was secure.

'And when they arrived in England,' shouted the Buffer, 'the buggers wouldn't leave our women alone. Sex maniacs they are.'

'Jealousy will get you nowhere, Buffer,' shouted Wiggy fighting against the wind as he tightened a rope attached to the swaying lifeboat. 'Anyways,' he went, 'why the hell did they call 'em "Dough Boys"?'

'I dunno,' the Buffer yelled, wiping seawater from his face, 'probably because they got more money than our lads, now let's get inboard afore we get fuckin' soaked to death.'

In the wardroom the officers received the news with equanimity.

'Jolly good, what?' beamed Sub Lieutenant Oliver, his plummy voice raised slightly, 'this means more soldiers, more food and…'

'More VD,' Coburn interrupted warily. 'After they came over in 1917, they spread it around like wildfire. Married women caught it also,' he added spilling tea into his saucer.

'I don't care what they bring,' said Manley, gripping the side of a chair while sipping his tea, 'as long as they bring us more ships.'

During the night the wind continued to howl as the flotilla bounded through the high rolling sea. As dawn broke Land's End was a faint blur on the port beam. The heavens opened up sending walls of rain belting down, turning the sea into a myriad of tiny explosions.

'Looks like we're in for a right bastard,' commented Manley, who was sharing the morning watch with Sub Lieutenant Harper-Smyth. Peering though his binoculars he noticed flashes of fork lightning on the horizon away to starboard.

'At least it'll keep the U-boats and the Luftwaffe away, sir,' replied Harper-Smyth, stamping his feet and blowing into his hands.

Shortly after "Call the hands" at 0600 Stirling appeared on the bridge. Nodding casually to the two officers he lowered himself into his customary chair.

'Signal to all escorts, "Alter course ten degree to starboard", Number One,' shouted Stirling, feeling rainwater drip from the peak of his cap onto his duffle coat. 'I want to keep us well clear of Brest.'

Manley repeated the order to the wheelhouse while Leading Signalman Tansey Lee, using his Aldis lamp, signalled the rest of the flotilla.

'When do we enter the Bay of Biscay, Number One?' Stirling asked thoughtfully, knowing that when they did so radio silence would be in force.

'On our present course and speed we should reach the southern edge of the Bay around twenty hundred, sir,' Manley replied, 'and I'm happy to report the barometer seems to be rising.'

'Thank goodness for small mercies,' Stirling replied caustically, 'I take it there's been no Asdic reports.'

'No problems there, sir,' Manley reported with a faint smile, 'the weather is obviously keeping the U-boats away.'

But the state of the weather and the presence of U-boats would not be the last of Stirling's problems.

# CHAPTER THIRTY-THREE

During the next two hours the wind dropped slightly and the rain stopped. But the mountainous seas continued to batter the flotilla. *Sandpiper* and the other ships would rise in unison and as if lifted by a hidden hand, balance precariously on the peak of the wave. Then with a sickening sideways roll the ship would descend into the trough, quiver and begin the process again.

'The sooner we reach calmer waters,' cried Ape, trying in vain to dodge another cloud of spray, 'the better my stomach will feel.'

'Shame on you, my dear fellow,' shouted Sub Lieutenant Harper-Smyth, who was sharing the afternoon watch with Ape. 'I thought you Aussies all had webbed feet. All that surfing and all.'

Ape was about to reply when the stout figure of Leading Wireless Operator Bungy Williams appeared on the bridge. In one hand he held a signal, the other shielded his eyes from the rain. 'Message from *Petrel,* sir,' he said, catching his breath then handing it to Ape.

'Bloody hell!' exploded Ape as he read the signal. '*Petrel* has trouble with her condensers again and can only make ten knots.' He wiped the lens of his binoculars and managed to pick out the dark outline of *Petrel.* 'And she's falling behind,' he shouted. 'The old man won't like this.'

Stirling was in his sea cabin writing up the ship's log when the squeaky noise of the voice-pipe disturbed his concentration.

'Yes,' he said, unhooking the metal tube from the bulkhead, 'what is it?'

'Officer of the Watch, sir,' Ape quickly replied apprehensively, 'message from *Petrel*. It reads, "*Recurrent trouble with condenser. Can only make ten knots maximum. Request instructions.*"'

'Thank you, Pilot,' Stirling replied, frowning thoughtfully as he spoke, 'I'll be up immediately.' Stirling, wearing his duffle coat, grabbed his cap and wrapping a towel around his neck left his cabin.

'How far away is *Petrel?*' he shouted to Ape as he arrived on the bridge.

'About six cables from the rest of the us, sir,' Ape replied, peering through his binoculars. (Six cables is three-fifths of a mile.)

'Radio to *Petrel*,' shouted Stirling, 'say, "How serious is it? Can you repair problem? If so how long will it take?"'

Williams memorised the message and quickly left the bridge.

'Just what exactly is this condenser, sir?' Ape asked, wiping water from his face.

'It's a system of heat exchange that removes the latent heat from exhaust steam so that it condenses and can be pumped back into the boiler. If damaged this can affect the efficiency of the engine and boilers.'

'Really, sir' Ape replied trying to sound as if her understood Stirling's answer.

'Now,' said Stirling, nervously stroking his chin, 'how far away are we from the nearest English port?'

Ape quickly consulted his chart then replied, 'We're just over two hundred and fifty miles south of Penzance, sir.'

Leading Wireless Operator Williams appeared and handed Stirling a signal.

'*Blast it,*' cried Stirling, glancing warily at Ape who was close by, 'the condenser has completely packed up and it'll take at least twenty-four hours to repair.'

A startled expression immediately spread over Ape's face. '*Twenty four hours, sir!*' he replied alarmingly, 'that'll mean us having to stop.'

'Yes, I'm fully aware of that,' Stirling replied gravely.

Stirling realised he had to make a decision that could affect the success or failure of the mission. If he ordered the flotilla to slow down and wait until *Petrel*'s engineers had fixed the condenser the flotilla might be detected by U-boats or even attacked by a Focke-Wulf Condor. Alternatively, he could order *Petrel* to return to England with *Plover* as escort, thus reducing his small armada to four sloops. This would also mean the loss of the destroyer's high-range anti-aircraft guns. He decided to do the latter.

'Radio signal to *Petrel*,' said Stirling, 'repeated to *Plover, Redshank, Curlew, Shearwater, Sparrow,* Admiralty and C in C Western Approaches, say, "*Petrel's condenser defective. Repair time uncertain. Speed reduced to ten knots. Have ordered Petrel to return to England, forthwith. Plover to escort.*"'

Half an hour later a signal from Admiral Horton was received which read: "*Message received and understood. Will arrange air cover when the two ships reach the channel. Continue mission, Godspeed.*"

A series of messages of "*Good luck*" signals flashed to *Petrel* and *Plover* as they left the flotilla. With a heavy heart Stirling watched as the remaining four sloops pulled away leaving the two ships sailing slowly in the opposite direction.

'They look so bloody lonely, don't the, sir?' Manley muttered ruefully.

'Indeed they do,' sighed Stirling, then raising his voice, said, 'increase revolution one-third. Steer south by south-east.'

During the night the flotilla skirted the outer waters of the Bay of Biscay. As dawn broke the sea was calmer, the wind dropped and the grey granite sky was now an eye-smarting blue. Just after 0700 Stirling came onto the bridge.

Squinting up at the strong morning sun he said, 'Better pipe hands to change into number tens,' He added with a smile, 'Shorts and white shirts will make a pleasant change from overalls and sweaters. How far are we from the Azores?'

'Roughly three hundred miles, sir,' Manley replied after consulting Ape's charts.

Turning to Ape, Stirling asked, 'What's our present position, and speed, Pilot?'

Ape, quickly consulted his charts and replied, 'Latitude 53 degrees 22 minutes north, longitude 003 degrees 20 west, speed fifteen knots, sir.'

'Thank you,' Stirling replied, then, pausing slightly, he glanced cautiously at Manley and said, 'Signal the group, say, *"At 1300, I intend to launch a single new depth charge. In doing so increase speed to avoid shock wave. Be prepared for a much larger explosion than normal and report any damage."* Better inform Sub Lieutenant Harper-Smyth to set the charge at 300 feet and have his team ready.'

'Very good, sir,' Manley replied and left the bridge.

Five minutes later Manley returned, his faced wreathed in smiles.

'What's so funny?' Stirling asked Manley, picking up the ship's intercom.

Manley gave a short laugh. 'When I told Harper-Smyth, his face became as white as a sheet. He even asked if he and his team qualified for danger money.'

Stirling shook his head slightly and smiled. Then clearing his throat told the crew about the exercise, adding, 'Everyone except the depth charge party are to keep clear of the quarterdeck. That is all.'

By 1245 Sub Lieutenant Harper-Smyth and his team stood on the quarterdeck anxiously waiting for the telephone to ring giving the order to fire. The guardrails on the end of the quarterdeck had been removed. The bright green, barrel-shaped depth charge rested on a steel launcher. The tension increased as Harper-Smyth cast a quick glanced at his wristwatch. 'One minute to go, PO,' he said, feeling his mouth suddenly go dry.

Just then a rating turned to PO Weedon and in a timid voice, asked, 'What if the bloody thing blows half the quarterdeck up, PO?'

'If that happens, my lad,' the PO replied philosophically, 'it'll take us with it. But don't worry, you won't feel a thing...'

The ringing of the telephone interrupted him and Harper-Smyth immediately unhooked it, paused momentarily, then, looking wide-eyed across at PO Weedon, yelled, '*Launch!*'

The four ratings immediately tipped the launcher and nervously watched as the depth charge rumbled along the steel rollers and disappeared over the stern of the ship. The runner was then hastily brought inboard and the guardrails re-attached.

Suddenly, as if being chased by some unknown sea monster, the four sloops increased speed churning up the blue waters and sending a frothy bow wave over their respective fo'c'sles.

The explosion that followed sent a huge pall of dark seawater soaring into the sky which reaching its zenith, blossomed into a grey, watery mushroom. For a while a huge fountain of foam hung in the air before slowly collapsing into the sea.

By this time the ships were about five hundred yards away. The quarterdeck parties had been dismissed but on the bridges everyone reactively ducked as the unnerving warmth of a shockwave hit their faces.

On *Sandpiper*'s bridge everyone gave a great sigh of relief as they watched the tidal wave fail to reach the ship's stern and fall into a series of smaller white horses. Feeling a tingle of cold sweat run down his spine, Stirling turned to Manley and said, 'Well, Number One, at least we know what to expect.'

The lookouts on either wing gave each other a started glance.

'I don't know about you, Nobby,' said one of them, licking his lips nervously, 'but I'm gunna sleep with my lifejacket on tonight.'

'Might as well keep it on for the rest of the trip, mate,' Nobby sarcastically replied. 'You never can tell what'll happen onboard this ship.'

Stirling gave a satisfied glance at Manley, smiled and said, 'Steer ten degrees southwest. I want to avoid the Azores and Madeira even if they are supposed to be neutral.'

'Pity we're not crossing the equator, sir,' said Ape making a notation in the deck log, 'I'd have like to have seen the ceremony.'

'You could have been King Neptune,' replied Manley with a grin. 'All trussted up in a grass skirt and crown wielding a large fork, it would have made a great photo to send home, eh Pilot?'

'Actually, sir,' interrupted OOW Sub Lieutenant Oliver, who in his usual plummy voice, added, 'the fork you mentioned is called a Trident, meaning "three prongs".'

'Bloody know-all,' Ape jokingly replied. 'Are you sure you don't mean three pricks?'

'Ignorant Antipodean,' grunted Oliver using his sextant to take a noon fix.

The warm weather and blue skies brought off-duty ratings, who would otherwise be below in their hammocks or playing cards or uckers, onto the upper deck. Bedding was aired and mess decks dried out and cleaned.

'This is the life, eh Nobby,' mumbled Able Seaman Buster Brown. He and several other ratings clad in white shorts and sandals were lying on the port waist, eyes closed, soaking up the sunshine.

'Too bloody true, mate,' replied Able Seaman Clark, feeling the warm breeze fan his weather-beaten face. With a sigh and a salacious grin he added, 'All I need is Betty Grable to rub me down with sun lotion.'

'To be sure, I'd rather have Rita Hayworth, so I would,' chimed in Able Seaman Patrick Duffy, his face partially covered by a dog-eared copy of *Tit-Bits*. 'She's got bigger tits than Betty Grable.'

'For fuck's sake,' cried three-badge Able Seaman Darby Allen, lying close by on a hammock cover, 'pipe down, yer givin' me a hard on.'

With a smirk playing around his lips, Buster replied, 'At your age you should be grateful.'

'Cheeky bastard,' Darby replied giving Buster a playful kick on the shins, 'why don't you bugger off and make sure the rum hasn't evaporated?'

Chief Stoker Digger Barnes and Nick Carter, a tall stoker from York, had come up from below for a quick smoke and a breath of fresh air. Carter wore an off-colour cap cover tied on his head like an elderly man on Blackpool beach. Each man wore overalls rolled down to their waist, the whiteness of their sweaty bodies contrasting sharply with their tanned faces. Both of them were leaning against the guardrail smoking.

'You can almost see the bottom of the ocean, it's so clear,' said the chief taking off his battered cap and wiping his brow with the back of his hand. 'I've never seen so many fish, there must be millions of them darting about down there.'

'And sharks,' Carter answered dryly, exhaling tobacco smoke and watching it idly drift away. 'Still,' he added with a sigh, 'I'd give the world for a fishing rod.'

On the bridge Stirling sat on his chair smoking. He and OOW Lieutenant Anderson were entranced watching several dolphins leap in and out of the water a few yards in front of the ship. Not far away a shoal of flying fish swept along the surface of the sea, then, as the ship approached, they darted away in all directions like pieces of jagged shrapnel.

'Amazing creatures, those dolphins, eh sir,' remarked Anderson, wiping his brow with a handkerchief. 'They always seem to be smiling. Old sailors thought they were a sign of good luck.'

'Here's hoping they're right,' Stirling replied tersely.

An hour later darkness quickly descended. The heavens became a vast panoply of glittering stars, which together with the pale yellow glow of a full moon changed the placid dark green sea into daggers of twinkling light.

By the 11 December the flotilla was approximately 428 nautical miles from its objective. So far the voyage had been relatively uneventful. There were no signs of the Luftwaffe or the presence of U-boats.

The time was shortly after 2000. Sub Lieutenant Harper-Smyth had the second dog watch having just relieved Lieutenant Anderson. The ship was darkened and the only light was a pale blue glow coming from a shaded bulb over the navigators' chart table in a tiny recess aft of the bridge. The tall, ghostly figure of Leading Signalman Tansey Lee, clad in a duffle coat, stood by the binnacle, staring hypnotically into the darkness. Harper-Smyth lit a cigarette, took a deep drag and relaxed in the captain's chair. On either side of *Sandpiper* he could see the black silhouette of the four sloops, their masts and funnels outlined against the dim light.

'Beautiful, isn't it, Lee,' he said watching as the bows cut through the inky black sea sending lines of phosphorous fizzing down either side of the ship. 'So peaceful, it's hard to believe there's a war on.'

'If you say so, sir,' grunted Tansey. 'Personally,' he replied stretching his arms and yawning, 'I'd rather be below in me mick havin' forty winks.'

Harper-Smyth smiled lazily then, watching the smoke from his cigarette dissipate in the wind, muttered, 'Peace, perfect peace, but what will tomorrow bring?'

They were about to find out!

# CHAPTER THIRTY-FOUR

Stirling was fully clothed and resting in his bunk when he heard the explosion. The concussion of the blast bounced against the bulkhead causing the ship to rock violently. The sudden movement lifted Stirling up and almost flung him onto the deck.

'Good Lord!' Stirling exclaimed opening his eyes and grasping the side of his bunk. For a fleeting second he though the ship had hit a mine. In one quick movement he levered himself onto the deck and left his cabin. Arriving on the bridge his attention was immediately drawn to a billowing mushroom of yellow flames glowing in the dark, two miles away to port. Even at that distance Stirling could feel the warm caress of the heat on his face. The glimmering flames lit up the darkness, the reflection of which turned the sea into a flickering mass of yellowy waves.

Using his binoculars Stirling cried, 'It's *Curlew,* it looks like she's hit something.'

At that moment Ape, Manley and Surgeon Lieutenant Coburn arrived on the bridge.

'What's happening, sir?' Manley asked his voice filled with concern as he gazed in horror at the mass of smoke and flames stark against the night sky. No sooner had he spoke than another ear-splitting detonation erupted from the same area sending another pall of yellow flames and smoke soaring into the air. Everyone except Stirling instinctively ducked. Focussing his binoculars he watched in horror at what was left of *Curlew.*

'*Good God in heaven!*' he cried, his voice bordering on hysteria. 'She's gone, completely disappeared.' He paused, gathered his senses then shouted, 'Hard a starboard, Number One. Signal the other ships to join ourselves and search for survivors.'

Throughout *Sandpiper* men had felt the shock-wave hitting the side of the bulkhead like a sledgehammer. Men instinctively leapt from their hammocks and bunks, grabbed their lifebelts and hurried onto the upper deck.

'Jesus Christ!' shouted Able Seaman Nobby Clark, shielding his eyes against the fiery glow of the flames, 'it must 'ave been a fuckin' torpedo or summat.'

'Maybe there's been a collision with another ship,' offered CPO Chippy Harry Tweed, staring unbelievingly at the coruscation turning night into day.

'Or a mine,' cried Ordinary Seam Nipper Clark, as he inflated his life jacket.

'Whatever it is,' added the gravelly voice of Chief Bosun's Mate Sammy Taylor, 'it's certainly done for all the poor buggers onboard her.'

It was a feeling shared by all who watched. Men they had sailed with on previous ships, argued, and at times, even traded punches, were aboard *Curlew*. Each man gazed helplessly at the shimmering flames deeply conscious they had lost good friends.

In a matter of minutes the four sloops surrounded the area where *Curlew* once lay. The full moon cast a clear glow on the calm waters, but all each man saw was a mass of debris, body parts and flotsam.

'Dear God, sir,' muttered Manley, slowly shaking his head while glancing warily at Stirling, 'what the hell could have caused that?'

'What indeed, Number One,' replied Stirling, staring pensively at the remains of what was once a proud ship. Suddenly Stirling remembered the admiral telling him the new depth charges were still in the experimental stage. A thought too dangerous to contemplate flashed through him. What if the explosions were caused because the Torpex was unstable? Each of the four remaining sloops could be carrying a time bomb! The implication of this sent a cold shiver down his spine. With fear in his eyes he turned to Manley, took a deep breath and said, 'Go with Harper-Smyth and check those extra depth charges we took onboard.'

The inference of Stirling's order was not lost on Manley. 'You don't mean to say the explosions could have been…' said Manley, staring wide-eyed at his captain.

'Just do it,' snapped Stirling abruptly and turned away. If what he feared was true Stirling realised he was faced with a momentous decision. If the Torpex was faulty he could jettison them overboard. This would mean using the conventional depth charges to sink the Milk Cow, providing of course, they were able to locate it. Alternatively, he could carry on and pray nothing happened. This would be putting the lives of five hundred men in grave danger. He was also unable to break radio silence and seek guidance. Another thought struck him. How, with only four sloops at his disposal, could he hope to locate the enemy submarine? And if another sloop were to explode…

Twenty minutes later, slightly out of breath and sweating, Manley and Sub Lieutenant Harper-Smyth arrived on the bridge.

'The new depth charges are all secure, sir,' he reported, 'none have broken loose, so…'

'Yes, yes, thank you, Sub,' Stirling replied irritably, 'no need to elaborate.'

PO Yeoman Tate and lookouts Able Seaman Dinga Bell and Able Seaman Jackson couldn't help but overhear the conversation between the two officers. Out of earshot of the officers Dinga Bell glanced guardedly at PO Yeoman Tate and murmured, 'D'yer think there might be summat wrong with them new depth charges?'

'I bloody well 'ope not,' Tate replied cautiously.

'Jesus Christ,' gasped Bell, nervously licking his lips, 'if it is then we could go up any second!'

'The other ships report no survivors, sir,' Manley said, his tanned features set in stone. 'Poor beggars, all 125 of them, it hardly seems possible.' The worried expression in his eyes betrayed his feelings. 'If it was the depth charges that caused the explosion then we...'

'Yes, yes,' retorted Stirling, staring blankly ahead of him, 'I fully realise what you mean.'

Aware of the terrible responsibility resting on the captain's mind, Manley hesitated before continuing, 'What er... do you intend doing, sir?'

'I know what you're thinking, Number One,' Stirling replied, his hand shaking slightly as he lit a cigarette, 'but I have my orders. We will carry on and complete our mission.'

'And if another ship blows up?'

Stirling gritted his teeth, then answered, 'That's a chance we'll have to take. Signal the rest of the group, say, *"The loss of Curlew and her men is a terrible blow. But we must carry on and complete our mission. I have every confidence in all of you and I'm sure we will succeed."*'

However, the commanding officers and crews of the other ships were not so sanguine. *Redshank* replied, *"With respect, new charges may be faulty. Suggest we ditch half of them."* Shearwater and *Sparrow* signalled similar misgivings and even suggested jettisoning the new depth charges. Stirling's reply to them was received with trepidation. *"Fully aware of the dangers. Check mechanism on all new depth charges. Do not, repeat, do not jettison."*

Upon receiving Stirling's signal, *Shearwater*'s captain, Lieutenant Commander Hasting's dark brown eyes narrowed. He glanced apprehensively at his First Lieutenant. 'I only hope Stirling knows what he's doing, Number One,' he said, frowning while slightly shaking his head.

His First Lieutenant's reply was philosophical in the extreme. 'Well, sir,' he replied raising his eyebrows and sighing deeply, 'if anything happens to us it won't make any difference.'

The rumour that the depth charges may be faulty soon spread throughout each ship. Nerves became on edge. Mess decks became quieter as tension rose. Tempers flared. Onboard *Sandpiper* Able Seaman Patrick Duffy accused his friend Able Seaman Darby Allen of cheating at cribbage. In a fit of anger he brushed the cribbage board onto the deck and pushed Darby on the chest sending him tumbling onto the deck. Wacker Payne, the leading hand of the mess, quickly intervened.

'For fuck's sake,' shouted Wacker, grabbing hold of Duffy's arm, 'what's up with you. Pick up the board. It'll be night rounds in ten minutes.'

'Jesus Mary and Joseph,' grunted Duffy bending down to help Darby up from the deck, 'I wish we'd never taken those new bloody depth charges onboard. It's like sitting on a powder keg, so it is.'

'Oh belt up,' Wacker replied curtly, 'the captain knows what he's doing.'

'Says you,' Duffy sarcastically replied, handing Darby a cigarette.

On the bridge Manley and Stirling were only too aware of the uneasiness spreading throughout the ship. 'How far are we from the Cape Verde, Pilot?'

Ape bent over his chart and using a pair of dividers and metal slide rule, he quickly replied, 'Approximately six hundred and fifty-eight nautical miles, sir.'

'And what's the speed of the group?'

'Steady at fifteen knots, sir,' said Ape. Anticipating Stirling's next question he added, 'At this speed we should be some thirty miles off the quadrant in four days.'

Aware that the ship was rife with rumours about the depth charges Stirling decided to try and reassure the crew by making an announcement. He unhooked the voice-pipe and nervously cleared his throat.

'This is the captain speaking,' he said trying his best to sound calm. 'It has come to my notice that a rumour is going around the ship concerning the stability of the new depth charges. Some of you think this might have caused the loss of *Curlew*. Well let me assure you these have been thoroughly checked and are safe.' He paused momentarily hoping he sounded convincing and to allow his words to sink in. 'The group expect to arrive close to the Cape Verde Islands in four days. Once again, the depth charges have been deemed safe,' he stressed. 'I will keep you informed. That is all.'

'What about signalling the other commanding officers to give a similar talk to their crews, sir?' Manley suggested, glancing expectantly at Stirling.

'I agree, Number One,' Stirling solemnly replied, lighting a cigarette. 'At least it might make them feel better.'

Out of earshot of the two officers, PO Yeoman Tate turned to Able Seaman Soapy Waters, the port lookout, rolled his eyes upwards and muttered, 'Some fuckin' hope.'

With *Sandpiper* in the van the small flotilla resumed their position in line ahead.

'Come and see me, please Number One,' said Stirling sitting in his chair on *Sandpiper*'s bridge. 'I'll be in my sea cabin.'

The time was 2130. Manley had completed night rounds and was standing next to Stirling smoking and staring blankly into the darkness reflecting on the loss of *Curlew*. He, like Stirling and the other officers and men, had lost good friends. He took a deep drag of his cigarette wondering what could possibly have caused such a terrible tragedy.

Ten minutes later Stirling was engrossed in compiling a letter to the wife of Lieutenant Commander Jeremy Gifford, *Curlew*'s captain. As he wrote he felt a lump the size of a football in his throat. In his mind's eye he saw the smiling face of Gifford with his fair hair and deep-set blue eyes. Gifford was married with two young boys. With a weary sigh he sat back, pen poised in his hand, and wondered how he could explain Gifford's death. The somewhat impersonal telegram the next of kin would eventually receive would not mention the details. It would simply say, *"It is with deep regret the Lords of the Admiralty have to inform you of the death of ..."* How could he possibly describe Gifford's death to her when he himself wasn't sure?

A sharp knock on the door interrupted his thoughts. The door opened and in came Manley.

'Ah, Number One,' Stirling said, looking up and placing his fountain pen by the side of his unfinished letter. 'Come in and sit down.'

'Thank you, sir,' Manley replied, easing himself into a chair while looking at the worried expression on Stirling's face. Clearly, the strain concerning the loss of *Curlew* was weighing heavily on the captain's shoulders and it showed.

Stirling sat back in his chair, pursed his lips then looked across at Manley's heavily tanned face. 'What do you think might have caused that explosion?' he asked, nervously stroking his chin. 'Do you think it could have been a primed shell in the magazine?'

'No, sir, I don't,' Manley confidently replied, 'Brian McCormack, *Curlew*'s Gunnery Officer, was too efficient to allow that to happen,' he paused, then quietly added, 'he was also a very close friend…'

For a few seconds Stirling didn't reply. Then taking a deep breath, he said, 'Do you think it could have been those new depth charges. Please be frank.'

'What else, sir?' Manley replied, feeling his mouth suddenly go dry. 'Perhaps a stray mine,' he added, answering his own question.

'Is that the consensus of the other officers?' Stirling asked, taking a cigarette from an open packet, giving one to Manley and lighting both with a match.

'By and large, sir,' Manley answered, turning in his head to one side and exhaling a feather of smoke. 'One or two thought *Curlew* might have been torpedoed, but there was nothing on the Asdic screen.'

With doubt etched in his tired eyes, Stirling lent forward and in a hoarse voice, said, 'Tell me, Bill, do you think we should jettison the depth charges?' As he spoke ash from his cigarette tumbled onto his leather-bound blotting pad.

Stirling's question using his Christian name took Manley momentarily by surprise. 'No, sir, I don't,' Manley finally replied.

'As you mentioned when we sailed, sinking that supply boat would force the enemy subs to return to base to refuel, thus safeguarding the convoys and saving lives.'

'Even if it means risking the lives of all the men?' Stirling said, taking a deep drag of his cigarette.

'As Chief Bosun's Mate Taylor remarked when I met him after listening to your speech,' said Manley his intense, deep-set blue eyes fixed on Stirling's face, 'that's the risk we all have to take. The crew are naturally uneasy, sir, but rest assured they'll not let you down. You've trained them too well for that.'

# CHAPTER THIRTY-FIVE

A hundred miles to the west of Stirling's small force U-459 continued on her southerly course. The time was 1200 and from a clear, eggshell blue sky the dazzling sun shone down on a silvery sea. Leaning his muscular, six-foot frame against the guardrail of the conning tower, Kapitan Oberleutnant Bruno Studt felt the warm trade wind caress his handsome, weather-beaten face. He removed his cap, wiped his brow with the back of his hand then ran his fingers through his thick blond hair. Listening to the steady throb of the vessel's electric motors, he stared down at the four spare 533 mm torpedoes, secured in large copper canisters either side of the deck. How bare the wide metal casing looked without the high velocity 37 mm gun carried by conventional U-boats. With a wry smile he reminded himself that this was no ordinary submarine.

Stored below in watertight compartments were four more torpedoes and ammunition. There were also gallons of lubricant, spare parts, a machine shop for repairs and drinking water that could be transferred by hose plus a refrigerator to preserve meat and vegetables. They also carried a doctor and a small operating room. Her valuable cargo would enable Doenitz's precious U-boats to prolong the "Happy Time". This was the name given by the U-boat commanders who, with impunity, were wreaking havoc to the convoys in the mid-Atlantic.

Bruno Studt was a thirty-one-year-old U-boat "ace", already awarded the Knight's Cross with Oak Leaves, for his successes in the Atlantic commanding a conventional submarine. He was married to Anna and had a two-year-old son, named Heinrick. As a student at Berlin University he revelled in the Fuehrer's denouncement of the Versailles Treaty and promises of a New Order. After graduating with honours in naval history, he joined the Nazi Party. In 1930 he entered the naval college at Bremen and became a junior officer. After taking a course in undersea warfare in Willhelmshaven he was promoted to leutnant. His speciality was navigation and his enthusiasm and ability soon attracted the attention of his superiors.

In 1939 he was given command a U41. During the first six months of the war he sunk a record quantity of Allied shipping. In the summer of 1940 Doenitiz promoted him again and appointed him Kapitanleutnant of U-459, a new type of supply submarine with a displacement of 1,120 tons.

Standing next to Studt was Oberleutnant Karl Muller, his second in command, a small, thickset officer with dark, brooding eyes and a sallow complexion. Both officers felt the gentle shudder of the submarine dipping heavily in and out of the dark green waters, sending a foamy wave flowing down each side of the vessel's cigar-shaped body, each containing over two hundred tons of fuel oil.

'Another beautiful day, eh sir?' Muller remarked, using his powerful Zeiss binoculars to scan the sky and horizon. On either side of the narrow, somewhat cramped conning tower a lookout did the same. Studt and Muller were bareheaded. On the shoulders of their open-necked khaki shirts silver epaulettes denoted their rank. With each movement the silver eagle clutching a swastika in a gold band, worn above a left pocket, glistened in the sun.

Both men had previously served together earlier and like Studt, Muller was a member of the Nazi Party and a staunch supporter of the Third Reich.

'Indeed it is,' Studt replied, placing a cigarette in a black, long-stemmed holder. After gripping it between his teeth he turned slightly allowing Muller who, despite the breeze, managed to light it with a small gold lighter.

Studt gave an impatient sigh. 'How long before we reach our rendezvous point?' he asked watching as a slight gust of wind dissipated the stream of blue tobacco smoke. Even though he had earlier checked the ship's chart he wanted to be certain they were on course to meet U-boats U-78 and 59.

'We should arrive in quadrant seven during the night of the sixteenth, sir.'

'Good,' Studt replied, his pale blue eyes wrinkling in a satisfactory smile. 'And the weather?'

'Calm, with a full moon, I'm happy to say, sir,' Muller answered smiling slightly while jutting out his firm, well-shaven chin.

'Excellent,' Studt said, taking a deep drag of his cigarette, 'that'll save sending up a recognition flare.'

Meanwhile a third of the submarine's 560 crew were on duty. The remainder were either sitting or sleeping in quarters that were much bigger and more comfortable than in conventional U-boats. Most of the crew were draftees. Protests against being sent to U-459 were met with severe punishment or even worse, an appointment to a submarine on Arctic patrol. However, each officer was a volunteer and had his own quarters and bathroom.

In the for'd section Hans Steiner, a tall dark-haired Junior Lieutenant with a pale complexion was checking the trinometer, a device that indicated the submarine's trim. Next to him stood

Hauptobermatt Hans Mayer, a small, serious-looking chief petty officer with a thin face and deep-set grey eyes.

'I still say we're slightly overladen with oil and fuel, Chief,' Steiner remarked noticing the marker on the machine resting on the red dial.

'What does the kapitan say?' replied Mayer, furrowing his brow.

'He doesn't seem unduly concerned,' said Steiner, tapping the dial before making a note on a report attached to his clipboard. Then, glancing at Mayer, he gave a slight shrug of his shoulders and added, 'But I'm sure he's aware that it could slow down the dive should we be attacked.'

'At these latitudes the chances of that happening are remote,' Mayer answered, his eyes wrinkling into a confident smile.

'Hmm, I hope you're right,' Steiner replied pensively, 'but with the amount of fuel and ammunition we carry, one well-placed bomb would send the sub sky high.'

# CHAPTER THIRTY-SIX

As usual, Monday 13 December dawned warm with a misty heat haze dividing the blue, cloudless sky from the sea. The time was a little after 0800. On *Sandpiper*'s bridge Lieutenant Allan Prospero Evans was in the process of relieving Sub Lieutenant Harper-Smyth of the morning watch. PO Yeoman Tate stood near the binnacle using his binoculars to study the three other sloops sailing in line abreast away to port. On the port wing lookout Able Seaman Soapy Waters was doing the same.

'Course steady on south 250 degree, Ape,' Harper-Smyth reported stifling a yawn, 'barometer a hundred millibars and will no doubt rise. Latitude 35 degrees, 17 minutes north, longitude 193.4 degrees, 9 minutes west. Speed 16 knots. The mist should clear in an hour or so. It's all in the log.'

'Cheers, sport,' said Ape. Glancing up at the pale blue, cloudless sky, he added, 'The sea looks as calm as Melbourne City Lake on a summer's day.'

With a touch of sarcasm, Harper-Smyth replied, 'I wouldn't know, dear boy, having never been there.'

At that moment Stirling appeared followed closely by Manley.

'Morning, Pilot,' Stirling said, heaving himself into his chair. 'How far are we from the Verde Islands?'

'We should sight Ponta Moreia in two days, sir,' Manley replied, 'that is,' he paused monetarily and shot a sly glance at Ape and added, 'that is if our esteemed Antipodean's calculations are correct.'

'*Shearwater* signalling, sir,' shouted Leading signalman Tansey Lee, his binoculars pressed tightly to his eyes. 'Message reads: "*Have developed a defect in the propeller shaft. Chief ERA informs me it might take at least twenty-four hours to repair. Request instructions."*'

'Christ almighty!' cried Stirling, looking alarmingly at Manley, 'first *Curlew* now *Shearwater*, that's all we bloody-well need.'

Once again Stirling was faced with a difficult decision. If the group slowed down and hoped that *Redshank*'s problem was resolved they might miss the rendezvous with the German tanker. As it was with only four ships the search could prove impossible.

'Reply,' snapped Stirling, shooting Taylor a pensive glance, '*what is the maximum speed you can make?*'

The reply that read, *"eight knots"* served to increase Stirling's dilemma.

'If we slow down, sir,' said Manley, 'it could…'

'Yes, I know, Number One,' Stirling interrupted impatiently, 'but we can't just leave her, if a U-boat appears she'd be helpless.'

'If we waited, say, twenty-four hours and the shaft still isn't fixed, sir,' Manley went on uneasily, 'what then? We'd have lost a day and maybe miss finding the supply tanker.'

Stirling gritted his teeth while pensively stoking his chin. 'I'm well aware of that,' Stirling replied irritably. 'I think we'll give her twelve hours, if *Shearwater*'s still in trouble, I'm afraid I'll have no choice but to go on. Better signal her to that effect and also inform the other two ships what is happening. And reduce speed to eight knots. In the meantime,' he went on, 'lookouts will be doubled. If Asdic detects a U-boat, we'll have to protect *Shearwater*.'

The tight-lipped expression on Stirling's face showed the strain he was under. Manley therefore offered a consoling remark, 'I'd say that was a fair compromise, sir,' he said quietly.

'Let's hope it's the right one,' Stirling replied nervously gripping the sides of his chair.

Once again tension arose throughout the ships.

Onboard *Shearwater* Chief ERA Bill Durning, a tall, man whose grey eyes matched his sparse hair, and Lieutenant (E) Peter Davey a small, fair-haired RNVR officer, plus his team of engineers worked tirelessly throughout the day. By 1800 having stripped the propeller shaft down they emerged from the bowels of the ship, their faces and overalls smeared with dust and grease.

'It looks like we'll have to work through the night, sir,' said the chief, using a piece of cotton waste to wipe his sweaty brow. 'As you saw the crack is right aft and awkward to get to.'

'Hmm,' pondered the lieutenant, 'if we do that the noise of our hammering will be heard under water for miles, and you know what that could mean.'

'Aye, but it's a chance we'll have to take,' replied the chief, 'or we'll be here for the duration.'

Meanwhile in *Sandpiper,* Stirling was sat in his sea cabin writing up the ship's log when Manley knocked and entered.

'Bad news I'm afraid, sir,' he said, shaking his head. He then told Stirling about the delay in repairing *Shearwater*'s propeller shaft.

With an air of resignation Stirling dropped his fountain pen on his blotting pad and sat back. 'That's it then,' he said folding his arms. 'I am loath to do it, Number One, but we'll have to go on without her and hope she catches us up.'

'What about breaking radio silence to ask for an escort to come to her aid,' Manley tentatively suggested.

Stirling solemnly shook his head. 'Too dangerous,' he replied, 'every bloody U-boat in the vicinity would pick up the transmission. Better signal her, say, *"Regret but have to leave you. Hope you understand. Godspeed."*'

Shortly afterwards came *Shearwater*'s reply. *"Understand your problem. Press on. Good hunting and Good luck."*

Stirling's decision not to break radio silence was the correct one. Fifty miles to the north of the group U-78 was submerged and steering a steady southerly course. U-59 was on the surface thirty miles from quadrant seven and would be the first to rendezvous with the German tanker.

With a sloop either side of *Sandpiper* the group now shorn of four of its original number made good progress towards their goal. The day before they were due to reach quadrant seven Stirling decided to contact the other sloops using the ship-to-ship telephone. Each message read, *"During the next twenty-four hours we expect to detect the enemy. As you know, the new depth charges should be powerful enough to breach her hull if the tanker is submerged. If she surfaces attack her with gunfire. We might even have to ram her. But no matter what, at all costs the tanker must be sunk. Good luck to you all."* During "stand easy" Stirling also announced this to *Sandpiper*'s crew.

In the seaman's mess Leading Seaman Wacker Payne looked uneasily over his mug of tea at Able Seaman Duffy and said, 'I don't like the sound of "at all costs", Paddy.'

'To be sure,' Duffy replied warily while crossing himself, 'neither do I.'

It was a sentiment shared by all the crew.

## CHAPTER THIRTY-SEVEN

Forty miles, south of the Stirling's three sloops, the U-459 arrived at quadrant seven. The submarine, driven by her powerful diesel engines, was cruising below the surface doing ten knots. The crew had finished supper and were closed up at their respective posts. Having been submerged during the day the air was warm, muggy and smelt heavily of diesel oil. In the operations room KPR Oberleutnant Studt, his slightly wrinkled white cap turned back to front, gripped the round metal hand bars of the powerful Askania navigation periscope. Adjusting the device on the handle to improve his focus of the strong lens he carefully scanned the horizon. A few yards away Muller stood next to the thick, shiny steel barrel of the attack periscope.

'No sign of either submarine, Karl,' he muttered, his voice quiet and slightly concerned.

'They could be anywhere in the area,' Muller reflected dryly, 'perhaps if we surfaced you could send up a flare.'

'I agree,' replied Studt, folding the hand bars and turning his cap around. From his back pocket he took out a handkerchief, wiped the sweat from his brow then in a clam voice, said, 'Stand by to surface. Open top valves.'

At once a well-drilled team of sailors went into action.

Operators sat on the port side facing panels of coloured dials and gauges watched over by hawk-eyed petty officers. Opposite several sailors stood ready to turn the small wheels attached to pipes that would allow compressed air into the ballast tanks.

Further along in the heart of the submarine technicians prepared to switch on the powerful engines that would turn on the dynamos that would drive the vessel when on the surface. It was a task that needed precision, accuracy and a keen eye.

'Top valves opened, sir,' came the strident voice of a sailor his eyes carefully watching a set of dials. Suddenly the hissing sound of compressed air through the valves could be heard. Shortly after this the submarine began to gradually move upwards.

'Hydroplanes reversed and steady,' shouted another sailor.

'Air pressure in the lower tanks reduced, sir,' cried someone else.

From the engine room a young officer reported, 'Water being blown from the tanks, sir.'

Peering through the soft rubber aperture of his periscope Studt watched impatiently for the inky black water to give way to the greyness of the evening.

'We're not rising as quickly as we should,' said Studt, 'and the trim doesn't feel even. Can you feel it Muller?'

'Yes, sir,' Muller replied, steadying himself against a stanchion. 'Maybe it's due to the strong current.'

'I doubt it,' Studt angrily replied, 'you'd better try and find out why this is happening.'

'Could it be because we're slightly overloaded, sir,' Muller tentatively replied. 'I think Storeman Oberleutnant Kraus did express his concerns before we sailed.'

'Nonsense,' answered Studt, his voice faltering slightly, 'but check it out all the same.'

'Very good, sir,' Muller answered sharply. 'Just as soon as we're surfaced.'

A few seconds later, Studt, still peering through the periscope shouted, 'Conning tower above the surface, open hatchway.'

Muller whose duty this was, climbed up a steel ladder and exerting all his strength turned the tight circular wheel of the hatchway. When it was free he pushed it upwards. As he did so he narrowly avoided a residue of cold water pouring onto his face. He then climbed down and allowed Studt to enter the conning tower. As he did so he took a welcome breath of evening air as a warm breeze fanned his weather-beaten features. The conning tower stood thirty feet above the steel casing. Dark green water splashed over the fat, snub nose of the submarine then drained away on either side and vanished in the evening mist. The only sounds were the gentle hum of the engines and the hissing of the sea. High above in the sky a myriad of twinkling stars had begun their nightly vigil and on the western horizon the half moon shape of the sun bathed the ocean in a golden patina.

'Beautiful, isn't it, sir?' came the voice of Muller, who like two seamen lookouts had also arrived.

'Yes, it is, Karl,' Studt replied eagerly scanning the sea with his binoculars. 'But I'm afraid there's no sign of any of our friends. If we don't sight her by tomorrow evening I suggest we send up a flare. If she's submerged she might see it through her periscope.'

Just then Radioman First Class Hans Grabler, a tall, flaxen-haired young man with pale blue eyes arrived on the bridge. 'Radio message from headquarters in Lorient, Kapitan,' he said handing Studt a signal while snapping his heels and standing to attention.

Keeping his binoculars clamped to his eyes Studt said, 'Thank you, what does it say?'

Grabler nervously licked his lips and replied, *'"U-78 will meet you your time 16 December 1930 approx. Lat 18 deg 26 min N. Long 03025 deg 15 min W. U59 attacked and sunk enemy warship. Has sustained minor damage and is returning to base. Heil Hitler."'*

'Thank you, Grabler,' he said lowering his binoculars.

The radio operator raised his right arm and gave the Nazi salute the turned smartly and left the bridge.

'A pity about U-59,' said Studt, 'but it means we can sail for the Canaries and rendezvous with two more U-boats straight away after we've supplied U-78.'

'All being well, sir, ' Muller replied with a satisfied smile, 'we should be home in a few weeks.'

'Nevertheless we should be ready to crash dive at all times,' stressed Studt, 'as usual we'll use the quick-release hoses as they have a telephone cable running through them.'

'Very good, sir,' Muller answered curtly. 'Everything will be ready.'

'Thank goodness for the calm sea,' replied Studt feeling the submarine roll slightly while cutting through the water. 'As you know, transferring fuel and stores at sea can be hazardous, especially in rough weather. Remember what happened in the Caribbean during our last trip.'

'Indeed I do,' Muller replied reflectively. 'We lost two men overboard as did U-463 a month later.'

'I'm still not happy about the trim,' Studt remarked, his brow frowning slightly, 'we seem to be rolling a little too much to port.'

'I'll do as you ordered, sir, and have a word with Klaus,' replied Muller.

'I don't know what Klaus was worried about,' said Studt, grasping hold of the guardrail against the roll of the submarine. 'We've managed quite well so far. Besides our cargo is badly needed for our brave comrades to continue sinking the enemy ships.'

Muller nodded in agreement, but he was only too aware that overloading could dangerously affect the trim. He also knew that the characteristic of any submarine is that it has very poor "reserve buoyancy"; that is, it takes the admission of a small amount of water to cause the craft to sink. And if overladen with fuel diving could be cumbersome.

'I agree.' Muller replied calmly, 'if you'll excuse me, sir, I'll go and have a word with Kraus.'

Muller left the bridge and made his way down a wide steel ladder into the heart of the vessel. As he did so the steady throb of the engines became more acute. For a few seconds he blinked allowing his eyes to become used to the strong neon lighting.

Unlike conventional submarines that were cramped and uncomfortable, the tanker was relatively spacious. Muller shot a glance round the control room. In the centre, the oiled steel periscope shafts glistened in their deck housings. Ratings in blue shirts and officers in khaki, were concentrating on dials and meter readings as the boat, rolling slightly, cut through the water. A petty officer called the planesman, sat at a panel operating a stick that kept the vessel on even keel. Marine engineers monitored gauges for the trim valves and propulsion system, and seamen, some of them not much more than eighteen, peered at amber radar screens.

Two other officers engrossed in conversation stopped talking and stood to attention as Muller walked passed. After giving the officers a quick nod, he climbed down another ladder leading into a long compartment clustered with pipes and instruments.

U-459 was a floating storeroom. On either side, shelves containing wooden boxes were packed tightly together. Glancing through an open hatchway Muller could see the shiny, cylindrical shapes of four torpedoes secured in metal cages. Continuing along a wide passageway he passed several locked compartments, which he knew were full of everything from ammunition to medical supplies. He arrived at an open door of yet another room full of boxes. Sitting at a desk was a broad-shouldered officer with short blond hair. In front of him was an open ledger. He looked up as Muller entered.

'Hello Karl,' he said, as he spoke his pale blue eyes wrinkled into a smile. 'Any sign of the sub?'

'Not yet,' Muller replied, casually leaning against the side of the door. 'Just checking to see if you're still worried about the ship being overloaded,' he added, trying to sound unconcerned. 'The captain is convinced everything is all right, er... is it?'

'Not really,' Klaus replied sitting back in his chair, and shaking his head. 'Even when we discharge the fuel oil, the water we take in to keep the correct buoyancy is lighter than oil, and that can be a problem, especially if we have to crash dive.' He paused momentarily and lit a cigarette. 'I've already told this to the captain,' he went on, lifting his chin and blowing out a steady stream of blue smoke, 'but he doesn't seem concerned.'

'I see,' Muller replied uneasily, then with a quick shrug of his shoulders added, 'if the captain's happy why should we be worried, eh? See you at lunch.' He smiled weakly, closed the door and left.

At 0800 the next day Studt was on the conning tower eagerly scanning the horizon hoping to spot the dark image of U-78. A lookout either side of the bridge did the same. At that moment Radioman Grabler arrived slightly out of breath holding a signal sheet.

'Message from U-78, sir,' he said, snapping to attention and saluting. 'It says, *"Have noted your position. Will arrive pm 16 December and take position on your port quarter. Starboard inlets will be ready to receive your fuel hose. Heil Hitler."'*

'Excellent!' exclaimed Studt, slapping the edge of the guardrail. 'Hard a port, better pipe hands to their stations. We'll meet her as she approaches. And tell the engineer to prepare the quick-release hose, we'll transfer it across by rubber dinghy. Also inform the stores officer what is needed.'

'Do you wish to fire a recognition flare, sir?' Muller asked.

'Yes,' Studt replied, 'we'll surface at 1800. Send one up at just before sunset.'

'Very good, sir,' Muller smartly replied, 'if all goes well we should be on our way north by this evening.'

'What do you mean, "*If* all goes well?"' Studt replied irritably, 'the sea is calm and we are completely alone. What could possibly go wrong?'

# CHAPTER THIRTY-EIGHT

Fifty miles away from U-78, Stirling and his small flotilla continued south sailing in line abreast. *Sandpiper* was in the van and slightly ahead. *Sparrow* was two miles on her port side with *Redshank* the same distance away on the opposite side. The time was 2100 on 15 December.

'We'll be entering quadrant seven early tomorrow morning, sir,' Ape said to Stirling.

'Very good, Pilot,' Stirling replied. 'Better warn the morning lookouts.'

Day had been suddenly transformed into dusk as the orange glow from the sun faded leaving behind a pale blue hue stretching across the western horizon. The first stars had appeared enabling OOW Sub Lieutenant Harper-Smyth to take an evening navigation fix. Lookouts, radar and Asdic operators were closed up.

'Do you wish the ships to alter their positions, sir?' Manley enquired, who like Stirling and PO Yeoman Tate were using their binoculars to sweep the horizon.

'I think so, Number One,' Stirling cautiously replied. 'Tell them to widen their present station to five miles.' Remembering his concerned remark to the admiral before they left England, he added, 'Even though it'll be like looking for a needle in a haystack. Maybe lady luck will shine on us...' He was abruptly interrupted by the sound of the Asdic intercom.

'Contact approaching five miles to the north,' came the strident voice of Leading Seaman Wacker Payne from the Asdic compartment. 'It looks like a surface vessel.'

'My God!' he exploded, remembering the admiral mentioning the presence of the *Graf Spee* somewhere in the South Atlantic. 'Surely it can't be a German raider this far south. What's her speed?'

'She's moving quite fast, sir,' Payne replied, 'I'd say about twenty knots.'

'Better sound the alarm, Number One,' said Stirling without moving his head. 'If it's an enemy warship it could bugger up everything.'

By this time the unidentified warship was less than a mile away.

'She's flashing a signal, sir,' shouted PO Yeoman Tate. Keeping his binoculars against his eyes, he slowly read out the message.

'"*USS destroyer Cyras Vance – Good to see you – Regret to tell you your ship Shearwater sunk by U-boat – Captain, three officers and twelve men lost – have one hundred and ten survivors onboard – attacked U-boat but she escaped – am aware of your task to sink U 459. – Can I help? – Commander Oscar P. Daniels, captain.*"'

The loss of *Shearwater* stunned everyone on the bridge. For a few seconds nobody spoke. The tense, forlorn expressions on the faces of those on duty told its own story.

Stirling broke the silence. 'Good Lord!' he gasped his brow creased while solemnly shaking his head, '*Shearwater* sunk. I should never have left…'

'You had no choice, sir,' Manley stressed, placing an understanding hand on Stirling's shoulder. 'If we'd remained we might have been sunk also, and then where would we have been?'

Regaining his composure Stirling took a deep breath. 'Yes, I suppose you're right, Number One,' he murmured quietly. 'Reply to the signal, say, *"Your help very welcome. Hope to sight U-459 pm tomorrow. Do you have many depth charges left? Commander R. Stirling, RN. Group Commander."*'

The reply came almost immediately. *"Enough to help you sink the bastard!"*

Stirling shot a wry smile at Manley. 'Reply, *"Splendid. Please take station on my port bow. Intend to increase speed to fifteen knots."* Better inform *Redshank* and *Sparrow* about *Shearwater*,' Stirling added stonily. 'Tell them the American has joined us and say the survivors will be transferred to us when the situation allows it.'

Twenty minutes later the destroyer painted a dull grey, came closer, the twin sets of 4.5 gun barrels gleaming menacingly in the early evening sunlight. A huge white bow wave curled over he sharp bows and from her yardarm the Stars and Stripes fluttered wildly in the strong breeze. On her upper deck the crews from *Sparrow* and *Redshank* waved wildly as the destroyer took up her position.

'Just like the cavalry in the films,' Able Seaman Jackson mockingly remarked, who like many of *Sandpiper*'s crew, was on the quarterdeck cheering and waving. 'It's a wonder someone isn't blowing a bloody bugle.'

'Don't be so fuckin' stupid,' chimed in SBA Appleby who had left the sick bay to see what was happening. 'We're already three ships short so if you ask me, the Yanks are more than welcome.'

'Sweet Jesus, you're right there, Doc,' remarked Able Seaman Patrick Duffy, 'maybe they'll send us over some of their lovely ice cream.'

'And a few bottles of Coca Cola,' added Able Seaman Buster Brown grinning like a Cheshire cat. 'I'm quite partial to a drop of rum and coke.'

Throughout the day the group, now strengthened by the arrival of the destroyer, continued their way south. The sea continued to be relatively calm and high above the sun's warm rays beat down from a clear blue sky. Shortly after 1900 Stirling decided to hold a meeting in the wardroom of his officers and brief them about his proposed plan of attacking U-459.

Each officer stood up as the tall, imposing figure of the captain entered.

'Good evening, gentlemen,' Stirling said with a smile, 'do sit down and smoke if you want to.'

Sub Lieutenant Jock Weir removed a dark brown briar pipe from his jacket pocket and lit it with a match. Straight away he, Coburn, and Ape who were sat on either side of him began to cough as they became engulfed in a cloud of pale blue smoke.

'Good Lord,' cried Harper-Smyth, quickly wafting the air, 'why the deuce have you suddenly taken up using a pipe and what the hell are you smoking?'

'This pipe belonged to my father and if you must know the tobacco it's called Old Holborn,' Weir grunted, taking another puff and glaring at the young officer.

'Smells more like old socks, to me,' chimed Ape, coughing slightly.

'Whatever it is,' grinned Coburn furrowing his brow while grinning, 'it's a danger to public health.'

'Right, gentlemen,' Stirling said, lighting a cigarette, 'I've asked you here to give you the details of my attack plan when we meet the German.' He paused watching the expectant expression on the faces of his fellow officers. 'To begin with we can rule out any element of surprise as their radar will have picked us up. I therefore expect she'll have submerged, so this is what I intend to do.' He paused and felt the tension in the air again. 'We will approach the enemy in line abreast. *Cyras Vance* will take a position a mile ahead of us and can deal with any emergencies should they arise. If the tanker is submerged and we have her firmly in Asdic contact I will approach her then stop. With their engines just turning over to give five knots, *Sparrow* and *Redshank* will move stealthily into position. Only when the range and bearing of the enemy coincide, will I give the order to fire. Any questions?'

'One, sir,' said Manley, raising a finger, 'What about if the German is on the surface. I believe they are much faster than we are?'

'Should that happen,' Stirling quickly replied, 'the American, who can do up to twenty-five knots, will attack using her 4.5 guns.'

'And if the blighter surrenders, sir?' asked Ape, a hopeful gleam in his eyes.

'Then, my antipodean friend,' Stirling answered, his weather-beaten features breaking into a wide smile, 'we'll share her prisoners around the sloops, commandeer her fresh food and vegetables and head north.' After another pause, Stirling added firmly, 'I will use the ship-to-ship phone to inform *Redshank* and *Sparrow* of these instructions. Now,' he added, smiling while playfully licking his lips, 'who's going to offer me a Horse's Neck?'

# CHAPTER THIRTY-NINE

Shortly before 1700 on 16 December U-459 started to surface. The deck began to tilt as the hydroplanes lifted the nose of the submarine. Gradually the submarine burst through the calm sea, its bold pennant number, painted white, clearly visible either side of the conning tower. Rivulets of foamy blue seawater streamed from its superstructure like miniature waterfalls. Then, levelling out, the huge bulge around each side of its central hull settled majestically into the sea.

On the western horizon the anaemic yellow sun was slowly sinking while high above in the fading blue sky a myriad of stars began to light up the heavens.

Studt opened the hatchway and climbed into the conning tower. Under his feet he could feel the gentle vibration of the vessel's electric motors that would be used for manoeuvring on the surface. Behind them came Muller and two duty lookouts. After the muggy warmth below the night air felt chilly. Anticipating this both officers and the lookout wore caps and overcoats. For a few seconds everyone took a deep breath of fresh air while blinking to accustom their eyes to the dim light.

'No sign of U-78,' Studt said scanning the darkening horizon with his binoculars. 'Better send up that signal flare you suggested.'

'Very good, sir,' Muller replied.

Without waiting to be told, one of the lookouts bent down and using a small steel key opened a large watertight metal box. From inside he removed what appeared to be an oversized pistol. He then took out a thick cartridge and placed it inside the stubby barrel.

'Flare ready, Mein Kapitan,' the lookout snapped.

'Thank you,' Studt replied, his binoculars still pressed against his eyes. 'Fire...'

Just then the buzzer from the bridge phone interrupted him

'Radar reports submarine on the surface ten miles to port, sir,' came the clear voice of the Radioman Hans Grabler.

'Excellent, thank you,' Studt replied a satisfied smile on his face.

'Do you still want to fire a flare, sir?' Muller asked.

'Yes,' Studt answered, nodding his head, 'it'll enable our friend to vector in on us easier.'

The sharp retort of the signal pistol pierced the evening air as a streak of white smoke from the pistol soared upwards. Studt lowered his binoculars and with the other three watched as it disappeared upwards. Reaching its zenith the flare suddenly burst into a colourful cascade of sparkling light. For a few minutes the display hung in the air, then one by one as if snuffed out by an unseen hand each light disappeared.

'Pipe all hands to transferring stations,' ordered Studt, lighting a cigarette. 'I want to be away as soon as possible.'

No sooner had the pipe been made than the deck casing became a hive of activity. Hatchways were opened and the quick-release hoses attached to the oil pumps along with those secured to fresh water tanks. Wide openings were made ready for torpedoes to be hoisted by chains onto the deck. Using an air compressor, the rubber dinghy was quickly inflated and secured to the submarine's side by a painter. Under the keen eyes of Oberleutnant Kraus boxes of fresh fruit, bread and vegetables were brought up together with boxes of spare parts should they be needed.

'Submarine two miles away on the starboard quarter,' yelled one of the lookouts from the conning tower.

Studt glanced at his expensive waterproof Rolex watch, 'Seventeen thirty, perfect timing, Muller,' he said with an air of confidence, 'as you mentioned, we should be on our way north very soon.'

Thirty miles away Stirling's four ships continued their journey southwards. *Sandpiper* was in the centre with the USS *Cyras Vance* two cables in front.

High up in *Sandpiper*'s crow's nest, Able Seaman Lofty Day had the last dog watch. This was the watch favoured by sailors as it meant they had no duties till the morning, hence the saying – "last dog and all night in". From this vantage point the whole of the ship's upper deck was laid out before him reminding him of a model he had once made. The rolling of the ship exaggerated the swaying movement of his perch. And directly ahead he could just see the foamy white tide race fizzing down either side of the ship's bows in sharp contrast to the inky black sea. From a cloudless sky, a full moon dappled the sea in jagged white lights and a warm breeze fanned his face. Moving his binoculars slowly from left to right then back again, he carefully scanned the horizon directly ahead of him. He, like the rest of the crew, knew they were heading into danger and consequently, his level of concentration was acutely high. Suddenly he stopped and quickly trained his binoculars back, certain he had seen something. Sure enough, barely visible was a small cascade of whiteness lighting the horizon. Feeling his heartbeat increase he grabbed the bridge voice pipe and yelled, '*What looks like a distress signal on the horizon dead ahead, roughly twenty miles, sir.*'

Below on the bridge Day's words immediately brought everyone to attention. Eyes strained as binoculars were trained ahead of the ship.

'There it is, sir,' cried Manley, 'he's right. It does look like a distress signal.'

'Distress signal my foot, Number One!' Stirling exclaimed, rubbing his hands together with obvious glee. With smug expression on his face, he added, 'It looks like we've found that needle in a haystack and lived up to the ship's motto.'

'What the deuce it that, sir?' Manley asked, 'I'm afraid I can't remember.'

'Endure and ye shall find,' Stirling replied with a wide grin.

'Signal from the other two ships, sir,' called out PO Yeoman Tate, 'they also report seeing the light and request instructions.'

'Reply,' said Stirling, '"All ships increase revolutions one-third." Then signal our American friend to take any action he thinks appropriate.'

'Aye, aye, sir,' Tate replied reaching for his Aldis lamp.

'I'd stake my pension on that being the tanker, Number One,' stressed Stirling, 'and at our present speed we'll soon be picked up by her radar. What time is it now?'

'Eighteen forty-five, sir,' Manley replied.

Lowering his binoculars Stirling turned to Manley. 'Better tell the crew we've sighted the enemy,' he said gravely, 'we'll go to action stations in twenty minutes.'

The news that the tanker had been discovered came as a relief throughout the ship. Everyone knew about the mission and as each day passed the tension increased. Despite the reassurances from the captain the crew were still in constant fear of one of the new depth charges exploding. For once the sound of the alarm bell came as a welcome relief.

Within minutes every department in the ship was closed up at their stations.

'Thank fuck for that, Jumper,' gasped Able Seaman Patrick Duffy to Able Seaman Buster Brown who was checking the sight on the port Oerlikon, 'to be sure, at long last we'll get rid of them green buggers on the quarter deck.'

'Too bloody true, Paddy,' Buster replied, hastily feeding in ammunition belt into the gun's breech socket, 'maybe now I'll be able to get a decent hard-on.'

SBA Brum Appleby ensured the first aid parties were mustered then returned to the sick bay and placed several surgical instruments in the sterilizer.

'Can't be too careful, can we, sir,' he said giving Surgeon Lieutenant Coburn a reassuring smile.

'Quite so,' came Coburn's sanguine reply, 'but don't forget to switch on the kettle and make some kye.'

On the quarterdeck Sub Lieutenant Harper-Smyth's blue eyes blinked nervously as he watched his team prepare for action. On either side of the quarterdeck a row of depth charges were secured to the bulkhead by metal clips. The last three on the port side were the green painted Mark VIIs. Under the watchful eye of PO Dusty Miller four ratings, using a small hand trolley, removed these and wheeled them to the side of the metal roller, ready to be launched.

'If the size of the explosion the one we launched before is anything to go by, sir,' remarked PO Miller glancing apprehensively at Harper-Smyth, 'the three ships firing them together should be enough to blow the bloody U-boat clean out of the water.'

'I hope you're right, PO,' Harper-Smyth replied, pensively stroking his chin while grinning weakly.

## CHAPTER FORTY

U-78 easily spotted the recognition flare sent up by U-469 and had taken a position some fifty yards on the tanker's port side. The difference in size between the two vessels was starkly obvious. U-459 with her massive superstructure, bulging bulkheads and squat conning tower dwarfed the smaller U-78.

Both vessels had switched on the upper deck lighting and at five knots, were cruising in unison. The captains of both submarines stood bareheaded on the guardrail of their conning towers and communicated using a loud hailer. The captain of U-78, a tall, dark-haired officer, who like many of his crew had a full beard, grinned and shouted, 'Good to see you,' he yelled, giving Studt a salutary wave, 'we'll need about five hundred tons of oil and as much fresh water as you can spare and six torpedoes.'

'Excellent,' Studt replied loudly, his voice barely audible over the purring sound of the vessels electric engines. 'Everything is ready, we should be finished in a few hours.'

Under the close supervision of Muller, the quick-release hoses were passed across from U-459 via the rubber dinghy, secured around bollards and attached to the oil inlets of U-78. Oberleutnant Klaus and the bosun's mate watched closely as fresh water hose was also ferried over along with watertight boxes of stores. During this process the crews of both vessels exchanged friendly banter.

'When do you expect to get back to Lorient, Boris?' yelled one sailor onboard U-78 to a friend onboard U-459.

'God only knows, Ludwig,' shouted Boris, who along with several other sailors was hauling the hose onboard. 'A week or two, but when you return give Lorraine, the pretty frauline we met in that bar, a kiss from me.'

Ludwig threw back his head and gave a salacious laugh. 'I'll give her more than a kiss, Boris,' he replied bending his arm and making an obscene gesture.

At that moment the excited voice of the Asdic operator came over the conning tower intercom.

'Four surface craft approaching ten miles to the north, sir!' he exclaimed, 'they look big enough to be destroyers.'

An expression of incredulity suddenly spread across Studt's face. '*Mein Gott!*' he exclaimed staring wide-eyed at Muller. '*How can this be? Enemy ships this far south, warn U-78.*'

But U-78 had also picked up the approach of the enemy. Using his loudhailer her captain yelled, 'Get going, Bruno. I will try and divert the enemy away from you. Good luck.'

'Thank you,' Studt shouted, knowing full well that U-78 would be relatively defenceless against the onslaught of four Allied warships.

U-78 slowly pulled away from the tanker while sailors manned her single barrelled 1.8cm gun for'd of the conning tower.

The shrill, honking noise of the tanker's klaxon ordering the tanker to dive, struck fear into the minds of the crew. Each one had experienced the shuddering impact of a depth charge attack and knew what to expect.

Men in the process of raising torpedoes on chain hoists, stopped and began to reverse the procedure. The rubber dinghy was dragged, partially loaded with stores back onto the tanker's deck. Fuel and oil hoses were disengaged from U-78 and hauled onboard the tanker.

Watching anxiously from the conning tower, Studt thumped the edge of the guard in frustration, well aware that this was a painfully slow process.

'*Hurry things up, Karl,*' he yelled to Muller who was on the casing overseeing the operation. '*Asdic tells me the enemy are ten miles away and closing fast.*'

As the last fuel hose was hauled onboard Studt breathed a sigh of relief and hurried down into the control room. The last member of the crew to enter the submarine reached up and secured the hatch. Studt then shouted, 'Up periscope.' Bending down he peered anxiously through the reinforced glass aperture; he could just see the top of a masthead appearing in and above the rolling waves.

'Take her down to two hundred feet, Karl,' he shouted.

The order was passed to the engineers and the well-drilled routine of diving began.

Ballast tanks began to blow sending clouds of foamy air bubbling either side of the submarine. A marine engineer, his eyes studying the sea level shown on a wide, amber screen, slowly turned a small wheel that depressed the hydroplanes.

The deck tilted slightly. Studt shouted, 'Down scope,' and stood up. Like Muller and those men standing he held onto anything at hand and waited as the submarine began to descend. Suddenly the vessel tilted slightly to port and slowed down.

'What the devil is happening,' Studt yelled, glaring alarmingly at Muller, his face taut and anxious, 'why the delay?'

Before Muller could answer, the strident voice of Storekeeper Oberleutnant Kraus came over the intercom.

'The trim is unbalanced, sir,' said Kraus. 'If we had offloaded more stores to U-78 the trim would be all right, that's why we're listing.'

'How long will it take you to stabilise everything?' Studt asked, feeling his heart pounding in his chest.

'At least an hour, sir,' Krause replied.

'Mein Gott!' he exclaimed, 'that's far too long. By that time the enemy...' he paused, then stressed, 'you must do it quicker. Time is essential.'

'Very good, Kapitan,' Kraus answered warily, 'but I did warm you we were overloaded...'

'Yes, yes,' Studt interrupted angrily, 'just get it done!'

Shooting a worried glance at Muller, he snapped, 'How far away is the enemy?'

'About ten miles, sir,' Muller replied, frowning.

'Increase ballast tank action,' Studt said, 'we must be down to at least three hundred feet before they attack.'

Throughout the submarine men waited, their shirts wet with perspiration, hanging onto anything as the vessel very slowly descended. At one hundred and fifty feet Studt had the periscope raised. The sight that met his eyes startled him. With the aperture half obscured by the dullness of the water, he saw a destroyer approaching. Behind, barely visible, came the bow waves of Stirling's three sloops.

'Maximum hydroplane angle, Karl,' he ordered, feeling beads of cold sweat running down the sides of his face, 'we must get down quicker.'

But the descent continued to be painfully slow.

'Strong propeller noise a mile away, Kapitan,' cried the hydrophone operator, glancing apprehensively over his shoulder. 'And closing fast.'

'Take her down to 400 feet, Muller,' Studt snorted nervously. Unhooking the vessel's intercom, he gave the order every submariner dreaded, *'Stand by for depth charge attack, all hands brace themselves!'*


*Cyras Vance* was the first of the four ships to go into action. Radar Operator O'Reily, a small, fair-haired rating from New Jersey spotted U-78.

'Submarine on the surface dead ahead two miles sir,' he reported, his voice trembling slightly. This was his and the destroyer's crew's first sight of the enemy and like everyone, he was understandably nervous. 'She's blowing her ballast tanks but appears to be stationary.'

The day previously Commandeer Phillip Daniels, a tall, dark, thirty-year-old officer from Ohio, had been given permission from his superiors in San Diego to divert from his patrol duty and attack U-58. After the U-boat had escaped he picked up the survivors of *Shearwater*. One of these, a young midshipman, informed him of Stirling's mission.

Standing on *Cyras Vance*'s closed bridge, Commander Daniels focused his binoculars directly ahead of him. Next to him stood Lieutenant Commander Harry Willis, his Executive Officer, a sturdily built officer with blue eyes and a crew cut. Close by was a tall, pale-faced ensign, and a heavily tanned Petty Officer Signalman.

'Sound General Quarters, Harry and signal *Sandpiper,* say, *"U-boat on surface one mile ahead, about to engage with guns. Tanker submerged,"* and hoist the battle ensign,' he added ruefully, 'just to let them know Uncle Sam's here.'

'Aye, aye, sir,' Willis replied grinning proudly, and nodded towards his signalman, who immediately carried out the order. As he did so the alarm bell sounded sending men scurrying to their action stations.

No sooner had Stirling received Daniel's signal than gunfire could be heard and seen coming from the American destroyer.

'Two contacts a mile away, sir,' came the cockney voice of Leading Seaman Waker Payne from the Asdic compartment voice-pipe. 'One contact on the surface moving away at speed, the other submerged roughly two hundred fathoms.'

Stirling suddenly had an idea. Glancing expectantly at Manley, he said, 'Tell Harper-Smyth I intend to use a four pattern attack using the old depth charges. And signal *Redshank* and *Sparrow* to do the same.'

Manley raised his eyebrows in surprise, 'The old ones, sir,' he replied, his voice stern and questioning, 'but surely...'

'Bear with me, Number One,' Stirling said smiling wryly, 'and let's see what happens.'

From the bridge of the three ships everyone could see the American destroyer all guns ablaze, closing in on U-78. Tall plumes of water began erupting around the submarine as she gathered speed, returning fire as she did so. Suddenly, a cloud of black smoke and yellow flame belched forth from her conning tower. Then another explosion poured upwards from her stern. The vessel appeared to stop and slowly tilt to port. Men could be seen jumping into the water as U-78 turned turtle and quickly disappeared under the water in a massive bubble of oily water.

Meanwhile the three sloops closed in on their prey.

'Contact four hundred yards ahead, roughly two hundred fathoms deep, sir,' Payne reported, 'and descending.'

'We're practically above the bugger, sir,' cried Manley.

'Exactly,' said Stirling, his eyes narrowing, 'launch depth charges.'

# CHAPTER FORTY-ONE

Four hundred feet below the surface the crew of U-459 knew what to expect. Most had been through similar experiences before in the Atlantic. Even so, the tension was palpable as each man holding onto anything at hand, waited, pale-faced and anxious for the inevitable bone shuddering cacophony that would soon follow. And then it came: ear-splitting explosion after explosion, banging against the bulkhead like a sledgehammer. But to everyone's relief, the overall effect of the shock waves was surprisingly weaker than they expected.

'The depth charges they're using are no match for our re-enforced steel hull,' said Studt, a sly smirk on his sweat-stained face. 'I think we'll remain at this depth and see what happens.'

'What about sending up some oil and a few uniforms?' suggested Muller, nervously licking his lips.

'Too soon,' Studt answered cautiously, 'the British are no fools. If they know what type of submarine we are, they'll expect a lot more than that.'

'What if they decide to wait us out, sir?'

With a wry smile, Studt replied, 'Then we'll simply outrun them with our superior speed. However, let's make it harder for them. I want total silence throughout the ship.'

From the bridge of the three sloops each officer and rating watched apprehensively as the explosions turned the inky black sea into mountains of white water before settling into a series of widening concentric ripples.

On *Sandpiper*'s quarterdeck, PO Dusty Miller grinned at Sub Lieutenant Harper-Smyth and shouted, 'If that don't make the buggers change their underpants, sir, nowt will.'

Ignoring Miller's sarcastic remark Harper-Smyth scanned the seething waters hoping to see evidence that would prove the tanker was sunk.

'Nothing in the water as yet, PO,' he remarked, glancing at Miller.

'Remember, them's were the Mark V depth charges, sir,' he replied, then grinning he added, 'just wait till the buggers get a taste of the big uns.'

'Strong contact two hundred yards, bearing five zero, sir,' reported ASDIC operator Leading Seaman Wacker Payne.

With a steely glint in his eyes Stirling turned to Manley and said, 'Signal *Redshank* and *Sparrow,* give them the tankers bearing and say, "*Lay off one hundred yards. Order silence throughout ship. Move at five knots towards target and fire Mark VII depth charges when ordered. Set at 400 and 600 feet. Keep one in reserve for emergencies. Will indicate with a flare when to attack. Increase revolutions two-thirds after firing. Good luck."*'

'Six hundred feet is the maximum depths any submarine can go, sir,' said Manley giving Stirling a quick, questioning glance. 'Do you think it will go that deep?'

'I would if I were him,' Stirling replied confidently. However, he knew if his intuitive feeling was misplaced the tanker would be safe and the mission would be endangered. Swallowing nervously he unhooked the ship's intercom, 'Captain speaking,' he said, clearing his throat, 'in a short while we will be firing the new depth charges at the enemy. We will approach the tanker doing five knots. During this time I want total silence throughout the ship. That is all.'

Stirling's "creeping attack" was about to be put into action.

Darkness had fallen leaving a pale haze on the western horizon. High above in a clear sky the reflection of moon and stars turned the sea in a carpet of sparkling lights.

Tension showed on the faces of everyone in the ships knowing the culmination of the mission was close at hand. In every department men whispered to each other as if the sound of their voices could penetrate the ship's hull and be heard by the enemy.

Strangely enough no man felt fear. Each knew his job and had confidence in his captain borne out of hours of training and discipline. In a matter of minutes the tactics practised by the group, albeit now greatly reduced, would be tested. Meanwhile, everyone held their breath and waited.

With *Sandpiper* in the van the three sloops moved imperceptibly through the sea.

'Range fifty yards, bearing zero one five, sir,' whispered Ape peering through the azimuth ring of the compass repeater.

Stirling felt his mouth go dry knowing if the attack failed the tanker would escape.

'Thank you, Pilot,' Stirling replied, trying his best to sound calm. 'Tell me when the range and bearing coincide with the position of the sub.'

The feeble vibration of the engine was barely audible as the ship moved stealthily towards its underwater prey. On the bridge nobody spoke. Only the individual thumping of their hearts and the beads of sweat running down their faces reflected the mounting anxiety.

A few minutes later Payne's muted voice came over the intercom. '*Range and bearing twenty yards, sir.*'

'Stand by with the flare, Number One,' snapped Stirling.

Manley unhooked the Very pistol and placed a cartridge inside the barrel then, taking a deep breath, raised his right arm.

A few seconds later Stirling yelled, *'Fire and launch depth charges!'*

Manley pulled the pistol trigger sending a streak of explosive whiteness soaring into the night sky. Seconds later six Mark VII depth charges from each sloop tumbled into the water. As ordered the sloops then increased speed.

'Surely no submarine could withstand the strength of these depth charges, sir,' Manley remarked, giving Stirling a hopeful glance.

Grasping the sides of his chair with both hands, Stirling replied ruefully, 'If they do, that barge on the Thames is looking…' Suddenly, detonations like miniature earthquakes interrupted him. The noise, loud and terrible, could be felt vibrating throughout the ship. Seconds later walls of white seawater erupted like gigantic fountains near the spots where each depth charge had been dropped. For a few seconds each eruption hung in the air, poised like vaporous shrouds before slowly collapsing into the sea into widening pools of fizzing water.

In each sloop Asdic operators reported the sharp noise of what sounded like metal cracking and creaking as though a giant hand was crushing the tanker.

Onboard *Sandpiper,* Payne could hardly contain his excitement. 'It sounds as though the bugger's breaking up, sir,' he cried.

And so it was.

The first shock waves rocked U-459 and all the lights went out. The emergency lighting also failed leaving the crew to grope frantically in the dark. Cries echoed around as many were flung against the bulkheads or onto the deck.

Studt, clinging desperately onto the periscope, suddenly realised he had been caught in a trap. The use by the enemy of ordinary depth charges had been a ruse lulling him and his crew into a sense of false security. Clearly, what was being used now was far more lethal.

'*Got in Himmel, Karl!*' he yelled, his voice shaking with fear. '*What on earth are they using?*'

Feeling blood oozing from his nostrils Karl, lying on the deck, shouted, '*God only knows Mein Kapitan, but we should get clear as fast as we can.*'

But it was too late.

The last thing Studt saw before being overtaken by oblivion was a blinding yellow flash. Nobody heard the mind-bending cacophony as the submarine gradually disintegrated. Nobody had time to scream or yell. In an instant more explosions provided a sudden release from the terror. Bodies were torn apart by pieces of jagged metal; the bulkheads fragmented into large, ugly hunks of steel. The Mark VII depth charges had proved deadly efficient. Almost instantaneously U-459's crew of four hundred and eighty officers and men were killed.

Everyone on the bridge of the three sloops watched as huge bubbly fountains of oil turned the sea into a morass of blackness. But what followed churned the stomachs of the most hardened sailors. Amongst the mass of debris scores of bodies, some headless, others without arms or legs, slowly surfaced. Even in the darkness streams of blood could be seen creating slimy patterns in the dank, oily sea.

The sight sickened everyone. Onboard *Sandpiper,* men such as long-serving CPO Sammy Taylor were stunned.

'Blimey, Dixie,' he gasped, turning to the tall figure of Able Seaman Dean, 'I was a boy seaman at Jutland on the *Iron Duke,* and saw ships blowing up, but for the life of me, I've never seen anything like this.'

Ratings closed up on the gun platforms looked on in silence. Nobody cheered, the sight was too terrible for words.

'There but for the grace of God, go I,' mumbled Seaman PO Dusty Miller to himself, on the quarterdeck.

On the bridge Manley, like the others on duty, stood pale-faced and shocked.

'Those poor beggars,' he sighed wearily, glancing at Stirling, 'whoever volunteers for submarines must be insane.' He immediately bit his lip remembering Stirling's son was a submariner. 'Sorry, sir, I didn't mean to...'

'It's all right, Number One,' Stirling quietly replied. Over the past few days he had been so concerned with sinking the tanker, he hadn't had time to think about Mark. But now, watching the remains of human beings floating grotesquely in the water, he felt a shiver of fear run through him. Please God, I beg you, he silently prayed, don't let my son end up like this...

'Do you want anything brought onboard as proof, sir?' Manley asked hesitatingly.

'Yes,' Stirling replied hoarsely. 'Get someone to hook up that cap floating near the side of the ship.'

A few minutes later Able Seaman Darby Allen arrived holding a soggy white cap. Seawater was still dripping from the cluster of oak leaves on its peak. And on the top was a dark stain. Stirling accepted it and held it in his hand realising it must have belonged to U-459's captain. The name *Bruno Studt, Kapitan*

*Oberleutnant,* written inside on a crinkly wet silk lining confirmed this. Stirling turned it over and carefully ran his hand across the cover. He then looked sombrely at Manley and said quietly, 'I wonder what kind of man he was, Number One.' After a slight pause he handed it to Manley and said, 'Send a signal to Admiral Horton, C in C Western Approaches and say, "Mission complete".'

Half an hour later came the reply. '*Well done all. Splice the Mainbrace,*' but to Stirling's abject dismay, there was no mention of Mark.

# CHAPTER FORTY-TWO

The following morning, 17 December, the *Cyras Vance* lowered its sea boat and transferred *Shearwater*'s survivors to the three sloops. The crew of *Sandpiper* lined the guardrails and cheered as the destroyer came alongside.

Using a loudhailer Stirling thanked Commander Daniels and wished him and his crew a safe journey home. Twenty-five ratings were accommodated in *Sandpiper*'s passageways. The sole surviving officer, the young midshipman who had informed the destroyer's captain of the mission, was given a tot of rum and a cot in the sick bay.

The passage northwards was uneventful except for a drastic change in the weather. By the time they arrived at Gibraltar on 23 December the barometer was dropping and it was raining. However, the mail waiting for them served to cheer them up. Stirling, anxious for news of Mark, ripped open the three letters from Pamela. Sadly, none was forthcoming. Her last letter ended, *"It has been a fortnight since Mark was reported missing. But we must still live in hope, darling. I pray every night for his safe return."*

After refuelling and a quick "rabbit run" (a naval term used for buying presents to take home), in Gibraltar, the small flotilla sailed for England. For the next two days the three sloops skirted around the Bay of Biscay.

On *Sandpiper*'s bridge Manley glanced cautiously at the dark clouds racing across the dull grey sky. 'We were lucky to miss any

U-boats or aircraft on the way out, sir,' Manley remarked to Stirling, 'and if we manage to keep fifteen knots, we should be back in dear old Plymouth in two days.'

Stirling was about to reply when the shrill voice of Able Seaman Lofty Day in the crow's nest yelled, *'Aircraft in the sky away to starboard!'*

'You may have spoken too soon,' Stirling gravely retorted, who like Ape and Manley, hurriedly scanned the sky with his binoculars.

Gradually the black dot became clearer.

'Stone the crows!' Ape cried alarmingly, 'it's a bloody Stuka, sir, I'd recognise those gull wings anywhere. It was one of them bastards that sunk the *Perryworth*.'

'Sound action stations, Number One,' Stirling ordered gravely, 'and tell Guns to stand by to open fire.'

In the sickbay, SBA Appleby hurriedly placed a set of surgical instruments in the stainless steel steriliser. Sitting on the deck the first aid team, clutching their steel helmets, gave each other searching looks.

'Maybe it's a drill to keep us on our toes,' Steward Potts remarked, glancing hopefully around at PO Steward Slinger Wood and Writer Chats Harris.

'Well,' replied Slinger, nervously licking his lips, 'we'll soon find out.'

Surgeon Lieutenant Coburn, who was sat at his desk, ignored them. Glancing warily at Appleby, he said, 'Better make sure there's plenty of morphia in the medical valise, just in case...'

Meanwhile on *Sandpiper*'s bridge all eyes watched as the bomber circled around like a vulture about to dart onto its prey.

'Signal all ships to open fire,' said Stirling, lowering his binoculars and lighting a cigarette.

'But it's about ten thousand feet and out of range, sir,' cried Manley looking askance at his captain.

'I bloody-well know that,' Stirling retorted impatiently, 'but it might scare the bastard away. And order the ships to do a ten degree zig-zag, just in case.'

A few seconds later the 4.5 guns of the three ships belched fire. Almost immediately the sky became pockmarked with tiny bursts of black smoke.

'Christ almighty!' PO Yeoman Tate yelled alarmingly, 'the sod's turning. It's beginning to dive!'

'*Everyone take cover!*' Stirling shouted, leaving his chair, removing his cap and clamping on his steel helmet.

Everyone instinctively ducked while glancing upwards as the spider-like shape of the Stuka which, despite the barrage, was plunging towards the ship. At that moment the unmistakable, ear-splitting wail of its so-called "Jericho Trumpet", rent the air. (This was a propeller-driven device fixed either to the undercarriage or the wings. Its piercing whine was designed to intimidate the enemy.)

On and on came the enemy plane, yellow sparks flickering from the edge of its wings spurting deadly machine-gun fire.

'*My God!*' someone cried, '*the bugger's coming straight at us.*'

The next few seconds seemed like an eternity, but passed in seconds. The Stuka, its black crosses clearly visible on the underside of its dark green wings and fuselage, swooped down. The sharp metallic sound of bullets piercing the sides of the bridge echoed ominously around. Before banking and quickly disappearing into the sky, two black cylindrical bombs, each containing 550 lbs of TNT dropped from the underside of each wing. For a second they twisted slightly before angling downwards.

Watching the bombs descend beads of cold sweat ran down Stirling's face, his eyes filled with fear.

Missing by inches the bombs exploded either side of the ship's bridge. Jagged pieces of the missiles' casings cut into the ship's side and flew, dagger-like, into the air.

'Signal all ships to cease fire,' he shouted, his voice barely audible over the *thud, thud* of gunfire. Seconds later a dull pain spreading up his leg made him look down. To his horror he saw his left shoe covered in blood. Suddenly he lost balance and grasped the arm of the chair.

'Are you all right, sir?' Manley cried, reaching out and taking hold of Stirling's arm.

'It's my foot,' gasped Stirling, his face contorted with pain. 'Shell splinter, I think,' at which point he began to feel faint and fell against Manley.

'Good God,' Manley cried seeing blood pooling around Stirling's shoe. 'Get the doc up here quickly,' he shouted, adding, 'you'd better lie down, sir.'

Ape joined Manley and together they carefully lowered the captain down onto the bridge platform.

Surgeon Lieutenant Coburn and SBA Appleby arrived, both slightly out of breath and sweating. Straight away Coburn knelt down and immediately saw a jagged piece of metal poking through an open wound on the base of Stirling's left leg.

'My God, what a mess,' Coburn thought, frowning while staring at pieces of the lower tibia and fibula, bones that formed part of the ankle, protruding though the skin. Coburn immediately realised not only had Stirling a very bad wound, he also had a compound, comminuted fracture of his ankle. (This is an open wound in which the bone is broken in more than one place.)

From his valise Coburn took out a small ampoule of morphia and a bottle containing anti-gangrene serum. He opened a small oblong-shaped tin and removed two metal syringes with graded glass barrels. After wiping the top of each bottle with a surgical swab, he filled the syringes with fluid and expelled any air. Using a pair of plain forceps, he changed both needles. He rolled up Stirling's right trouser leg, cleansed an area with a swab of surgical spirit, then one after the other, inserted the needles. By this time Stirling's eyes were closed and his face ashen.

Glancing charily at Appleby, he cried, 'Quick, he's going into shock. Get a tourniquet around his upper leg, leave his shoe on and put a shell dressing on his wound.' The bridge platform was on a slope facing for'd. Coburn looked at Manley and retorted, 'Thank goodness his head is lying lower than his legs, that'll help to reduce the shock.' Coburn knew that shock was a potential killer. The condition was the result of blood pooling in the lower extremities thus starving the upper part of the body and brain of oxygen. Raising the lower part of the body could redress the balance.

Appleby applied a tourniquet making a mental note of the time in order to release it later to allow the blood to flow, thus avoiding gangrene. In order to prevent pressure against the piece of metal, using pads of cotton wool he arranged a circular dressing around its point. He then sprinkled sulphanilamide powder into the wound then covered it with a large shell dressing.

'Do you want him moved below?' Manley asked, looking anxiously at Stirling's bandaged ankle.

'No,' Coburn answered flatly, 'that might increase the pain and shock. We'll keep him here for a while. Bring blankets and a pillow from his sea cabin and fetch a set of splints and the portable oxygen unit from the sickbay, chop, chop.'

PO Yeoman Tate appeared by Manley. 'Two men on the port Oerlikon injured, sir,' he reported, 'the first aid lads are there, but one of them seems in a bad way.'

'On your way to the sickbay go and see to them,' said Coburn to Appleby, 'and let me know how they are.'

As he spoke a rating appeared holding blankets and a pillow. Without disturbing the injured ankle, Coburn gently eased a blanket underneath Stirling. As he did so, Stirling opened his eyes, stared glassily at Coburn and in a weak voice asked, 'How am I, Doc? Is it serious…?'

'You've got a shell splinter in your ankle, sir,' Coburn answered, 'I'm afraid it'll have to stay there until we get you ashore to a hospital.'

'Can't feel a thing,' Stirling muttered, forcing a smile.

'That'll be the morphia I gave you working, sir,' said Coburn, nervously licking his lips.

Petty Officer Slinger Wood arrived carrying a resuscitation box, a carton of cotton wool and a set of long wooden splints.

'Appleby is with the two injured, sir,' he said kneeling beside Coburn. Gasping for breath and sweating he went on, 'Able Seaman Duffy has a bullet in his arm and Able Seaman Brown has a chest wound. Appleby has bandaged them up and they're being taken to the sick bay. He also told me to bring these,' he added, laying down the oxygen box and splints.

Coburn unhooked the lid of the box and removed a small oxygen cylinder. Attached to the end of a red rubber tube was a small mask. He quickly attached the other end of the tube to the oxygen valve and using a small lever, slowly turned on the oxygen.

After ensuring the flow wasn't too strong or quick he placed the mask over Stirling's nose and mouth.

'Breath slowly and deeply,' he said, 'I'm going to give you an injection of sodium pentothal. That'll put you to sleep while I splint your foot up.'

Twenty minutes later, with Stirling asleep, Coburn, with the help of PO Wood, had placed Stirling's left ankle and leg in a well-padded splint and bound it firmly with bandages.

'How far are we away from England, Number One?' Coburn asked, wiping his brow with the back of his hand.

Manley shot a questioning glance at Ape.

'If we increase speed, we should arrive off Penzance by 0600 tomorrow, sir,' Ape answered confidently.

'Christmas Eve, eh Pilot, some home coming?' Manley soberly replied. 'Send a signal to C in C Plymouth. Say, *"Commanding officer and two ratings badly injured. Request ambulance and doctor meet Penzance, 0800 tomorrow."*'

# EPILOGUE

At first everything was a greyish blur, then gradually objects came into focus; a harsh, yellow electric light directly above him hurt his eyes making him blink; rows of coloured paper decorations crisscrossed the pale green ceiling and thick blackout curtains were drawn across a window. The pungent smell of antiseptic hung in the warm air and the short, white cotton gown he wore was bunched uncomfortably under his arms. He tried to swallow but his throat was sore and his mouth felt like sandpaper. He then tried to sit up but found it difficult because the bed was raised and he was lying flat at a slight gradient. However, this didn't prevent him from noticing an arched bulge under the bedding at the foot of the bed.

After quickly screwing up his eyes he saw a tallish man in a white coat and with a pale brown complexion looking down at him. Behind him stood a small, portly nurse wearing a benign smile. Over a blue shift she wore a white starched apron and a small crinkly cap was perched precariously on her head.

Running his tongue across his cracked lips Stirling muttered, 'Where… where am I?'

The doctor's round, fleshy face wrinkled into a warm smile.

'I am Doctor Shyamal Mukherjee,' he replied. His excellent English was tinged with a slight Asian accent, 'And you are in Penzance General Hospital. How are you feeling?' As he spoke he reached down and taking hold of Stirling's wrist felt his pulse.

'Very thirsty,' Stirling managed to mumble as the doctor removed his fingers.

The doctor nodded to the nurse. 'Just a few sips at first,' he said and moved sideways allowing the nurse to pick up a glass carafe resting on Stirling's bed locker and pour water into a small cup with an overhanging lip. Eager for a drink, Stirling immediately raised a hand and placed it around the cup.

'As the doctor said, a little at first,' protested the nurse as he attempted to take a good gulp, 'or you'll be sick.'

Afterwards, Stirling sank back into his pillow. With a weary sigh he gave the nurse a grateful glance and uttered, 'Thank you, that tasted like nectar. But tell me,' he added raising his eyes and looking enquiringly at the decorations, 'what day is it?'

'Saturday, 26 December,' the nurse replied, gently dabbing his mouth with a piece of gauze, 'Boxing Day.'

'You've been here for almost two days,' the doctor added, 'under sedation.'

With a puzzled expression Stirling, said, 'I remember injuring my foot, passing out and vaguely hearing voices and being moved, then nothing else. But how badly am I hurt and why is the bed at an angle?'

The doctor placed both hands into the pockets of his coat, and shot a concerned glance first at the nurse then at Stirling. It wasn't every day he had to tell a man he would be crippled for life.

He gave a nervous cough and said, 'I'm afraid, Commander,' he said hesitatingly, 'the bones of the lower part of your tibia and fibula were badly fractured. I did my best but sadly I had to amputate your leg just above the ankle joint.'

The word, *amputate* sent a cold chill running through Stirling's head. He felt his stomach contract and for a few seconds held his breath. Thoughts of Pamela flashed through his mind.

How on earth would she cope being married to an invalid? And as for a future in the navy, that of course was at an end.

'My God,' he finally muttered, feeling the blood drain from his face, 'was there nothing you could do?'

'I'm afraid not,' the doctor replied, slowly shaking his head.

'Why am I lying at an angle?' Stirling asked.

'The bed is tilted to prevent post-operative shock,' replied the doctor, 'and this,' he went on, tapping the curvature at the end of the bed, 'is a metal cradle to keep the pressure off your leg.'

Gradually the severity of his injury became clearer. 'I don't suppose you've got a cigarette and anything stronger than water, have you, Doc?'

With a slight, apologetic shake of his head, the doctor replied, 'Sorry, no smoking as you're still recovering from the anaesthetic, but if you feel up to it, you have a few visitors waiting outside. It's five o'clock and they've been there on and off all afternoon.'

Stirling nodded and replied, 'Of course, send them in.'

The first person Stirling saw when the door opened was Pamela, his wife. A green, Robin Hood cap rested firmly on her head and under an ankle-length brown, cashmere coat she wore a thick checked, Harris Tweed skirt. A silver chain and a small cross around her slender neck rested on the top of a cream-coloured jumper. In one hand she held a pair of dark leather gloves and over her left shoulder hung a black leather handbag. Behind Pamela came the burly, six-foot figure of Captain Creasy. Both were smiling as they came in.

'Darling?' Pamela cried, her eyes glistening as she hurried to Stirling's bedside, 'how are you feeling?' Before he could answer their arms went around each other and ignoring the bristles on his unshaven chin, she kissed him warmly on the lips. They broke away, slightly breathless, and for a moment stared longingly into each other's eyes. Stirling was about to ask if there was any news about Mark, but he hesitated, fearing her reply would spoil the happiness in her eyes. Anxious though he was, he decided to wait and pick his moment.

'Doctor Mukherjee explained what had happened, darling,' Pamela said, her fingers entwining tightly around his, 'but it doesn't matter, the main thing is you are alive.'

'I suppose you're right,' Stirling replied quietly. He looked up and smiled weakly at Creasy. 'Thank you for coming, George, how is the crew and the group?'

'*Sandpiper* is in dry dock under repair,' Creasy answered, 'and your Number One, Bill Manley, has been given an extra stripe and is her new captain. The crew all send their best wishes. *Sparrow* and *Redshank* are alongside Gladstone Wharf.'

'How are the two that were injured?'

'I'm sorry to say, Able Seaman Brown died,' Creasy replied frowning, 'a machine-gun bullet in the chest, I believe.'

'Poor chap,' Stirling replied sadly. He paused, and with a poignant sigh remembered the panic onboard *Sandpiper* Brown had caused when he lost the key of the rum store. 'And the other one?'

'Able Seaman's Duffy's arm wound is healing well,' Creasy replied, 'he's in a ward nearby.'

'I'm glad to hear it,' Stirling replied. Then, glancing ruefully at the bulge in his bedding, went on, 'I suppose it's a bowler hat and a pension, for me now, eh George?'

'Nonsense, dear boy,' retorted Creasy, his craggy features breaking into a broad smile. 'Officers with your experience are hard to come by.' Taking out a small sheet of paper from his pocket, he glanced at Stirling and went on, 'I received this signal from Admiral Horton. It reads: *"My best wishes to Bob for a speedy recovery. He has been promoted to captain with a bar to his DSO. When fit he is to report to me for duties as Operations Director."'*

Stirling sank back in his pillow, lost for words. Suddenly all his fears about Pamela and having to leave the navy vanished.

'That's wonderful news,' he finally managed to say, ' but God only knows when I'll be fit. Somehow I can't imagine me crawling around Derby House on crutches.'

'Oh, darling,' said Pamela, squeezing Stirling's hand while fighting back tears, 'they can do wonders these days with false legs and ankles, anyway darling,' she went on, 'Nelson only had one eye and an arm, and her didn't do badly, did he?'

'I'll bear that in mind,' replied Stirling with a wry smile. After a slight pause, he took a deep breath. Now was the time to ask the question, the answer to which he was dreading. In a sombre voice, he said, 'How... how is Mark. Is there any news?'

Pamela turned and glanced expectantly up at Captain Creasy. 'By the way, old boy,' he said, turning and walking towards the door. 'We forgot to tell you, you have another visitor.'

The door opened and there stood the tall heavily tanned figure of his son dressed smartly in his uniform. For a few seconds Stirling was too stunned to speak. *'Mark, I can't believe it!'* Stirling finally cried, as Mark hurried to his bedside. Pamela stood up allowing Stirling and Mark to embrace each other.

'But what happened?' Stirling asked after they had broke free. 'Your mother and I...'

'I'm sorry, Dad,' Mark interrupted, shaking his head, 'but it's a long story. We were on patrol in the Meddy when two Focke-Wulfs attacked my sub. Before it sank I was thrown from the conning tower into the sea. Luckily, two others and myself found a huge log floating nearby. For hours we clung to it before being rescued by a fishing trawler. The crew were Maltese but the captain was an Italian who was pro-British. They gave us rather dirty sweaters to wear and took us to Malta. Unfortunately the captain forgot to remove the Italian flag and we were arrested by the military police. Would you believe it, they thought we were spies! They kept us in a cell for over a week. After a visit from a naval commander I finally convinced them who we were. That's why you or Admiral Horton didn't hear anything. Sorry, to spoil your Christmas, Dad.'

'Christmas my foot,' he cried, warmly hugging his son again. Fighting back tears he glanced over Mark's shoulder at Pamela and said, 'Seeing you both is the best Christmas present I've ever had.'